# KILLIGREW
# AND THE SEA DEVIL

# KILLIGREW AND THE SEA DEVIL

Jonathan Lunn

**headline**

First published in Great Britain in 2005
by HEADLINE BOOK PUBLISHING

10 9 8 7 6 5 4 3 2 1

Cataloguing in Publication Data is available from the British Library

ISBN 0 7553 2069 7

Typeset in Times by Avon DataSet Ltd,
Bidford-on-Avon, Warwickshire

Printed and bound in Great Britain by
Mackays of Chatham plc, Chatham, Kent

HEADLINE BOOK PUBLISHING
A division of Hodder Headline
338 Euston Road
London NW1 3BH

www.headline.co.uk
www.hodderheadline.com

For Sarah Keen

# ACKNOWLEDGEMENTS

It's time to knock on the head the old lie that writing novels, unlike writing film scripts, is not a collaborative process. While a novelist by definition spends most of his (or her) time sitting alone in a room telling himself (or herself) stories, we are all dependent on a variety of dedicated, talented and hard-working people who help the work in progress along to the stage where it is fit and ready for publication.

The past year has been particularly difficult for me, encompassing as it has the departure of my former editor, Sarah Keen, from Headline: a loss which at the time seemed quite bad enough, but was then totally eclipsed by the tragic death of my agent, James Hale. While neither could ever be replaced, full credit is due to Martin Fletcher of Headline and Andrew Hewson of Johnson & Alcock for bravely trying to fill their shoes as editor and agent respectively; both have proven themselves equal to the task.

Thanks are also due to Alastair Wilson and Yvonne Holland for keeping an eye on the technical and literary details respectively; and when one strays into the territory of the other, as they invariably do, I'm never less than delighted to discover that once again their sharp eyes and capacious minds have preserved me from humiliation; where mistakes do occur, the responsibility is all mine.

Thanks are also long overdue to Helena Towers, my publicist, whose enthusiasm, efficiency and overall *niceness* is a constant delight not only to myself but also to the editors, reviewers and booksellers with whom she brings me into contact.

Undying gratitude to Susan Yamamoto for the two maps and for being so supportive over the past few years. And an especial thanks to the League of Gentlemen – Jeremy Dyson, Mark Gatiss, Steve Pemberton and Reece Shearsmith – for permission to use the name and rules of 'Go Johnny Go-Go-Go-Go'.

Finally, thanks to the following for inspiration: David Arnold, John Barry, Paul Bowers, Pierce Brosnan, John Buchan, Sean Connery, Graham Crowden, Roald Dahl, Fyodor Dostoyevsky, Daphne du Maurier, Bruce Fierstein, Ian Fleming, George MacDonald Fraser, Jerry Goldsmith, Nikolai Gogol, Basil Greenhill and Anne Giffard, Bernard Herrmann, Aleksandr Herzen, Christopher Hibbert, Jack Higgins, Alfred Hitchcock, Lawrence Kasdan, Ernest Lehmann, Herbert Lom, Alistair MacLean, Richard Maibaum, Tom Mankiewicz, James Mason, John McTiernan, Roger Moore, Bill Nighy, Aleksandr Pushkin, L.T.C.

Rolt, Julia Sawalha, Dr Seuss, Donald Thomas, Publius Vergilius Maro, Jules Verne and – last but by no means least – the late, great Albert 'Cubby' Broccoli.

## Commander Christopher I. Killigrew

1824 – Born. 1837 – Entered the Navy. 1840 – Aide-de-Camp to Commodore Charles Napier in Syria. Distinguished himself at St Jean d'Acre. 1842 – Served at the capture of Woosung and Shanghae, and in the operations on the Yang-tse-Kiang. Distinguished himself at the storming of Ching-Kiang-Foo, and obtained in consequence his first commission. 1843 – Took part in an attack on a large piratical settlement on the Island of Borneo. 1845–7 – Active in the oppression of slavery. 1847 – Made a Lieutenant. Employed at the destruction of the Owodunni Barracoon. 1849 – Actively engaged against the pirates in the South China Sea. 1852–53 – Took part in Sir Edward Belcher's Arctic Searching Expedition. Promoted to Commander in consequence. 1854 – Appointed to the *Ramillies*. Commander Killigrew's person bears the marks of no fewer than eight wounds.

### The Killigrew Novels

Killigrew R.N.
*The Guinea Coast, 1847*

Killigrew and the Golden Dragon
*South China Sea, 1849*

Killigrew and the Incorrigibles
*The South Seas, 1850*

Killigrew and the North-West Passage
*The Arctic 1852–3*

Killigrew's Run
*The Baltic, 1854*

Killigrew and the Sea Devil
*The Gulf of Finland, 1855*

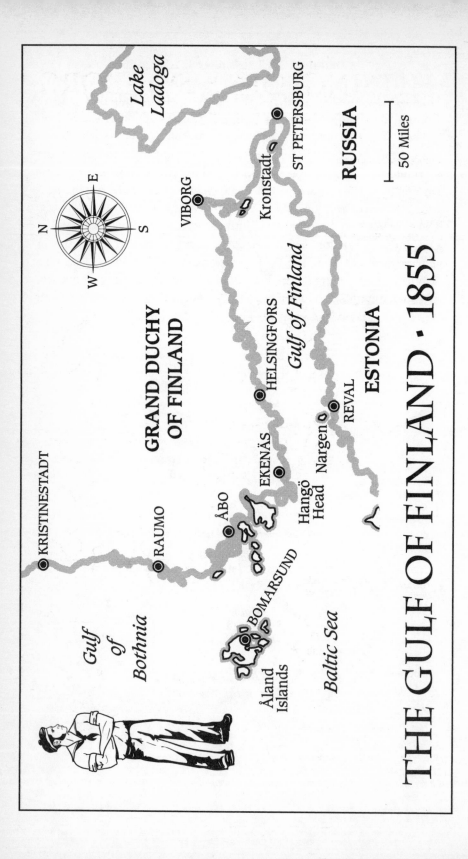

# THE GULF OF FINLAND · 1855

Lake Ladoga

ST PETERSBURG

RUSSIA

50 Miles

VIBORG

Kronstadt

GRAND DUCHY
OF FINLAND

Gulf of Finland

HELSINGFORS

ESTONIA

KRISTINESTADT

RAUMO

ÅBO

EKENÄS

Hangö
Head    Nargen

REVAL

Gulf
of
Bothnia

BOMARSUND

Åland
Islands

Baltic Sea

N · E · S · W

# HELSINGFORS & SVEABORG

## – 9TH AUGUST 1855 –

A. Helsingfors University
B. Cathedral
C. Esplanade
D. Senate Square
E. Senate
F. Imperial Palace
G. Stålberg's House
H. Naval Base
J. Observatory

**HELSINGFORS**

B
A D E
C F
G

North Harbour

H
Skatudden

South Harbour

Kronbergsfjärden

J

Langorn

Little Svarto

Stora
Rantan

West
Svarto

1 2 3

4

East
Svarto

Sandhamn

**SVEABORG**

Vargon

5

Gustafvard

1. Artillery Bay
2. Gunboat Sheds
3. Arsenal
4. Citadel
5. Fort Gustaf

Bakholmen

*British
Gunboats*

*British
Gunboats*

Abramsholm

*British
& French
Gunboats*

Otterhall

*Skogsholm*

Mortar Vesssels

Dragon

Euryalus

Skogskar

Vulture

*British
Gunboats*

0    500  1,000        2,000

Yards

N

W        E

S

*Allied Fleet
at anchor*

Magicienne

Grohara

# Prologue

# Reindeer Games

---

Kit Killigrew suddenly knew that he was tired. He always knew when his body or his mind had had enough, but in his line of work it was not always possible to act on the knowledge. He had the feeling that today was going to be just such an occasion.

Shrugging off the urge to find a warm, quiet place where he could lie down and catch up on much-needed sleep, he pulled up the bottom of his sealskin jacket to get at the pockets of his trousers and took out his miniature telescope. He rubbed the palm of a gloved hand over the eyepiece and raised it to one eye, studying the village through the clouds of condensation that billowed from his mouth: the snow was piled thick on the roofs of the log cabins and barns, and here and there wood smoke twisted lazily from chimneys. The place was peaceful enough ... if you went by appearances.

He returned the telescope to his pocket, took the ski poles from where he had propped them up against the trunk of a pine tree, and pushed himself off over the snow. He had heard that in mountainous Norway, the folk often skied downhill at breakneck speeds, using the poles only to steady themselves and leaving the rest to gravity. It sounded exhilarating, and Killigrew promised himself that when the war with Russia was over he would find the time to travel to Norway and try it for himself.

But this was the Duchy of Finland – if not as flat as Norfolk, then certainly closer to its topography than Norway – and he had to push the skis forward one after the other to cover the half-mile to the village.

Tomorrow, he knew, his ankles would ache from the unusual movement; but tomorrow could look after itself.

He halted at the back of the barn on the outskirts of the village and crouched to unbind the skis from his half-boots. Putting the skis and ski poles in the lee of a feed trough, he made his way around the side of the barn and strode briskly up the lane. There were not many folk in the streets – it was too cold to be out without good reason – but those farmers he did pass gave him sidelong glances of curiosity.

Vice Admiral Napier had probably chosen this place because it was so far from the beaten track, and therefore discreet to his way of thinking. But Killigrew, who was no stranger to this kind of cloak-and-dagger work, would have preferred a larger town, or even a city like Åbo, where there were too many people for everyone to know everyone else's affairs, and a stranger could pass unnoticed. At least the Finns believed in minding their own business, and were too polite to stare. Nevertheless, Killigrew could not shrug off the feeling that there were a hundred pairs of eyes watching him intently through the cracks in the shutters over the windows looking out over the lane. Finland was part of Russia, after all, and since Britain and its ally France were currently at war with Russia, and Commander Kit Killigrew was a British naval officer in civilian rig, if captured by the authorities he was eligible to be shot as a spy.

Which, he thought ruefully, was effectively what he was.

The inn stood towards the middle of the village and had probably done so since the Middle Ages. It was built around three sides of a courtyard, with the stables forming the fourth side of the square. Killigrew passed through the archway into the courtyard, looking around to get a sense of the layout of the place. Wooden steps led up to a gallery with rooms leading off on two sides, and tables and benches were set out to one side where the inn's patrons could sit and eat in the summer, although now the area was covered in snow.

The door to the main part of the inn was off to his left. He pushed it open and stepped into a low-beamed room with tables and chairs and a log fire roaring in the hearth, the only part of the inn built of stone. A Christmas tree decked with ribbons and baubles still stood in one corner. An attractive blonde woman sat on a stool behind the counter, reading a book, while a young man wearing an apron wiped down the tables.

Killigrew pulled back the fur-lined hood of his jacket to reveal the face of a man in his early thirties, dark brown eyes set in an angular, lean-jawed face beneath thick, black hair. 'Good morning,' he said in Swedish. In this part of Finland, most people spoke Finnish, but Swedish – the language of the middle and upper classes, and of the south coast – was still understood, a hangover of the days when the duchy had been part of Sweden: that had been forty-five years ago, before the Swedes had been forced to cede the duchy to Russia.

'Good morning,' the woman returned. 'What can I do for you?'

'Do you have any *glögg*?' '*Glögg*' was Swedish for 'mulled wine'.

Her eyes narrowed. 'In Finland we call it *glögi*.'

He gave the countersign: ' "A rose by any other name . . ." '

She nodded. 'Come with me,' she told him, coming from behind the counter and walking towards the door. 'Look after the place,' she told the youth in the apron. 'I'll only be a few minutes.'

He nodded.

Killigrew followed her out into the courtyard. On the far side, she opened the door to the stables. He followed her in.

'Is this your first trip to Finland?' she asked, striking a match to light an oil-lamp. The yellow flame revealed that the stables were roomy, with horses in some of the stalls, reindeer in a pen at one end, and a hayloft overhead.

Killigrew closed the door behind him. 'Right now, I'm more concerned that it may be my last.'

She turned and found herself staring down the barrel of the revolver in his fist. 'Mind if I search you?' he asked.

'Do I have any say in the matter?'

He shook his head. 'Hands against that wall and spread your legs.'

She complied, and he started to run his hands over her body, patting her down for concealed weapons.

'This is rather intimate, considering we haven't even been formally introduced,' she remarked.

'The name's Killigrew,' he told her. 'Kit Killigrew, at your service.' He straightened and pulled up the bottom of his jacket to tuck the revolver back inside the waistband of his trousers. 'Now: where's Jurgaitis?'

'He's not here yet.'

'He was supposed to be waiting for me.'

'I cannot help that. Did he have far to come?'

'Far enough.'

She shrugged. 'Then we will have to wait.'

3

'How do you pass a spare hour or two in Finland?' he asked archly.

Before she could reply, he heard footsteps outside. He glanced towards the door in time to see a shadow fall across the narrow gaps between the planks in the walls of the stables as someone approached. He pushed the woman away from him so that she sprawled across a bale of hay: if there was going to be any shooting, he did not want her to get hit.

By the time the door opened, he had already drawn his revolver once more and levelled it at the man who entered. Killigrew dropped into a crouching position, but he straightened as soon as the light of the oil-lamp fell across the man's face. The newcomer was the same age as Killigrew, tall, blond and well built. He had several days' growth of beard on his chin and from the look of his clothes he had been sleeping rough for the past few days.

Killigrew tucked away the revolver again. 'Nick . . .!'

Nicholas Jurgaitis took two tottering steps forward and collapsed into Killigrew's arms. 'Hullo, Kit,' he said weakly, as Killigrew lowered him gently to the floor. 'Wondered who Napier would send. Should've guessed it would be you.'

'What's the matter?'

Jurgaitis gestured weakly at his stomach. 'Knife wound. Couldn't very well go to a surgeon. Fothered it as best I could, but I think it's gone bad . . .'

Killigrew tore open the front of Jurgaitis' coat and the frock-coat underneath to reveal that the waistcoat below that was stiff with dried blood, and there was a rank smell that was more than just body odour, so bad that Killigrew struggled not to gag.

He gripped Jurgaitis by the shoulder. 'Hold on, Nick,' he said desperately. 'I've a boat waiting down by the coast. There's a medicine chest on board. We'll get you fixed up . . .'

Jurgaitis shook his head. 'I'm done for. It's gangrene: you know it and I know it. Feel in my coat.'

'In your coat?'

'In the lining: secret plans.'

'What plans?' Had Jurgaitis somehow managed to steal the Russians' war plans while he had been working at the Admiralty in St Petersburg? Somehow it seemed too good to be true.

Killigrew fingered Jurgaitis' coat until he felt what he was looking for. Taking out his penknife, he slashed at the lining and pulled out a large piece of paper, folded into eighths. A quick glance revealed technical drawings of some kind; Killigrew did not have time to study them more closely. 'What is it?'

'Get that drawing to Napier,' gasped Jurgaitis. 'He'll know . . .' He broke off as a fit of coughing racked his body. Blood bubbled between his lips.

'I'll take those, if you don't mind,' said the woman.

Killigrew glanced up and saw her standing over him with a small pocket pistol in one hand, pointed at him.

'Your revolver first: nice and slowly. Toss it over there.' She jerked her head to indicate one corner.

He obeyed. 'Third Section?' he asked her. Only the Third Section of the Tsar's Chancery – the Russian secret police, known from Finland to Alaska as 'the White Terror' – could be so villainous as to employ a woman as a spy.

She nodded and extended one hand. 'The plans.'

He held them out to her, putting them close to her hand but not actually in it. She groped for them, glanced down . . .

He brought his left hand down on her right wrist, forcing the pistol aside. She squeezed the trigger instinctively. The shot went wide, startling the animals and filling the air with acrid smoke. Dropping the plans, he spun her round and twisted her arm up into the small of her back until the pistol fell from her fingers.

'I've never killed a woman,' he hissed angrily in her ear, 'but there's a first time for everything.'

Hearing more footsteps behind him, Killigrew whirled, pulling her in front of him, one arm crooked around her neck, the palm of his other hand against the back of her head.

Three men entered the stable, two of them carrying rifled muskets that they unslung and levelled at Killigrew: Finnish *jägers*, judging by their uniforms. The third – Killigrew recognised him as Lieutenant Kizheh – wore a greatcoat over the sky-blue uniform of an officer of the Third Section and limped badly, walking with the aid of a cane.

'That's no way to treat a lady,' sneered Kizheh.

'No lady would work as a spy for the Third Section,' Killigrew countered.

'Ditto a gentleman work as a spy for the British Royal Navy,' Kizheh countered.

'And how's our mutual friend Colonel Nekrasoff these days? I'm surprised he didn't make the effort to come and arrest me in person. I must have made him look damned foolish to his superiors after I spirited the Bullivants out from under his nose last year. Was he obliged to take up residence in Siberia?'

Kizheh shook his head. 'He's well enough; I'm sure he'll be pleased to see you when I take you back to the Kochubey Mansion for . . . interrogation.' The lieutenant smiled broadly. 'Commander Christopher Killigrew! I had hoped to arrest one of Vice Admiral Napier's spies in addition to this traitor here,' taking out a revolver, he indicated Jurgaitis, 'but I never hoped in my wildest dreams it would be you!'

'Tell your men to drop their muskets, or I'll snap her neck!'

The lieutenant shook his head, and tutted. 'An officer and a gentleman? Murder a woman in cold blood? I think not, Commander.'

'Just now my blood's anything but cold, Lieutenant.'

'Unlike mine.' Kizheh brought the revolver up sharply and squeezed off a shot. Killigrew felt hot blood splatter across the side of his face as the top of the woman's skull exploded. Suddenly limp, she slipped from his arms to crumple on the floor, leaving him exposed. He raised his hands, fully expecting the lieutenant to shoot him where he stood, and glanced to where a hayfork was propped against the wall nearby.

Kizheh saw it too. 'Don't even think about it,' he warned Killigrew pleasantly.

'Wouldn't dream of it.' Butter would not have melted in the commander's mouth.

The lieutenant indicated Jurgaitis. 'Check him,' he told one of the *jäger*s.

The man slung his rifle across his back and crouched over Jurgaitis. 'He's still alive, but only just.'

'How will we get him back to Helsingfors?' asked the other *jäger*.

Kizheh levelled his revolver at Jurgaitis' forehead and pulled the trigger. Killigrew flinched as his friend's body juddered and lay still.

The lieutenant indicated the folded drawing at Killigrew's feet. 'Pick up that paper and bring it to me,' he ordered the *jäger*.

The man unslung his rifle once more, levelling it at Killigrew as he approached. With Kizheh keeping him covered, there was little Killigrew could do, but the *jäger* still kept his eyes on the commander as he groped for the plans, not taking them off him until the drawings were in his hand and he was well out of the commander's reach. Over his shoulder, he handed them to the lieutenant, who tucked them in an inside pocket.

'All right, let's go,' Kizheh told Killigrew, and gestured at the door with his revolver. 'After you.'

The commander walked across towards the three Russians. As he drew level with Kizheh, he kicked the cane out from under him. The lieutenant fell and Killigrew snatched the cane from his hand, using it to bat the oil-lamp from the post on which it rested. It smashed against the wall, dousing the second *jäger* with burning oil. As the man screamed, the other *jäger* whirled. Killigrew brought the cane down sharply against his head, knocking him down. Kizheh struggled to rise with the revolver in his hand; Killigrew grabbed him from behind, crooking one arm around his neck and prising the gun from his fingers. Holding the muzzle to Kizheh's forehead, he reached inside his coat to retrieve the plans, tucking them inside his jacket.

'No: after *you*.'

The two of them followed the screaming *jäger* from the blazing stables. The *jäger* threw himself down in the snow outside, rolling over and over to extinguish his burning clothes. The rest of the *jäger*s were waiting in the courtyard outside, about a dozen of them. They unslung their rifles, but seeing Kizheh with a gun to his head they hesitated.

'Tell your men to throw down their muskets,' Killigrew snarled.

'This is ridiculous,' Kizheh sighed calmly. 'You're outnumbered, surrounded, and on enemy territory. Just how far do you expect to get?'

'Far enough.'

One of the *jäger*s cocked the hammer on his rifle. Killigrew levelled the revolver at him warningly, and Kizheh seized his chance. He rammed an elbow into Killigrew's stomach and broke free. He screamed at his men as he hobbled away from the commander: 'Shoot him!'

Killigrew was the first to obey, shooting the man who had cocked his hammer. He kicked over one of the wooden tables and ducked behind it. The rest of the *jäger*s discharged their rifles in a ragged volley, the bullets splintering through the wooden boards, one of them coming close enough to pluck at Killigrew's sleeve. He stood up before they could reload, blazing away with the revolver and knocking two of them down before the hammer fell on a spent percussion cap. He threw the gun at a third, turned, and sped across the courtyard. Jumping on a table, he ran across it, his feet slipping awkwardly in the snow, and hurled himself from the far end.

He caught hold of the gallery above and swung from it, hauling himself up on to the railing. Balancing on the rail, he straightened and reached up for the eaves above. His fingers scrabbled at the snow-covered shingles, legs kicking in the air below as he struggled to pull himself up. At last he managed to get a knee over the lip of the roof, then one foot followed by the other, and he stood up. The *jäger*s had already reloaded their rifles and they started shooting. Bullets soughed past Killigrew's head as he ran over the apex of the roof, dropping down out of sight on the other side. He slid down the roof, and launched himself from the eaves at the back of the inn to land on the balls of his feet on the ground below, rolling over in the snow.

As he ran around the backs of the log cabins, he could hear booted feet clattering on the cobbles in the courtyard. 'Split up and search the whole village until you find him!' Kizheh was shouting. 'Ten kopecks for the man who brings me his head!'

*Skinflint*, Killigrew thought with a grin, making sure he had the plans securely tucked inside the guernsey beneath his jacket.

He reached the barn where he had left his skis and crouched down to bind them on his feet, his fumbling fingers shaking with cold and excitement. He had finally secured the last binding when he heard a footfall, and looked up to see one of the *jäger*s step into view from the side of the barn.

The *jäger* levelled his musket. 'Stand up – slowly!'

Killigrew stood up – quickly. He grabbed one end of the feed trough as he did so, flipping it end over end so that it fell against the *jäger*, knocking him down. The *jäger* had barely hit the ground before Killigrew picked up his ski poles and pushed off over the snow.

He had covered perhaps a few hundred yards before they came after him. The first he knew of it was when shots rang out behind him and he saw the bullets kicking up little spurts of snow. He glanced over one shoulder to see half a dozen reindeer-drawn sledges coming after him. The sledges were low, barely large enough for a grown man to sit in, but perfect for travelling across country in the Finnish winter. The *jäger*s drove them with one hand on the reins and another holding a carbine with the stock hard against their shoulders. They did not seem to have much difficulty shooting while on the move, and gripped the reins between their teeth when they needed to reload. Even as he looked, one of the sledgers brought his carbine up to his shoulder and fired, without releasing the reins in his left hand. Killigrew heard the crack of the carbine and saw smoke plume from the muzzle. The bullet came close enough for him to hear it sough through the air: they had to be using rifled muskets; but even so, they were good shots.

Drawn by the reindeer, the sledges moved much faster over the snow than Killigrew could hope to on skis. There was a thick belt of trees off to his right and he made for them: the sledges might be swifter, but

8

they would be less manoeuvrable. He only had to make it as far as the trees, he told himself, and he would stand a chance.

He zigzagged right and left, trying to throw off their aim, but by the time he reached the trees they were only a hundred yards behind him. Even as he shot between two trunks, a bullet smacked into a bough overhead and sent the snow heaped on the branch cascading down into his eyes.

He slalomed in and out of the trees gingerly at first – there had been no forests in the Arctic where he had learned to ski – but he could not afford to be cautious with six Finnish *jägers* in reindeer-sledges breathing down his neck. He pushed as hard as he could with the ski poles, powering himself over the snow at break-neck speed.

The ground sloped down, enough for gravity to give him a helping hand. He tried to take a path that would be impossible for the sledges to follow, ducking under branches lower than a reindeer's antlers or using snow hummocks to launch himself over fallen tree trunks, almost crashing into a bush on the other side of one. When the track became straight enough for him to risk another glance over his shoulder, however, he saw his pursuers were still gaining. He glimpsed three of them, moving through the trees in a skirmishing line, the nearest less than fifty yards off now.

Abruptly there were no more trees in front of him, and the ground dropped away sharply to reveal a sunken road. One of the sledges moved up the track below him: a *jäger* had cut around the outside of the forest to head him off. He had not seen Killigrew yet, but it was only a matter of time. The commander's first instinct was to brake: he ignored it, and pushed off the edge of the slope with his ski poles, aiming for the sledge.

The *jäger* saw him and tried to level his carbine from the still-moving sledge. Killigrew's skis glanced off the barrel of the gun, throwing the man's aim off. The commander landed on the other side of the road, falling heavily on his side. But the *jäger* had been thrown from the sledge. Still gripping the reins, he jerked the reindeer around. The beast turned sharply, the sledge skidding on the icy track before hitting a rock. It bounced into the air, spinning, and smashed against the side of a tree.

Sprawling in the snow, the *jäger* fumbled for his carbine. Killigrew flung one of his ski poles like a spear, taking the man in the throat. Steaming blood pumped on to the snow, almost black against the whiteness.

Another carbine barked, the bullet narrowly missing Killigrew. He glanced up to see a second *jäger* had halted at the top of the slope above him. As the man reloaded, Killigrew skied across to where the first *jäger* lay dying. He snatched up the carbine, aimed and fired; the man tumbled from his sledge and rolled down the slope to lie still at the bottom.

Two more sledges appeared a hundred yards down the road and turned to meet him. Glancing in the other direction, he saw the other two sledges appear. Past the road the ground sloped down again to the coast, less than fifty yards away now. Beyond, the sea ice stretched out into the distance, a smooth, unbroken expanse of white. A few miles off, Killigrew could just make out a black speck that might have been the *Sankt Georg*, the fishing boat that had brought him here and would – he hoped – take him away again. But if he tried to ski towards her, the *jäger*s would overtake him before he got halfway.

He glanced at the sledges of the two men he had killed. The first was smashed beyond repair; the second at the top of the slope above him, and by the time he had climbed up there the other four would be upon him. Taking his clasp-knife from his pocket, he skied across to the reindeer that had been drawing the first sledge. Skittish, it shied away, but he managed to calm it. He slashed through the harness that attached it to the wreckage of the sledge, and then pocketed his knife, taking the reins in one hand and the traces in the other.

'Giddyap!'

The reindeer did not understand English, but got the general idea from the way Killigrew flicked the reins. It sprang away, drawing him after it on his skis.

'I do not like it,' the skipper of the *Sankt Georg* said in his broken English, flapping his arms about his body to keep warm.

'You ain't being paid to like it,' Petty Officer Wes Molineaux told him. 'And paid well, I might add.'

A seaman from the back streets of Seven Dials, Molineaux looked out of place on the deck of a Swedish fishing boat – a stout-hulled, fore-and-aft rigged *galease*, fifty feet from stem to stern. Molineaux had not spoken a word of Swedish when the boat had set sail from the Åland Islands just over a week ago, although he had picked some up since then, the skipper being the only other person on board who spoke English.

In retrospect, Molineaux reflected, Mr Killigrew could have picked

10

someone better to help him on this mission – Vice Admiral Napier had given him his pick of any man from the British fleet – but Molineaux had been the commander's first and last choice. The two of them had met while working undercover for the Slave Trade Department seven and a half years ago. Since then they had shared all manner of adventures together in the far-flung corners of Her Majesty's Empire: some routine, some anything but. Now, once again, they were on one of their less routine assignments, up to their necks in the kind of cloak-and-dagger misadventures that Napier seemed to take especial delight in embroiling them in.

But – being black – Molineaux did not exactly blend in with the crew of the Swedish fishing boat.

Despite his reservations about this particular mission, Molineaux had been delighted that Killigrew had chosen him for this job: it was flattering to be picked out of an entire fleet, especially when the man doing the picking did so because he knew his life would depend on you coming through for him. Not that Molineaux had not proven to the commander that he could depend on him time and time again, but Killigrew had saved the petty officer's own life enough times to make keeping score irrelevant. Molineaux would not have presumed to describe himself as one of Killigrew's friends, but the petty officer had hopes that one day he would earn a boatswain's warrant, and Killigrew was one of the few officers willing to let him prove himself worthy of it. Besides, the commander had a knack for getting himself out of scrapes rivalled only by his knack for getting himself into them in the first place. Whatever else you could say about Killigrew, life was never dull when he was around.

'What's that?' The skipper pointed to where some dark specks in the distance advanced across the ice towards them.

Molineaux adjusted the aim of his telescope, and a grin spread across his face when he picked out a figure on skis being dragged across the ice by a reindeer. Four reindeer-drawn sledges were in hot pursuit, and Molineaux saw the occasional muzzle flash in the early morning gloom.

He handed the telescope to the skipper. 'See for yourself.'

'Is that who I think it is?'

'It ain't St Nick, that's for sure! Draw us in to the ice.'

While Molineaux headed below to fetch his rifled musket, the skipper ordered his men to pull on the mooring ropes until the fenders on the side bumped against the ice. By the time the petty officer returned on

11

deck, the *jägers* were within range: he raised the rifle to his shoulder and fired. He hit the nearest in the chest and had the gratification of seeing him fall back out of his sledge.

Killigrew reached the edge of the ice about two hundred yards ahead of his pursuers. 'Whoa!' He hauled on his reindeer's reins and skithered to a halt a few yards from where the boat was moored. As Molineaux reloaded his musket, the commander used his knife to cut the bindings on his skis. He paused to fondle the reindeer's ears affectionately. 'Bravo, Blitzen!'

Molineaux laughed. 'You certainly know how to make an entrance, sir!'

'But now I'm more interested in making an exit; the sooner, the better.' Killigrew took a run up, leaped from the edge of the ice and hooked his hands over the *galease*'s gunwale. Molineaux hauled him inboard, and the skipper ordered his men to unfurl the sails while Killigrew slumped in the lee of the gunwale.

The skipper crossed to the helm and spun it, putting the *galease* on a north-westerly heading to take the best possible advantage of the south-westerly winds. The strong breeze rapidly carried them away from the coast, and by the time the other sledgers reached the edge of the ice the fishing boat was all but out of range. They unslung their carbines and fired after it anyway, without making any of their shots tell.

Once the danger was past, the skipper put the *galease* about – they would have to tack to reach the Åland Islands – and ordered one of his men to take the helm. There was no danger of pursuit: the ships of the Russian navy would be frozen in their harbours at Kronstadt and Sveaborg by now, with no chance of breaking free before the spring.

Molineaux took Killigrew down to the saloon, where one of the fishermen supplied the commander with a blanket to drape round his shoulders, and a steaming mug of cocoa.

'What about the cove you were s'posed to meet?' asked Molineaux.

'Didn't make it,' Killigrew told him tightly.

'Wasted trip?'

'Perhaps.' Killigrew reached under his guernsey, took out a large piece of paper and unfolded it. He stared at it with a thoughtful expression. 'Perhaps not.'

# I

# Secret Weapons

From the Åland Islands, Killigrew and Molineaux travelled by steamer to Danzig, where Killigrew purchased them both railway tickets to Stettin and showed them to the guard at the barrier.

'You'd better give me my ticket, sir,' Molineaux said once they were on the platform and had seen their traps loaded into the baggage van. 'I dunno about these Prooshan trains, but in England they sometimes have cads in the third-class carriage what checks you ain't trying to get a free ride.'

Killigrew gave him a deprecating look. 'After what we've been through together, Molineaux, you're not seriously suggesting I'd expect you to ride in third while I travel first are you?'

'First class? Are you sure, sir?'

'Oh, for heaven's sake, Molineaux! It's not as if I can't afford it now I'm on a commander's pay.'

'Very kind of you, sir.'

'Nonsense. I shall be glad of your company.'

Molineaux and Killigrew chatted easily on the journey from Danzig to Stettin, and if it had not been for the coarser cloth of Molineaux's clothes, the colour of his skin, and the fact he threw the occasional 'sir' into his side of the conversation, an eavesdropper fluent in English might have taken them for social equals. They discussed poetry, a subject on which Molineaux's knowledge far outweighed Killigrew's, as he was conversant with every English poet from the anonymous author of *Beowulf* to Alfred Tennyson.

The conversation turned to the army's mismanagement of the

campaign in the Crimea, a revelation that had surprised neither, as they shared the bluejackets' contempt for 'sodgers', although their contempt was not unleavened by pity for the sufferings of the brave men who had risked life and limb at Inkerman, the Alma and Balaclava. The previous year's naval campaign in the Baltic had not been without its horrors, but seemed like a church outing compared to the kind of news they had received from the Black Sea.

They reached Stettin shortly after noon. After dining at one of the cafés in the town they caught a train to Berlin, where they spent the night at a hotel on the Unter den Linden. Early the following morning they took a diligence to the Potsdamer Bahnhof and travelled by train via Hanover and Cologne to the Belgian border, where they passed through customs without incident and the train continued on to Liège. Molineaux dozed, his feet up with a newspaper under his boots so they would not dirty the seat opposite, and as Killigrew gazed out of the window at the snow-covered Ardennes his thoughts turned to the Honourable Miss Araminta Maltravers.

They had met at Cowes four years ago. That had been the year of the Great Exhibition, the year Killigrew had discovered that he did not have to be on the quarterdeck of one of Her Majesty's ships to find true happiness. It had not been long before a passionate affair had turned into a romance. He could not remember which of them had first mentioned marriage, but before he knew it they had become engaged, despite the opposition of her parents: Viscount and Viscountess Bullivant.

But in his bitter experience, happiness was something that never lasted; and perhaps it was this knowledge that had driven him to pre-empt fate by breaking off his burgeoning relationship with Araminta and volunteering to join Sir Edward Belcher's expedition to rescue the missing Franklin expedition. It had always been his dream to join one of the Arctic exploring squadrons, and he had even put his name forward for Franklin's expedition when it had set out, although he had been rejected at that time.

How to break the news to Minty had been another matter altogether. In the end he had lost his nerve. Well aware that he might never return from the Arctic, he had not wanted to leave her widowed before she was even married, so he had told her nothing, convincing himself that making her hate him was the kindest thing he could do. The first she had learned of it was when she had seen his name in the newspaper as one of the officers who had already sailed in Sir Edward Belcher's

14

squadron. If he did survive, he had told himself, he could explain his reasons for jilting her and, perhaps, pick up where they had left off.

But Belcher's expedition had been almost as big a disaster as Franklin's, except that at least most of Belcher's men had returned. By the time Killigrew had got back to England, weak from malnutrition and scurvy, more than a year after he had set out, Society gossip was linking Araminta's name romantically with that of Lord Dallaway, and Killigrew had discreetly kept his distance.

An invitation from Vice Admiral Sir Charles Napier had made it easier for him. By the late summer of 1853 talk of war with Russia had already been in the air, and Napier had known that if Britain sent a fleet into the Baltic she would need experienced pilots to guide them through the shoals in the Gulf of Finland. Killigrew had travelled to Helsingfors, posing as an ichthyologist to recruit pilots from the duchy's community of fishermen and merchant seamen. At the time it had been something of a lark, and he had not thought of himself as a spy at all. Only later had he encountered the Third Section.

That had been the following year, after war had finally broken out, and Killigrew had been with the Baltic fleet by then, the second in command of HMS *Ramillies*. Apart from the capture of the Åland Islands, they had not seen much fighting and had lost more men to cholera than to enemy action.

And then Araminta and her parents had gone and got themselves captured by the Russians.

Lord Bullivant had been just one of several aristocrats for whom taking a yacht to the Baltic so they could watch the fighting seemed like a perfectly reasonable thing to do. The Russians had not agreed and wanted to try the Bullivants for espionage, so Napier had sent Killigrew ashore with a flag of truce to negotiate their release. After several alarms and excursions he had succeeded, although not without sinking his lordship's yacht and falling foul of Colonel Nekrasoff of the Third Section in the process. But none of that had seemed to matter when Killigrew had been able to hold Araminta in his arms once he was safely back on board HMS *Ramillies*.

But there had been four months left in the year before the onset of the winter ice would force the British fleet to withdraw from the Baltic until the following spring, and the Bullivants could not stay on the *Ramillies*, even those of them who would have liked to. So Araminta had gone back to England and Killigrew had stayed behind with the fleet in the Baltic. He had hoped to see her over Christmas –

he had had an invitation to spend the festive season at the Duke of Hartcliffe's country house in Somerset, and it was a fair bet that Araminta would be there. But just as the *Ramillies* had been preparing to leave the Baltic with the rest of the fleet, Vice Admiral Napier had summoned Killigrew on board the flagship with another invitation. He had made it sound so easy – nip ashore, collect Jurgaitis and bring him back to London. Jurgaitis was an old friend, so Killigrew could hardly refuse.

As the train approached the French border, Killigrew wondered what sort of reception he would get from Araminta if he turned up on the doorstep of her father's town house on the fashionable side of Grosvenor Square. His lordship was one of the leading lights of the Tory Party, and with parliament in session he and his family would be residing in town rather than at his country seat in Rutlandshire. But Araminta was of age, and if she agreed to receive Killigrew there was little her father could do to stop it.

It was now the last weekend in January 1855. Their parting five months earlier had been on a positive note, and it had not seemed unreasonable to hope that by the following summer she would be Mrs Killigrew. But she had not replied to any of the letters he had sent her since then, and the mail service between England and the fleet was usually pretty good. Killigrew knew all too well that relationships started under intense circumstances never lasted but, his relationship with Araminta predating the adventures they had shared in the Gulf of Finland, he hoped it was firmer than that. On the other hand, it had not taken her long to find a new beau while he had been in the Arctic; and for an heiress as eligible as the Honourable Miss Araminta Maltravers, it did not seem impossible that she might have fallen for the charms of someone from her own kind: richer than Killigrew, better-looking than Killigrew, a better prospect for marriage in more ways than he cared to consider. He tried to tell himself there was no point worrying about it now: all would shortly be revealed.

The next day was a Sunday and there were no trains, so Killigrew and Molineaux spent two nights at a hotel in Montmartre, exploring the city separately during the course of the intervening day. Killigrew knew Paris well, and Molineaux had also picked up French somewhere along the line, so the two of them were able to amuse themselves well enough.

On the Monday morning they rendezvoused on the platform at the Gare du Nord in plenty of time to catch the Double Express Service to

London via Boulogne, where a packet steamer waited to take them across the Channel. At Folkestone, Molineaux was about to join Killigrew in one of the first-class compartments when he caught sight of an altercation between a prettily distraught Frenchwoman and the guard, who clearly did not speak a word of French but seemed to think that if he spoke English loudly and slowly enough, she would understand.

Molineaux intervened. '*Pardonnez moi, mam'selle. Puis-je vous aider?*'

'*Vous parlez français, m'sieur?*'

'*Oui, mam'selle, bien sûr.*'

'*Je dois prendre le train à Londres.*'

'*Mais certainement, mam'selle. Le train ici, c'est le train à Londres.*'

'*Ah, merci, merci, m'sieur! Merci beaucoup!*'

Molineaux turned to Killigrew. 'I'd best go with her, sir,' he said with a wink. 'Make sure she gets off at the right station.'

The commander smiled indulgently. 'I'll see you at London Bridge.' He watched Molineaux go, and shook his head, chuckling wryly. He had been impressed by Molineaux's abilities as a seaman long ago, and had learned to turn the occasional blind eye to his impudence. Once he had promised himself that if he ever got the chance to help Molineaux in his career he would certainly do so, but looking back he could not help thinking that Molineaux had done more to advance his, Killigrew's, own career, if only by keeping him alive.

There were four first-class compartments in each carriage, opening straight on to the platform. Killigrew found an empty one, climbed inside, and settled down on one of the seats, taking the front and back pages of the previous day's *Manchester Guardian* and spreading them on the opposite seat so he could rest his boots there. He leafed through the remaining news pages, which were full of the terrible sufferings of the troops in the trenches before Sevastopol. The member of parliament for Sheffield, a Radical, had moved a resolution calling for a committee of inquiry to be set up to investigate the Tory Government's conduct of the war, and Lord Aberdeen's administration was looking very shaky indeed.

'I do beg your pardon. Is this the London train?'

Killigrew looked up from his newspaper to see a clergyman leaning through the door of the compartment, a tall, broad-shouldered fellow with a shovel hat and a pair of half-moon spectacles perched on his nose.

'It is indeed, Reverend. Hop aboard.'

The clergyman climbed into the compartment and closed the door behind him. He put his shovel hat on the hat rack, hung up his furled umbrella, and turned to Killigrew, looking pointedly at his cheroot.

'Does this bother you? I can put it out, if you like . . .'

The clergyman shook his head. 'Not on my account, please! But would you mind if we opened a window?'

Killigrew waved a dismissive hand. 'By all means. I'm not averse to a little fresh air myself.'

The clergyman opened the window and sat down opposite Killigrew, opening a copy of the Bible. At last the guard on the platform blew his whistle, and a hiss of steam sounded from the engine. A succession of clanks sounded as each coupling took up the strain, and then the whole carriage gave a slight jerk and they were on their way.

Killigrew gazed out of the window, watching the rooftops of Folkestone roll by, until the train had left the suburbs behind and was barrelling through the snow-covered Kentish countryside. A stiff breeze blew through the window, but both Killigrew and the clergyman were well muffled against the cold.

Killigrew tilted the brim of his wideawake down over his eyes so he could snooze, and looked forward to his reunion with Araminta. Of course, his first priority was to report to Napier as soon as possible; but already the winter sky was growing dark, and the Admiralty would be closed by the time the train reached London. He could go back to Paddington, spend an hour cleansing the grime of his long journey from his pores at the local hummum baths, change into some clean clothes, and it would still not be too late to call at the Bullivants' . . .

An exclamation from the clergyman snapped him out of his reverie. 'Bless my soul!'

Killigrew pushed up the brim of his wideawake with an index finger and met the clergyman's expression of alarm with a quizzical glance.

'I'd clean forgotten: we'll be coming up on the Sandling tunnel at any moment!'

The last thing they wanted was billows of smoke from the engine's smokestack filling the compartment with soot. 'Stay where you are, Reverend,' Killigrew told him, rising to his feet. 'I'll get it.'

He grasped the leather tab to pull it back up, but it was stuck. The clergyman stood up behind him; to help him close it, he assumed. He was trying to jerk it free when he glanced down and noticed a broken matchstick wedged in the crack, jamming it. The matchstick could not

18

have been there when he had opened the window only a few minutes earlier, which could only mean . . .

He started to turn, and at that moment the train entered the tunnel and the unlit compartment was plunged into darkness. Killigrew felt something cold and unyielding looped over his head and pulled tight against his throat. The clergyman hauled him backwards, pulling him off balance, and forced him down with his chest against the edge of one of the seats. Killigrew felt a knee between his shoulder blades, and then the cold, hard metal of the chain was cutting into his Adam's apple, choking him.

It was done as expertly as any *thug* garrotting an innocent traveller on the Grand Trunk Road between Delhi and Lahore. Too late Killigrew realised he should not have been taken in by the shovel hat; the man was far too broad-shouldered to be a man of the cloth. He flailed to break free in vain.

Drawing up one knee beneath him, Killigrew managed to brace it against the floor at the foot of the seat. He let himself go limp. The assassin was too much of an expert to stop garrotting him, but he grew more confident. Killigrew braced his hands against the seat and, in conjunction with his leg, heaved himself backwards with all his might, carrying the assassin with him. The two of them crashed against the side of the compartment, and Killigrew heard glass smash as the assassin's head collided with the window. The earthy reek of smoke filled the compartment, the clatter of the wheels on the track echoing against the walls of the tunnel.

The fading sunlight filled the compartment once more as the train emerged from the tunnel. Killigrew rammed an elbow into the assassin's ribs and managed to break free. The assassin came at him again as he turned, the fob chain of a watch stretched taut between his gloved hands. Killigrew caught him by the wrists, but the assassin was stronger. He forced the commander back against the door, pinning him there. Before Killigrew could brace his arms, the chain was digging into his throat once more. He felt himself choking, the assassin's face an impassive mask dissolving in the red haze that filled his vision.

Realising he had only a few seconds of consciousness left, he aimed a kick at the man's crotch. But the assassin expected nothing less and twisted to receive the blow on one leg. Killigrew's attempts to pull the chain away from his throat were in vain. In desperation, he reached behind him until his groping fingers clasped the door handle.

He opened it.

As the door swung open behind him, he felt himself falling back. He caught hold of the door jamb and hung out from the side of the carriage, painfully conscious of the gravel bed of the railway rushing past beneath him at breakneck speed, close to forty miles an hour. The wind whipped the wideawake from his head in an instant.

The assassin tried to prise his fingers off the jamb. With his other hand, Killigrew reached up and grabbed the top of the door to brace himself. But he lost his footing on the threshold as the door swung out further and found himself dangling from one arm. He swung his other arm up and hung there, staring through the open window to where a train coming in the opposite direction hurtled towards him.

The assassin leaned out from the door, trying to grab him and drag him back inside the compartment. Killigrew would be hanged first. He thought about throwing himself from the train, but the rocky embankment below the track offered escape only at the cost of a broken neck. There was only one way to go.

Up.

He hauled himself up the side of the door with his arms, ignoring the painful protests of an old injury in one shoulder, until he could get his foot on the window-sill. He boosted himself up until his hips were against the top of the door – still swinging wildly with the swaying of the train, it was almost impossible to keep his balance – and he could reach across to grab the luggage rail that ran around the flat roof of the carriage.

The other train was almost upon him.

With one hand gripping the rail, he reached across with the other and entwined his fingers in the netting that held the luggage in place on the roof. Kicking himself clear of the door, he hauled himself over the rail, clambering over the neatly arranged luggage. He swung his legs clear less than two seconds before the rush of air from the locomotive slammed the swinging door against the side of the carriage and ripped it clean off its hinges with a crack like a rifle-shot, loud enough to be heard over the shriek of the passing locomotive.

The toecaps of Killigrew's half-boots scrabbled against the netting as he hauled himself to the centre of the roof. Gripping the netting tightly, he lay there gasping for breath. But he knew he could not afford to rest: the assassin was clearly bold and determined, and would not waste time before climbing up after him.

The wind made Killigrew's eyes smart. He looked towards the head of the train in time to see the arch of another tunnel bearing down on him. He threw himself flat and hugged the luggage through the netting, trying to melt into it. The roof of the tunnel roared overhead, plunging him into darkness once more. Acrid smoke stung his eyes and clawed at his lungs as the brickwork slashed past barely inches above his back. He glimpsed a light somewhere ahead, and moments later the train emerged from the tunnel.

He gulped the fresh air into his lungs, blinking tears from his eyes as he peered up ahead. No more tunnels for a while, as far as he could see. He eased himself gingerly into a sitting position, facing towards the side of the train, waiting for the assassin to show his face above the level of the roof so the commander could ram the heel of his half-boot into it. At least, with the door gone, it would be more difficult for him to climb up . . .

But why climb up on that side, when there was a perfectly sound door on the other . . .?

Killigrew twisted in time to see the assassin ascending behind him. There was barely time to brace himself for the onslaught, except the assassin rose to his feet, struggling to keep his balance on the bucketing carriage, and reached inside his frock-coat. Going for a dagger or a pistol; Killigrew did not know which and was not going to wait to find out. He threw himself at the man, catching him around the waist and bearing him down to the roof. The two of them tumbled perilously close to the edge.

The assassin rolled on top, straddling Killigrew and pinning him down. He belaboured Killigrew's face with his beefy fists before reaching under his coat again and pulling a large knife from his belt. He tried to plunge it down into the commander's face, and Killigrew barely caught him by the wrist in time. It took the strength of both arms to keep the blade at bay. Killigrew jerked his head to one side and relaxed his arms, allowing the blade to come arcing down and bury its tip deep in a steamer trunk less than an inch from his ear. Then he sank his teeth into the man's wrist and bit down with all his might.

The man screamed and Killigrew tasted blood in his mouth. He thrust his assailant off, crawling several feet across the luggage before turning to face him. The man had risen to his feet again and drawn the knife from the trunk. Killigrew had little choice but to rise to meet him, the wind buffeting his back as he stood up. He tugged off his greatcoat as the man came at him again. There was no need to throw it: all he had to do was let go and it flew from his hands to wrap itself around the assassin's head. The man flailed wildly with the knife, but Killigrew had already turned to run – or at least totter – towards the front of the train. He picked his way over the netting-covered luggage until he reached the end of the carriage.

There was no time to stop and measure the gap: he leaped without thinking, launching himself from the edge of one roof to land on the other. It was not much of a leap, at least not in terms of the breadth of the gap, but the wind was against him, as well as the uneven surface of the netting over the luggage packed there. One foot slipped out from beneath him and he stumbled, falling heavily and rolling over the side. Feeling himself slipping from the roof, he caught hold of the rail with one hand, and the breath was knocked out of him when he slammed against the side of the carriage.

He hung from one arm for a few seconds, flailing wildly until he caught hold of the rail in the other hand. He found himself dangling opposite the window of another first-class compartment. He tried to get the occupants' attention in the hope they would lower the sash and let him in, but peering through the window he saw there were only two people in there, a man and a woman, and both so intensely locked in a carnal embrace they probably would not have noticed if it had been a hippopotamus in lawn sleeves hanging outside the window.

The assassin leaped across the gap between the two carriages and landed on his feet, swaying only slightly before turning to stand over Killigrew. Grinning, he raised one foot over the commander's right hand where it gripped the rail. Killigrew transferred his grip to the netting and braced his feet against the side of the train, giving the netting an almighty tug. It was pulled out from beneath the assassin's feet and he landed on his back across the luggage.

Killigrew pulled himself up on to the roof and turned in time to see the assassin coming at him again, knife in hand, his back to the front of the train. The commander looked past him, and his eyes opened wide with fear. He threw himself flat on the roof, clasping his hands over his head. Seeing this, the assassin did not waste time glancing over his shoulder to see the low bridge hurtling towards him, but likewise threw himself flat.

Which was a mistake, because there *was* no bridge; Killigrew's act had fooled him completely. As the assassin lay on his stomach, waiting for the non-existent bridge to pass overhead, the commander stood up and ran across his back, whirling to grab him by the ankles and swing him off the roof of the train. The assassin twined his fingers in the netting to stop himself from going over, but the netting tore, so that he found himself swinging against the side of the carriage, with only a few strands of the netting still in place. He started to haul himself up, only to find the side of a steamer trunk blocking his way on to the roof. Looking up, he saw Killigrew had set the trunk on its end, and now stood behind it.

'No!' screamed the assassin.

Killigrew gave the trunk a kick. It toppled over the side and hit the assassin on the head, breaking his grip on the netting, and both trunk and assassin plummeted from the side of the train to tumble down the embankment. The trunk burst open, spilling shirts and handkerchiefs to the wind; the assassin rolled over and over, disappearing into a patch of brambles beneath the embankment.

Killigrew watched the brambles as they receded into the distance, and then slumped on the roof of the carriage, breathing hard.

Most likely the assassin had been an agent of the Third Section. It came as no surprise to learn that there were Russian spies operating in England, although it was alarming to discover they included assassins as well as observers and political agitators. It seemed unlikely that the man had been sent specially to England to murder Killigrew; Nekrasoff had had plenty of time to send a coded telegram to one of his agents with a description of the commander and instructions to await his arrival at Folkestone, the most likely point of entry into the country for anyone returning from the continent.

It was ironic in a way. Conscious that the Russians might try to retrieve the plans before he could hand them over to the Admiralty, Killigrew had kept a weather eye open for trouble all the way from Danzig to Boulogne; only when he had set foot on English soil had he relaxed his guard. That had been foolish of him, he now realised; the Russians would have expected nothing less, so it was the obvious place to ambush him.

The train was slowing. He looked up to see them entering the next station on the line: Ashford. He waited until the train had come to a complete halt before levering himself up and dropping down from the roof of the carriage to land on the platform next to an astonished elderly couple.

'Shockin' conditions in third class these days,' he told them, shooting his cuffs, before collecting his holdall and going in search of a less draughty first-class compartment.

* * *

23

Rear Admiral Michael Seymour arrived at the Admiralty in a common hansom. This, he felt, was hardly befitting a man of his importance and dignity, but his carriage was broken – something to do with a cracked axle, according to his damn' fool of a coachman – and it would take hours to repair; and Seymour had a very important appointment with the First Lord that he could not afford to miss.

The cab pulled up in front of the main entrance and Seymour waited for the cabbie to climb down and open the door for him.

The cabbie did not move from his seat. 'This is it, Capting,' he announced, as if Seymour had never seen the building before. 'The Admiralty.'

'I'm well aware of that.' Seymour sighed. Apparently he was expected to open the door for himself. He got out. A thick snowfall was blanketing London, and two of the Admiralty's 'messengers' – as the general-purpose flunkeys there were known – were brushing snow from the cobbles in front of the building.

Seymour turned back to look up at the cabbie, who was thickly muffled in greatcoat and comforter. 'What do I owe you?'

'Four shillings and ninepence, guv'nor.'

'Daylight robbery,' grumbled Seymour. He drew some change from his pocket and gave the cabbie five shillings. The cabbie looked at the coins in contempt, then pocketed them and made to whip the horse on.

'Hold on a minute!' protested Seymour. 'What about my change?'

'What, thruppence?' the cabbie exclaimed derisively. 'What about my tip?'

'I'll give you a tip: if you want to receive a gratuity, I suggest you learn to distinguish rank. I'm an admiral, not a captain.'

'Bleedin' skinflint!' The cabbie tossed him a sixpence. 'There's half a grunter for you. You obviously need it more'n I do!' He whipped up the horses and drove away.

Seymour had almost made it to the main entrance of the Admiralty when something knocked his cocked hat from his head. Cursing, he stooped to retrieve it, and a second snowball exploded against the seat of his trousers. He straightened sharply and whirled in time to see a couple of street urchins running off down Whitehall, laughing.

'You damned ragamuffins!' he called after them, shaking his fist while brushing snow from his posterior with his other hand. 'Count yourself lucky I don't call for a police constable!'

He entered the Admiralty. In his early fifties, Rear Admiral Michael Seymour was one of the youngest flag officers in the navy – having been promoted to post rank at the tender age of four-and-twenty – a tall man with a patrician face and greying hair swept back from his temples, iron-grey side-whiskers creeping across his prominent cheekbones like cant hooks.

He stepped into the marble-floored entrance hall, unbuttoning his coat to reveal his full-dress uniform with its wealth of gold piping. A flunkey hurried to greet him: one of the 'messengers' who safeguarded their lordships' appointment books and wangled expertly for bribes.

'I've an appointment with Sir James,' Seymour explained in response to the messenger's enquiry as to his business at the Admiralty.

'And you are?' the messenger asked politely.

The admiral glowered at him. 'Seymour. Rear Admiral Michael Seymour.'

'Very good, sir. Sir James is waiting for you in the boardroom.'

Seymour shrugged off his coat and handed it to the messenger before heading upstairs. It was a pity the incident with the obnoxious cabbie and the ragamuffins had spoiled what promised to be a red-letter day, and he tried to dismiss them from his mind. He had a pretty good notion what the First Lord of the Admiralty wanted to see him about.

When the Baltic Fleet had returned to Portsmouth back in December, Vice Admiral Sir Charles Napier had gone at once to meet the First Lord, Sir James Graham. No one else had attended the meeting, so exactly what had passed between the two men was known only to them, but since it had resulted in Napier hauling down his flag as commander-in-chief of the Baltic Fleet, it could be safely assumed there had been a full and frank exchange of views.

Napier and Graham had been friends once, which was presumably one of the reasons why the vice admiral had been appointed commander-in-chief the previous year in spite of his reputation for being a loose cannon. Napier's orders had been to keep the Russian Northern Fleet bottled up in the Baltic and to 'look into the possibility of doing something in the Åland Islands'. Napier had carried out his instructions to the letter: the Russian ships had not dared emerge from behind their maritime fortresses to face the Anglo-French fleet, and the 'something' he had done in the Åland Islands had been to reduce the fortress at Bomarsund and capture the archipelago from the Russians.

But the problem with having a reputation for exceeding orders was that after a while people expected it from you as a matter of course, and when the Allied fleet had not bombarded Kronstadt and landed in St Petersburg, public opinion in England had turned against the former

25

hero. The war was going badly in the Crimea, and when everyone's hope that it could be brought to a swift conclusion by a decisive blow against St Petersburg had been dashed, Lord Aberdeen's Tory Government had needed a scapegoat. It had turned to the Admiralty, since the First Lord was a Whig, and Graham had quickly passed the blame on to his former friend Napier.

Seymour had been Napier's second in command, Captain of the Fleet, so he was well aware of the difficulties the vice admiral had faced, exacerbated by the dilatory, contradictory and sometimes downright foolhardy instructions he had received from the Admiralty. But he had no sympathy for his former chief. As far as he could see, Napier was the victim of his own bombast. It was his own fault for making such vainglorious speeches about what he was going to achieve in the Baltic beforehand.

And now that Napier was gone, the Admiralty needed a new commander-in-chief for the Baltic Fleet.

Seymour smiled confidently as he advanced on the door to the boardroom. He had a good idea who the new commander would be. Since Napier's dismissal just before Christmas, he had been hard at work in the clubs of London, distancing himself from his superior's perceived failure with anyone of importance who would listen. 'Poor old Napier – getting too old for that sort of thing – lost his nerve – needs someone younger, with a bit more "go" – someone with experience of campaigning in the Baltic.' He licked a fingertip and smoothed his eyebrows.

'Rear Admiral Michael Seymour, to see Sir James,' he told the messenger standing at the door to the boardroom.

'Very good, sir.' The messenger opened the door and ushered him through. 'Rear Admiral Seymour,' he announced.

The First and Second Lords of the Admiralty – Sir James Graham, MP, and Rear Admiral the Honourable Richard Saunders Dundas, CB – rose to their feet to greet him.

'Admiral Seymour!' Graham said jovially. In his early sixties with thick black eyebrows above what would have been described on a woman as 'come to bed eyes', the First Lord of the Admiralty was one of those men who went through life with a hint of a crooked smile on his lips, as if life were a joke and he was one of the few people clever enough to get it. 'Do take a seat.'

'Thank you, my lord.' Seymour joined them at the table.

'As you know, we've been looking for someone to take command of the Baltic Fleet ever since Napier hauled down his colours in high dudgeon,' said Dundas. He was a couple of years younger than Seymour, with wild salt-and-pepper hair receding from his high-domed forehead and crow's-feet crinkling the corner of his eyes beneath thick, black brows.

'We're not going to make the same mistake we made with Napier,' put in Graham. 'We need a steadier pair of hands on the helm, as it were. Someone younger and more vigorous. But not someone without experience.'

'Quite so, Sir James,' said Seymour. 'I couldn't agree more.'

'I did not have to look far for a suitable candidate.'

Seymour smiled. 'Whomever you have decided to appoint, Sir James, I shall be more than happy to serve under,' he said, with what he thought was suitably becoming modesty.

'I'm glad to hear it,' said Dundas. 'I know I'll be able to rely on you, and the experience you gained of campaigning in the Baltic last year will be invaluable.'

'You're too kind, Sir Richard.'

'So, let's get down to brass tacks. How long do you think the ice in the Gulf of Finland will keep the Russians locked up in the harbours?'

'Oh, at least until April, sir.'

Dundas nodded. 'I thought we'd send the fleet out in two squadrons, an advance guard setting out in mid-March, while you and I follow in the *Duke* a week later with the rest of the fleet.'

'Er . . . you intend to accompany the fleet, Sir Richard?' Seymour asked in astonishment.

Dundas laughed. 'But of course! I wouldn't be much of a commander-in-chief if I stayed behind in England, would I?'

Seymour turned to Graham. 'You mean . . . *he's* the new commander-in-chief?'

'But of course! Who did you think we meant?'

'But . . . you can't! I mean . . . he's a member of the Board of Admiralty!'

'Not any longer. He's resigned in order to take up his new position as commander-in-chief of the Baltic Fleet.'

'Naturally, I'll keep you on as captain of the fleet,' Dundas hurried to assure him.

'You're too kind,' Seymour said again. Neither Graham nor Dundas noticed the sour note in his tone this time.

'Splendid! Now, as I was saying, we'll leave Portsmouth in two squadrons. Our main objective for the campaign ahead is to keep the Russian fleet bottled up in its harbours. The last thing we need is the *Emperor Peter I* sailing up the Thames to bombard the Palace of Westminster!'

'You'll need to achieve more than that if you're to avoid the same disgrace as Napier did, though,' Graham told Dundas. 'You must attack Sveaborg at the very least. Perhaps even Kronstadt. Naturally, I'll leave it to the two of you – in conference with your French opposite numbers, of course – to decide which of the Russian fortresses you decide to attack. But attack one you must. Public opinion demands victories, so a victory is what you must give them . . .'

Seymour listened with only half an ear as British public opinion – rather than strategic advantage – dictated their plans for the forthcoming campaign. He kept a smile pasted on his face, although inside he was seething. How dare Graham appoint Dundas over his head? True, Dundas had been promoted to rear admiral a year before Seymour and thus had seniority; but that was only because he had reached the rank of post-captain only nine years after joining the navy, and that thanks to the fact his father, Lord Melville, had been a former First Lord of the Admiralty. Why, the great war with France had been over by the time Dundas had joined the navy! At least Seymour had fought against the French. Hadn't he boarded *La Sultane* when he had been a midshipman?

'Well, I think that covers everything for now,' said Graham, and Seymour snapped out of his bitter reverie to see that the First Lord was ringing a small glass bell to summon a clerk. 'You'll receive your written instructions as soon as you've hoisted your flag on the *Duke*,' he told Dundas.

The clerk entered and started to tidy away the First Lord's papers. 'What's my next appointment?' asked Graham.

'That's the last one for today, my lord. Although there is a Commander Killigrew to see you.'

'Killigrew, Killigrew . . . oh, yes, I remember. Met him when he returned from the Arctic after that *Venturer* débâcle. Does he have an appointment?'

'No, sir.'

Graham looked pained. 'Now really, Trench, you know better than that. I can't see anyone without an appointment.'

'I know, sir, but he was most insistent. He said it was a matter of the utmost importance and that he had to see you at once.'

'It's always a matter of the utmost importance.' Graham sighed. 'Tell him to make an appointment and I'll see him when I can. And tell my coachman to bring my carriage to the door.'

'Very good, sir.' The clerk took Graham's dispatch box and retreated from the boardroom.

Graham, Dundas and Seymour headed for the entrance hall.

'You're quite right not to see that fellow Killigrew,' said Seymour. 'Nothing but trouble, that one.'

'You know him?' asked Dundas.

'Know him? Unfortunately! He's Crichton's second in command on the *Ramillies* . . . one of Napier's creatures. The man's nothing but a dangerous lunatic . . .'

'Napier?' said Graham. 'Or Killigrew?'

'Both of them,' growled Seymour. 'Napier sent Killigrew to negotiate Lord Bullivant's release when his lordship's yacht was captured by the Russians last year, and that fool almost got them all killed with his ridiculous antics. Tried to take on a Russian paddle-sloop with an unarmed yacht, had it sunk from beneath him, and ended up getting stranded on some uninhabited island.' He laughed, making a snorting sound like a sow with asthma. 'They'd all have been killed by the Russians if a French frigate hadn't chanced by to rescue them.'

'I wonder he wasn't court-martialled,' said Graham.

'I was all for it, sir,' said Seymour. 'So was Lord Bullivant. But Killigrew was Napier's blue-eyed boy.'

Graham, Dundas and Seymour made their way outside, where snow continued to fall in thick flurries. 'I don't suppose I could trouble either of you for a lift, could I?' Seymour asked the others. 'My carriage is laid up at present, and after the dreadful altercation I had with some ruffian of a cabbie, I'm not sure I want to trust myself to public transport.'

'Where are you headed?' asked Graham.

'The United Services.'

'That's all right: I'm on my way to the Reform Club.' Graham's footman jumped down from the back of his carriage to hold the door open for them. They climbed inside and sat down facing one another.

Graham turned to the footman. 'Pall Mall, Whittingham.'

'Very good, sir. Pall Mall, Mr Barrett!' the footman called up to the coachman, swinging himself up on the back of the carriage. The coachman whipped up the horses and they rattled away up Whitehall.

'Haven't eaten at the United Services for a while,' mused Graham. 'How's the food there these days?'

'Not bad,' said Seymour. 'Not bad at all. Mind you, the wine cellar leaves a lot to be desired. Had a very *ordinary* bottle of St-Emilion the other day—'

'Good evening, gentlemen!' Killigrew said breezily, thrusting his head through the window to Seymour's right. The rear admiral jumped as if stung. 'Mind if I join you?' Standing on the running board as they clattered into Trafalgar Square, the commander opened the door and swung inside, plumping himself down on the seat next to Seymour.

'Killigrew!' exclaimed the rear admiral, hurriedly moving to sit beside Graham. 'How dare you, man?'

'Yes, what's the meaning of this intrusion?' demanded the First Lord.

'Please, gentlemen,' pleaded Killigrew. 'I beg you to forgive the unorthodox nature of my approach, but I really must speak to you both on what may be a matter of the utmost national importance.' He fumbled inside his coat and took out what looked like some kind of technical drawing. 'Would you mind taking a look at this, sir?' he asked, handing it to Graham.

'What the blazes is it?'

'I don't know.'

'You don't know?' Graham echoed incredulously. 'Is this your notion of a joke, Killigrew?'

'No, sir. It could be some new secret weapon—'

Seymour groaned. 'Oh, Lor'! Not *another* secret weapon!'

Graham handed the drawing to Seymour without glancing at it. 'Killigrew, do you have any notion of how many dire warnings we've received about the secret weapons supposedly in the possession of the Russians?' he demanded impatiently. 'Infernal machines, asphyxiating shells, portable buoyant wave-repressors, repeating submarine cannon firing self-plugging lateral explosive shells . . . all fantasy, all the product of some opiate-swilling pamphleteer's overheated imagination. Where did you get this one?'

'Lieutenant Jurgaitis gave it to me, sir.'

'Lieutenant Jurgaitis?'

'Half-Livonian chap who resigned his commission in the navy to defect to the Russkis,' explained Seymour.

'Half-Lithuanian, sir,' corrected Killigrew, earning himself a dirty look from the admiral. 'But he wasn't a traitor: he only pretended to defect to the Russians in order to gain access to their Admiralty as a spy. Vice Admiral Napier will confirm it: it was his idea.'

'Napier!' snorted Graham. 'I've said everything I ever want to say to that pompous old fool. What do you make of it, Seymour?'

'It's very indistinct. What's this brown stuff on it?'

'Dried blood, sir,' said Killigrew.

'Eurgh!' The admiral dropped the drawings on the floor.

Killigrew retrieved them and handed them back to Graham. 'It's obviously some sort of contraption, sir. Whatever it is, Jurgaitis must have thought it was important because he gave his life so that I could bring these drawings safely back to England. And the Russians must have felt the same way, because they went to a good deal of trouble to try to stop them from falling into our hands.' Killigrew told them briefly about his mission to Finland, and the Russians' attempts to reclaim the plans.

'Secret weapons!' Seymour snorted when he had concluded. 'Woman spies! Ski chases! Brawling on the rooftops of moving trains! Is this your notion of naval service, Killigrew?'

'I think we've heard quite enough of this nonsense.' Graham hammered his cane against the ceiling. They pulled up on Pall Mall and the footman jumped down to hold the door open for Killigrew. 'Of course, I shall want a full report of your activities from the moment you left the *Ramillies* to the moment you returned to England at your earliest convenience,' Graham added in the same tone a schoolmaster might have instructed a pupil to write out 'I must not waste the teacher's time with tall tales' ten thousand times.

'What about the . . . the contraption, sir?'

'What about it?'

'It could be some new weapon of unspeakable power, sir. It has to be researched.'

'And it will be, I assure you, Commander Killigrew,' Graham said blithely. 'We'll get our top men working on it right away.'

Killigrew did not look satisfied. 'Who?' he insisted.

Graham glared at him, and replied with slow deliberation: '*Top* men.'

31

# II

# Death in Paddington

---

Killigrew watched Graham's carriage disappear into the falling snow and sighed, feeling suddenly weary. Jurgaitis had always thought of himself as a Briton, whatever his ancestry. He had given his life for his country, and his country did not even care. The commander turned the collar of his frock-coat up against the falling snow and hunched his shoulders, walking through St James's until he came to Piccadilly, where he was able to flag down a passing hansom and head for home, stopping *en route* to purchase some groceries.

For the past four years – of which he had spent two and a half at sea – 'home' had been a set of rooms in a house off Praed Street, where rents had dropped alarmingly when it was announced that the Great Western Railway would be extending their main line deeper into the city, terminating at – you guessed it – Praed Street, where the new terminus had just been opened. The landlady lived on the ground floor and did not approve of her tenants entertaining guests of the opposite sex, but Killigrew had soon discovered she depended upon the creaking fifth step to enforce this rule, as well as to catch tenants whose rent was in arrears. He had paid up until the end of the previous year, thinking that he would return with the fleet by Christmas; so it had come as a pleasant surprise when he returned a few weeks later than expected to find she had not thrown his stuff out into the street and relet the rooms.

He avoided the fifth step now, since he would not be able to pay his rent until he had reported on board HMS *Ramillies* to collect his own arrears. As he had learned from a clerk at the Admiralty the *Ramillies*

32

was at Sheerness for a refit, that would have to wait until later in the week.

The suite of rooms was modest: he had to be able to afford it even when he was on half-pay, and besides, he spent so little of his time there it was not worth renting anything more than a kitchen, bedroom and parlour. The threadbare furniture and mismatched furnishings betrayed the fact it was rented accommodation, and there were few personal touches – shelves of books ranging from the *Aeneid* to the latest Dumas *père*, and souvenirs of his travels: doilies of Maltese lace upon the table; a jewelled dagger from the Levant (useful as a letter opener); a Chinese puzzle box; an amulet made from polar bear's teeth; and a carved wooden West African fertility totem pressed into service as a bookend.

The rooms were cold and musty after being uninhabited for so long. His sea-chest had been delivered from the station while he had been at the Admiralty, and there was a pile of mail just inside the door, thrust under by the landlady at some point: invitations to Christmas balls he had missed, final demands from money brokers who had bought up his debts from various tradesmen, and begging letters. Who wrote the last of these and what made them think he could help them would always be a mystery. Most of them were from lunatics who had come up with hare-brained schemes to explore the Poles, and thought he was just the man to lead their expedition. When Killigrew had asked Sir John Ross about what he could expect when he went to the Arctic three years ago, that venerable explorer had forgotten to mention the letters from crackpots. He could not help thinking he could have used them the first (and definitely the last) time he had gone to the Arctic: they made good firelighters. Once he had a fire burning in the hearth, he poured himself a glass of whisky and sat down in one of the threadbare easy chairs to enjoy a cheroot.

He had just got comfortable when, inevitably, there was a knock at the door. He pushed himself to his feet and was about to answer the knock when a thought occurred to him. He was not expecting anyone, and after his encounter on the train earlier he could not be too careful. If it was Russian spies come to stop him from delivering the plans to the Admiralty, they were too late: but they might not realise that.

He fetched a revolver from his sea-chest, tiptoed to the door and threw it open sharply, grabbing the man standing on the other side and dragging him inside, throwing him into a chair and pointing the pistol at him. He did it so quickly and efficiently, he did not realise that 'he' was a 'she' until he looked and saw the Honourable Miss Araminta Maltravers glaring up at him.

'Well! That's a fine way to greet your fiancée!'

Closing the door behind her, he quickly lowered the revolver. 'Sorry. Being attacked on a train by a pastor does rather put one on edge.'

'A pastor?' she exclaimed, and smiled. Nearly thirty now, she was a tall woman with light brown hair and a strong-jawed face, long lashes framing her cool grey eyes and a hint of freckles dusted across the sides of her nose. 'It must have been one of Mr Kingsley's muscular Christians.'

'Very droll.' He smiled. 'Minty. You know one of the things that makes you different from other women? Other women are never quite as beautiful as you remember them to be. Why is it you always seem to be *more* beautiful than I remember?'

She rose to her feet. 'Oh, you remembered me, did you?'

He spread his arms to embrace her. 'Couldn't keep you out of my mind.'

She moved towards him, but instead of entering his arms, she gave him a stinging slap across the cheek.

'Minty! What was that for?'

'You know jolly well! It's a month since the *Ramillies* returned to Portsmouth. You didn't think to get in touch before now?'

'What do you mean, get in touch? I only got back today. I swear it. I had to stay behind in the Åland Islands for a few weeks. Look!' He pointed to his sea-chest. 'I haven't even unpacked it yet.'

She regarded the chest with suspicion. For a moment she looked tempted to take his word for it, but she knew him too well for that, and crossed to lift the lid. 'And you couldn't write to me?'

'Not really. I was on a secret mission. Ask Sir Charles Napier: he'll tell you.'

She looked alarmed. 'Nothing too dangerous, I hope?'

'No more dangerous than coming home to the woman I love,' he said, raising a hand to his cheek. He knew that if he looked in the mirror he would see the crimson imprint of her hand there. 'Anyhow, it's not as if you'd replied to any of the letters I'd sent you before then, so I was starting to wonder what the point was.'

'What letters?'

Killigrew stared at her. 'I must have written three dozen letters to you after you went back to England. Don't tell me you didn't receive *one* of them?'

She stared at him, open-mouthed. 'Not one. Are you sure you sent them to the correct address?'

'The Honourable Miss Araminta Maltravers, Bullivant House, Grosvenor Square.'

She clenched her jaw and her fists, nodding. 'Papa must've intercepted them. That . . . why, I'll . . . when I catch up with him . . . ooh!' She was speechless with rage.

Killigrew almost felt sorry for the viscount. When he had first met the Bullivants, his lordship had lorded it over his wife and daughter just as much as he did over his tenants on his estates in Rutland, but during their adventures together in the Gulf of Finland the previous summer, Killigrew had seen a change come over the viscountess and her daughter. Lord Bullivant's attitude had been less than helpful throughout the brief but perilous ordeal, and it had been as if something inside the two women had snapped, and they had tacitly decided they were not going to take any nonsense from him any more. By the time the dispatch boat had come to take them off the *Ramillies*, Bullivant had had the look of a broken and thoroughly hen-pecked man.

Araminta ran into Killigrew's arms. 'Oh, Kit! I'm sorry I ever doubted you.'

'I'm sure you can think of some way you can make it up to me.'

She kissed him: not a formal peck on the cheek, but the passionate kiss of a man and a woman who had been lovers in the past, and would be again in the future. In the very near future, Killigrew hoped.

'Hungry?' he asked.

'Famished!' She allowed him to take off her *sortie de bal* and hang it from the peg on the back of the door.

'Me too. I'll make some supper.'

He went into the kitchen and started unpacking the groceries while she sat down at the upright pianoforte in one corner of the parlour. The piano had been there when Killigrew had moved in, and would probably remain there long after he had moved on. Having no musical talent himself, he had used it to keep books on before Araminta had become a regular visitor to his rooms. Now she started playing 'I Dreamt that I Dwelt in Marble Halls': sentimental pap, in Killigrew's opinion, but she played so exquisitely he would have been happy to listen if it had been 'Home, Sweet Home'; but that was a shade of sentiment too far even for Araminta.

He suspected she played the tune out of a mischievous sense of irony. The truth was she *did* dwell in marble halls – when she was at her father's country estate, at least – and his town house was nothing to be sniffed at, either.

But she loved Killigrew all the same.

He loved good music well played, and had he had the least musical accomplishment he would much have preferred to be a concert musician than a naval officer, a sentiment that would have given his grandfather apoplexy. But he had known from childhood that he had never been destined for an artistic life: generations of portraits of naval officers on the walls of the gallery at Killigrew House in Falmouth had told him that.

'Where do your parents think you are tonight?' he asked her, cracking some eggs into a mixing bowl. The suite of rooms was small enough that a man whisking eggs in the kitchen could have a conversation with someone playing the piano in the parlour without any great vocal effort on the part of either.

'The Panopticon, with Lord Hartcliffe and his mother,' Araminta replied without missing a note.

'How is Hartcliffe?'

'Not good. He had a blazing row with his father over Christmas.'

'Hartcliffe always has blazing rows with his father over Christmas. It's a Hartcliffe family tradition.' Killigrew did not need to ask what the row had been about. Hartcliffe's elder brother had married an American woman, to the disgust of his father, the duke, who had disinherited him and even arranged an Act of Parliament so that Endymion was made his only heir and thus gained the title Lord Hartcliffe. His lordship had been at sea at the time, serving with Killigrew on board HMS *Tisiphone* in the South Seas, otherwise he might have pointed out the folly of his being made heir to the Dukedom of Hartcliffe: even if Lord Hartcliffe had been remotely interesting in becoming duke one day, his natural inclinations made it highly unlikely he would ever produce an heir of his own. By the time the duke had learned the truth, his elder son had disappeared into the wilds of the American frontier.

'I hear there's some Scottish chap set up an inquiry agency in Chicago,' said Killigrew, adding some butter to a saucepan. 'Pinkstone, I think his name is, or something like that. He's supposed to be very good. I keep meaning to dig out his address for Hartcliffe.'

'What good would that do? I mean, even if you could get in touch with Augustus, there's no guarantee he'd be any more interested in becoming duke than Endymion is.'

'You should never underestimate the power of *noblesse oblige*,'

Killigrew told her, lighting one of the rings on the gas stove and turning it down to melt the butter.

'And you should never underestimate the duke's stubbornness. Honestly, from what Hartcliffe says, he's as bad as Papa. You really think he'd swallow his pride and welcome home the prodigal son?'

'If it meant keeping the family estates in the family? Yes, I think he would.' Killigrew speared a piece of bread with a toasting fork and entered the parlour, propping it up in front of the fire.

'Scrambled eggs on toast again?'

'You always said you liked my scrambled eggs,' he said defensively.

'I do. But I thought that you'd have prepared something a little more special for our reunion?'

'If I'd known you were coming, I'd've booked a table at Rules.'

'What do you mean, if you'd known I was coming? You *invited* me, remember?'

'My dearest Minty, far be it from me to suggest you're anything other than welcome, but I didn't invite you. I was planning a quiet night in, so I could be fresh and rested when I called on you tomorrow.'

She stopped playing and turned to face him. 'Then why in the world did you send me a note?'

'Note? What note?'

'This note!' She dug in the pocket of her skirt and took out a small, crumpled note that she thrust into his hands. 'And don't try and tell me that isn't your handwriting! I should think I know it well enough by now.'

He stared at the note, a nasty cold feeling stirring in the pit of his stomach. It *was* his handwriting. It was even his notepaper – or the same brand, at any rate.

But he knew he had not written it.

He took her *sortie de bal* down from its peg and tossed it at her. 'Come on. We're leaving.'

She stared in astonishment. 'Kit? What's going on?'

'I don't know, but I'm fairly certain it would be better if we weren't around to find out.' He turned out the gas under the saucepan. Then, taking his revolver, he thrust it in one of the pockets of his frock-coat, grabbed her by the hand and opened the door.

To find Colonel Radimir Fokavich Nekrasoff coming up the stairs with Killigrew's attacker from the Double Express Service, whose unsmiling face was now one mass of bramble-scratches.

Araminta let out a gasp of shock. She knew Nekrasoff from her adventure in the Baltic the previous summer; more importantly, she knew what he was capable of.

Killigrew reached for his revolver, but Nekrasoff was faster. 'Please don't,' he said urbanely. 'No one has to die.'

Moving in front of Araminta, Killigrew slowly raised his hands.

A door opened in the hallway below. 'Gotcha!' said Mrs Antrobus. 'Oh, I'm sorry! I thought you were someone else.' Killigrew could not see her from where he stood on the landing, and from the sound of it she could not see the revolver in Nekrasoff's hand. 'Er . . . who are you?'

'Deal with her,' Nekrasoff told his burly companion, without taking his eyes off Killigrew.

The other man raised his hands placatingly. 'It's quite all right, ma'am,' he said. His English was, if anything, even better than Nekrasoff's. 'We're detective police officers from Scotland Yard . . .'

As the other man descended to confront Mrs Antrobus, Nekrasoff gestured with his revolver for Killigrew to back into his rooms.

The commander was too stunned to do anything but comply. He had found himself looking down the barrel of a gun plenty of times before, but it was never a situation one took lightly. Besides, that was usually in the far-flung corners of the British Empire, when he was on duty. This was Britain, damn it; London!

Nekrasoff paused on the landing, facing Killigrew through the open door. 'Keep going.'

As Killigrew obeyed, he saw Araminta had already snatched the poker from the fireplace and was standing against the wall by the door, ready to smash Nekrasoff in the face with it. It was a risky tactic, but it might be their only chance, and Killigrew's fear for her mingled with admiration.

Nekrasoff hesitated on the threshold, however, trying to look past Killigrew into the rooms beyond. He rolled his eyes in exasperation. 'Miss Maltravers, would you be so kind as to put down whatever makeshift weapon you've snatched up and move away from the door to where I can see you?'

She stared at Killigrew in disbelief. Nekrasoff pointed his revolver at the other side of the wall. He had guessed her position exactly; and at that range there was every chance that the bullet would pass through the wall and through her as well.

'You'd best do as he says,' sighed Killigrew.

Araminta propped the poker against the wall and moved behind him once more.

38

'That's better.' Nekrasoff stepped into the parlour, and smiled. 'Well, here we all are: together again.'

'I wish we could say we were pleased to renew your acquaintance,' Killigrew said drily.

The other man came through the door and closed it behind him, nodding at Nekrasoff. The colonel gestured to one of the easy chairs with his revolver. 'Sit down, Miss Maltravers.'

She shook her head. The big man put a hand on her chest and shoved her back into the seat. Killigrew managed to take two steps towards him before Nekrasoff thumbed back the hammer of his revolver.

Killigrew froze.

The big man took a length of rope from his coat pocket and started to tie Araminta up.

'Up against the wall, Commander,' ordered Nekrasoff. 'Feet spread, leaning on your fingertips.'

Killigrew obeyed. Nekrasoff kept the muzzle of the revolver pressed against his spine as he frisked him expertly, quickly finding the revolver in his coat pocket. 'Ah! I see you were expecting me.' He threw the gun into a corner.

'If I'd been expecting you, Nekrasoff, I'd've brought a rusty knife!'

Straightening, the colonel smiled. 'Turn round.'

Killigrew turned. The big man had finished tying Araminta into the chair.

Nekrasoff pushed Killigrew towards the other chair. 'Do sit down.'

The big man put a huge hand on one of Killigrew's shoulders, forcing him down into the chair. The next thing Killigrew knew, the man was wrapping ropes around him, tying him fast. Killigrew tensed his muscles: Petty Officer Molineaux had once told him that if you did that, the ropes might have some slack in them when you relaxed.

'There!' Nekrasoff said in satisfaction as soon as the big man had finished tying Killigrew up. 'I feel much safer now.'

'I wish I could say the same,' said Killigrew. He wriggled surreptitiously: as far as he could tell, tensing his muscles had not done a blind bit of good.

The big man picked up the poker and crouched on the hearthrug, thrusting the tip of the poker into the hottest part of the fire.

'You know what comes next, don't you?' asked Nekrasoff.

'If you've come for the plans, you're too late,' Killigrew told him. 'I handed them in at the Admiralty this afternoon.'

A flicker of emotion crossed Nekrasoff's face, too swiftly for Killigrew to work out what emotion it was. 'Yes, I thought you might have done,' he said mildly. 'It makes no difference. Those plans are unimportant: another of the grand duke's little toys. But what *is* important is the name of the man who helped Jurgaitis in Helsingfors.'

'I didn't meet Jurgaitis until he reached Kristinestadt,' said Killigrew. 'How should I know who helped him in Helsingfors?'

'Come now, Mr Killigrew. We both know you were in Helsingfors before the war, posing as an ichthyologist while trying to recruit pilots for your fleet. Presumably whoever helped you then helped Jurgaitis last month.'

'No one helped me.'

Nekrasoff crossed the room to lean over the back of Araminta's chair. 'Are you quite sure about that? Such a pretty face . . . it would be a shame if we had to damage it.'

Killigrew felt nauseous. 'Damn you, Nekrasoff! I'm the one who rescued the Bullivants last year, and I'm the one who got those plans to our Admiralty. Your quarrel's with me, not her. If you want to torture someone, torture me!'

'Oh, but I tried that last summer, remember? With little success, I must admit.'

'Because I didn't know anything, damn your eyes! You asked me where Napier planned to attack next, and I told you even he hadn't made his mind up. Didn't he prove that by not attacking anywhere?'

'You told me Kronstadt.'

'I had to tell you something: you were trying to drown me at the time! You seem to think I'm some kind of hero, impervious to pain. Well, I'm not, I can assure you. All you have to do is wave that poker in my face, and I'll tell you everything you want to know, if I can.'

'Yes, but you would say that, wouldn't you? I think applying it to Miss Maltravers' face will prove much more efficacious. By the way, I understand it you've already met my associate, Mr Ryzhago?'

Still crouching in front of the fire, the big man grinned over his shoulder at Killigrew. 'I had the pleasure of Mr Killigrew's acquaintance on the train this afternoon.'

'Ryzhago isn't his real name, of course,' said Nekrasoff. 'Were I to tell you his real name . . . well, suffice to say his father's name is so well known in St Petersburg Society that I dare say even you might have heard of it. He's been one of my top agents in England for years. If you're wondering where he learned to speak English so fluently,

I can answer your question easily enough. His father had somehow got the lamentable notion in his head that Britain's public schools were the finest in the world, so he sent his son to Eton.'

'I've always said that place was a breeding ground for the worst scum in society,' sneered Killigrew, still struggling surreptitiously against his bonds. 'Murderers, rapists, lawyers, politicians . . . you name it!'

Nekrasoff smiled. 'A lesson his father learned too late, alas. I can assure you that Ryzhago is living proof that brains and brawn can be combined in one body; but English not being his first language, he did rather struggle during his first few terms. And they do have a tendency to flog pupils who don't come up to scratch. Personally, if I had children, I should sooner send them to Siberia than to a British public school!'

'A purely academic question,' said Killigrew, 'as I can't imagine any woman so lacking in taste that she should want you as the father of her children!'

Nekrasoff shrugged the insult off. 'The net result of all these beatings at such an impressionable age, I'm afraid to say, is some confusion in poor Ryzhago's mind about the difference between pain and pleasure. I first encountered him when I was working in the Department of Public Morals. There was one very nasty incident at one of the licensed brothels in St Petersburg . . . one which catered for clients with very particular needs.' Nekrasoff thought for a moment. 'Come to think of it, it always *was* very popular with diplomats working at the British Embassy. Unfortunately, poor Ryzhago there got rather carried away in the throes of his passion, and started to dish out a little of what he had gone there to receive.'

Ryzhago scowled, clearly disliking to have his peccadilloes discussed in such an offhand manner, but from the way he withdrew the red-hot tip of the poker from the fire and turned to advance on Araminta, it was clearly not Nekrasoff he was going to take his anger out on.

'You see, the thing about Ryzhago is, he's a great believer in the words of Our Lord when He said it is more blessed to give than to receive,' concluded Nekrasoff. 'Particularly when it comes to inflicting pain. His father was more than happy for me to give his son a new identity and enlist him in the Third Section. Don't you agree that it was better to employ Ryzhago in a capacity in which he could be of service to his country than to embarrass his family with the shame and humiliation of a public trial? Now, are you quite sure you wouldn't like

41

to share the name of the man who helped Jurgaitis in Helsingfors with us?'

Mesmerised by that poker, Araminta blanched. 'Don't tell him, Kit.'

Killigrew shook his head, sick with horror. 'If I knew anything I would, Minty, believe me. Damn you, Nekrasoff! We both know you're going to kill us anyhow. Why should I tell you anything?'

'Because you want Miss Maltravers to avoid unnecessary suffering beforehand?'

Ryzhago moved the poker close to her cheek. Even though it had already cooled to a dull red glow, it was still hot enough to bring beads of perspiration from her brow at a distance of a couple of inches.

'All right, all right!' sobbed Killigrew. 'Qvist! His name was Qvist. Lars Qvist. He was one of the cleaners at the University of Helsingfors.'

Nekrasoff smiled. 'I knew it had to be someone who worked at the University.'

Ryzhago took the poker away.

The colonel frowned. 'But then, as you said just now, you *had* to say *something* . . .' He nodded at Ryzhago.

'No!' Killigrew screamed as Ryzhago pressed the poker to Araminta's cheek, but his scream was drowned out by hers as her flesh sizzled.

Mercifully, she fainted.

Tears streamed down Killigrew's face. He swore vilely at the colonel.

'Dear me,' said Nekrasoff. 'Not the sort of language I'd expect from an officer and a gentleman.'

Killigrew lifted his head to glare into Nekrasoff's eyes. 'You'd best kill me now and be done with it, Colonel. Because if you don't, I'm going to come after you, and when I catch you, you're going to take a long time to die.'

Nekrasoff crouched before him, smirking. 'Oh, I don't think so. You see, this time you're in over your head. Out of your depth.' He straightened and moved behind Killigrew. 'We won't be meeting again.'

Killigrew felt something smash against the base of his skull. The room spun around him, and he felt a momentary nausea before the waves of blackness washed over him and carried him out to sea like so much flotsam.

Someone was hammering at the door. The noise seemed to match the pounding in Killigrew's skull. He groaned: it was the closest he could come to expressing a coherent thought.

The hammering stopped; the hammering on the door, at any rate. 'Mr Killigrew? We know you're in there, sir. Open this door!'

*Open it yourself*, thought Killigrew. He tried to say it too, but his tongue seemed to have swollen in his mouth and turned to cotton wool.

The pounding on the door resumed. Killigrew opened his eyes. He lay face down on the floor, the threadbare rug stretching away before him. Everything was as he had left it, except for the people. There was no sign of Nekrasoff or Ryzhago; or of Araminta, for that matter. Even the ropes that had bound her to the chair had gone. Only the stench of charred flesh still lingered in the air to let him know it had not been just a nightmare.

They had taken Araminta!

He knew he had to get after them. He had no idea what he was going to do, but he knew that lying on the floor was not going to get it done.

'All right, lads, break it down!' said a voice outside the door. The pounding became less frequent, but heavier.

Killigrew tried to get up. It proved to be the hardest thing he had ever done. Climbing to the truck of the *Dreadful*'s mainmast as a midshipman had nothing on climbing to his feet now. He realised he had to take it in easy stages. Palms against the floor and . . . push! He raised his chest up, and his head swam sickeningly. Fighting back the bile that rose to his gorge, he managed to bend his legs and get up on his hands and knees.

The door burst open and a man staggered in, almost tripping over him. The man wore the swallowtail coat and stovepipe hat of a peeler. There were two more bobbies in the hallway outside, and two men in chesterfield overcoats, the elder wearing a chimney-pot hat that had seen better days, the younger wearing a Bollinger hat on his head.

All four of them followed their colleague into the room. Two of the peelers caught Killigrew under the armpits and hauled him to his feet.

'Search the place!' ordered the man in the chimney-pot hat.

It did not take them long. The man wearing the Bollinger crossed to the bedroom door and froze on the threshold, crumpling against the jamb. 'In here, Mr Jordan.'

The detective crossed to the door, then pushed past him into the bedroom. Killigrew tried to follow him, but the two peelers held him fast.

After what seemed like an eternity, Jordan re-emerged, taking off his chimney-pot hat to dab at his brow with a wadded handkerchief. He looked sick and tired.

43

'What?' demanded Killigrew. 'What's in there?'

Jordan looked up at him, and his eyes were full of cold loathing. 'I think you know, Mr Killigrew.'

Killigrew had a nasty feeling he did. 'I have to see.'

Jordan shrugged. 'Show him, boys.'

The two peelers escorted him to the bedroom door.

Araminta lay on the bed, her face contorted into a rictus of agony. There was the stink of death in the room, the stink of faeces and urine. Her face was already turning grey; Ryzhago's watch-chain had left its cruel mark upon her throat.

'Commander Killigrew?'

Araminta was dead.

It was not the first time a woman he had loved had died because he thought he could save the world from itself, but, if anything, that only made it hurt all the more. The self-pity – the feeling that he was cursed – would come later, a part of his mind told him. The part that was still rational, that had somehow defied the odds to cling on to sanity while his whole world – everything he had pinned his hopes and dreams for the future on – came crumbling down around him. A woman he loved, and who loved him, for a wife . . . surely it had not been too much to ask?

Araminta was dead.

'Commander Killigrew?'

But before the self-pity, the self-recrimination. She was dead because once again he had allowed a woman to become caught up in his stupid cloak-and-dagger games. Death held no terrors for him, but there were worse things to befall a man than death, and this was the worst of them. Was God testing him, like Job? Or punishing him, like Solomon? But if only he could have had the wisdom of Solomon!

Or was he trying to make sense of something that made no sense? Was he merely trying to mitigate his feelings of guilt by sharing them with God? Perhaps his friend Strachan, a devout atheist, was right . . . at times like this, it was hard to believe in God. Things just happened. Atoms collided in space. Famines and diseases racked the planet. And in a seamy bedroom in Paddington, the daughter of a viscount was garrotted with a fob chain because her lover thought he could play games with Russian agents.

'Commander?'

No amount of rationalisation could assuage his guilt. Would she still

44

be alive if Killigrew had not given Nekrasoff a made-up name? It seemed unlikely that the colonel kept a complete list of the university's staff in his head. More likely he had planned to kill Araminta all along. The only mystery was why he had not killed Killigrew while he was about it.

What mattered was that Araminta should never have got mixed up with him in the first place. Worst of all, it was as if a part of him had known that all along. Perhaps that was why he had broken off their engagement three years ago, before sailing off into the Arctic. They belonged to two very different worlds: hers a world of balls and titles and monogrammed carriages, his a world of danger and intrigue and sudden, brutal death. He had flattered himself he could move seamlessly between those two worlds, that he was as much at home in a ballroom as he was on the quarterdeck of a man o' war in battle; but now the latter world had somehow spilled over into the former, with the most dreadful consequences.

Araminta was dead.

'Sir?'

He finally became aware of a portly, middle-aged man standing over him. Killigrew looked up at him blankly.

'Inspector Jordan of the Detective Branch at Scotland Yard,' the man introduced himself in a husky voice. He indicated the fair-haired plain-clothes officer standing beside him. 'This is Sergeant Dunwoody. Sorry to keep you waiting. Do you mind if we ask you a few questions?'

Killigrew shook his head numbly and rose from the bench in the waiting room at the police office on Marylebone High Street. He followed the two officers into an office where Jordan gestured to a chair at the table and Dunwoody pulled it out for him, like a waiter seating a patron at a restaurant.

Killigrew sat down. Jordan dropped some files on the table between them and sat opposite him. 'I've been through the statement you gave Sergeant Hawkins, and I wondered if you'd mind if we went through it again?'

Killigrew heard the words, but they made no sense to him. Nothing made any sense to him any more. He shrugged non-committally.

'Now, these two men who invaded your rooms . . . you say they were Russian spies?'

Killigrew made an effort to reply sensibly, knowing that the best way he could avenge Araminta's death was to do everything in his power to assist the police. 'That's right.'

45

Jordan grimaced. 'You see, the problem is, we can't find a single witness who can corroborate any part of your story.'

'What about Mrs Antrobus? The landlady?'

Jordan and Dunwoody exchanged glances. 'Not a very good witness, sir, seeing that she's dead too.'

*Jesus Christ! Not Mrs Antrobus as well!*

'What happened?' asked Jordan. 'Did she come to investigate the disturbance?'

Killigrew shook his head. 'She came out of her rooms as Nekrasoff and Ryzhago were coming up the stairs. The fifth step creaks: she always comes out to investigate, in case it's a tenant who owes her . . . owed her . . . arrears.'

'The fifth step,' Jordan echoed dubiously.

'Speak to Sir Charles Napier,' Killigrew told them wearily. 'Speak to Sir James Graham or Rear Admiral Seymour. They'll tell you. I was on a secret mission to Finland. I crossed the path of the Third Section – that's the Russian secret police – and they must have followed me back here.'

'Ye-e-es. You say you left Finland on the eighteenth?'

'Yes!'

'And you arrived back in London earlier today? Or yesterday, I should say now. Still . . . Finland to England in eleven days. That's quite impressive.'

'Yes, well, with stolen plans in my pocket and Russian spies on my tail, I didn't feel like tarrying to take in the sights.'

They looked at him, stony-faced.

'I left Finland by fishing boat and arrived in Danzig on the twenty-third. The next day I travelled by train and arrived in Berlin via Stettin. From Berlin it took me three days to reach Paris. The next day was a Sunday, so I had to wait until this morning – yesterday morning – to catch the Double Express.' He reached into his coat pocket. 'See? Here's the ticket stub.'

'Oh, we're not disputing your itinerary,' said Jordan. 'It's these Russian spies that trouble me. I can't work out how *they* got to London so quickly. Perhaps you could explain that one to us?'

Killigrew shook his head. 'If I made it, why couldn't they?'

'Because they couldn't come by the same route as you, could they? With all of Russia's Baltic ports iced-in, they'd have to travel overland, and there are no railways between Finland and Warsaw.'

Killigrew stared at them. It was true. Then how in the hell had

Nekrasoff . . .? 'Look, I don't know. Maybe he was already in London, and someone sent a telegram to tell him I was on my way back from Finland. All I know is that while we're sitting here asking and answering foolish questions, he's getting further away.' He buried his face in his hands. He was so tired . . . why did he have to waste his time with these idiots? 'Speak to Vice Admiral Sir Charles Napier,' he repeated. 'He'll confirm my story.'

'Oh, he already has—'

'Then why are we sitting here when we should be getting after Nekrasoff? There's still time, damn it!'

'At least, he's confirmed those parts of it he *could* confirm. We don't doubt what you tell us about your mission to Finland. Where we do struggle is with the presence of Russian spies here in London.'

Killigrew was ready to start tearing up the table that was between them. Ever since the war had loomed the previous spring, people had been seeing Russian spies under their beds. Now there really *were* Russian spies operating in Britain, why did he have to get the only two policemen who put spies in the same category as Father Christmas and the Tooth Fairy?

'Look, for heaven's sake! All right, perhaps to you . . . living here safe and comfortable in England while brave men die in the trenches of the Crimea . . . the war is something terribly distant that hardly touches your lives. But the fact is there *are* Russian spies operating in this country, and perhaps if you people spent less time wasting my time, and more time trying to track them down, you might stand a chance of catching Miss Maltravers' murderer before he leaves the country.'

'Oh, we'll get Miss Maltravers' murderer, sir,' Dunwoody said with heavy significance. 'Of that you can be sure.'

Killigrew stared at him in disbelief, understanding at last just what was going on here. 'You think *I* did it?'

'The victim was found in your rooms,' Jordan said quietly. 'By your own admission, you were the last person to see her alive.'

'No, Nekrasoff and Ryzhago were the last people to see her alive, because they're the bastards who murdered her! This is utterly insane! For God's sake, I was going to marry her! I loved her, damn it! What possible motive could I have for murdering her?'

'Why don't you tell us about Sophronia Ponsonby?'

'Who?'

Jordan took out another file and opened it to reveal a crumpled piece

47

of paper. 'We found this letter in the victim's hand. How she found it we can only speculate, but it's obvious that you continued to have at least one mistress after you became engaged to her. We've compared the paper to the notepaper supplied to the officers on board HMS *Ramillies* and it matches this exactly.'

'You can pick that paper up at any stationer's. This is ridiculous! I've never even heard of Sophronia Ponsonby! Look, that's not even my handwri—' Killigrew stared at the handwriting on the note. 'Jesus Christ! That's my handwriting!'

'You freely admit that, sir?'

'No, damn you! I mean, it *looks* like my handwriting. They forged it, obviously.'

' "They" being these vanishing Russian spies, I suppose?'

'Yes! Can't you see? They murdered her, then tried to make it look as if I did it! Look . . . whoever forged that letter is the fellow who forged the letter that tricked her into coming to my rooms! Compare the two letters, you'll see . . .'

'That they were written by the same person. We've done that already. We've also compared it with your own handwriting in the written statement you gave Sergeant Hawkins. As you yourself can see, they clearly match.'

'It was forged, I tell you! It *must* have been.'

'Why don't you just tell us the truth, sir? Miss Maltravers came to call on you the moment you returned from the Baltic. Somehow this love letter from yourself to Miss Ponsonby had come into her possession. She confronted you with it, there was a row, things turned ugly . . . perhaps she lashed out at you first; you were only defending yourself? You can tell us, sir. We'll understand. You'd be amazed how often we come across cases like this.'

Killigrew managed a bitter chuckle. 'Oh, I don't think you've ever come across a case *quite* like this one, Inspector. If you think I murdered the woman I love in a row over some woman named Sophronia Ponsonby, then you find this Sophronia Ponsonby and bring her to me, and ask her if she's ever seen me in her life. If she even exists, which I very much doubt. Sophronia Ponsonby indeed!'

'We're still following up that line of investigation,' admitted Jordan. 'However, I don't think it will be necessary.' He picked up the letter. 'This is all the evidence the counsel for the prosecution will need to send you to the gallows. However . . . admit your guilt, sign a confession . . . judges can be lenient in cases of a *crime passionnel*.

Perhaps with a good brief you might find your sentence commuted to transportation for life to the colonies.'

'I've seen the penal colonies,' Killigrew told him. 'Frankly, I'd rather die.'

'That's your decision, sir.'

'I want to see a lawyer.' *Jesus*, thought Killigrew, *I never thought I'd hear myself say that*. 'I'm not saying another word until I've seen a lawyer.'

Jordan sighed. 'Mr Christopher Killigrew, I hereby charge you with the murder of the Honourable Miss Araminta Maltravers. Have you anything you wish to add to—' Jordan broke off as a knock sounded at the door. 'Come in?'

A uniformed constable thrust his head around the door. 'Can I have a word, sir?'

'I'm in the middle of charging the suspect, Constable,' Jordan said testily.

'It's very important, sir. I think it has a bearing on the Maltravers case.'

Jordan smiled thinly at Killigrew. 'If you'll excuse me a moment, sir?' He rose to his feet and followed the constable out, closing the door behind him and leaving Killigrew alone with Dunwoody. The plain-clothes constable looked bored. He probably sent innocent men to the gallows every day, Killigrew thought bitterly.

Jordan returned a few moments later. 'All right, take him down the custody cells.'

Dunwoody stood up and motioned for Killigrew to rise.

'You realise this case will never reach a court of law, don't you?' Killigrew said as Jordan turned to the door. 'The scandal would destroy Lord Bullivant, and he's a personal friend of the Prime Minister's.' Playing a political card was the last thing he wanted to do, but he realised now his case was desperate and he had no other cards left to play.

Jordan turned back to face him. 'Lord Aberdeen, sir?' He shook his head sadly. 'For the moment there is no prime minister. Lord Aberdeen resigned yesterday.'

# III

# The Accused

---

Killigrew spent the next two hours sitting in a cell at Marylebone police office, trying to make sense of everything that had happened. Except that he knew there was little sense behind any of it, and nothing to tie it all together. It was all simply an unfortunate concatenation of circumstances. Lord Aberdeen's resignation had nothing to do with Miss Maltravers' murder. It should not even have come as a shock: pressure from the opposition over the government's handling of the war had been mounting for months.

So Aberdeen was gone. Killigrew could not have cared less: as far as he could see, the vast majority of politicians – be they Whig or Tory – were a bunch of pompous hypocrites; kick one out, and you could only replace him with another poltroon who told slightly different lies.

Napier was gone, too, ordered to haul down his flag and made into a scapegoat by Graham. That hurt. Napier had been Killigrew's patron, the one man of influence who had always tried to promote his career prospects, if only by putting him in harm's way so often that he had every opportunity to make a name for himself. But more important than that, Killigrew had liked the irascible old Scot, and respected him as a good admiral. Certainly Napier had been no Nelson; but Nelson was long dead, and with the possible exception of Rear Admiral Sir Edmund Lyons, of whose actions in the Black Sea Killigrew had heard good things, Napier was the best of an otherwise damned bad bunch.

And Araminta was gone. That was the *coup de grâce*. One of the things he had always fought for in the navy was the preservation of an England where that kind of thing simply did not happen. But that

England did not exist: it was a chimaera, a cloud-cuckoo-land; just another of the lies he told himself to justify his role in defending an Empire that served as a cloak for too many instances of exploitation and repression.

Why? Killing Araminta had not enabled Nekrasoff to retrieve the stolen plans (what *were* those plans?). It had not helped anyone win the war. Silencing a witness? Punishing Killigrew . . . for what? There was no sense to it. There was no sense to any of it.

At last – after turning these thoughts over and over in a mind battered by too many twists of fate and getting nowhere, just as his pacing back and forth in his cell got him nowhere – a key turned in the lock and the door opened to reveal the custody sergeant.

'You're free to go.'

'Free?' The word, like everything else, no longer had any sense for Killigrew. In a daze, he followed the sergeant upstairs, where his personal effects were returned to him.

On the street outside, he looked around for a hansom cab, but the only one in sight already had a passenger, a heavily muffled man whose face was largely covered by the comforter wrapped around his mouth and nose against the chill January weather, the brim of his Bollinger hat pulled down over his eyes. Killigrew walked up the street as far as the Marylebone Road and caught a horse-drawn omnibus to Paddington.

When he got back to his lodgings he paused on the landing outside the door. Nekrasoff and Ryzhago were doubtless halfway back to Russia by now; but he had thought they would leave him alone after he had delivered the plans to the Admiralty, and had been proven lamentably wrong. He pulled out his revolver, taking a deep breath before he unlocked the door to his rooms, afraid of what he might see. That Nekrasoff and Ryzhago had been in here, had murdered Araminta in here . . . he had heard that people who had been burgled experienced a feeling of violation on discovering that evil-doers, strangers, had been in their homes; but that was not the feeling that troubled him now. Since he had started living here, he had spent so much time overseas that he hardly thought of this as his home; if he had a home, it was his cabin on board HMS *Ramillies*. Nevertheless, some of his happiest memories revolved around the bedroom, and Araminta in it.

On the bed where she had been garrotted.

He choked back the bile that rose to his gorge and forced himself to go to the bedroom now, to get it over with. Her body was gone, of course, but the mattress remained. The first thing to do was buy a new mattress. He could not sleep on that one now. He was not sure he could ever sleep in these rooms now.

And then it finally sank in: *Araminta was dead.*

His legs buckled and he fell to the floor, blubbering like a child. And he despised himself for it, even though he knew he had as much right as any man to weep. When he had first started courting her, whenever some problem had troubled him, he had always been able to turn to her for advice, and she had always given it kindly but firmly, even when she knew perfectly well it was not what he wanted to hear, even if it was for his own good. And he had learned to trust her advice, and follow it, and had never regretted it. And now she was dead he wanted her advice – or her words of comfort, at least – but he could not turn to her because she was dead. She had been there when he had learned of the death of his grandfather, his last surviving immediate relative. She had let him mourn a week, and then told him: people die. Get used to it. Life goes on. Get on with it.

Harsh words, but true. She would not have been impressed to see him blubbering now. Touched, perhaps, but not impressed.

So he cuffed the tears from his cheeks and pushed himself to his feet.

Life went on.

He crossed to the window and looked down into the street below. A hansom was parked across the way. Killigrew could not see the occupant from that angle, but he fancied the cabbie looked like the one driving the cab he had seen on Marylebone High Street. He chuckled bitterly. No wonder the police had let him go: they were tailing him. Who did they expect him to lead them to, Sophronia Ponsonby? He shook his head with a grimace.

He took his full-dress uniform from the wardrobe, folded it and carried it to his local hummums. A Turkish steam bath, a cold shower bath, and a massage helped him clear his head as well as clean his body. Afterwards he put on his full-dress uniform and left his other clothes in the locker there.

When he emerged from the hummums, he saw the hansom parked on the opposite side of the street. He walked across to it. Sure enough, the heavily muffled man in the Bollinger hat turned out to be Detective Sergeant Dunwoody.

'I'm going home now,' Killigrew told him. 'I don't expect I'll be going out tonight.'

Dunwoody met his gaze levelly, but said nothing.

'Just so you know.' Killigrew turned away and looked for another hansom, but there was none in sight. He turned back to Dunwoody's.

'Since you're going my way anyhow . . . I don't suppose you could give me a lift to Paddington, could you?'

The detective sergeant sighed wearily, and moved up the seat. 'Come on, get in.'

'Man that is born of a woman hath but a short time to live, and is full of misery. He cometh up, and is cut down, like a flower; he fleeth as it were a shadow, and never continueth in one stay. In the midst of life we are in death: of whom may we seek for succour, but of thee, O Lord, who for our sins art justly displeased?'

The sun shone brightly in a February sky. Killigrew cast his eyes over the faces of his fellow mourners as the coffin was lowered into the grave. Lord Bullivant, glaring daggers at him as if he really believed it was Killigrew who had murdered his daughter; Lady Bullivant in bombazine, no tears for her child beneath the veil, but tragedy writ large on her grim features; and countless other friends and relatives, mostly aristocracy, all of them regarding Killigrew with lofty contempt or avoiding his eyes altogether.

He felt Mr Strachan's comforting hand on his shoulder to steady him, and mechanically reached up to pat it in acknowledgement. A tow-headed, blue-eyed man wearing wire-framed spectacles, Strachan had been the assistant surgeon on Killigrew's previous two ships, HMS *Tisiphone* and HMS *Venturer*. The young Scotsman leaned on an ebony cane to keep the weight off his wooden foot, which had replaced the flesh-and-bone one he had lost in the Arctic.

It was at times like this you really found out who your friends were. Some fellow naval officers had been talking in the library of the Army and Navy Club the other day, without taking the precaution of finding out who had been reading the newspaper in the high-backed chair turned away from the rest of the room; the fact that it was the *Manchester Guardian* should have given them a clue.

'. . . Read about a similar case he was mixed up in, in the Far East a few years ago. Another young woman who made the mistake of becoming romantically involved with him was killed. Bad business. Always was a question mark over that.'

'They say lightning doesn't strike twice.'

'Exactly! Then there was that whole Pall Mall child-killer thing.'

'Thought he was exonerated?'

'He was. But damned odd, all the same. Probably his grandfather, pulling strings.'

'Is it true his mother was a foreigner?'

'So I've heard. Greek, they say.'

'Greek! Ah, that explains it. Saw him in here earlier today, you know. Thought there was something shifty about him. I wonder the membership committee haven't done something about it yet.'

'I suggested it to Withers, but he said we had to give him the benefit of the doubt.'

'Well, he's in it this time.'

'Yes; and no grandfather left to pull strings for him.'

Killigrew had chosen that moment to fold his paper and rise from his seat, smiling pleasantly and wishing his fellow members a good evening. They had blanched satisfactorily as he passed, and rumour had it that one of them had been obliged to rush home for a clean pair of trousers afterwards.

Now the bishop was reciting the 'ashes to ashes' bit, and the chief mourners filed past the grave, each tossing a handful of soil on to the coffin.

As the collect was read, Killigrew glanced across to the church and thought about God. It was not a subject he usually chose to dwell on, but he had been raised in the Church of England and had always considered himself a Christian. Yet who could have faith in God at a time like this? Araminta's death had served no divine purpose; no purpose of any kind that he could fathom. Today he was not a Christian; not today or any other day from now on, because to him Christianity was a creed of forgiveness, and he did not feel much like turning the other cheek. The God he wanted to believe in was the God of the Old Testament, a God of wrath and vengeance.

'The grace of our Lord Jesus Christ, and the love of God and the fellowship of the Holy Ghost, be with us all evermore,' concluded the bishop. 'Amen.'

After standing in silence for a few moments, the mourners began to move away from the graveside to where their carriages waited outside the churchyard to take them back to Bullivant Hall. Most of them crowded around Lord and Lady Bullivant; no one had any words of comfort for the bereaved fiancé.

Captain Crichton had come to the funeral: he had known Miss Maltravers, but only for a short while, so it was reasonable to presume he was there to see Killigrew. As the other mourners departed – all but Strachan – Crichton approached, clutching his cocked hat awkwardly before him. In his mid-sixties, he was a tall man of imposing build with wild white hair and watery eyes that bulged from his fish-like face.

'Damnably sorry, Killigrew. Don't know what to say . . . she was a lovely girl . . .'

'Thank you, sir. That's much appreciated.'

'Not at all, not at all. By the way, have you spoken to Vice Admiral Napier since your return?'

Killigrew shook his head. 'I sent him a copy of the same written report I submitted to Admiral Dundas, but he hasn't replied yet. I've thought about calling on him in person, but I don't like to trouble him: he's got enough concerns of his own.'

'Molineaux said something about some secret plans you found?'

Killigrew nodded. 'The technical drawings for some kind of contraption. Heaven knows what it was supposed to be, but the Russians obviously think they're important because they went to a lot of trouble to stop me from handing them over to Sir James Graham.'

'And what did Graham have to say?'

'He was dismissive of the whole thing,' Killigrew said bitterly. 'Said he'd passed them on to his top men, and if you believe that you'll believe anything. Most likely they're tucked away at the back of a drawer somewhere in the Admiralty by now.'

'Can you blame him? I mean, so far we've received countless warnings of these damned infernal machines the Russians are supposed to have invented, but no one's actually run into one . . . perhaps that's what these plans are: the design for one of their infernal machines?'

Killigrew shook his head. During the previous summer's campaign in the Baltic, there had been much talk of infernal machines – explosive devices moored just below the water, that somehow exploded when a ship passed over them – although no ship had ever encountered one.

'I think it's something different,' he told Crichton. 'Something new. And if we're not careful, the first we'll know about it is when it sinks one of our ships. Let's hope that when Lord Aberdeen's successor is appointed, he appoints a new First Lord: one who's prepared to listen to reason.'

'Perhaps, but I wouldn't count on it. Sir James was able to deflect most of the criticisms of the way the campaign was handled in the Baltic on to Napier, so no one's calling for *his* resignation. And if the new prime minister is a Whig, like Sir James . . .'

'Lord Derby's the leader of the opposition, and he's a Tory.'

'Yes, but he'll probably have to form another coalition government, in which case he may just keep Graham on at the Admiralty. I know you don't like Sir James, but it's not as if he's done a bad job there, all in all. It's the usual horse-trading: Derby's offered Palmerston the post of Secretary of State for War—'

'Pam Secretary for War!' Killigrew snorted derisively. 'He'd be good at that.'

'Indeed. And Palmerston's accepted, on condition that the Earl of Clarendon stays on at the Foreign Office.'

'But Clarendon detests Derby! He'd never serve in his cabinet.'

'Exactly. It seems as though Palmerston's making mischief as usual.'

'Pam never makes mischief for its own sake, though. He must have an ulterior motive . . .' Killigrew pondered a moment. 'If the Tories were unable to pull together a coalition, the Queen would have to turn to him and ask him to be prime minister.'

'Little Vicky ask Pam to become PM?' Crichton laughed. 'It'll never happen. She's never forgiven him for the time he tried to tumble one of her ladies-in-waiting at Buck House. Besides, if Derby turns down the job, there are plenty of others she can invite to form a government: Lord Lansdowne, the Duke of Hartcliffe, even Clarendon himself.'

Crichton gazed across to where all the carriages but two had gone from the lane outside the churchyard. One was his own; the other was Sergeant Dunwoody's hansom.

'My constant shadow, now,' Killigrew explained, following Crichton's gaze. 'A plain-clothes sergeant of the Detective Branch at Scotland Yard.'

'Damnable nincompoops! They're wasting their time watching you, when we all know that the real culprits are halfway back to Russia by now.'

'Perhaps; but I'm rather hoping the fellow who forged the letter from this Sophronia Ponsonby turns out to be British.'

'British!'

'Think about it: if you were Colonel Nekrasoff, operating in what is effectively enemy territory, what would you do: bring a team of criminals with you with enough skills to meet every eventuality, or simply employ someone from the local labour market?'

Crichton nodded thoughtfully. 'Petty Officer Molineaux's always saying we have the best criminals in the world . . . perhaps he can suggest some names!'

Killigrew smiled. 'The thought had occurred to me.'

'Now . . . you won't do anything rash, will you, Killigrew? The fleet doesn't sail until April. Once you've cleared your name, it will be another matter entirely. We'll have a new prime minister by then. In the meantime, I'll drag my heels about finding someone to replace you on board the *Ramillies*. Do yourself a favour and play it by the book for once.'

'Wouldn't dream of doing it any other way,' lied Killigrew. 'As for the police, they'll find it difficult to keep tabs on me once I'm back on board the *Ramillies*.'

Crichton coloured. 'Ah. Yes, I was just coming to that. I've been asked to give you this.' He reached inside his coat and pulled out a letter bearing the Admiralty crest, with Killigrew's name written on it.

Bewildered, the commander tore it open to scan the lines within. The orders were curt and to the point: Killigrew was to be signed off the *Ramillies*' books and to report to HMS *Excellent* – the training ship permanently moored in Portsmouth Harbour – for a six-month course of instruction in diving.

'I don't understand,' stammered Killigrew. 'The fleet sails in two months . . .'

'They don't intend that you should sail with it,' Crichton explained grimly. 'The police don't want you leaving the country, and it seems someone at the Admiralty is more than happy to oblige.'

Killigrew crumpled the letter in his fist. 'My country's at war, and they want me kicking my heels in Portsmouth?' he snarled furiously.

'I'm damnably sorry, Killigrew. I've already sent a strongly worded letter of complaint to the Admiralty, but I doubt it will do any good.'

'Do I have any choice in the matter?'

'Well, they can't force you to attend the diving course. But it's that or going back on the half-pay list. And if you do that, they'll see to it you stay there for a long, long time.'

The commander nodded. 'For the rest of my career.'

After Crichton had taken his leave, he turned to Strachan.

'Thank you. For coming, I mean. You didn't have to. You didn't even know her.'

'I know *you*, don't I?' sniffed Strachan. 'At times like this, it's the living that need sympathy, not the dead. I just wish there were some words of condolence I could offer you. Something that could make sense of what happened. To lose one fiancée to a killer is bad enough, but to lose two . . .'

Killigrew nodded. It was as if Fate had seen fit to play some kind of cruel, twisted joke on him, and he wanted to react by making some bad joke in turn, to show he was not hurt; but he *was* hurt, hurt worse than he thought possible, and no joke would come.

Sensing Killigrew wanted a moment to himself, Strachan moved away, leaving his friend to watch the gravediggers cover the coffin with earth. They eyed him uncertainly. 'You, er . . . you want us to bide a bit, sir?'

Killigrew shook his head. 'No, no. You've got your work to do.'

They resumed shovelling the earth in. It was difficult to think of her lying in that ornate oak box, cold and lifeless, never more to breathe or to laugh, or to cry, or to dance, or make love . . .

Araminta was dead.

But Killigrew had no more tears left to cry.

At length, he turned away from the grave. Strachan waited by the lych-gate. The two of them started walking down the lane, the young Scotsman leaning heavily on his cane, while Sergeant Dunwoody's hansom followed them at a discreet distance . . . as if a lone hansom following two men down an empty country lane could be described as 'discreet' by any stretch of the imagination.

'So, how are you?' asked Killigrew.

'Fine . . . jings, I forgot to tell you! I'm a fully qualified surgeon now.'

'Congratulations! You know, if you applied for a posting as a ship's surgeon, you'd be a shoo-in . . .'

Strachan shook his head. 'I'm studying for my MD now. My seafaring days are behind me.'

'I'm sorry to hear you say that. You'd've made a damned fine ship's surgeon.'

'It's kind of you to say that, but . . .' Strachan tapped the side of his wooden foot with his cane.

'I'm sure that needn't be any impediment to a naval career. Besides, from the sound of things, the surgeons at Scutari need all the help they can get.'

'I'm sure Miss Nightingale and her associates will manage to get by without me.' Strachan glanced over his shoulder at the hansom. 'That must get very trying.'

'You'd be surprised how quickly you get used to it. Sergeant Dunwoody isn't such a bad fellow; he's just doing his job.' Killigrew managed a wan smile. 'And it isn't everyone who gets his own personal police escort! After what happened on Monday, I feel I need it.'

'Those Russians must be halfway back to St Petersburg by now.'

'I hope so,' agreed Killigrew. 'And yet . . .'

'What?' Strachan gave his friend a penetrating glance. 'Oh, so it's revenge you're after, is it? You know what the Chinese say: "Before setting out for revenge, first dig two graves".'

Killigrew bared his teeth in a savage grin that sent a shudder down Strachan's spine. 'They'll need to dig a lot more than two graves before I'm through.'

'And you think killing Russians will bring her back?'

'No. But it can't end here. I need justice, Strachan, and if God doesn't approve I'll seek help elsewhere. "*Flectere si nequeo superos, Acheronta movebo*." '

'The *Aeneid*?' asked Strachan. When Killigrew started quoting Latin tags, it was usually Virgil.

The commander nodded. ' "If I cannot move the gods, I'll stir up hell!" '

There were a number of brass name-plates beside the doorway of the building on an alley just off Lothbury in the City, but none of them drew attention to the office where Molineaux headed on the first Saturday in March. Although a place of business, it was not the sort of business that felt a need to draw attention to itself, for it had built up its reputation – for what that was worth – by word of mouth, and was disinclined to come by custom in any other fashion. While the nature of the business transacted by this concern was not in itself illegal, it had much to do with illegality and seemed to abide by the same rules of secrecy that governed much of the criminal world.

Molineaux had to make his way up several flights of narrow, crooked and unlit stairs to reach the office he sought. Captain Crichton had given him two days' leave so he could visit his family in London and attend to some business that the captain considered a duty of naval service, even though he knew the Admiralty would not see it that way. Crichton had even gone so far as to offer to pay him a day's wages out of his own pocket, which generous offer Molineaux had politely but firmly declined. Getting Killigrew's head out of the hangman's noose might be for the good of the service in Crichton's eyes, but for the petty officer it was a act of obligation towards a friend and, as such, an obligation he was more than happy to attend to, even if it meant revisiting some places he had never meant to return to.

Since he was officially on leave he was in his civilian togs, rather nattily dressed in railway-stripe trousers, a plaid waistcoat, an olive-coloured Doncaster coat and a Bollinger hat: a rig he could not have afforded on a petty officer's wages if he had not developed a profitable sideline in commercial endorsements in the wake of his brief celebrity as one of the heroes of the *Venturer* disaster in the Arctic.

There was only one door at the very top of the stairs, and since there was no name-plate on that either, he decided to knock in case he had got the wrong address.

'Come in!' a voice called from the other side. Recognising the voice, Molineaux opened the door with more confidence.

He found himself in a garret office with mismatched and battered furniture, the low, sloping ceilings and dormer windows indicating there was nothing above but the roof. The only person in the office was a man in waistcoat and shirtsleeves, and although both he and Molineaux were black, a stranger seeing the two men together would have been hard-pressed to discern that they were brothers. Although barely two years separated their births, Calvin Henson was more than a head taller than his brother – both Calvin and Luther had mocked Wesley as the runt of the litter when they had been children – and his face was more open whereas there was a vulpine quality to Molineaux's features. Indeed, apart from the colour of their skin, the only other physical trait they seemed to have in common was a pair of broad shoulders; whereas Molineaux had gained his in years of pushing at capstan bars, Henson had been born with his, although he had taken pains to maintain them with regular physical exercise. Not all his working life was spent behind a desk; as an assistant to an inquiry agent, he spent a good deal of time tracking down men who had welshed on debts, and since his quarry were rarely pleased to see him, it behove him to be physically fit enough to defend himself from their less-than-tender ministrations.

'Hullo, Wes.' Calvin smiled, although there was not much warmth in the smile. To Luther and Calvin, Wes had always been the black sheep of the family, first by turning to crime and then by running away to sea and leaving them to look after their mother in her old age. Not that she seemed to need much looking after, in Molineaux's opinion. Despite this, her love for all three of her sons was bestowed equally, even if she could only demonstrate it through nagging and clips round the ear hole.

60

'Cal,' Molineaux returned with a curt nod.

'What brings you here? Someone owe you some money? Or are you worried that your Lulu might be dabbing it up with some other coves when you're at sea?' Henson's tone was slightly mocking; he knew perfectly well that Molineaux's girlfriend was a singer at a penny gaff and kept herself on what could only be described as immoral earnings when her lover was away. Molineaux knew it too, and accepted it: he was not exactly faithful to her when he was overseas.

'I need information.'

'What sort of information?'

'The "Where can I find Deadly Nightshade?" sort of information.'

'Oh! Well, that sort of information ain't hard to come by. It's practically common knowledge. I may not even charge you for it.'

'You're too kind,' sneered Molineaux.

'But first you got to tell me why you want to know. Don't tell me you're going back to your old ways?'

Molineaux shook his head. 'You read the papers?'

By way of reply, Henson picked up the folded copy of The *People's Banner* at his elbow and held it up for Molineaux to see.

'Then you'll know that Mr Killigrew's being measured for a hempen cravat.'

Henson nodded.

'Yur, well, I don't believe he done it. But the only way we're going to convince a jury is if we can prove the letter found in Miss Maltravers' hand was a fakement. And that means finding the screever. Now, if it was Russian spies what done it, then you can be sure they'll have hired the best damn screever in London to do them a bang-up job.'

'That'd be Jem the Penman.'

'Right. Where do I find him?'

'You think if I knew that, I'd be sitting here? Have you got any notion how many coves we get in here who've been defrauded of hundreds of pounds by Jem the Penman?'

'That's why I've got to see Deadly. She'll know. I don't need to hang around the Rat's Castle no more to know there ain't a cross farthing earned in the Big Huey that she don't get a tol from.'

'Rat's Castle ain't there no more, Wes. They knocked it down when they built New Oxford Street.'

'Yur, so I heard. That's why I'm asking you where I can find her.'

Henson chuckled. 'She's moved up in the world since you were

around, Wes. Runs a conish buttocking ken in St James's these days.'
He gave Molineaux the address.

'Thanks, Cal. I owe you one.'

'Just watch yourself in there, Wes. They may have velvet drapes on
the windows and champagne behind the bar, but the bullies what runs
it are as tough as ever.'

Leaving the office, Molineaux cut down Old Jewry to Cheapside,
which bustled as always with city gents in chimney-pot hats and frock-
coats, ignoring the ragged beggars pleading for alms, ladies in shawls
and bonnets and with baskets over their arms inspecting the wares of
the barrows of the costermongers, flunkeys running to and fro with
messages, and a man and a woman playing a hurdy-gurdy and a violin
respectively while a child solicited donations from the disinterested
passers-by.

Molineaux could see a Chelsea and Shoreditch 'bus had just passed.
The traffic was slow enough for him to have caught it had he been of
a mind to run after it, but it was past noon, so he bought a pork pie
from a hot-pie shop and ate it in the street while he waited for the
next one.

He bought a cup from a coffee stall to wash his dinner down with,
flirting with the pretty young woman who served him. While he was
sipping his coffee, the shouts of a newspaper boy caught his ear above
the cries of the costermongers.

'Hextra! Hextra! Read all abaht it! Rooshian Hemperor hops the
twig!'

Molineaux bought a copy of *The Times*, but by the time he got his
change another omnibus had drawn up to collect a passenger, so he
folded the newspaper under one arm and swung himself on board just
as it set off once more, and settled down in one of the seats. He paid the
conductor his thruppence and unfolded the newspaper. Tsar Nicholas
had succumbed to pneumonia the previous day, and would be succeeded
by his eldest son, the Tsarevich Alexander.

'Does that mean the war's over?' asked a mechanic, reading over his
shoulder.

Molineaux snorted derisively. 'If you believe that, you'll believe
anything.'

He leafed through the rest of the pages while the omnibus carried
him along the Strand, before he hopped off at Regent Street and cut
down Charles II Street to St James's Square. The address his brother
had given him was a fine Georgian town house, five storeys high and

almost certainly knocked through into the adjoining houses on either side. Molineaux pulled the doorbell and presently it was answered by a burly-looking fellow whose broken nose and cauliflower ear belied the respectability of his butler's uniform.

He took in the colour of Molineaux's skin with a disdainful sneer. 'The tradesmen's entrance is round the back.'

Molineaux leaned in close to whisper in the butler's ear. 'I'll let you into a secret, cully,' he murmured, and brought a hand up to grab the man's scrotum through the fabric of his trousers. 'I ain't no bleedin' tradesman!'

The butler gave a strangled gasp and backed into the hallway. He reached inside his coat, but Molineaux caught him by the wrist and twisted his arm up into the small of his back. Clasping him firmly in a half-nelson, he marched him across the hall and through the door on the far side. The room beyond was a saloon, with velvet-covered furniture and crystal chandeliers. At that time of day it was empty but for a man polishing glasses behind the bar, but the emptiness only served to emphasise the stench of stale tobacco and sweat lingering from the previous night.

Molineaux slammed the butler against the bar and pinioned him there. The barman put down his glass and tea towel to reach under the bar, but Molineaux felt inside the butler's coat and pulled out his revolver, levelling it straight between the barman's eyes.

'If you're going to give me a slug, cully, make it gin 'stead o' lead!' He thumbed back the hammer. 'Where's Deadly?'

'Don't know what you're talking about,' the barman said surlily.

Molineaux fired a shot past the barman's ear, shattering the etched-glass mirror on the wall behind him.

The barman flinched, but quickly recovered himself and glanced mildly over his shoulder. 'That's seven years' bad luck.'

'It'll be a 'ternity of bad luck for you, if I have to pull this trigger a second time. Keep your fams where I can see 'em and move away from the barking iron I don't doubt you got stowed under the counter.'

A door opened off to one side and a tall, horse-faced man with red hair and military whiskers stepped through. 'What the hell's all the racket about?' he demanded, and then grinned when he saw Molineaux. 'Cowcumber Henson! As I live and breathe!'

'Hullo, Carrots. Long time no see.'

'Not nearly long enough, Wes! It's all right, Bob; Wes here's an old pal. As a matter of fact, Wes was the toast of the swell mob before either of you had faked your first cly; and he was a damned sight better at it too. What brings you here, Wes?'

Molineaux dropped the revolver into a sink of soapy water behind the bar. 'I wanted a word with Deadly. Is she in?'

Carrots nodded and gave his head a jerk, motioning for Molineaux to follow him back through the door from which he had just emerged. The two of them went down a short corridor and knocked on the first door to the left.

'Who is it?' a woman's voice called from the other side.

'Carrots. There's an old pal out here eager to renew your acquaintance.'

'Come in.'

Carrots opened the door and ushered Molineaux through into a room that was scarcely less plush than the saloon they had just left, if marginally more tasteful, barring the portrait of a reclining nude framed high on one wall.

The woman who had modelled for the portrait sat in a plush leather chair behind a mahogany desk with an inlaid leather surface, wearing a white blouse and a smart skirt. If Molineaux had not known better, he might have mistaken her for a respectable woman. Belladonna Porter – alias Deadly Nightshade – had to be nearly forty now, but remained as handsome as ever, and if she had fleshed out at all since the last time he had seen her, it was in all the right places.

As soon as she saw him, she smiled with delight. 'Cowcumber!' She rose to her feet and moved out from behind her desk to give him a peck on one cheek. 'No need to ask where you've been hiding yourself these past seventeen years.'

He grinned. 'Hullo, Deadly.'

'Missing the flash mob, are you? I can still use a dab fam like you, assuming you ain't let your old talents go rusty.' She indicated the man who sat in one of the other chairs with his elbows on the armrests and his fingers steepled. His togs were gentry, but Molineaux was not fooled: the eyes were as hard as the diamond pin in his cravat. 'Mr Pierce here's got wind of a prime lay, and he's looking for a dab cracksman.'

Smiling, Molineaux shook his head. 'I'm straight now, Deadly.'

'Are you sure? There could be a lot of 'gent in it for you.'

'Thanks, but no thanks. Can we voker in private?'

Deadly nodded. 'If you'll excuse us?' she said to Pierce. 'I'll be in touch. Carrots, tell Ned Agar I've got a prime lay for him.'

Carrots nodded and went out of the room after Pierce, closing the door behind them.

Molineaux glanced at the two-way mirror on one wall, through which he could see the saloon where Bob was sweeping up the shards of the broken mirror behind the bar and the butler was massaging his twisted shoulder. A moment later Carrots and Pierce emerged and crossed the room. 'Still up to your old tricks I see,' Molineaux remarked.

Deadly moved closer to him; closer than propriety might have permitted. 'Oh, I've learned a few new ones since the old days,' she whispered huskily.

'I dare say. You've come a long way since you were Sammy the Swell's moll.'

'And you're just a common lagger.' 'Lagger' was cant for 'sailor'; to the flash mob, sailors were the men who took convicted criminals to the penal colonies in the Australias. 'Bit of a comedown from being Cowcumber Henson, ain't it?'

'Excuse me! For your information, I happen to be a uncommon dab lagger.'

She moved away from him briskly, crossing to the sideboard where a row of crystal decanters stood. 'Take the weight off your stumps, Wes. Pull up a pew. Can I offer you a wet?'

'That depends . . . it's not going to be laced with arsenic, is it?'

'Wes! Would I do that to you?'

'That depends on whether or not you're still harbouring a grudge over the Haymarket job.'

'I always assumed it was Foxy that double-crossed Sammy on that one.' She laughed. 'Hell! If you'd made off with the bosh, I doubt you'd be working as a lagger now. For what that fiddle was worth, you could've bought your own ship!' She shook her head. 'Sammy double-crossed you and Foxy before Foxy double-crossed us all. He was lagged and the crushers caught up with Sammy a couple of years later.'

Molineaux nodded. 'I heard Sammy got cramped at Newgate.'

'And I hear Foxy cocked his toes in the colonies a few years back.'

'I know. I'm the one that hushed him.'

Deadly stared at Molineaux in disbelief. '*You* hushed him? I don't believe it. You and Foxy was always as thick as thieves.'

'It's a long story.'

'Did he ever tell you what he did with the bosh?'

Molineaux nodded. 'He swapped it for a dummy he'd hidden amongst the rubbish in the alley behind the theatre – he done it so smart even I didn't see the switch, and I was standing right beside him at the time – and went back for the ream article after. Hid it in the attic of a drum on Dyott Street.'

'You mean . . . it's still there?'

Molineaux shook his head. 'I already checked. Oh, I promised myself I wouldn't: told myself I'd put that life behind me, and that I needed to stay away to prove it to myself. But . . . well, curiosity's a powerful thing.'

'And was it still there?'

'The whole drum was torn down when they built New Oxford Street.'

Deadly laughed merrily. 'Easy come, easy go. Well, either way, you and me are square now, Wes.'

'In that case, I'll have some of that whisky you've got there.'

'Whisky! I remember when it was always gin with you, Wes.' She took the stopper from one of the decanters and poured out a couple of measures. 'I thought it was all rum, bum and baccy in the navy?'

'Never had a taste for any of those things,' Molineaux said mildly.

She brought two glasses of whisky away from the sideboard and handed one to him before resuming her seat behind the desk, all business now. 'So, Wes; if you ain't interested in coming back to the cross lay, what brings you to my humble abode?'

'I'm looking for a screevesman.'

'I can recommend any number.'

'I'm looking for one in particular. His tally's Jem the Penman. Word on the street is he's the one that dotted Commander Killigrew's card for the Paddington croaking.'

'I don't granny anything of that. It weren't done with my blessing, but you know how it is with cramping. There's too many amateurs even for me to keep a lid on it!'

'The coves what cramped Miss Maltravers were no amateurs, believe me!'

'What's your interest?'

'Killigrew's a pal of mine. So was Miss Maltravers, in a way. I ain't going to stand by and see him nap a blinder for it.'

'So you think the letter found in the victim's fam was a fakement, and you need to find the screevesman who faked it to prove this Killigrew's on the square.'

'That's about the long and the short of it.'

'What makes you think it was Jem the Penman?'

'The coves what cramped Miss Maltravers would've hired the best: they could afford it. And they say Jem the Penman's the best.'

'All right, let's say it was Jem the Penman; and let's also say that I know who he is and where you can find him. Why should I tell you? You're only going to blow upon him to the crushers to save your pal Killigrew from a Newgate neck-cloth. I don't chirp, Wes: it's bad for business. You should know that.'

'Not even if the coves what hired Jem the Penman were Russian spies?'

'Russian spies? Where do Russian spies come into it?'

'They're the ones as cramped Miss Maltravers. Oh, not for any military advantage: just out of spite, acos me and Mr Killigrew got her and her parents out of Finland last year. They found out Mr K was sweet on Miss M, so they found a way to fix 'em both.' Molineaux sipped his whisky. 'Now, if you're happy with the thought of Russian spies prowling through the night committing all sorts of crimes on your turf, then by all means keep Jem the Penman's ream tally from me.'

She stood up and crossed to the two-way mirror, staring at nothing in particular. Molineaux remained in his chair, content to let her chew it over for a moment.

Finally she turned back to face him. 'If I tell you, you didn't hear it from me.'

'That goes without saying!'

Deadly gave him the name. She even threw the initials after it into the bargain. The name meant nothing to Molineaux, but on hearing the initials his jaw dropped.

# IV

# Killigrew in the Underworld

The water at the bottom of Portsmouth Harbour was so silty that even at three fathoms Killigrew could hardly see his hand in front of his face. But he did not have to look hard for the thirty-two-pounder carronade: this was an exercise in salvage, not underwater location. Spotting it through the clouds of silt that billowed around his weighted boots with every step, he tapped the instructor on the arm and pointed to the gun. The instructor gave him the thumbs-up – it was impossible to see a nod when one's head was enclosed by the brass Siebe helmet – and the two of them made their way across to it, kicking up fresh clouds of silt at each step.

The instructor handed Killigrew the end of one of the ropes, and the commander got down on his knees to pass it under the barrel to fasten it into a sling. He had to rely on feel as much as sight to see what he was doing, with the sound of his own breath rasping in his ears as an accompaniment to the rhythmic sighing of the pump at the other end of his air hose, and the great weight of the water above him pressing the rubber and twill canvas diving suit against his body.

At last he had fastened the cable to the sling, tugged it a couple of times to make sure it was secure, and gave the instructor the thumbs-up. The instructor moved closer to check the fastenings for himself, and then gave another thumbs-up and gestured in the direction of the diving platform. The two of them made their way across to it, and no sooner had Killigrew given a couple of pulls on the communication rope than the platform began to rise.

When they emerged from the waves, without the water to buoy it up

Killigrew's helmet became heavy once more, and he was conscious of his weighted belt and the weights hanging from his corselet. He climbed up on to the deck where two of his fellow trainees worked the air pump, his heavy boots awkward and difficult to lift in the air as he climbed up the accommodation ladder until he stood on the deck. He sat down on a stout bench so one of the other men on the deck could unscrew the nuts that fixed the helmet to his corselet. Killigrew blinked at the bright sunshine as the heavy helmet was carefully lifted from his head.

'How do you feel, sir?' asked the supervisor on deck.

'Never felt better,' Killigrew assured him, truthfully enough.

The supervisor clapped him on the back and turned to the instructor, who had followed Killigrew up on deck and had his own helmet removed in turn. 'How did he do?'

'Steady, confident and thorough,' the instructor said. 'How quick?'

'Want to guess?'

'Five and a half minutes?'

'Not far off. I make it five minutes and twenty-seven seconds. But the proof of the pudding is in the eating. Let's see what he's landed.' The supervisor ordered two other trainees to man the winch. Presently the carronade was hauled up from the inky depths, and the trainees on deck cheered and clapped Killigrew on the back.

'Not bad, sir,' said the supervisor. 'Keep this up, and we'll make a half-decent diver of you yet. All right, that's enough for today. Those of you who've been granted shore leave had better be back here by eight bells in the morning – and I want you all fit and rested, so no late night carousing ashore! Diving and the demon drink do not mix.'

Killigrew returned to his cabin to get changed back into his uniform, and was brushing his hair when there was a knock on the cabin door.

'Come in?'

The door opened to reveal Molineaux grinning on the doorstep, back in his petty officer's uniform. 'Hullo, sir!'

'Molineaux! What the devil are you doing here?'

'I'm on my way back out to the Our Emily.' HMS *Ramillies* was anchored out in Spithead with the other ships gathering for the fleet, due to sail for the Baltic in three weeks' time. 'Persuaded the cox'n to stop here so I could tell you what I managed to find out. How's the diving instruction coming on, sir?'

'Oh, it's the most terrific fun,' Killigrew told him in all sincerity. 'It's good to be working with my hands for a change, instead of strutting up and down the quarterdeck giving orders, or doing paperwork in my cabin. And the complex mathematical formulae it seems to involve help keep my mind off . . . well, you know. That said, you realise I'd much rather be getting the *Ramillies* ready for her next voyage with you and the others. I've got a score to settle with those Russian bastards. Still, the sooner I get off this murder charge, the sooner I can resume my duties on board the *Ramillies*.'

Molineaux frowned. 'You haven't heard, then?'

'Heard what?'

'They've appointed a new commander to replace you. It wasn't Cap'n Crichton's doing,' he added hurriedly. 'He kicked up merry hell about it when he found out the Admiralty had gone over his head. Said it wasn't their business to go appointing him a new second in command without consulting him.'

That was certainly true, although Killigrew could not imagine Crichton being so indiscreet as to say so to a petty officer. 'Now, Molineaux, I hope you haven't been listening at keyholes!'

' 'Course not, sir. Got it off the jolly who was on duty outside the cap'n's day-room, didn't I? And he didn't mean to eavesdrop, I'm sure; but you know what old Nose-Biter's like when his blood's up. He don't exactly keep his voice low.'

'True enough. Still, never mind that: did you have any luck tracking down this forger?'

'I got his tally.'

'Capital work! Let's have it, then.'

Molineaux gave him the name. And the letters after it.

'You're joshing me.'

'On the level, sir. Think about it: a cove in that lay needs all sorts of criminal pals. How better to make their acquaintance, all the while keeping up a respectable front for his friends and neighbours?'

'I suppose it makes sense. It's just incredible to think that a man in that line of work might be using it as a cover for criminal activity.'

'Oh, you'd be amazed how many of the purportedly respectable gentry coves you rub shoulders with at the Army and Navy are really hardened criminals.'

Killigrew thought about it. 'Well, perhaps not that amazed,' he told Molineaux. 'Did you get an address for him?'

Molineaux shook his head. 'No, but he shouldn't be that difficult to find. I'll bet Mr Strachan's uncle knows how to track him down.'

The petty officer could not keep his boat waiting any longer, so Killigrew walked him on deck and watched as he was rowed out to where the *Ramillies* was moored. It was a hard blow to learn that someone had been appointed to replace him on the block-ship. Even if he could satisfy the jury of his innocence at his trial, there was no berth waiting for him on one of Her Majesty's ships afterwards, unless a vacancy came up on a ship of the line – third rate or higher – where the captain was willing to appoint Killigrew as his second in command; and there had been precious few of those even before he had been accused of murder.

He had his nose rubbed into his situation every time he went up on the *Excellent*'s deck, for hardly a day passed without another ship arriving to join the fleet gathering at Spithead. Rear Admiral Dundas' flagship, the *Duke of Wellington*, was already there, anchored under bare poles with the other ships of the line, corvettes and sloops gathering around her; and all of the larger ships had a gunboat or a mortar-vessel as a tender. What was most remarkable of all was that every single ship had a funnel or two rising amidships: whether equipped with paddle-wheels or a screw, there was not a ship leaving with the fleet in April that was not a steamer.

Having got permission from the *Excellent*'s captain to go ashore that weekend, Killigrew rose at first light on Saturday morning and dressed in his civilian rig: a black cotton-print shirt decorated with a pattern of tiny white skulls and crossbones, gothic designs being all the 'go'; railway-stripe trousers; a waistcoat in the dark-hued hunting tartan of his native Cornwall; a tobacco-coloured frock-coat and a new greatcoat of Mackintosh cloth. Finally, he set his broad-brimmed wideawake hat – bran-new from James Lock & Co. – on his head at a jaunty angle, checked his appearance in the small mirror over the wash-stand in his cabin, and made his way up on deck.

As he was rowed ashore, he saw the children retrieving the round shot from the previous day's gunnery practice from the mudflats off Whale Island, skiing over the mud with wooden boards strapped to their feet. Their families made a good living selling them back to the *Excellent*, and one of them – the Grubbs – had even invented a special device for extracting the shot from the mud.

A carriage was drawn up in front of the Pier Hotel on the Hard when Killigrew emerged from the dockyard gates. It had been there ever since the commander had arrived on board *Excellent*, although the horses had to be changed regularly so they could get some exercise. He crossed to it now, peering through the window: the two constables inside, dressed in plain clothes, were fast asleep, wrapped against the cold, with the debris of their supper – greasy, crumpled sheets of newspaper – strewn around their hobnailed boots. With so many bluejackets and marines stationed off Portsmouth to create havoc in the city's taverns and brothels each night, it amazed Killigrew that the Hampshire constabulary could spare two men to keep a permanent watch on him. But barroom brawls were the stuff of routine in Portsmouth; it was not every day they got a Society murder.

He declined to disturb their slumbers, making his way through Portsmouth's narrow and crooked cobbled streets to the railway station, where he caught a train to Waterloo and took a hansom from the rank in front of the station. It took him across Waterloo Bridge, turning right at Somerset House on the north bank of the Thames and dropping him off at Temple Bar. Bewigged barristers clutched their briefs as they strode through the Inner Temple, trying to look purposeful. Being slightly less fond of lawyers than he was of man-eating sharks, Killigrew did not know his way around the Inns of Court, and had to ask one of the barristers for directions. He made his way to King's Bench Walk, where he found the building he sought. There were a number of brass plaques on the wall, and casting his eyes over them he found the one he was looking for: 'Mr James Tabard, QC'.

He entered and made his way up the stairs to knock on the door of Tabard's chambers.

'Come in!' a rich, plummy voice called from the other side. Had Killigrew received that reply while knocking on the door of a Chinese flower boat, he would have been in no doubt that the speaker was a barrister.

He opened the door and went in. Tabard's chambers were comfortable and well appointed rather than grandiose and elegant, but Killigrew suspected that only reflected the personality of their owner. Mr Tabard himself looked very much at home in one of the plush leather easy chairs, a portly man with a fringe of greying hair around a bald pate and the beaming, rubicund face of a Mr Pickwick. Nevertheless, Killigrew was surprised by how tall he was when he stood up to greet him, and it was easy to imagine him leaning over the gentlemen of a jury to dominate them.

'Mr Tabard?' asked Killigrew, in little doubt as to the answer.

'I am he, Mr . . .?'

'Killigrew. Commander Christopher Killigrew, of Her Majesty's Navy.'

'Goodness gracious! Not the chap who killed the polar bear?'

Killigrew suppressed a grimace: he was never going to hear the end of that. 'I am he,' he replied, faintly mocking the barrister's use of that phrase.

'A pleasure to make your acquaintance, sir.' The two of them shook hands. Tabard's grip was a little too firm for Killigrew's liking, as if he felt he could prove something by it, which to the commander's mind indicated that he felt he had something to prove. 'Do take a seat.' Tabard gestured to the chair across from his own on the other side of the fireplace where a log fire crackled in the hearth. 'And how may I be of service to you, Mr Killigrew? I'm afraid I can only give you half an hour in the present instance, as I'm due in court this afternoon.'

Killigrew smiled. 'In a professional or personal capacity?'

Tabard laughed. 'You have a singular wit, sir. Can I offer you a libation?'

'A little early in the day for me,' said Killigrew.

The barrister shrugged and crossed to the drinks cabinet, pouring himself a glass of claret from one of the crystal decanters. 'I am aware, of course, of your . . . shall we say, *alleged* involvement? . . . in the murder of the Honourable Miss Araminta Maltravers, naturally. I don't know how familiar you are with the workings of the law, but if you need a barrister to defend you in court, it is customary to go through a solicitor . . .'

'The police have not yet brought charges.'

'Then you are to be congratulated, sir. A sure sign that the Crown's case is a weak one.'

'I was merely after some legal advice. Your name was given to me by one of the sailors on board my last ship: Petty Officer Wes Molineaux.'

Tabard frowned. 'I cannot say I know the name.'

'You surprise me. I would have thought a man in your line of work would get to know a great many criminals.'

Tabard grinned. 'One does indeed. But still, the name Molineaux . . .?'

'Alias Wesley Henson, alias Cowcumber Henson? But then, he was never charged by the police, either, so he never had need of the services of a man such as yourself. But to get down to brass tacks: it's in my own interests to clear my name before the police charge me with murder. You won't have read in the papers that a letter of an intimate tone was found in Miss Maltravers' hand purporting to have been written by me to a Miss Sophronia Ponsonby.'

'You claim you never wrote the letter?'

'I never heard of a Miss Sophronia Ponsonby. The letter was forged, and if I can find the man who forged it, that would clear my name, would it not?'

'It would indeed! Am I to understand you know the identity of this man, then?'

'Let's just say I'm very close to him.'

'Indeed?' The smile did not flicker on Tabard's face, but now it was frozen in place and the laughter in his twinkling eyes had died. 'Do you have a name for this felon?'

Killigrew nodded. 'It was given to me by Petty Officer Molineaux.'

Tabard suddenly pushed himself to his feet. 'Would you have any objection to our repairing to my library? This reminds me of the case of Cobleigh versus Regina, and I think at this juncture it would be useful to consult a precedent.'

'By all means.' Killigrew followed Tabard through into the next room. Shelves laden with arcane tomes of law covered three out of four walls. The barrister sat down behind his desk; Killigrew perched on the edge of its inlaid leather surface. Tabard looked put out at this lack of formality, but did not say anything.

'Wouldn't you like to know the name of this forger?' Killigrew asked him.

'Would it mean anything to me?'

'As you yourself admitted, a man in your line of work gets to know a great many criminals.'

'Very well, what is his name?'

'Jem the Penman.'

Tabard stared at Killigrew for a moment, and then threw back his head and laughed heartily.

'Have I said something to amuse you?'

'Forgive me, Mr Killigrew.' Tabard produced a silk handkerchief and dabbed tears of mirth from his cheeks. 'Have you ever had an ague, Mr Killigrew? A medical friend of mine tells me that whenever a patient has a fever of some description, without sufficient symptoms to make a more accurate diagnosis, then a physician will merely diagnose it as an ague. There are so many ailments about which medical science remains ignorant even in this day and age . . . in the medical profession, saying a patient has the ague is merely a form of shorthand for saying, "I don't know what ails this fellow".'

'So it is with this Jem the Penman. Like physicians, the police detectives of Scotland Yard cannot bring themselves to admit of any ignorance, so whenever they come across a case of forgery they ascribe it to this "Jem the Penman". He's a bogeyman, Mr Killigrew. He is Scotch mist, he is a white elephant, he is a chimaera, he is the cat's mother.'

'He is sitting right in front of me.'

'I'm not sure I follow you, Mr Killigrew. But if you'll permit me, there's something I'd like to show you which I think will illustrate my point . . .' Tabard opened one of the drawers of his desk and reached inside it.

Killigrew swivelled on the desk, swinging his legs over it to kick the drawer shut with a heel, slamming it on Tabard's hand. As the barrister screamed, Killigrew slammed the heel of his other boot into his face, sending his chair shooting back on its castors to crash against the bookshelves behind him. The shelves collapsed, and dozens of thick tomes cascaded down on his head. He cried out as his chair went over backwards.

'Don't look so surprised, Jem,' Killigrew told him. 'Surely you must have known that sooner or later you'd feel the full weight of English law bearing down on you?'

He opened the drawer and took out the pistol Tabard had been reaching for: an ancient flintlock piece with little evidence of oil on its workings. Tabard used the criminal associates he made working as a barrister to help him by breaking safes or picking pockets to get him blank cheques and copies of signatures so he could forge cheques for huge sums, always using an unwitting dupe to cash the cheques in a way that they could never be traced back to him. As deplorable as it was, at least it was not a crime of violence; Tabard had the soft look of a man who did not care for violence, and for a moment Killigrew felt ashamed at having used force against him. Until he remembered the stench of Araminta's flesh burning and the sight of her garrotted corpse, lying in a pool of her own bodily waste on his bed.

He jumped down from the desk and grabbed Tabard by the cravat, hauling him to his feet and slamming him back against what was left of the shelves behind him.

'You . . . you maniac!' stammered Tabard. 'I've had some ruffians in here in my time, but you're the worst of them!'

Killigrew rammed the muzzle of the pistol against Tabard's right nostril. 'I'm so glad we understand one another.'

'Even if what you say is true . . . you haven't a shred of proof.'

'Proof? Proof is for someone who wants a conviction.' Killigrew thumbed back the hammer of the flintlock. 'I'm more interested in revenge.'

'Kill me, and you'll never prove your innocence!'

'Are you willing to write out a confession?'

In spite of his bruised face, Tabard managed a triumphant smile. 'Do you take me for a fool?'

'You'd better, because without it I'm a dead man anyhow – in which case I've nothing to lose by taking you with me. As well to be hanged for a sheep as a lamb. I'd advise you to say a prayer, Mr Tabard, but I wouldn't want you to waste your breath: there's a sign on the Pearly Gates that says "No lawyers"!'

'Merciful heavens! All I did was forge a couple of notes in your handwriting. I had no conception it would lead to Miss Maltravers' death, I swear it!'

'Sorry, Tabard. Save your rhetoric for Satan.'

'Wait, wait, wait! You say you want revenge . . . wouldn't you rather be avenged against the man who ordered Miss Maltravers' death, and the man who performed the deed? I can give you their names.'

'I already know their names. And since they're in Russia, and I'm here, and thanks to your penmanship I'm not likely to live until the war's over, they're out of my reach. So I'll just have to make do with you.'

'They're not in Russia! They're still here in London!'

Killigrew's heart almost leaped, but he caught himself: Tabard would say anything to save his own skin now. 'Where?'

'I can't tell you . . .'

With the muzzle of the pistol, Killigrew squished Tabard's strawberry nose against his face. 'Try,' he suggested.

'I mean, I don't know! They always contacted me.'

'Then how do you know they're still in London? When did they last get in touch with you?'

'Two days ago.'

'More than enough time for them to have left the country. You'll have to try harder than that.'

'They wanted me to make them a Prussian passport.'

'And you agreed?'

Tabard shook his head. 'I may have forged the odd cheque in my time, Mr Killigrew; but to falsify a passport from another country . . .? Even my skill has its limits.'

'But I'll wager you know someone who could!'

The barrister nodded. 'I was able to recommend the services of a former client of mine, a Hebrew gentleman who owns a printing shop on Bedford Street: a Mr Emmanuel Leventhal.'

'I think I shall have to pay a call on this Mr Leventhal,' Killigrew mused out loud. 'And if I find out you've lied to me, I shall be coming back.'

Leaving Tabard to chew on that, Killigrew left the Inner Temple and made his way back to the Temple Bar. It was a little over half a mile to Covent Garden, so he decided to spare himself the expense of a hansom and to get some exercise into the bargain by joining the crowds that bustled along the Strand. It was past noon, so he stopped at Simpson's Divan and Tavern for a mutton dinner washed down with a glass of claret. After enjoying a post-prandial cheroot to give the rich food a chance to settle, he resumed his journey, turning right on to Bedford Street a little after one. The thoroughfare was crowded with shoppers bustling between Covent Garden and the Strand, and a large, discordant barrel organ belting out 'Turkey in the Straw' scarcely blotted out the cries of the costermongers.

Leventhal & Son, Printers was on the west side of the street, wedged, aptly enough, between a publishing house and a bookshop. There were samples in the bay window: letterheads, calling cards and invitations to balls, faded by sunlight; given how little sunlight must have reached the window even at noon, it seemed reasonable to assume they had been there a long time.

A bell jangled as Killigrew pushed the door open, and the smell of printer's ink wafted from the workshop at the back. He closed the door behind him, muffling the cacophony of the barrel organ.

A podgy-looking fellow with greasy blond hair and the lugubrious expression of an overweight bloodhound emerged from the back of the shop, his fingers and apron black with ink. 'Good afternoon, sir. And how may I be of service?'

'Mr Leventhal?'

'Yes, that's right.'

'Mr Emmanuel Leventhal?'

'Manny to my friends, sir. Forgive me if I don't proffer my hand.'

'Are you Leventhal or Son?'

'Son, sir. My dear departed father was carried off by the cholera last summer. I keep the sign to honour his memory. How may I be of service?'

'I need a printing job done.'

'Well, you've come to the right place. What was it? Calling cards? Invitations? Letterheads? We offer a variety of typefaces and different shades of paper and matching cards, all the best quality at very reasonable rates.'

'How about passports?'

Leventhal coloured. 'I think you need to apply to the Home Office for one of those.'

'Jem the Penman sent me.'

The printer looked about shiftily and leaned across the counter, lowering his voice to a hiss. 'Well, you can go right back to him and tell him not to send anyone else, because I'm clean now, d'you hear? I don't do that no more!'

'And what about the two gentlemen Mr Tabard sent to you two days ago?'

This time Leventhal coloured such a dark shade of crimson that Killigrew was willing to believe him when he said he was trying to go 'straight': the man was such a terrible liar that if a policeman came in to order some letterheads, the printer would probably end up confessing to every crime he could think of. 'Don't know what you're talking about, mister.'

'Do you read the papers, Mr Leventhal?'

'On occasion.'

'Perhaps you've read about the Paddington Strangling?'

'I don't know anything about *that*,' Leventhal said firmly.

'The two men Mr Tabard sent do. They're the one's who did it.'

The colour drained from Leventhal's face as swiftly as it had suffused it only seconds earlier. But then he seemed to brighten. 'Ha!' he said. 'I knew it!'

'You knew they were the ones who murdered Miss Maltravers?'

'No, I mean, I knew Commander Killigrew couldn't've done it.'

That took Killigrew aback. 'What makes you say that?'

'Commander Killigrew? The cove what led the Venturers out of the Arctic? A murderer?' Leventhal snorted derisively. 'If you'll believe that, you'll believe anything.'

'I can only hope the jury shares your scepticism if it ever comes to trial, Mr Leventhal.'

'Why? What's it to you?'

'I'm Commander Killigrew.'

The printer snorted again. 'Oh yur? And I'm the King of Rooshia!'

'No, really. Why else do you think I'd be so interested in tracking down these men?' Killigrew took out his pocket book and extracted a pasteboard calling card. 'My card.'

Leventhal took it from him, his eyes flickering from the commander's face to his card and back to his face again. An expression of awe appeared on his features and he giggled nervously. 'Well, I'll be jiggered! You really are him, in'tcher? Commander Killigrew . . . it's a great honour, sir . . . I'd consider it a special honour if you would permit me to shake you by the hand . . .' He proffered his own hand, then remembered how inky it was and hurriedly withdrew it, wiping it on the front of his apron. 'Begging your pardon, sir, but this 'ere card – it ain't exackly the best quality. Now, I can see how a gentleman like yourself could be taken in, but if you'll permit me to say, this pasteboard ain't the best. See how easily it creases? And if you look closely at the print, you can see how ragged it is around the edges, not a quality printing job at all. Now, I would consider it an especial honour if you would permit me to print you a hundred cards on the very finest laid, free of charge . . .'

'That's far too generous of you, Mr Leventhal, but I really couldn't—'

Leventhal held up a commanding hand for silence. 'No, sir, I absolutely insist. Do you know what an honour it would be for me to be able to list you as one of my customers?'

Killigrew smiled. 'A man under suspicion of murder?'

The printer snorted yet again. 'Murderer, my eye! I hardly think that the man who marched across eight thousand miles of Arctic wilderness is going to let a little thing like a murder charge hamper him.'

'Eight hundred miles,' Killigrew corrected him.

'Why, I'm willing to bet the case gets thrown out of court before the first week is out!'

'I wish I shared your confidence. It would help immensely if I could produce the real murderers.'

'And you think those two gentlemen that Mr Tabard sent done it?'

'One in his mid-forties, with wavy black hair and dark eyes, the other in his thirties, tall and well built, with blond hair and blue eyes?'

Leventhal nodded thoughtfully. 'Yur, that sounds like them. They came in here only yesterday.'

'They're Russian spies.'

Leventhal's jaw dropped. 'Rooshians! *Oy gevald*! Mr Killigrew, you must believe me, I had no notion . . . I thought they were English gentlemen; if I'd known they was Rooshian spies, I'd've thrown 'em out of here in short order, I can tell you! Why, like as not I'd have set the crushers on 'em!'

'Like as not they'd've killed you before you got the chance,' Killigrew told him. 'Where can I find them?'

'I don't know. They didn't give me an address.'

'Is that usual for your customers?'

'It is when they want illegal documents!'

'Tabard said something about a Prussian passport. I don't suppose there's any point in asking who this passport is intended for?'

'I thought it best not to aks.'

'But they must have given you a description?'

'Age, thirty-three; height, six foot one; dark hair, grey eyes. The passport's to be in the name of Niklaus Hergerscheimer.'

Given that the name was almost certainly as false as the passport itself would be, Killigrew was not all that interested in that. 'Presumably you must have given them a date as to when it would be ready by?'

Leventhal nodded. 'Nearly four months from now.'

'Four months! They can't be in much of a hurry.'

'It's a specialist job,' protested the printer. 'First I've had to get hold of a real Prooshian passport to use as a template.'

'You mean that some pickpocket of your acquaintance has been waiting down at the docks for some poor devil to arrive from the *Zollverein*, so he can steal one?'

'One pickpocket! An 'ole team of them, more like. We was gonna return the passport when we'd finished with it; or hand it in at a police office, anyhow. I suppose you're going to report all this to the crushers?'

'And have them kill the trail stone-cold dead by arresting you and your pickpockets?' Killigrew shook his head. 'It's not you I'm after; it's the men who murdered Miss Maltravers. What arrangements did they make to collect the passport?'

'I'm meeting them at ten o'clock on Saturday the thirtieth of June at a place of their choosing. I hand over the passport and they give me the balance of the gelt they're paying me.'

'Where?'

'All right, all right! Hold your horses! I'm just coming to that, aren't I? If you'd only let me finish, I was going to tell you that I'm going to meet them at the—'

One of the window-panes shattered, throwing shards of glass across the shop and carrying the sound of a gunshot in from the street.

# V

# The Great Globe

---

Killigrew threw himself down behind the display in the window, his heart pounding. Drawing a revolver from the pocket of his greatcoat – he had started carrying it at all times since Nekrasoff and Ryzhago had turned up at his rooms – he glanced across to where Leventhal had been standing behind the counter, but there was no sign of the printer.

'Mr Leventhal? Are you all right?'

There was silence.

And then a voice came back from behind the counter: 'Some *schtarker* takes a shot at me, how do you think I feel?'

'But you're not injured?'

'I don't think so.'

'You'd better tell me where you arranged to hand over the passport.'

'What, *now* you want me to tell you?'

'Later might be *too* late.'

There was silence from the other side of the counter while Leventhal considered the implications of this. 'I've got a better plan,' he called back at last. 'Why don't you deal with the *schtarker* with the gun, and then I tell you?'

'If you told me now, there'd be no need for the . . . um . . . *schtarker* . . . to shoot you.'

'You going to tell *him* that?'

Killigrew was too busy listening to reply. It was not that everything had gone quiet outside, quite the opposite: the passers-by who had been shocked into silence by the sound of the shot had now resumed their street-cries and conversations, as if nothing had happened.

'Whoever it was, I think he's gone,' he told Leventhal.

'Why don't you stick your head up and find out?'

'Why don't you stick yours up?' Killigrew replied testily.

'Because I'm not a naval officer. I don't get paid to get shot at.'

'I'm only on half-pay.'

'Good! Maybe you'll only get half-shot!'

Tentatively, Killigrew raised his head above the level of the display. A second pane was shattered as a bullet splintered the chipboard inches from his nose. He ducked back down hurriedly.

'I think he's still there,' said Leventhal.

Killigrew did not bother to dignify the comment with a reply.

'How about you, Mr K?' called Leventhal. 'You still there?'

'Oh, yes, I'm not going anywhere.'

Outside, after some initial screams – the people in the street realising that the first shot had not been their imagination, someone really was shooting out there – all had fallen silent, the street suddenly deserted. The scene had an air of unreality about it. *This is going to make an interesting couple of paragraphs in my memoirs*, Killigrew thought ruefully. *The Battle of Bedford Street: How I was pinned down in a Covent Garden printer's shop.*

'You want to know something?' called Leventhal.

'Is it pertinent to our current predicament?'

There was a pause. 'I think so, yes.'

'Go on, then.'

'I don't think it's me he's trying to kill.'

'Of course it's you he's trying to kill. Obviously he thinks you've got some vital piece of information that will help me, and he's trying to stop you from passing it on.'

'If he wants to stop me from giving you a vital piece of information, wouldn't it make more sense for him to shoot *you*? Besides, they still want this passport, don't they?'

'Good point.'

Killigrew looked around for something – anything – he could use to get him out of this situation. Short of sending the marksman a calling card or an invitation to a ball, there was not a lot that was going to be much help. 'Have you got a stick?'

'A *schtick*?'

'You know: something long and thin.'

'Would a straight-edge do you?'

'Perfect!'

82

'Coming your way!' A steel-edged ruler came flying over the counter to land a couple of feet from where Killigrew lay. He pulled it closer to him under the heel of one half-boot, then took off his hat and put it on top of the stick, slowly lifting it into view in the window. But the mystery marksman was not falling for that one.

Killigrew raised an eye to the bullet hole in the chipboard display. The street vendors and passers-by had scattered. He scanned the first-floor windows of the shops on the other side of the street. Seeing they were all closed, he lowered his gaze to where—

Another shot drilled a second bullet hole a few inches to the left of the first, and he ducked down instinctively, but this time he had seen the puff of smoke from a long, thin barrel protruding over the top of the barrel organ.

An expert rifleman, he knew, could reload his weapon in twenty seconds; and while this one had not actually killed anyone yet, he was coming pretty close. Still, twenty seconds was twenty seconds. Killigrew picked himself up and dashed out into the street.

Another shot came in his direction before he had even crossed the pavement, soughing within an inch of his head. He threw himself flat. So the marksman had a winger; that was something he had not counted on. How long until the first rifleman reloaded? He thought he still had a few seconds. The shot had come from somewhere near the bottom of the street – Bedford Street inclined down towards the Stand – so Killigrew picked himself up and ran to where a water cart was parked near the top. No sooner had he reached it than the first marksman fired again. The bullet chipped the cobbles at Killigrew's feet: the man was aiming at his legs, exposed between the wheels of the cart. Looking over the top of the barrel on the cart, Killigrew could now see the second marksman, reloading his rifled musket where he sat on top of a carriage parked towards the bottom of the street.

Killigrew levelled his revolver at the man on the carriage. He was not much of a shot, but he might be able to . . .

He caught himself. At that range, all he was likely to do was hit one of the innocent passers-by walking down the Strand.

He tucked the revolver back in his pocket and grasped the handles of the water cart, pulling it back off the chock wedged under one wheel to stop it from rolling down the street. He edged it around, and after giving it an initial shove it was a question of letting gravity do most of the work. He kept hold of the handles to guide it, but soon he was running to keep up. The man on the carriage squeezed off a shot at him, drilling a hole through the barrel that splashed two streams of water across the cobbles.

When Killigrew was less than ten yards from the barrel organ, he let go of the handles, tripped, and rolled on the cobbles. The water cart smashed into the organ, which in turn smashed into the marksman who had moved around the side of it. All three went over with a discordant crash.

Killigrew rose up on one knee. He was now far enough down the street to take a shot at the man on the carriage without being in danger of hitting anyone on the Strand. He squeezed off a couple of shots, splintering the coachwork of the carriage. The other marksman jumped down from the driving seat and ran down the street.

Leventhal emerged from his shop, brandishing what looked like a roller from one of his printing machines. Killigrew indicated the man who lay dazed and groaning amidst the wreckage of the barrel organ and water cart.

'Tie him up and wait by him until the police get here.'

Leventhal looked disgruntled. 'You're the sailor; why don't *you* tie him up?'

Killigrew proffered his revolver, grip-first. 'Very well. Take this and go after the other one.' He nodded to where the second man had almost reached the Strand.

Leventhal's eyes widened. 'Other one? All right, all right! I'll get some string!'

Killigrew thrust his revolver back in his pocket – only a half-wit looking to cause a fatal accident ran with a gun in his hand – and sprinted down the street after the second man. When he reached the Strand, he stood on tiptoes, searching the heads of the crowds. There was no sign of his quarry. He jogged a short distance towards Charing Cross, looking about, until his eye was caught by a commotion on King William Street, which branched off to his right. A blind bootlace-seller sprawled on the pavement, his wares scattered across the cobbles, and the little girl who had been selling lucifers and fusees with him shook her fist after a figure running up towards Chandos Street.

Killigrew broke into a run, jinking in and out of the shoppers in his path. At the top of King William Street, the marksman made a sharp left on to Adelaide Street. By the time Killigrew had reached the junction, the man was already fifty yards off, ducking down the side of St Martin's-in-the-Fields before he reached the Strand again.

Killigrew's only chance of catching him lay in trying to guess where he would go next. He was heading for Trafalgar Square, but Killigrew guessed his quarry would not try running across the square: it was too open, and it would probably not occur to a killer in a hurry that his pursuer would not dare risk a shot in that crowded place. So he would have to turn right, up St Martin's Lane.

Killigrew took a short cut down the alley on the north side of St Martin-in-the-Fields. He had almost reached St Martin's Lane when the marksman appeared, running across the mouth of the alley. Wisely, he had abandoned his rifle somewhere so it would not mark him out in the crowd. Seeing Killigrew bearing down on him from his right, he instinctively turned left, dashing through the traffic on the street to disappear into the alley at the back of the National Gallery.

Killigrew followed him, dodging between an omnibus and a hearse, and hoping the latter was not an omen. The hearse driver swore at him as his lead horses reared in fright, but Killigrew had already entered the alley. His quarry was just a dozen yards ahead of him now, turning right up Castle Street, and then left down Orange Street.

As fit as Killigrew was, his feet and thighs were staring to ache, and he was running short of breath. But his quarry could be in little better condition. The two of them turned right again, past the Sablonière Hotel into Leicester Square. The marksman ran straight across to the rotunda housing James Wyld's Great Globe at the centre of the square, pushing past the people queuing to enter the portico at the north side. They shouted after him in annoyance.

Killigrew drew his revolver, holding it pointed in the air as he too pushed through the queue, shouting, 'Excuse me, excuse me! Police business!' That was more or less true, and if anyone did not believe him and summoned a real policeman, he would have no objection to a little assistance.

The marksman had already pushed over the attendant who was collecting entrance fees. 'Fetch the police!' Killigrew told the attendant, skipping over him. 'Warn them he's dangerous!' Without waiting for the attendant's reply, Killigrew followed his quarry into the circular passage that ran around the outer part of the rotunda, where a variety of maps, globes and atlases were on display.

Killigrew had visited the Great Globe with Araminta a couple of months after it had first opened, at the time of the Great Exhibition. Those had been happier days, a brief period when Britain did not seem to be at war with anyone, and he had squired her all around his favourite city in the world: Rules, Simpson's, the Greenwich Tavern, the ballet, the opera, and of course numerous visits to the Great Exhibition itself to take in the thousands of items on display at the Crystal Palace in Hyde Park.

He pushed the thought to the back of his mind. She was gone now, and he had a job to do. He searched the crowds of people moving slowly amongst the displays, oblivious to the fact there was a killer in their midst. Two, if you counted Killigrew.

An idea occurred to him. He fired a shot into the floor. 'Everyone down on the floor, *now*!' he shouted.

A woman screamed. Instead of everyone dropping to the floor, they all started trying to run for the exits. Killigrew was almost knocked off his feet by the rush. *Capital notion, Kit!* he told himself wryly. He was going to lose his quarry in the crush . . .

No: there the fellow was, being swept into the globe itself by the people who went that way in an effort to escape the lunatic with a revolver. Killigrew went after him.

The Great Globe was . . . well, imagine the world turned inside out, and shrunk down to a fraction of its size. The interior was not quite spherical – Killigrew had read it was about sixty feet high and forty in diameter – but there was no telling if you did not already know that. The geography of the world had been modelled in relief on the interior surface of the sphere, at a scale of one inch to ten miles, and a series of four observation platforms rose up like a tiered wedding cake from the centre of the floor, so you could see all parts of the map other than the rough outline of what little was known of Antarctica's geography on the floor. Strategically placed gas lamps struggled to illuminate such a vast space, and the place was dim.

While the visitors on the platform continued to peer at the sides oblivious to the commotion in the passages outside, the people on the floor milled about uncertainly. A little boy in a sailor suit was crying, clutching at his nanny's hand. Killigrew quickly slipped his revolver back in his coat pocket and searched the faces of the other people there for the cloth cap and rough features of his quarry, but all he saw were the side whiskers of gentlemen beneath stovepipe hats and the faces of women hooded by their bonnets.

'There he is!' a bearded gentleman exclaimed, and pointed an accusing finger at Killigrew. 'That's the feller!'

Footsteps sounded on the iron staircase leading up to the first platform. Killigrew looked up to see the man he was after pounding up the steps. Hearing the gentleman identify Killigrew, the marksman must have thought he himself was the victim of the accusation.

'Police business!' Killigrew pushed the bearded gentleman aside and ran up the steps after his quarry.

They reached the first platform, running alongside the railing to where the next flight of steps led to the platform above. A young man with a cane was sent sprawling as the marksman ran into him. Killigrew jumped over the young man before he had a chance to get up again.

Two more flights of steps led up to the topmost platform, slightly smaller than the one below to allow for where the sphere curved in at the top. Killigrew reached the top of the stairs in time to see his quarry cornered against the far rail.

'Nowhere left to run!' Killigrew shouted across, to the astonishment of the bewildered visitors there.

The man looked around desperately, and vaulted over the railing to land on the platform below.

Killigrew swore and ran halfway back down the stairs, vaulting over the banister and rolling on the platform in time to see his quarry running for the next flight. Those people who were still on the platforms tended to be crowded around the railing – no one had come to look at the middle of a platform (although the confrontation between Killigrew and his quarry was starting to draw their attention) – so the space there was relatively clear. Killigrew picked himself up and launched himself across, catching the man around the waist in a flying rugby tackle before he reached the steps. They slammed against the railing. Killigrew managed to land a punch in his quarry's midriff, but then one of the visitors steamed in.

'I say, that's enough of that, you two ruffians! Can't you see there are women and children present?'

He swung his cane at Killigrew's head. The commander ducked beneath it, but then the marksman punched him in the jaw, knocking him back against the railing. He toppled over it, felt himself falling, and barely managed to catch the rail in time. He dangled from one hand, level with the equator, and gazed down to New Zealand, some thirty feet below him.

Manny Leventhal emerged from the doorway in the South Pacific Ocean, followed by half a dozen bobbies, one of them waving a rattle furiously to summon further assistance. Leventhal looked up and saw Killigrew dangling from the platform above. He pointed up at him, and ran for the stairs, the peelers struggling to keep up.

Killigrew glanced across to where the marksman now struggled with the visitor armed with a cane. When the two of them parted, the cane was in the marksman's possession and he swung it at the side of the visitor's head, knocking him down. The spectators gasped, and after that no one felt like interfering.

The railings were too narrow for Killigrew to squeeze through back on to the safety of the platform. He managed to get his other hand on the rail, but then the marksman whirled with the cane and slammed it down between his hands. He drew back for another swing, and Killigrew had to let go of the railing, hanging off the stanchions below. The marksman lashed out with one foot, crushing Killigrew's fingers against the rail. The commander gasped and had to let go with that hand, dangling from the other.

He looked up to see his opponent standing above him, sweeping the cane back over one shoulder to swing it over the rail at Killigrew's head. Then the assassin's eyes widened in terror, and the next thing the commander knew the man was toppling over the railing. Killigrew drew his head in as the man fell past him, head first, screaming. The scream was cut short when he thudded against New Zealand and slid down the Pacific Ocean towards the Antarctic. A woman shrieked in horror, while the nanny tried to cover the eyes of her charge who, being a ten-year-old boy, did not want to be prevented from gawping at the dead man.

Killigrew managed to catch hold of one of the other railings with his crushed hand; it stung like the devil, but there were no bones broken as far as he could tell; and he had some experience of broken bones. Not that he wanted any more, so he was relieved when he looked up to see Leventhal leaning over the rail, reaching down to clasp his hand. It must have been the printer who had caught the marksman by the heels and tumbled him over the railing.

He hauled Killigrew to safety and the two of them sat down with their backs to the railings, gasping for breath. One of the peelers stood over them, arms folded and grim-faced, wanting some answers. Killigrew made a gesture that managed to be an acknowledgement of his presence, an appeasement, and a request for a chance to catch his breath before explaining, all in one.

He glanced over his shoulder. Through the railings, he could see the other peelers creating a cordon around the marksman's body. 'Is he dead?'

'He ain't dancing a jig, Mr K,' panted Leventhal.

'Damn! I wanted to take him alive!'

'Would you prefer it . . . if it was you down there . . . with your neck bent double . . . and him up here . . . still breathing?'

'I needed him to answer some questions.'

'We got the other one.'

Killigrew nodded, and glanced at Leventhal. 'I thought you people didn't believe in violence?'

'You must be thinking of the Quakers, Mr K. You ever *read* the Old Testament? Gideon, David, Samson? All Jews.'

'Well, I'm obliged to you, Mr Leventhal. You just saved my life.'

'Think nothing of it. Why, if I'd let you tackle them fellers alone, tonight you'd've been sitting in your club telling your pals over a glass of port and a cigar about how some dirty little Hebrew didn't help you tackle a couple of armed killers.'

'You did far more than most would have done.'

'Of course. What *you people* don't understand is what a full-time responsibility it is, being Jewish.' The printer indicated the waiting bobby. 'Your department, I think.'

Killigrew was kept waiting in a cell to himself at Bow Street Magistrates' Court for nearly twelve hours before the door opened and Detective Inspector Jordan entered. He had a face like thunder.

Killigrew covered a yawn with a bandaged hand and stretched his aching limbs. 'Is something wrong?'

'Your story seems to be true in its particulars as far as we can ascertain. The man you captured on Bedford Street is William Richards, alias Brassy Bill; the man who died at the Great Globe is a known accomplice of his, Charles Croker. Both were recently tried for murder at the Old Bailey but acquitted, thanks to the eloquent defence on their behalf by—'

'James Tabard, QC?' anticipated Killigrew.

Jordan scowled at having his thunder stolen. 'Yes.'

'And what does Mr Tabard have to say for himself?'

'Not much. He swallowed a whole phial of prussic acid shortly before we arrived. Killed himself out of remorse for having assisted two Russian spies to murder an innocent woman and frame an innocent man, according to his suicide note.'

'I don't believe it,' said Killigrew. 'He's a barrister. Barristers don't suffer from remorse.'

'I'd've thought you'd be pleased. It puts you in the clear.'

'It still doesn't make sense. Tabard was the sort who'd brazen it out, not take his own life. Where did he get a phial of prussic acid at such short notice, anyhow?'

'We've checked with the apothecaries in the vicinity of the Inns of Court and haven't found any record of prussic acid being sold to a Mr Tabard. Of course, he might have purchased the acid under an assumed name, but my guess is he was murdered. The barristers living in the adjoining chambers heard raised voices shortly before we arrived, and there are bruises on Tabard's throat, jaw, shoulders and arms consistent with his having been pinned down while someone poured the acid down his throat. And the suicide note's written in a very shaky hand, as if written under extreme duress.'

'Then why are you releasing me? I'd've thought I'd be your prime suspect.'

Jordan shook his head. 'You've got a cast-iron alibi: you were in here at the time. We know precisely when Tabard was killed because he was seen alive when he let two men into his chambers at three o'clock. The raised voices were heard about ten minutes after that. Then everything went quiet, and at twenty-three minutes past they emerged again. We arrived there at half-past.' He grimaced again, clearly painfully conscious that he had missed out on making the arrest of his career.

Killigrew frowned. 'Why so precise?'

'Pardon?'

'About the time they left, I mean. You said "twenty-three minutes past". Not "twenty past," or "twenty-five past," but "twenty-three minutes past".'

'Because the two men seen emerging from Tabard's chambers stopped to ask the witness the time: that's why he remembers it so precisely.'

'Doesn't that strike you as rather odd?'

'What do you mean?'

'Put yourself in their shoes. You've just forced a man to write a suicide note then held him down and poured prussic acid down his throat. Would you stop to ask the time as you left the building, and risk the danger that the man you asked would be able to give your description?'

'Well, lucky for you they did, because the description given by the witness is a fair tally for the one you gave of Nekrasoff and Ryzhago.'

Killigrew nodded. 'Covering their tracks. What about Leventhal?'

90

'That's slightly trickier. Technically, since he hadn't actually begun forging the Prussian passport, he's not actually guilty of any crime; and even if he had, I'm not sure there's any law against forging the passport of a foreign country. But we can get him on receiving stolen goods.'

'The real Prussian passport his confederates stole for him to use as a template?'

Jordan nodded.

'Actually, I was wondering if you could turn a blind eye to that.'

'We leave turning blind eyes to you naval lads. One way or another, we're going to throw the book at that greasy Hebrew bastard.'

'That "greasy Hebrew bastard", as you call him, saved my life, Inspector.'

'That's very nice, sir,' Jordan retorted coldly. 'You can speak up as a character witness at his trial.'

'What about this meeting he arranged to hand the passport over to Nekrasoff at . . . I never did find out where they were going to meet.'

'The Crystal Palace, sir. The Egyptian Court, to be precise. I think we can safely assume that meeting's been cancelled.'

'Why not get Leventhal to turn Queen's evidence? If it *was* Tabard that sent those two men to kill me, there's still a chance that Nekrasoff doesn't know we know about the passport. You could have plain-clothes men waiting at the Crystal Palace to arrest Nekrasoff when he turns up. I know it's a long shot, Inspector, but surely it's got to be worth a try?'

'Nekrasoff will know we know about the passport when he reads about Leventhal's arrest in the press tomorrow. The *People's Banner* already has the story. Gunfights in Covent Garden, a punch-up in the Great Globe – you can't keep incidents like that under wraps. The important thing is, this fellow Nekrasoff won't be getting his false passport now.'

'The important thing is finding out who that passport was intended for, surely? From the description Leventhal gave me, it wasn't Nekrasoff or Ryzhago. And I'm sure there are other forgers in London that Nekrasoff can go to.'

'And I'm sure we'll find Nekrasoff before he has a chance to use it. We've got men watching all the ports and we're checking all the known forgers.'

'What about the unknown ones?'

'You go back to Portsmouth and do your job, Commander. Leave us to do ours.'

'Do my job! It's thanks to your bungling, Inspector, that I'm going to spend the whole of the summer kicking my heels on board HMS *Excellent* while the fleet returns to the Baltic!'

# VI

# The *Merlin*

─────────────

'Did Vinny tell you what happened to the lads from the *Cossack*?' Seth Endicott asked Molineaux on the deck of HMS *Ramillies*.

'No. What?'

'They sent a boat ashore at Hangö Head to drop off some of the prisoners they'd taken – you know, merchant cap'ns off prizes – and there was a battalion of Russian infantry waiting for them ashore, and when the boat reached the pier the officer commanding the Russkis shouted: "We don't care for your flag of truce, we'll learn you not to fight against Russians!" and then he ordered his men to open fire on the boat.' A lanky Liverpudlian with greasy fair hair, Endicott had recently been promoted to gunner's mate following his predecessor's death from the epidemic of smallpox that had raged through the fleet, and now wore a petty officer's badge of distinction on the sleeve of his jacket. 'And afterwards, when they'd rounded up the prisoners, they took the bodies of the dead and the dying and threw them into the sea!'

'Yur, well, we know the Ivans ain't no respecters of a flag of truce,' said Molineaux, and frowned. 'How do they know?'

'Eh?'

'How do they know what the Russian officer said, if the Ivans killed half of them and took the rest prisoner?'

'Oh! One of the lads they wounded managed to hide ashore overnight and rowed back to the *Cossack* the next morning.'

'Haven't you two got anything better to do than lollygag around all day, gossiping like a couple of old washerwomen?' demanded Commander Tremaine, looming up suddenly.

The two petty officers regarded Killigrew's replacement with studied insolence. 'No, sir,' said Molineaux.

It was true enough. Since the British fleet had arrived in the Baltic two months earlier, the *Ramillies* – a third-rate ship of the line converted to a block-ship – had been engaged in the tedium of blockade duties, while the crews of the frigates and sloops of the fleet amused themselves as best they could by cutting merchant ships out of undefended Finnish harbours, or exchanging shots with troops ashore.

For the past two weeks, the *Ramillies* had been at anchor with the rest of the British fleet – now joined by the French contingent – off Kotlin Island, a sliver of land some six miles long. The fortress of Kronstadt stood on the east end of Kotlin, dominating the approaches to St Petersburg where the Gulf of Finland narrowed towards its end. The Allied ships of the line had anchored in line of battle some three miles beyond the western tip of Kotlin, presenting their broadsides to any ships that approached from that direction. Four frigates and two sloops formed a second line a mile closer to the island, but still well out of range of Kronstadt's guns.

The Russians had four ships of the line, three frigates and three brigs anchored behind the maritime fortress, moored in a line to the east where they could gain from the protection of Kronstadt's guns and protect the fortress in turn by serving as floating batteries. But they dared not come out to face the Allied fleet, and the Allied ships dared not try steaming past the granite-faced batteries of Kronstadt to go in and get them. The seamen of the Allied fleet had more to fear from smallpox and chicken pox than they did from enemy action, and as Lieutenant Frederick Adare stood on the quarterdeck, eavesdropping on the two petty officers' conversation, he had even found himself wishing he had been with the men from HMS *Cossack* who had gone ashore only to be massacred or captured: at least they had seen some action.

'Well . . . at least have the decency to pretend to be busy,' Commander Tremaine told the two petty officers testily.

'Pretend to be busy,' echoed Molineaux.

'Begging your pardon, sir,' said Endicott, 'but if it means that much to you, couldn't you pretend we're busy, like?'

Adare struggled to suppress a smile.

'That's enough lip from you, Endicott!' snapped Tremaine, wagging a finger in the Liverpudlian's face. 'I've had quite enough of your impudence!'

'Aye, aye, sir!' Endicott saluted smartly, and as the commander turned on his heel to stalk back to the quarterdeck, the Liverpudlian made obscene gestures at his back.

'A little harsh on them, weren't you, sir?' Adare asked Tremaine. 'They're both good men. They just want to see some fighting; they can't help it if the tedium wears down their tempers.'

'That's no excuse for insubordination! If you ask me, Commander Killigrew let things get a little too slack on this ship.'

'The Old Man never had any complaints about the way Mr Killigrew handled the men, sir.'

'Then he's as much to blame as Killigrew is.'

'Sir,' Adare commented non-committally. He had mixed feelings about Killigrew's replacement by Tremaine. The son of a senior clerk in the Post Office, Adare had always known he was going to have problems fitting into a service that was dominated by the sons of naval officers, landed gentlemen and titled peers. Indeed, so keenly had he felt the snobbery directed at him as one of the 'middling sort', he had been thinking about resigning his commission altogether when Captain Crichton had given him a berth on the *Ramillies*. Either Crichton did not care what a man's social background was, or – perhaps more likely – he had enough trouble remembering what his father did for a living, and played it safe by treating everyone with equal geniality. Killigrew, meanwhile, as president of the wardroom mess, had not tolerated any kind of snobbery – a true gentleman, he detested it as simply being bad manners – and he treated everyone with respect, from the captain down to the lowliest ship's boy. And in turn the men had respected him for it.

The queer thing was, the ratings could be the biggest snobs of all. Like the servants below stairs at his father's house in Dublin, they had their own hierarchy that had to be respected by all who were in it. They certainly had none of the respect that they automatically accorded the other officers for Adare. 'He ain't a proper gentleman,' he had heard one seaman remark, thinking he was out of earshot, and even Able Seaman Hughes, who constantly sought (in vain) to convert his shipmates to communism yet fawned obsequiously in the presence of officers, was noticeably less obsequious when dealing with Adare.

That had been the case when Adare had first joined the *Ramillies* sixteen months ago; and on every ship he had served on before then. It was not so bad now, and Adare knew he had Killigrew to thank for that: when the seamen had seen Killigrew treating Adare with respect, they had begun to do the same; grudgingly at first, but slowly he had begun to win them round.

Now Killigrew had gone, to be replaced by Tremaine – the biggest snob of all – Adare no longer had that safety net. But Tremaine had done so much to make an enemy of everyone on board with his strict adherence to every rule and regulation, and his inability to turn a blind eye to the most minor of infractions, the more the hands saw the commander treating Adare with contempt, the more they gave their tacit support to the lieutenant against the outsider, the cuckoo who had invaded their once-happy nest. Detestable though Tremaine was, his presence was almost welcome to Adare. Best of all, the commander had no sense of humour whatsoever, which made him an easy mark.

Adare glanced for'ard, in the direction of the Russian ships anchored beyond Kronstadt, and frowned. He took the telescope from the binnacle and levelled it, taking care not to let the eyepiece actually touch any part of his face. 'Is that the Russian fleet getting ready to weigh anchor?' he wondered out loud.

'What? Let me see!' Tremaine snatched the telescope from Adare's hands to see for himself. He peered past Kronstadt for a few moments, and then lowered the telescope again. 'I don't see any smoke coming from their funnels, and there's no sign of them crossing their yards.'

'I must've been mistaken,' said Adare, struggling to keep a straight face.

Endicott glanced at Tremaine, and instantly creased with laughter. He nudged Molineaux, who took one look and likewise doubled up.

Tremaine glared at them. 'What the devil's the matter with you two?'

'Nuttin', sir,' said Endicott, wiping tears of laughter from his cheeks with his sleeve. 'I just thought of a funny joke, that's all.'

'And what's your excuse?' Tremaine asked Molineaux.

'I thought of the same joke as Seth, sir.'

'Have you two been sucking the monkey? Come here so I can smell your breath!'

Snickering, the two petty officers stepped on to the quarterdeck, struggling to keep straight faces. When Tremaine thrust his nose close to their lips, however, they collapsed with fresh peals of laughter.

'Right, I've just about had enough of you two!' snarled the commander. 'Mr Adare, send for the master-at-arms. I want these two men under arrest, now.'

'Aye, aye, sir.' Somehow, Adare managed to keep a straight face. 'Pass the word for the master-at-arms.'

The master-at-arms came on deck, and promptly collapsed when he saw Tremaine's face.

Crichton emerged from the after hatch. 'Did I hear someone pass the word for the master-at-arms?' he asked. Then he saw Tremaine's face, and everything became clear. 'Ah-ha! Been in a fight have we, Mr Tremaine?' he asked with a smile.

'Fight, sir? No . . .'

'In that case, I think you'll find that some joker has smeared the eyepiece of the bring-'em-near in the binnacle with boot blacking.'

'What?' Tremaine rubbed his eyes and looked at his hands to see the blacking smeared on the white kid leather of one of his gloves. He rounded furiously on Adare. 'This is your doing! I'll pay you back for this!' Crimson-faced, he turned and stumbled down the after hatch.

As soon as the commander had gone, Adare could no longer suppress the gales of laughter that had been welling up inside him.

'A tad on the childish side, don't you think, Mr Adare?' Crichton said with a smile.

'Sorry, sir.' Adare wiped his eyes with a handkerchief. 'Not very original, I know, but I couldn't resist it. He does rather set himself up for it.'

'I suppose you put blacking on the mouthpiece of the speaking trumpet, too?'

'Want me to clean it off, sir?'

'Good heavens, no! By the way, I've been invited to go aboard the *Merlin* today; Sulivan's taking us in to take a closer look at the Russian defences. Fancy coming along?'

'I'd be delighted, sir.'

'Splendid! I don't imagine we'll see much excitement, but it beats kicking our heels on the *Ramillies* all day, eh? Mr Pemberton, would you assemble the crew of my gig? Mr McGurk, pass my regards to Mr Tremaine and tell him I'm going aboard the *Merlin* with Mr Adare. He's in command in my absence.'

'Aye, aye, sir.' Midshipman McGurk made his way below.

The gig was lowered from its davits and Adare shinned down the lifelines with the crew before they rowed the boat to the foot of the accommodation ladder, where Crichton descended with more dignity if less panache to join the lieutenant in the stern sheets.

'Reminds me of when I was a snotty in the *Ramage*,' Crichton remarked to Adare as they were rowed across to the *Merlin*. 'We used to fill the salt-shaker in the cockpit with baking soda, put a tissue over the top, prod it down a little and pour some concentrated lemon juice inside, put a circle of card inside the top of the shaker so the juice won't come out, replace the lid – but don't screw it down – trim off the tissue paper sticking out around the edges, and warn everyone else in the cockpit not to use it. As soon as the victim gives it a shake, the baking soda reacts with the lemon juice and spews foam everywhere, blowing off the lid.' He cleared his throat. 'Not that I'd expect an officer of mine to get up to such shenanigans.'

'No, sir.'

'I particularly wouldn't want him to do it on Friday night when I'm dining in the wardroom, so I get to see what happens.'

'I'll bear it in mind, sir,' said Adare, making a mental note to ask the steward if he had any tissue paper.

A surveying ship, the *Merlin* was 125 feet from stem to stern, a small paddle-steamer dwarfed by the ships of the line. The *Ramillies'* gig was one of ten bearing captains from the other ships of the fleet, and Crichton and Adare had to wait their turn before they could climb on board, where Admiral Pénaud – the commander of the French contingent – was already waiting with his own captains.

'Hullo, Sulivan,' Crichton greeted the *Merlin*'s captain once they were on board. 'Have you met my second, Mr Adare?'

'It's an honour, sir,' said the lieutenant, saluting Sulivan, an intense-looking Cornishman whose dark hair was starting to turn grey at the temples. He already knew Sulivan by reputation. The fleet's surveyor, he had served as a midshipman under Commander Fitzroy on several voyages, including the one Mr Darwin had made famous in his celebrated book, *The Voyage of the Beagle*. He had made a name for himself the previous year by surveying a channel through the Åland Islands, making Vice Admiral Napier's attack on the fort at Bomarsund possible.

Adare was not the only junior officer who was a guest on board the *Merlin* that day; several of the other captains had brought a junior with them, and Adare recognised Lieutenant Slater from the *Buzzard*, with whom he had served on board HMS *Bolitho* before the war. The two of them greeted one another warmly.

The *Merlin* was about to steam away from the fleet when a gig arrived bearing a lieutenant from the flagship, HMS *Duke of Wellington*, and a civilian in his mid-fifties wearing a frock-coat and chimney-pot hat and clutching a sketch pad. 'Rear Admiral Seymour presents his compliments, sir, and asks if you'd mind taking Mr Carmichael with you, sir?' asked the lieutenant.

'The sketch artist from the *Illustrated London News*,' Sulivan explained to Crichton in a low voice. 'My compliments to the rear admiral, and tell him I shall be delighted to have Mr Carmichael aboard. Send him up, Lieutenant!'

Sulivan lifted the speaking tube from the binnacle and blew into it before lifting it to one ear and listening for a moment, then speaking into it. 'Turn ahead, half, Mr Lowther,' he told the engineer. He listened for a response, then hooked the tube back in its place moments before the engine below decks throbbed into life and the paddle-wheels on either side of the hull plashed at the waves, driving the *Merlin* forward. 'Three points to port, Gilham.'

'Three points to port it is, sir.' The quartermaster nodded to the two seamen at the helm, and they spun the wheel, bringing the *Merlin*'s head around to starboard until she pointed east-north-east. As she steamed around the flotilla of gunboats riding the waves closer still to Kotlin, she was joined by her escort: HMS *Dragon* and HMS *Firefly*, and the *d'Assas*: a steam frigate, a paddle-sloop and a French corvette respectively. The *Firefly* followed close in the *Merlin*'s wake, while the *Dragon* and the *d'Assas* kept a course parallel to the two smaller ships.

While they were steaming across towards Kotlin Island, Mr Carmichael sketched Admiral Pénaud with Sulivan and the other captains posing on the quarterdeck. Presently Tolboukin Lighthouse came up off the starboard bow: a cylindrical, seven-storey tower rising up from a cluster of buildings that huddled on a rocky islet half a mile off the west end of Kotlin. As they passed, Adare glimpsed the granite forts bristling with guns that rose sheer-sided from the waves to the south of Kronstadt. There were signs that the Russians had begun constructing similar forts to the north. Previously they had believed the water there to be too shallow to permit the passage of ships, but Sulivan had disproved that by sounding in HMS *Lightning* the previous year.

There was also evidence that the Russians had not been idle during the winter on Kotlin itself. As the *Merlin* steamed along the north coast of the island, Sulivan and the other officers observed that several new batteries had been built across the island halfway along its length, presumably to prevent the Allies from landing troops on the west end from which they could set up their own batteries to bombard Kronstadt the way Bomarsund had been bombarded the previous summer.

The *Merlin* was proceeding under steam and sail, and as one of the hands moved aft to adjust a brace, he bumped into Mr Carmichael, who had finished sketching the officers on the quarterdeck and was now wandering about the windward waist. Knocked off balance, Carmichael staggered into another seaman, who responded by expressing himself in exceedingly salty language, much to the artist's evident embarrassment.

'Mr Carmichael, why don't you sit on the fore-side of the paddle-box?' Sulivan suggested to the artist. 'You'll get a better view from up there, and you can rest your sketch pad on your knees.'

As the *Merlin* rounded a headland halfway along the length of the island, the ships of the Russian fleet came into view.

'Come two more points to port,' Sulivan ordered the quartermaster.

'Two points to port it is, sir.'

'Let's see how close they'll let us get. Dickens, make sure the lookouts keep a sharp eye on those enemy ships, in case one of them decides to weigh anchor. You never know, they may yet surprise us.'

'Aye, aye, sir.'

'Dickens, did you say?' Crichton murmured to Sulivan.

'My chief bosun's mate, Arthur Dickens.'

'He's no relation of . . . ah . . . you know?'

'Not that I'm aware of. I never thought to ask. Still, you never know: I believe that the author hails from Kent, as does Chief Petty Officer Dickens, so I suppose it's entirely feasible.'

The *Merlin* steamed at a leisurely pace parallel with the north-east shore of Kotlin for the next hour and a half, until by a quarter-past three they were parallel with the east end of Kronstadt, close enough to see the flotilla of Russian gunboats and mortar-vessels harboured in the fortress' lee. Sulivan gave the order to drop anchor, and got busy with the other officers on deck, sketching the fortifications with a practised hand.

After looking for himself, Crichton handed a telescope to Adare so he could see. They were just over half a mile off the main fortress, near enough for the lieutenant to make out the soldiers in shiny helmets and white coats manning the battlements as they bustled back and forth.

They had been at anchor for three-quarters of an hour when a cry came from the lookout at the masthead. 'Sail ho!'

Sulivan took the speaking trumpet from the binnacle to call back. 'Where away?'

'Fine on the starboard bow!'

Sulivan levelled his telescope to where a paddle-steamer approached from the direction of St Petersburg, grey smoke puffing from her funnel beneath the lowering sky. Sulivan handed his telescope to his second in command. 'What do you make of her, Creyke?'

'Flapper of some sort, sir. Difficult to say how many guns she's got.'

'Best not to take any chances. Beat to quarters!'

As the marine drummer summoned the crew to their battle stations, Sulivan took the telescope back from Commander Creyke for another look, and gasped in astonishment. 'Good heavens!'

'What is it?' asked Captain Mundy of the *Nile*.

'The flapper: she's a pleasure steamer.'

'I beg your pardon?'

'See for yourself.' Sulivan handed him the telescope. 'You can see the gawkers lining the rails: men in chimney-pot hats, and women in ball gowns.'

Mundy looked through the telescope and saw Sulivan was telling the truth. 'Good gracious! You're right!'

'They must've come from St Petersburg to view our fleet.'

'What do they think this is, is naval review?' Captain Erskine of the *Orion* spluttered indignantly. 'Don't they know this is the seat of war? Why, we should order the *Dragon* to engage 'em. Serve 'em right if a few near-misses gave 'em a shower-bath, what?'

'It would be a waste of shot,' said Sulivan. 'Let them watch. We'll learn more from watching them than they'll learn from watching us.'

Once the officers on board had seen all they had come to see, Sulivan took the *Merlin* to another point off the coast of Kotlin to draw the Russians' attention from the point they had examined earlier. Just as the surveying ship was turning to rejoin the rest of the fleet, a distant boom echoed across the waters of the gulf.

Adare turned to see a Russian gunboat emerge from behind the eastern end of Kronstadt, a plume of smoke disseminating from the muzzle of the gun on her deck. Closer to the *Merlin* – but still more than half a mile away – a great spout of water rose up where the shot landed.

The Russians were not in the habit of taking pot shots; Adare guessed the shot was intended to provoke them into giving chase, perhaps to lead them close to some of these infernal machines he had heard about.

But Sulivan was too experienced a captain to fall for that one. 'As you were,' he told the quartermaster. 'Steady as she goes.'

'Aye aye, sir.'

'Perhaps Captain Sulivan should not get *too* close,' Carmichael said anxiously to Captain Mundy on the paddle-box.

'Not to worry, Mr Carmichael. We're well out of range of their guns.'

'Are you sure about that?'

Mundy smiled. 'Captain Sulivan knows what he's doing, I assure you.'

The *Dragon* and the *d'Assas* maintained position on a parallel course once more, while the *Firefly* followed in *Merlin*'s wake. The Russian coast was just over a mile away to the north-east after they had been steaming for three-quarters of an hour. Adare levelled a telescope at it: a low-lying, dreary-looking place, as far as he could see, all swamps and forests. The Russians were welcome to it, as far as he could—

The roar of the explosion filled his ears and the deck shuddered beneath his feet, making him stagger. He lowered the telescope in time to see a huge fountain of water rising over the level of the bulwark from below the port bow.

'Jesus Christ!' exclaimed one of the seamen on deck. 'What the 'ell were that?'

'There!' exclaimed Carmichael, ashen-faced. 'A shot has struck us!'

'I doubt it,' said Mundy. 'I didn't hear the shot.'

'Take over, Mr Creyke,' Sulivan told his first lieutenant, dashing down the after hatch. 'I'll check in the engine room.'

'Sounds as though the engine's running all right to me,' sniffed Erskine. 'Something must've hit us . . .'

'Or we hit something,' added Crichton.

The vibrations of the deck beneath their feet ceased as the engine was stopped, although the *Merlin* continued to glide forward under her own momentum. 'We're not aground, at least,' said Adare.

Sulivan emerged from the after hatch. 'Damage report, Chips!'

'Aye, aye, sir.' The carpenter hurried below decks to see if they were holed.

'Well, the engine still appears to be working,' Sulivan announced to the officers on the quarterdeck.

'That was an explosion!' said Erskine, climbing up to the port-side paddle-box to investigate. 'Must've been one of those infernal machines we've been hearing some much about.'

'Signal the *Firefly* to stand off, Underwood,' Sulivan ordered one of his seamen.

'Are we sinking?'

'No need to alarm yourself, Mr Carmichael,' Sulivan said confidently. 'I don't think we're holed. We'll know for certain soon enough.'

'Ah-ha!' Erskine exclaimed from the port-side paddle-box. 'Come and take a look at this, Sulivan! I can see a stone . . .'

'A stone?' Sulivan echoed incredulously. 'Take a sounding, Meakin,' he added to the leadsman as he crossed the deck to the port bulwark to see for himself.

Adare heard the lead plop into the water off the bow as the leadsman slung it, measuring the depth in the line that ran out through his fingers. 'By the mark five, sir!'

'There's definitely something down there,' Sulivan agreed with Erskine, leaning over the port bulwark. 'Mr Bullock, ask Mr Lowther to turn astern, half.'

'Aye, aye, sir.' One of the *Merlin*'s lieutenants blew into the speaking tube on the binnacle and listened for the engineer's response. 'Turn astern, half, Mr Lowther.'

The *Merlin*'s engines started up again. No sooner had she begun to reverse through the water, however, when a second explosion shook her and water fountained up immediately below the starboard paddle-box, rising several feet above the hammock-netting. The *Merlin* gave a jerk beneath Adare's feet, and the masts shook alarmingly as the ship heeled over, sending the men beneath them scurrying for cover.

'Stop her!' ordered Sulivan.

Adare sniffed: suddenly there was a strong smell of rotten eggs in the air.

'Smell that?' asked Crichton. 'Sulphur!'

Sulivan nodded. 'There's no doubt about it now: infernal machines,' he said, heading for the after hatch once more. 'Not so chimerical after all, it seems. I'm afraid we've blundered into an infernal machine field.'

Adare followed Sulivan below to offer his assistance and they met one of the petty officers on the lower deck: the man looked terrified.

'What's the matter, Farley?' demanded Sulivan.

'We're holed, sir! There's water coming in!'

Sulivan and Adare made their way below to see the extent of the damage for themselves. Most of it was in the engine storeroom: where two diagonal girders crossed one another, one made of wood and the other of iron, the iron one was bent in from the side and the wooden one was broken. The explosion must have bent the side in for a moment, before the wooden timbers sprang back to their original positions. A heavy tank of tallow had been torn from the side to which it was cleated and thrown three feet across the storeroom against the opposite bulkhead along with all the paint-tanks and casks. The shelf-piece under the deck head was split and broken, and water was pouring in from somewhere above.

'Find that hole and fother it, Farley!' Sulivan ordered crisply.

Adare followed the petty officer up to the engineer's mess place on the deck above. It really was a mess now: the sideboard and lockers were smashed, the mess-traps and private stores they contained scattered across the deck, which was strewn with shards of crockery and glass, along with the pickles and sauces some shattered bottles had previously contained.

There was no sign of a breech in the hull, but Adare could hear the trickle and splash of water coming from the next compartment. He opened the door to reveal the engineers' bath, and laughed with relief: the pipe leading from the water tank to the tap was broken. 'There's your leak!' he told the petty officer.

The damaged pipe did not take long to plug. Adare made his way back on deck and told the officers gathered there that there was no real damage.

The *Firefly* hauled to within a cable's length of the *Merlin* to see if she could lend assistance when a third explosion erupted under the paddle-sloop's bow.

'Signal the *Firefly* again, Underwood,' ordered Sulivan. 'Find out if they've sustained any damage.'

'Aye, aye, sir.'

The signal hoist was raised, and presently the reply came back in the negative.

'Somebody up there likes us,' said Mr Carmichael, glancing heavenwards.

'Either that, or the Russians aren't using sufficiently powerful charges in their infernal machines,' Crichton remarked drily.

'Impossible to say without knowing how close to the hull these things were when they exploded,' said Sulivan. 'All right, let's see if we can get back to the fleet without running into any more of these infernal machines. Too dangerous to press on without knowing exactly what we're dealing with here.'

# VII

# Infernal Machines

---

'Stroke!' ordered Adare.

The oarsmen pulled on their oars, gently; enough to give the cutter some headway, but at no great pace. Then they lay on their oars, waiting for the lieutenant to repeat the order, while the crew of the second cutter – rowing parallel to the first a few dozen yards away – did likewise. Adare looked to Molineaux, who crouched in the bows, dangling a rope over the prow. The other end of the rope was held by a petty officer in the bows of the other cutter, but it was weighted in the middle so it would catch the line mooring any infernal machines hidden beneath the water between the two boats. When the two cutters ran out of momentum and the petty officer shook his head, Adare repeated the order.

'And . . . *stroke*!'

One more pull on the oars propelled the boats forward a few more yards. Again Molineaux shook his head.

'And . . . *stroke*!'

The *Ramillies*' cutters were just two of dozens of boats that crept across the surface of the water between Kotlin Island and the Russian mainland to the north. The enterprising commander of a Russian gunboat could have had a field day, ramming them one after another, if it had not been for a couple of British frigates anchored to oversee the operation, close enough to give the boats cover if necessary.

It was 21 June, midsummer's day and so far from feeling cold – even here in the Baltic – Molineaux was grateful for an excuse to take his jacket off and sit in his waistcoat and shirtsleeves. More than a week had passed since the *Merlin* and the *Firefly* had run into the minefield, and since then the *Ramillies* had been dispatched with HMS *Exmouth* and a couple of gunboats to look into the mouth of the River Narva, where they had been engaged in a swift exchange of shots with a regiment of artillery ashore. The Russians had come off worse, the British ships sustaining no serious casualties at all.

The rest of the fleet, meanwhile, had sailed to Nargen Island off the Estonian Coast, where the *Exmouth*'s flotilla had rendezvoused with them before returning to weigh anchor off Kronstadt once more. At times like this, Molineaux wondered if Dundas and Seymour had the faintest idea what they were doing. Certainly as far as the infernal machines were concerned, their initial approach to the problem had been to ignore it until it went away; the flaw in this plan had been brought sharply home to them the previous day, when HMS *Valorous* had discovered yet another infernal machine the hard way. The paddle-frigate had sustained relatively minor damage, but even if Dundas and Seymour did not see that sooner or later the Russians were going to realise they were not putting enough explosives in the machines, Captain Sulivan did. With Pénaud's help, he was able to persuade the two British admirals of the necessity of sweeping for the mines and, if possible, retrieving one or two for examination.

The *Ramillies*' cutters continued their slow progress across the water, quartering backwards and forwards in the intricate search pattern Sulivan had laid down. During the course of the past hour they had managed to dredge up a sledge, half a cartwheel, and some bladder-wrack, but no infernal machines.

'This is a bloody waste of time,' Endicott declared at last. 'There's nuttin' down there. I reckon the Ivans only put those infernal machines down where they could be sure the *Merlin* would run into them, knowing that we'd spend weeks dredging every inch of the sea before we dared send one of our ships into it.'

'You may be right, Endicott,' Adare said grimly.

'Hold it, hold it, hold it!' said Molineaux. 'I got a bite!'

'Lie on your oars!' Adare told the crews of both cutters. He took the glass-bottomed bucket from the bottom of the boat and picked his way over the thwarts to join Able Seamen Hughes and Iles in the bows. Leaning over the side, he immersed the end of the bucket into the water, and ordered his cutter to move towards the other. They had covered half the distance when he spied what looked like a disc floating in the gloom about three feet below the surface cutter. Then he saw that the disc was in fact the base of a cone floating upside down, another rope running down into the inky depths below.

'I think we've found one,' he said softly. He withdrew the bucket and handed it to Endicott, who took a look for himself.

'Just looks like a buoy to me,' said the Liverpudlian.

'Yes. Except that buoys are supposed to float on the surface where they can be seen, not half a fathom below it.'

'So that's an infernal machine, is it?' said the Liverpudlian. He sounded disappointed. 'Strange . . . it don't look much, when you think about all the fuss these dooflickers have caused.'

'It isn't much, if the lack of damage to the *Merlin* and the *Firefly* is any indication,' agreed Adare. 'On the other hand, if one blew up beneath this cutter, I think we'd soon know about it. That is, if we ever knew anything ever again.'

'Doesn't bear thinking about, does it?' said Endicott. 'Eh, now what do we do? Try to, you know, hook it up with the grapnel, like?'

'Are you crazy?' asked Petty Officer Kracht, the *Ramillies'* blacksmith. 'Do that, and you might just set the *verdammt* thing off!'

A German by birth, Jakob Kracht was the kind of man who could take one of McGregor's finest chronometers apart . . . and then put it back together so that it worked even better than before. Unable to get their tongues around the guttural sounds of his name, his shipmates called him 'Jim Crack' in tribute to his skill at fixing things. Molineaux had had a feeling that Kracht's technical know-how was going to come in handy if they found an infernal machine, which was why he had brought him out with the cutter.

The petty officer started to strip down to his undershorts.

'Er . . . you're not thinking what I think you're thinking, are you, Molineaux?' asked Adare.

'That depends, sir. If you were thinking that I was thinking of going over the side to take a closer look, you're dead right. We've got to get one of these things intact so we can take it apart and find out what makes it work; so first one of us has got to find a way of getting it into this boat without blowing us all up.'

Adare nodded glumly. 'That's what I was afraid you were thinking.'

'Be careful,' said Riggs, the carpenter's mate.

'Thanks for the tip,' Molineaux said wryly. He took a deep breath and was about to dive over the side when Kracht caught him by the arm.

'See if you can work out what makes it explode,' suggested the blacksmith. 'It's got to work in one of two ways: either it's set off from shore using a galvanic charge carried along a wire, or there's some way it registers contact with the hull of a ship and ignites. See if there are wires to carry a galvanic charge coming out of it.'

Molineaux nodded and turned to Riggs. 'Hear that? That's *helpful* advice, Jerry. Maybe you should take a leaf out of Jim Crack's book.' He turned back to the blacksmith. 'What if there *aren't* any wires coming out of it?'

'Then – as Jerry says – be very, *very* careful with it.'

Molineaux grimaced and dived over the side. The water was bitterly cold, even in June, but at least the Baltic was less salty than most other seas, so it did not sting his eyes so much when he opened them under water. He swam down and trod water at a depth of about half a fathom, looking the device over. The cone was two feet deep and fifteen inches across the top. A rope ran down from the base of the device into the murk below, presumably leading down to some kind of anchor to prevent it from floating to the surface. Molineaux examined the rope closely, but found no sign of any wires.

He swam back to the surface and clung to the side of the cutter. 'No wires . . . must be set off by contact with a hull. I think I can bring it to the surface. Pass me my fi'penny, Seth.'

Endicott nodded and fished in the pockets of Molineaux's jacket, taking out his clasp-knife. The petty officer looped the lanyard around his neck and let go of the cutter's side, treading water. 'Better back off now, sir. If this thing comes up under the keel, they'll be sweeping bits of us up off the streets of St Petersburg for days to come.'

Adare nodded and ordered the rest of the men to backwater. They took up their oars and rowed clear. Molineaux waited until they were a safe distance off, then opened his clasp-knife and gripped it between his teeth like any proper pirate. He duck-tailed beneath the water and swam down beneath the device. Steeling himself, he caught hold of the rope and began to saw through it, reflecting that if it exploded now, at least his death would be swift and painless.

The last strands parted, and the device floated slowly up to the surface. Molineaux surfaced beside it, and waved for the cutter to come back. They rowed alongside. 'Handsomely does it now, lads.'

'Be careful of these horns,' warned Kracht, indicating two rods projecting sideways from the top of the inverted cone. 'These must be the triggers that set it off.'

Molineaux waited until they had got the device in the boat before climbing back aboard. 'Maybe I should dismantle it,' offered Kracht, producing his own clasp-knife and approaching the infernal machine. 'If we know how these things explode, perhaps we can find some way to—'

'*Don't you dare!*' snarled Adare. 'Our orders are to take one on board the *Exmouth* as soon as we can get our hands on one intact. There'll be no monkeying about with its workings!'

Endicott threw Molineaux a towel so that he could dry himself off while the two cutters rowed back to the fleet. The petty officer was dressed again by the time they approached the *Exmouth*'s side.

'Boat ahoy!' the marine on sentry duty at the entry port called down to them.

'No, no!' Adare called back.

An officer appeared at the entry port. 'Permission to come aboard?' Adare called up from the stern sheets, and indicated the cone-shaped device tenderly wrapped in a towel at Molineaux's feet.

The officer nodded, and a rope was lowered from a yard-arm. Molineaux tied the end of it to the ring at the base of the cone.

'Haul away, boys!' Adare called up. 'Handsomely does it!'

As the device was hoisted up the *Exmouth*'s side it started to swing perilously close to the bulwark. 'Handsomely, I said, handsomely!' Adare called up angrily from the side ladder. It would be just their luck to be the men who helped to sink Admiral Seymour's 90-gun flagship, Molineaux thought wryly.

Once the device had been swung in over the bulwark, out of sight, Adare turned to Kracht. 'Are you sure you want to be the one who tries to take it apart?'

The blacksmith nodded. 'Someone has got to do it. Might as well be me, *hein*? Or do you know someone in the fleet who is better qualified?'

Adare shook his head. 'All right, follow me up. We'll offer your services to Admiral Seymour. You'd best come too, Molineaux, in case we need another pair of hands. I don't know any steadier than yours.'

Molineaux sighed and followed Adare and Kracht up the accommodation ladder to the entry port, where they were just in time to see the device lowered to the deck with a thud that made them both wince. Adare made his obeisance to the quarterdeck before turning to the *Exmouth*'s commander.

'Where do you want it, sir?' he asked, indicating the infernal machine.

'Oh, just put it with the others.' The commander gestured to where thirty more infernal machines stood on the deck amidships.

Molineaux and Kracht exchanged wry looks.

There was a huddle of officers on the poop, and the *Exmouth*'s commander approached them. 'Lieutenant Adare's here, sir. He's brought another infernal machine for your inspection.'

Seymour and Captain Hall turned away from the huddle, and Adare saluted them. They returned the salute curtly before turning back into the huddle, and Molineaux's heart leaped into his mouth when he saw what they were all studying: yet another infernal machine, balanced precariously on its apex, with the top prised off so they could study its workings.

'This is Petty Officer Kracht, sir,' Adare told Seymour, indicating the blacksmith. 'He's a regular wizard with anything mechanical. He's bravely volunteered to take one of these devices ashore and dismantle it, so we can learn how the mechanism works.'

'Ah. That's very good of him, Lieutenant, but I think we've pretty much worked it out for ourselves,' Seymour said loftily. 'At the top there's an air chamber to make it float, at the bottom a gunpowder charge – no more than eight or nine pounds of powder by the look of it; how the Russians think that's going to sink a ship is beyond me – and here in the middle is the firing device.' He stepped back up to the cone and reached down inside it.

'I'd be careful with that, sir, if I were you.'

'It's all right, Lieutenant, I know what I'm doing.' Seymour glanced up at one of the other officers, a captain in the Royal Marines. 'I suppose the liquid in this glass tube contains some kind of acid,' he said, tapping something inside the cone with a pencil. 'When it's broken, the acid ignites the primer.'

'Be careful, sir,' said Captain Hall. 'You might set it off.'

'Oh, *no!*' Seymour placed a finger against one of the horns. '*This* is the way it would go off—'

He pushed the slide in.

*Boom.*

A polar bear was the last thing Killigrew expected to see when he entered the room, and it brought him up short. The nightmares had faded, but even twenty-two months after his return from the Arctic, the sight of the beast was enough to send a frisson of icy fear down his spine. Then he realised that this particular specimen was long dead, even if the taxidermist responsible had made a fair job of giving it a lifelike appearance.

His next thought was that he was in the wrong room, so he backed out of the natural history department and set off once more through the maze of galleries in search of the Egyptian Court. He kept a weather eye out for Nekrasoff and Ryzhago as he went, and slipped a hand into the pocket of his greatcoat for the reassuring feel of the grip of his revolver.

The Crystal Palace in Hyde Park had been disassembled while Killigrew had been in the Arctic, only to be reassembled at Sydenham on an even grander scale, using twice as much glass, covering a hundred more acres and with an additional three storeys on top, as well as a basement containing machines, vehicles and carriages. Industrial courts celebrated the products of particular British cities and regions, while other courts illustrated the art and architecture of different periods in history. The Egyptian Court in the north transept was the most spectacular, with two rows of reproduction sphinxes gazing enigmatically at one another across the central aisle, real palm trees flourishing in the humid atmosphere of the giant glasshouse, and two gigantic statues seated with their hands on their knees – modelled on those at Luxor Temple at Karnak – towering over the far end.

Killigrew stood at the railing of one of the galleries overlooking the court and searched the faces in the crowd. Rude artisans in rough jackets and cloth caps wandered with their wives, sweethearts and children, munching on pies and swigging from bottles of Allsop's as they gazed in awed incomprehension at the exhibits. There was no sign of Nekrasoff or Ryzhago, or anyone who looked as though they might have been sent to collect the passport from Leventhal. Detective Inspector Jordan had been right: Nekrasoff had made alternative arrangements to get himself a forged passport, and this rendezvous was a waste of time. Still, there were worse ways of spending a Saturday afternoon away from Portsmouth than wandering through the glittering halls of the Crystal Palace.

Hearing someone moving behind him, he whirled to see three men standing there. He did not recognise any of them, but all three were looking at him with cold expressions on their faces. They had crept up on him so silently it was impossible to believe their intentions were benign.

111

'Commander Killigrew?' asked one, a long-jawed, sharp-eyed man. 'Yes?'

By way of explanation, the man merely opened his coat just long enough for Killigrew to see the revolver holstered under his left armpit. 'I wonder if you'd mind coming with us, sir?' he asked. His English was so flawless, Killigrew might have taken him for a native if he had not known better. 'Someone would like to talk to you.'

'Do I have any choice?'

The man smiled. 'Yes, but I wouldn't recommend the alternative.'

The four of them left the building – the long-jawed man leading the way, Killigrew following and the other two bringing up the rear – and made their way to where a carriage was parked on Crystal Palace Parade with a coachman already on the driving board. The long-jawed man climbed in first. Killigrew followed and sat down opposite, only for the other two to enter via opposite doors and plump themselves down on either side of him, so he was wedged between them.

Without awaiting any instructions, the coachman whipped up the horses and they rattled away along the road. Killigrew was conscious of the cold weight of his revolver against his thigh: if the man on his right had moved his own knee a couple of inches to the left, he would have felt it, too; in fact, it was amazing none of them had noticed the bulge in his coat. If he tried to draw it, the long-jawed man would be able to get his own revolver out first; Killigrew might have slipped a hand in his pocket and shot the man opposite him through the fabric of his coat, but then what? He would not be able to bring the revolver to bear on either of the men sitting beside him.

'Would you mind telling me where we're going, or who it is that wants to meet me?' Killigrew asked the long-jawed man.

'You have an appointment.'

'Business or pleasure?' He looked from the long-jawed man to the other man on his left, and back again, and when neither answered his question, he shrugged. 'Mystery tour, eh?' He tried to sound blasé, although his heart was pounding.

They headed north and soon entered the suburbs of London: Dulwich, Peckham, then up the Kent Road into Southwark and across London Bridge to the City. The streets were more crowded here, and the carriage slowed in the heavy traffic. There was a chance Killigrew could take his captors by surprise, jump out of the carriage and disappear into the crowd before the long-jawed fellow could draw his revolver and fire, but he decided against it. It was too risky: a better opportunity might yet present itself. Besides, the chances were the man they were taking him to see was Nekrasoff; and when they arrived, there was still a faint possibility that he could somehow turn the tables on them and round up the whole gang in one fell swoop.

*And pigs might fly*, he thought ruefully to himself.

The carriage passed down Cannon Street: they were heading east, into Whitechapel. They left the City on the other side by Aldgate, passing through the East End via Commercial Road until they turned on to West India Dock Road, which led them down to the Isle of Dogs.

At last the carriage entered a shipyard in Millwall and the driver reined in beside the office buildings. The whistle of a steam packet sounded in the distance as the four of them climbed out, and Killigrew could see the vast, scaffolding-covered side of Mr Brunel's latest ship, as yet unnamed, towering over the buildings to his right.

The place was all but deserted. Flanked by the three men, Killigrew entered a dusty office building where a diminutive caretaker swept the floor, whistling a vaguely familiar tune. Beyond the office, they walked down a long corridor lined with lockers until they came to a door at the far end.

Killigrew sensed that the man he was being brought to meet was on the other side of that door. It was now or never.

He jammed an elbow into the stomach of the man standing behind him, and threw a right cross at the jaw of another, throwing him back against the lockers. As the first man tried to straighten, Killigrew slammed a fist against the back of his neck, knocking him down to the floor.

The long-jawed man turned back from the door, in time to receive Killigrew's half-boot in the stomach as the commander lashed out with one leg. He closed in, delivering a right upper cut to that long jaw. The two of them grappled. Killigrew kicked the man's ankles out from beneath him and threw him down across the first man, who was trying to rise.

The second man came at him again. Killigrew kicked him in the chest, slamming him back against the lockers once more. Before any of them could recover, he ducked through the door and closed it behind him, wedging the back of a chair under the handle. He dropped to one knee, pulling the penknife from his pocket and opening the blade in one smooth movement, holding it by the blade ready to hurl at his nemesis.

The well-dressed man who sat at the desk reading some paperwork was seventy if he was a day, but rakishly dressed for all that, in fashionable railway-stripe trousers and a tartan waistcoat. His white hair and bushy side-whiskers were dyed a garish shade of orange. He hurriedly removed a pair of wire-framed spectacles and hid them from sight, peering myopically at the commander.

Killigrew recognised him, of course. How could he fail to, when this man had been caricatured a thousand times in *Punch*?

'L-Lord *Palmerston*?' he stammered, as someone hammered frantically at the door behind him.

'Commander Killigrew, is it? Well, stand up, man, stand up. I'm the Prime Minister, y'know, not the sovereign, what?'

Killigrew rose to his feet and pocketed the penknife. Behind him, the door burst open and the long-jawed fellow staggered through, looking flushed. 'Is everything all right, my lord?' he gasped.

'Everything's capital. Why? Is there a problem?'

'Mr Killigrew attacked us, sir.'

'I thought they were agents of the Third Section, my lord,' Killigrew apologised. 'The Russian secret police.'

'Didn't you identify yourselves to him?' Palmerston asked the long-jawed fellow.

'I showed him my treasury badge, my lord.'

'I beg to differ, sir,' Killigrew said coldly. 'But you did no such thing.'

The man opened his coat once more and this time, in addition to the revolver holstered under his arm, Killigrew saw the treasury badge pinned there. 'Oh!' he said, feeling very foolish.

'You mean to tell me the three of you allowed yourself to be drubbed by one man?' Palmerston asked the treasury agent. 'Why, that's capital work, Killigrew, capital! I can tell you're just the sort of feller I'm lookin' for, what? Thank you, you've done your duty,' he added to the agent. 'That will be all.'

'Very good, my lord.' The man bowed out of the room.

Killigrew became aware of three other men standing at the other end of the room. Palmerston rose from where he sat and introduced them. 'I don't think you've met Sir Charles Wood and his private secretary, Mr Baring . . .?'

It was nearly four months since Wood had replaced Sir James

Graham as First Lord of the Admiralty. He was in his mid-fifties, a tall man with receding grey hair, a long, thin nose and prominent cheekbones. Killigrew exchanged nods with the First Lord's private secretary, remembering that he was the son of Sir Francis Baring, the banker who had helped Pitt the Younger underwrite the cost of the Great War with France.

'I believe you already know Sir Charles Napier?' added Palmerston.

Napier was in his sixties, a stocky man with white hair and bushy black brows. Even though he retained his rank – he might no longer be commander-in-chief of the Baltic Fleet, but he was still a vice admiral of Her Majesty's navy – he was not in uniform, although that did not necessarily mean anything. 'Dirty Charlie' had always been notorious for his casual attitude to his own attire, even though he was strict about the appearance of his subordinates. Today he wore a printed cotton shirt, patterned with the figures of tiny ballerinas.

'Sorry to hear about your dismissal as commander-in-chief, sir,' Killigrew told the admiral. 'The Russians must be delighted,' he added, with a hard glare in Palmerston's direction.

Whatever had brought the Prime Minister and the First Lord of the Admiralty to a dockyard on a Saturday afternoon had to be pretty damned important. Another man might have been intimidated to find himself confronting such powerful and influential men, but Killigrew had too low an estimation of politicians to be impressed.

'Shall we go through into the next room?' Palmerston suggested, gesturing to a door. It led through to what looked like a boardroom, with plush-backed chairs arranged in a precise manner around a long mahogany table. The curtains were drawn over the windows at one end, and a clean white linen bed sheet hung over them opposite the magic lantern on the table.

'Do be seated, gentlemen.' Palmerston sat down on the chair that Baring pulled out for him. 'Now then, Killigrew . . . what d'ye know about these infernal machines, hey?'

'Only what I read in the newspapers, sir. Two of them are supposed to have exploded against the *Merlin*'s hull in the Baltic while she was reconnoitring Kronstadt, but no one was hurt and there was only minor damage.'

'So, ye've no' heard what happened on the *Exmouth* last week?' asked Napier.

'The *Exmouth*, sir?'

'Admiral Seymour's flagship,' explained Wood. There was a hint of a Yorkshire accent in his voice.

'He knows what the *Exmouth* is, Sir Charles,' Napier told the First Lord of the Admiralty, rather testily. Like many Scotsmen, his accent seemed to grow stronger the older he became, like Scotch whisky matured in an oak vat.

He turned back to Killigrew. 'It seems Seymour got one o' these things out o' the water and up on deck and was fiddling aroond wi' it tae find out what makes them explode.'

'Was he successful?'

'In a manner o' speaking. Fortunately no one else was seriously injured in the blast. The *Exmouth*'s surgeon assures us that Seymour may eventually regain the sight o' the eye.'

'In the meantime, we'll just have to get used to calling him "See-Less".' Killigrew knew the quip was in bad taste, but he would not have been Kit Killigrew if he had been able to resist it.

Napier glowered at him. 'Och, very poor, Killigrew. Even by your standards.'

'Sorry, sir. But someone had to say it.'

'Aye, but why the devil's it always got tae be you?'

'Well, at least he's fit for duty,' said Wood. 'At least, as fit for his duties as he ever was. Loss of sight in one eye didn't stop Nelson from becoming a great admiral.'

'Indeed, no, sir,' said Killigrew. 'If anything stops Seymour from being a successful admiral, I'm sure it won't be his eye.'

'Rear Admiral Dundas also had a close shave with an infernal machine,' said Napier. 'It seems that same day he tried to study the workings of one of the things in his cabin on board the *Duke of Wellington*. Fortunately, the powder charge had already been removed, so only the detonator went off. I'm told his eyebrows will grow back in due course.'

'Nincompoops,' growled Palmerston. 'The people of this country are lookin' to me to bring this damn' war to a swift and satisfactory conclusion, and I have to rely on nincompoops like Dundas and Seymour!'

'At least he had the decency to risk only his own life,' said Wood.

'That's not the point, Sir Charles. The point is, Dundas and Seymour had no business tinkerin' with those things in the first place. It's quite bad enough that the captain of the fleet managed to blow himself up, without the commander-in-chief doing the same! Do they *want* me to order them to hand over command of the whole fleet to Admiral Pénaud?'

'I hardly think that will go down well with the men of the fleet, my lord,' said Napier.

'Or with the voters here in England,' added Wood.

'I know, I know,' sighed Palmerston. 'Still, at least we didn't appoint the damn' fools. But that's not why I've called you here today. What's significant is that the reports of Napier's spies have been proved to be based on a real threat. If these infernal machines really do exist, what other secret weapons that the Russians are supposed to have in their armoury are also real?' He turned to Killigrew. 'Been readin' your report about your little jaunt into Finland back in January. Very interestin'. That drawing Jurgaitis gave you – seems Graham at least had the sense to pass it on to one of our top men to take a look at. *He* recognised the blessèd thing at once, and wasted no time in drawin' my attention to it once I was Prime Minister. Well, let's have him in, shall we?'

Baring opened another door and spoke to someone on the other side. 'If you'd like to join us, sir?'

A man wearing smart, sober clothing entered. He was in his late forties, a small, olive-complexioned man with receding hair.

'Sorry to keep you waitin', Brunel,' said Palmerston. 'I'm obliged for the use of your offices.'

'Not at all, my lord,' the engineer replied easily. 'I'm honoured that you took the trouble to travel all the way to Millwall for this. I'm aware that your time must be precious, especially having come to office so recently, and I could easily have attended you at Downing Street.'

'Too many pryin' ears at Number Ten,' snorted Palmerston. 'Still don't know which members of staff I can trust, and which ones will go off bleatin' to the Tories. Or – worse still – to the papers. If this contraption is as important as your telegram implied it might be, we could go settin' off a national panic if word gets out, what? Well, let's take a look at the confounded thing. You have the floor, Brunel.'

'Thank you.' The engineer struck a match and lit the candle in the magic lantern. 'Could I trouble you to turn down the gas, Mr Baring?' As the lights were dipped, Brunel moved to stand by the screen. 'The first slide, if you please.'

Killigrew saw the technical schematics he had brought back from Finland projected on to the sheet, the bloody thumbprint unmistakable in one corner. Whoever had developed it had done a fine job. It looked a lot less blurry somehow, and at that size it was possible to make out some of the details: vaguely cylindrical, with a large box at one end and a screw-propeller at the other.

'Well, Brunel?' said Wood. 'Any notion what the confounded thing might be?'

'Yes, Sir Charles. It's a submersible boat.'

# VIII

## On Her Majesty's Naval Service

'A submersible boat?' echoed Sir Charles Wood. 'You mean, a boat that can travel underwater? Is such a thing possible? Either a vessel floats, or it doesn't, surely? Are you trying to tell me this boat can sink and then float again? With men inside?'

'Indeed,' said Brunel. 'I'm sure I don't need to remind you of Archimedes' principle?'

Blank faces stared back at him.

The engineer sighed. 'Any vessel completely or partially submerged in a liquid is acted upon by an upward, or buoyant, force, the magnitude of which is equal to the weight of the liquid displaced by the vessel.'

'What does that mean in English?' demanded Palmerston.

'A ship floats because the weight of the volume of water it displaces exceeds its own weight,' explained Brunel. 'However, if we can create a watertight vessel which can vary its own displacement, it becomes possible to create a vessel that can rise and sink at will. Van Drebel built a working submersible as long ago as 1620 – King James the first is said to have accompanied him on a voyage up the Thames – and in 1776 Bushnell built the *Turtle*, which was used to attack HMS *Eagle* at New York by attaching explosives to her hull. The attack failed, but the theory was sound. Since then there have been several attempts to construct a submersible vessel, with varying degrees of success, not least of which was Fulton's *Nautilus*—'

'Be a good fellow and spare us the history lecture, Brunel,' cut in Palmerston.

119

'Was your associate Mr Russell no' working on something similar a while back?' asked Napier.

Brunel nodded. 'A little *too* similar, as it happens. But I'm afraid it sank with all hands during trials.'

'And now it seems the Russians have developed one as well,' Napier said grimly.

'Wouldn't have thought they'd be interested in something like this,' said Wood. 'Not exactly forward-thinking, these Russkis. Very backward, in fact, and proud of it. I'm told they regard Western technology as a corrupting influence.'

'Perhaps so, Sir Charles,' said Palmerston. 'But I understand the Grand Duke Konstantin is a very forward-thinkin' young man. Eager to modernise the Russian navy, whether their Admiralty likes it or not. I think if someone showed him the plans for an underwater boat, he'd give the project his patronage.'

Killigrew remembered Nekrasoff's remark about the grand duke's new toy. But he suspected that all this was missing the point. 'Mr Brunel, when you said that the underwater boat Mr Russell is working on was *too* similar . . .?'

'Better show 'em the other slide, Baring,' said Palmerston.

'This was taken from the plans for Russell's underwater boat,' explained Baring, inserting the second slide without removing the first. 'We had to do some fiddling about to get the two to line up, but from this I think you should be able to see—'

'Good God!' said Wood.

'An exact match,' remarked Napier.

'The Russians must have a spy in this shipyard!'

'I wish it were that simple,' sighed Palmerston. 'Perhaps you'd better tell them, Mr Brunel?'

The engineer took a deep breath. 'Four years ago – about the time of the Great Exhibition – a Bavarian engineer named Wilhelm Bauer approached Prince Albert, seeking patronage for an invention he wished to build: an underwater boat. He called it his "*Seeteufel*" – the *Sea Devil*. His Highness was sufficiently impressed to give Bauer a letter of introduction to Sir James Graham. Graham set up a committee of scientists and naval experts to consider the plans, and after some months it reached the decision – erroneous, in my opinion – that an underwater boat is simply unfeasible. Bauer then took his plans to Mr Russell. The two of them worked on the *Sea Devil*, but I'm sorry to report that it was not a happy collaboration. Herr Bauer was very protective of his designs and disinclined to share his secrets with Russell. He also repeatedly rejected my advice to submit his ideas to the patent office. Last year Russell grew impatient with Herr Bauer and dissolved their partnership, confident that he could build an underwater boat without Bauer's help.'

Palmerston nodded. 'I saw his design. Even suggested a few modifications of me own.'

'This would be the one that sank with all hands?' asked Killigrew. Butter would not have melted in his mouth.

'So it looks as though Bauer's given his designs to the Russians?' asked Wood.

'Indeed,' said Palmerston, glowering at Killigrew. 'Of course, by the time Russell and Bauer fell out, we were already at war with Russia. Customs and Excise were ordered to confiscate the drawings and the model of the *Sea Devil* if Bauer tried to leave the country. Couldn't have him sellin' his invention to the Russkis, what?'

'Then how the devil did they get hold of the drawings?' demanded Wood. 'I think we should have this fellow Bauer in for questioning.'

'Couldn't agree more,' said Palmerston. 'As soon as I found out that the Russians already had the plans, I sent a couple of Treasury agents to his lodgings in Greenwich to bring him in. Unfortunately, it seems someone had already tipped him the wink: the blighter's disappeared.'

'Skipped the country?'

'We don't know; but it seems reasonable to assume the worst. He couldn't have left the country without help, that much I do know.'

Killigrew snapped his fingers. 'Niklaus Hergerscheimer!'

'*Gezundheit!*' said Palmerston.

'Who's Niklaus Hergerscheimer?' demanded Napier.

'He's no one, sir,' Killigrew explained. 'He doesn't exist. Earlier this year, while I was making my own inquiries into the death of the Honourable Miss Maltravers at the hands of Russian spies, I ran into a forger who'd been asked to make a Prussian passport in the name of Niklaus Hergerscheimer by Colonel Nekrasoff, an officer of the Third Section. The police stopped the transaction by arresting the forger before I could get my hands on Nekrasoff. The passport must have been meant for Bauer.'

'I'm not sure I'm following this,' said Wood. 'What is this Third Section?'

'The Third Section of His Imperial Highness' Chancery, tae gi'e it its full title,' explained Napier. 'The Tsarist secret police. The Russians call it the "White Terror". It's a vast organisation: nearly every town

121

and village in the Russian Empire has at least one Third Section informer. Their agents are empowered tae look into anythin' considered tae be a threat tae the safety of the Russian state, from treason, subversion and espionage tae moral perversion and petty crime.'

'Do you mean to tell me there are Russian spies operating in England?'

'Without a doubt,' said Palmerston, who had been Home Secretary prior to his elevation to Number Ten. 'They maintain a ring of spies and informers in London – and indeed all the major capitals of Europe – to keep an eye on political dissidents like Herzen and Marx. We keep tabs on the spies we know about, but otherwise leave 'em alone as long as they don't break the law. If we deported 'em, the Russians might very well send over other spies we *don't* know about—'

Now Killigrew understood how Nekrasoff had been able to get to his rooms in Paddington so quickly. Clearly, he had already been in London to arrange Bauer's defection; a chance to get his revenge on Killigrew had been a bonus.

'And if they *do* break the law, my lord?' he cut in bitterly. 'I suppose you let British naval officers take the blame?'

Palmerston coloured. 'Yes, yes, a mistake was made. Lack of communication between government departments, what? But entirely understandable, given the political situation at the time. You have my unreserved apologies for any inconvenience you may have suffered, Mr Killigrew.'

'Inconvenience!'

'This is all very well,' Napier said impatiently. 'Except that Mr Killigrew brought his copy o' the drawings fra' Finland last January . . . months before Bauer disappeared. And the Russians must have got hold o' their copy weeks – if no' months – before that.'

Brunel indicated the image projected on to the bed sheet. 'To me this looks like the design Bauer first showed to Prince Albert when he started to seek a patron in London. It gives a notion of the feasibility of the vessel, without giving away any of its secrets. A sort of "taster", if you will, to whet the appetite of a potential patron.'

'So the question is, did the Russians receive a complete set of plans, or just this taster?' asked Wood.

'Just the taster, would be my guess,' said Killigrew. 'If they had the complete plans, why bother to take Bauer at all?'

'I think we must assume the worst, gentlemen,' said Palmerston. 'Herr Bauer is now working for the Russians, and if they haven't finished construction of this contraption, they must be well on the way by now.'

'Supposing the Russians *have* built one of these contraptions,' said Wood. 'Just how big a threat to our fleets does it represent?'

'That would depend on how far it could travel concealed under water,' Napier replied. 'Mr Brunel?'

'The only thing that would limit it would be the amount of air contained within the vessel.' Brunel checked his notes. 'In a sealed chamber containing ten cubic feet of air, a man could breathe for approximately one hour before he'd start to feel any ill effects due to lack of oxygen: laboured breathing, dizziness, confusion, unconsciousness and, ultimately, death by asphyxiation.'

'Not unlike the effects of sitting through one of Mr Gladstone's speeches,' sniffed Palmerston.

Brunel ignored the interruption. 'A submersible vessel of the dimensions we have here could not contain more than a thousand cubic feet of air, and that's being damned generous: the internal workings of the thing, and the ballast, would take up some of the space, not to mention the bodies of the crewmen themselves. If we're talking about a crew of about ten men, we're looking at approximately ten hours maximum, probably less. Of course, a man's rate of respiration increases when he's under stress or engaging in strenuous physical activity.'

'I think we can safely say that men sealed in a submersible boat under water will have an increased rate of respiration,' Killigrew said with a faint smile.

'How many knots can she do?' wondered Napier.

'She's powered by a couple of treadmills inside the hull, so her speed would depend on the energy and endurance of the crew,' said Brunel. 'I'd be surprised if it could manage more than a couple of knots.'

'So – assuming the crew wishes tae return tae base after completing their mission – she's got a range of fifteen miles at the most?' asked Napier.

'Probably much less,' agreed Brunel. 'And she'd have to surface every few minutes for the captain to get his bearings: he wouldn't be able to see more than a few feet through those portholes while submerged. Even if he could, it's unlikely that what he saw would make much sense compared to the view on the surface. Navigation when submerged would be largely by guesswork, because even a compass corrected in the latest mode according to the Astronomer Royal and Commander Evans would be most unreliable. In inshore waters she would be unlikely to be able to remain submerged for more than fifteen minutes at a time, without having to surface to check her position.'

Wood nodded. 'So there's no danger of this contraption submerging in one port, sailing – for want of a better word – fifteen miles under water to another port along the coast, sinking a ship there, and then returning to its home base, without surfacing once.'

'Nae,' agreed Napier. 'But if a fleet were blockading a port – like Sevastopol, for instance – there'd be nae stopping this vessel from emerging fra' the harbour, sailing up tae the flagship, attaching an explosive charge tae the hull, and then retiring. The first thing anyone on board would know of it would be when a hole was blown in the hull!'

'I'm afraid you have the nub of it, Sir Charles,' said Brunel. 'We needn't fear an army of Russians landing from a fleet of submersible boats floating undetected up the Thames; but it could present a very real threat to any one of our ships that came within striking distance of a port where this vessel was operational.'

'Thank you, Mr Brunel,' said Palmerston. 'You've been of inestimable service. Unless any of you gentlemen have any further questions for him?'

The others shook their heads.

The engineer was about to withdraw when Palmerston called after him. 'Mr Brunel? I'd be grateful if you said nothing of this to anyone outside this room. Including your associate Mr Russell. We don't want a national panic on our hands, do we, what?'

Brunel shook his head and went out.

'But this is catastrophic!' Wood exclaimed as soon as the engineer had closed the door behind him. 'Are you telling me we daren't send one of our ships within striking distance of a Russian port?'

'Jack Tar will be prepared tae take that risk,' asserted Napier.

'And well he may! He doesn't have to foot the bill for the ships that are lost. Do you have any notion how much a steam-driven ship of the line costs these days?'

'The cost ain't the point,' Palmerston said quietly. 'All it takes is for one ship – the flagship, perhaps – to be sunk, and the damage to morale within the navy will be incalculable. The Russians know that; they may even be countin' on it.'

'Do you really think they'd resort to such a sneaky, underhand method of attack?' asked Wood. 'Damme, it's unconscionable!'

'Why not?' asked Killigrew. 'We've tried to.'

Wood gave him a dirty look, but Palmerston smiled serenely. 'The Russians know they cannot beat us by conventional means. But neither can they afford to lose this war. We must assume the worst, gentlemen. But we need to know *more*. We don't even know if the damn' thing works, what? We need to know whether or not the Russians are building one, whether or not it's operational, where it's located, and – perhaps most important of all – if it has an Achilles heel we can exploit.'

'Difficult to see how we *can* learn more,' said Wood. 'The Russians are a damnably secretive bunch; even about everyday, unimportant things. If they *are* building one of these underwater boats, you may rest assured they'll keep it tightly under wraps.'

'Mm. I don't suppose you have any more spies in St Petersburg, Sir Charles?' Palmerston asked Napier.

'There is one man I know that might be prepared to help us. Whether or not he can be trusted is another matter entirely.'

'What we need is someone who can penetrate the Russian Admiralty,' said Palmerston. 'Or at least the shipyard where this contraption's bein' built. Someone we can rely on.'

Killigrew had a nasty, cold feeling in the pit of his stomach. He could see where this was leading.

'Too late in the day tae send in another defector like Jurgaitis,' said Napier. 'Whoever we sent, he'd be working under cover, wi' false papers.'

'He'd need nerves of steel,' said Wood. 'We'd need someone tough and resourceful; preferably with previous experience at this kind of work. Someone not afraid to be utterly ruthless when the need arose.'

'And someone who speaks Russian,' put in Napier, looking at Killigrew.

And suddenly, everyone was staring at the commander.

'Oh, no!' he said. 'You can't possibly think I'm going to go. I absolutely refuse. Find someone else.'

'There is no one else,' grated Palmerston.

'That's your problem. I've already been to Russia twice since this war began – well, Finland, at any rate – and on both occasions I was fortunate to get out alive.'

'Third time pays for all,' said Napier.

'Or pushes one's luck,' said Killigrew. 'This isn't Finland you're asking me to go to this time: it's St Petersburg. The heart of the Russian Empire. And the Third Section already has a file on me. I'd have to be insane to go back again.'

'Not even for your country?' wheedled Wood.

'The devil take my country! If I wanted to commit suicide, there are easier, less painful ways of doing it, albeit none so sure.'

'Confound it, man! Where's your patriotism?'

' "Patriotism is the last refuge of a scoundrel", Sir Charles,' quoted Killigrew. 'A scoundrel I may be, but I've not yet been driven to the last resort.'

'Dinna tell me you're afraid o' the Russians!' scoffed Napier.

'Afraid of the Russians? Of course I'm afraid of the Russians! You know they still have hanging, drawing and quartering over there? Let me be sure I understand you correctly: you want me to go to Russia alone and unsupported, find Bauer, kill him, destroy the *Sea Devil* and all copies of the plans, and then somehow get out of the country and safely back to Britain? Although I suppose the last part of that is entirely optional from your point of view.'

'I only wish I was young enough tae go maself,' said Napier.

*The old lunatic means it, too*, thought Killigrew. 'Any suggestions as to how I should proceed?' he asked.

'Under the circumstances, it only seems reasonable to allow you a fair degree of latitude in that respect,' Wood said smoothly.

'Ah. I'll take that as a "no", then. Still, Russia's only got an area of several *million* square miles. Any suggestions as to *where* I should start looking?'

'Try the coasts,' Palmerston said curtly.

Killigrew grimaced. He could see he was not getting out of this. He tried to look on the bright side. 'I suppose I do have a score to settle with the Third Section,' he admitted.

'If you should come across Nekrasoff, I don't want you running off on some kind of vendetta,' said Wood. 'Avenging Miss Maltravers will not bring her back.'

'You didn't get her killed,' Killigrew said bitterly.

'Neither did you. Don't make it a personal vendetta, Commander. It's an assignment like any other . . .'

'Hardly,' said Napier.

Wood ignored the interruption. '. . . And if you can't treat it as such, coolly and objectively—'

'Fiddlesticks!' cut in Palmerston. 'From what I hear of this feller Nekrasoff, he's forfeited his right to live. Now see here, Killigrew: Sir Charles is right . . . up to a point. Your job is to find out if the Russians have built the *Sea Devil* and – if so – to find out whether or not it works, and if it has a weakness we can use to defend our ships against it. But if you should run into Nekrasoff, then by all means execute him. In fact, I've a mind to make that a direct order. The world will not mourn his passing.'

'That is not government policy,' Wood said tightly.

'Fiddle-de-dee!' Napier snapped back. 'It teks a damned plucky feller tae undertake a mission like this. Ah've trusted in Killigrew's judgement in the past and ne'er had cause tae question his methods. If ye want him tae dee this, I suggest ye let him get on wi' it and handle things as he sees fit.'

'As you will,' Wood said truculently. 'But I don't want to know anything about it. And if he gets himself captured, we'll disown him. You needn't expect to be exchanged for any Russian prisoners of war, Killigrew. If you're discovered Her Majesty's government will deny all knowledge of your activities, and the best you'll be able to hope for is a swift death in front of a firing squad.'

'That's usually the way these things are done,' Killigrew agreed drily. 'If I'm going to go into Russia, I'll need to go in disguise.'

'False moustache and spectacles, you mean?' said Palmerston. 'That's a bit melodramatic, ain't it?'

Killigrew took a deep breath. 'I mean, I'll need to travel under an alias. That means I'll need papers: false passport, letters of introduction, official passes, et cetera.'

'Surely you don't expect us to supply you with that sort of thing?' Palmerston exclaimed indignantly. 'What, do you think the government has its own bureau of forgers somewhere?'

'I know of at least one forger who's currently a guest at Her Majesty's pleasure. Why not offer him a pardon in return for . . . ah, shall we say, services rendered?'

'The vessel is fifty-two feet long, with a beam of twelve and a half feet and a height of eleven feet. She's driven by a single propeller powered by four treadmills, two at either end of the interior, each with a diameter of seven feet. These are connected to the screw by a shaft through a gear train aft.' As Brunel spoke, he indicated the various features on the diagram of the *Sea Devil* on the image projected by the magic lantern.

It was nearly three weeks since Killigrew had attended the meeting with Palmerston and Sir Charles Wood. Since then he had been discharged from HMS *Excellent*'s books. While Emmanuel Leventhal had been working to produce a false passport for him, Killigrew had spent the three weeks brushing up his Russian and listening to interminable lectures from Brunel on how the *Sea Devil* worked.

'The trim is controlled by a weight fixed to a long screw: as the screw is turned, the weight is moved up and down the length of the vessel, shifting the centre of balance forward or aft. Depth is controlled by three cylindrical ballast tanks, ten feet long and four and a half feet in diameter, with a total ballast capacity of about twenty-eight tons. These levers here work pumps to flood the ballast tanks. This smaller cylinder here is a fourth ballast tank, for fine adjustment: by carefully controlling the amount of water taken into it, the vessel can be made to sink to varying depths. To surface once again, it is only necessary to pump the water from the tanks until positive buoyancy is attained once more . . . are you paying attention, Commander?'

'Hmph?' Killigrew looked up from the newspaper he had been reading.

'I said, are you paying attention?' Brunel demanded testily.

'Yes, of course.'

'Then perhaps you can tell me how you make the vessel surface?'

Killigrew blinked. 'Pump water from the ballast tanks until positive buoyancy is attained.'

Brunel scowled, and continued with the lecture. 'For'ard we see the observation cupola, fitted with glass ports and waterproof gauntlets to allow one of the crew to attach an explosive charge to the hull of an enemy ship using a rubber suction cup. If circumstances should not permit the charge to be fitted from within the vessel, it's also possible for a crewman to leave the vessel in a diving suit to act independently.'

'Wouldn't water flood the contraption as soon as the hatch was opened?'

Brunel shook his head. 'There's a sealed chamber in the vessel with two hatches, one leading into the vessel itself and one leading out. Essentially, it works on much the same principle as a canal lock. A sort of "*air-lock*", if you will. The diver dons his suit and helmet, enters the inner hatch, and seals it behind him. He attaches his air hose to a valve inside the chamber. The chamber is then flooded with water from outside the vessel, and the diver is able to open the outer hatch and operate as independently of it as his air hose will allow. Got that?'

'I think so,' said Killigrew.

The door opened and Napier entered, stumping along with the aid of a cane – a memento of an old war wound – and waving a bulging manila envelope in his free hand. 'Your documents, Killigrew. You're going tae Russia as an American journalist. I seem tae recall ye dee a fair Yankee accent?'

Killigrew nodded. When on half-pay ashore, he often amused himself – and others, it was to be hoped – by taking part in amateur theatrical performances to raise money for the charities supported by the millionaire heiress philanthropist, Angela Burdett-Coutts, and had acted in plays alongside Charles Dickens, a fellow amateur dramatist.

'The Russians will think twice aboot treating ye roughly as long as they think you're a son o' Columbia,' continued Napier. 'They depend on American arms even more than British ones. Being a journalist will give ye an excuse tae ask all kinds of invasive questions. Being an American one means it will take the Russians at least a month tae check your background.'

Killigrew was relieved to hear it; even with his recent practice, he was not sure his Russian was good enough for him to pass himself off as a native. 'And if I'm not in and out of Russia within the space of a month, I think it's safe to say I'll not be coming out at all.'

Napier handed the envelope to him. 'American passport – you're John Bryce of the *New York Herald*, by the way – letter of introduction from Mr Gordon Bennett, the editor; and various Russian documents that the Foreign Office think you'll need. Are ye sure ye can trust this feller Leventhal? These documents could say "Arrest me, I'm a Russian spy" for all we ken!'

Killigrew took the documents out of the envelope. 'They look genuine enough to me, sir. And Leventhal will be released?'

'As soon as ye get safely back from Russia.'

'That's not the deal I made, sir.'

'That's the only deal Leventhal's getting, believe you me. We dinna want him running off tae Russia in the hope of getting a reward when he tells them aboot how he made a false passport for a certain Commander Killigrew.'

'Leventhal saved my life, sir. It hardly seems fair that his freedom should depend on my getting safely out of Russia.'

'If this *Sea Devil* is as big a threat as we think it is, there'll be a lot more people whose lives depend on ye than just this Leventhal. I should like one of oor translators at the Foreign Office tae look them over afore ye go, just tae be on the safe side.'

'You said something about having a spy in St Petersburg, sir?'

'Aye: his name's Mscislaw Wojtkiewicz. Ostensibly he's a vodka distiller; although I suspect that's just a cover for other, less legal activities, if ye catch ma drift. But he spends a fair amount o' time moving in exalted circles in St Petersburg and he gets tae hear some very interesting rumours. It was thanks tae him we got oor first whiff of these infernal machines.'

'I can trust him, then?'

'Aye, if you're a fool. If it's help you're needing, there are British citizens living in St Petersburg; upright members of the business community. I'm sure if the worst cam' tae the worst ye could turn tae them.'

'They're only allowed to remain on the sufferance of the Russian government, and I'll lay odds there's three Third Section agents assigned to watch each of them full time. My getting in touch with them will only draw suspicion on both myself and them. Besides, most of them are arms merchants, selling the Russians the armaments they need to slaughter our boys in the Crimea. Men like that wouldn't hesitate to turn me in if they thought they could get another contract out of it.'

'As ye will. I'll set up an address for ye tae send telegrams tae, if ye've any urgent messages. Ye canna send codes via telegraph, and we daren't risk a cypher: ye may depend upon it that the Russians will check every word ye send; backwards, forwards, sideways and upside doon. Instead we'll use a system o' key words. Ye send your messages as if they were journalistic dispatches: write any old drivel ye like – Christ knows, that's whut most journalists seem tae dee – and I'll jist look for the key words: "located" means ye've found the *Sea Devil*; "satisfied" means it's in St Petersburg; "contend" means it's at Kronstadt; "subscribe" means it's at Sveaborg; "resolve" means it's at Reval; and "moribund" means ye've managed tae destroy it. Put "not" before any o' those words tae turn it intae a negative. I'm sure a man o' your literary skills should have nae trouble working those phrases intae an innocent-reading dispatch.'

To Killigrew, that sounded like a dig at the reports he had submitted to Napier in the past. 'Located, satisfied, contend, subscribe, resolve and moribund,' he repeated, to impress the words in his memory.

Napier turned to Brunel. 'Did that parcel I arranged to be delivered for Mr Killigrew arrive yet?'

'Yes, Sir Charles. It's downstairs in my workshop.'

'Let's go, then.'

The three of them made their way out of the boardroom, Brunel leading the way while Killigrew and Napier followed. In the workshop, the engineer's assistants worked making a variety of models of various engines and contraptions of Brunel's devising. One of his assistants sat at a bench, annotating some plans. Brunel tapped him on the shoulder.

'How are those drawings coming along, Mr Jacomb?'

'Very nicely, sir. They should be ready to send to the War Office by two o'clock.'

'Good. Would you fetch Admiral Napier's parcel from the safe?'

'Yes, sir.' Jacomb stood up and headed through a door into another office.

Napier peered at the plans he had been working on. 'Whut are these?'

'Plans for a prefabricated hospital for Scutari, Sir Charles,' explained Brunel. 'It should ease the conditions for our brave boys wounded in the Crimea.'

'Prefabricated?' said Napier.

'The walls, floors and ceiling are constructed here in England, and then shipped out to Scutari to be assembled on the spot. Each section of the hospital is designed as a self-contained unit, so even if those dunderheads at the Army Commissariat manage to separate the units, those that do arrive at the correct destination will still be of some use . . . Don't touch that!' he added, seeing Killigrew toying with a model ship.

'You're a little old to be playing with toy boats, aren't you?'

'That's not a toy! I'll have you know you have in your hands the model for a revolutionary type of gunboat. With any luck it will result in the fall of Sevastopol and end this ghastly war. It's transported to the Black Sea in a steam collier that's been converted so that the bows open up to allow the gunboat to emerge from within. The armoured turret contains a single breech-loading twelve-inch gun firing three rounds per minute.'

'Ingenious!' Killigrew examined the underside of the model. 'Where's the screw?'

'A rudder or a screw might become damaged or fouled, leaving the vessel vulnerable,' Brunel explained with the air of a man explaining something that ought to be perfectly obvious to a child of ten. 'I'm working on a system of jet-propulsion that does away with the need for a screw and a rudder.'

Killigrew and Napier both blinked. 'Er . . . "jet-propulsion"?' echoed the admiral.

Brunel nodded. 'The vessel is propelled by three jets of steam: one main jet for forward propulsion, and two smaller lateral jets for manoeuvring. Of course, the jets could only work for a short distance.'

'I see,' Killigrew said dubiously. He had heard that the division between genius and insanity was not so much a line as an overlap; Brunel had clearly entered the overlap. 'Bauer had an office here?'

'Yes, upstairs. Why do you ask?'

'I should like to see it, if I may. Even if I confine my search to St Petersburg, it's still a big city with a good many shipyards. It's a long shot, but there's a chance that if Bauer left in a hurry, he might have left behind some clue as to where I should start my search for him.'

'I've already got someone else working in that office now,' said Brunel.

'What are ye hoping tae find, a letter to Bauer from the Grand Duke Konstantin, recommending a good hotel in St Petersburg?' asked Napier. 'Detectives from Scotland Yard have already gone through the personal belongings Bauer left behind with a fine-toothed comb.'

'I should like to have a look through it all anyhow,' said Killigrew.

Brunel's assistant returned carrying a parcel wrapped in brown paper tied up with string, and handed it to the engineer. 'Thank you, Mr Jacomb,' said Brunel, using a pair of scissors to cut the string on the parcel. 'Oh, do we still have that box of bits and bobs that Bauer left behind?'

'I think so, sir. Would you like me to go and check?'

'I'd be obliged.'

Jacomb hurried away again, and Brunel tore the wrapping off the parcel to reveal a mahogany box.

'Ah, good,' said Napier. 'Give me your gun, Killigrew.'

The commander dug into the pocket of his frock-coat and took out his revolver, handing it to Napier.

'Aye, I thought so,' sighed the admiral. 'This damned Deane and Adams again. I've tolt ye aboot this before.' He handed the revolver to Brunel. 'Ye tell him . . . for the last time.'

Brunel weighed the revolver in his hand. 'Rather bulky to carry in your pocket. Not very waterproof, either.' He tossed the revolver down contemptuously on Napier's desk.

'Any comments, Killigrew?' asked Napier.

Killigrew took a deep breath. 'I disagree, sir. I've been using the Deane and Adams for eighteen months. I've never missed with it yet. Well, hardly ever.'

'Maybe no',' said Napier. 'But it misfired on ye the other day and ye nearly spent six months in hospital in consequence. Ye'll carry Lefacheaux . . . unless of course ye prefer tae go back tae standard naval duties?'

'No, sir.' Killigrew said firmly. Now that he had resigned himself to undertaking this mission, he was determined to take the opportunity to avenge Araminta's death. 'I would not.'

'Then from now on ye carry a different gun,' Napier told him. 'Show him, Mr Brunel.'

The engineer opened the mahogany box to reveal a revolver. 'Now, pay attention, Commander Killigrew: a Lefacheaux pinfire revolver. Just like an ordinary revolver, but with one small yet vital modification: these.'

He showed Killigrew a fistful of small, funny-looking objects, brass cylinders with lead bullets embedded in one end.

'A combined bullet-and-cartridge-in-one. No more fumbling with powder and ramrod: the charge is housed in the brass cartridge, much like the pellets and charge in a shotgun cartridge. To load, open the top-hinged loading gate and place the hammer at half-cock.' Brunel broke open the revolver. 'As you can see, the cylinder contains six chambers, just like a Colt. Simply insert a round into each chamber, with the brass-wire pins at the base of the cartridges in the notches facing outwards. When the hammer falls, it strikes the pin, which rests against a percussion cap inserted in a small compartment in the base of the cartridge. When you've fired all six shots, eject the empty cartridge casings using the sliding rod here. You'll find that with practice you can reload in a matter of seconds, even in the heat of battle. Here, you try it.' He handed the revolver to Killigrew.

'Open the top-hinged loading gate . . . place the hammer at half-cock . . . insert the rounds into the chambers.' Killigrew loaded the revolver and snapped it shut. 'Seems straight-forward enough.'

'Also, note the absence of a trigger guard. When not in use, the trigger folds forward along the base of the frame, making it less bulky and easier to slip into a pocket. There's a secret compartment in the base of this holdall, to help you smuggle the revolver through customs.'

Jacomb returned carrying a large box full of odds and ends, and overturned it on one of the workbenches. 'This is all the stuff Bauer left behind.'

Killigrew and Napier sifted through it. Most of it was stationery and draughtsman's equipment: pencils, pencil sharpener, rulers, a slide rule, a set of logarithm tables, compasses, set-squares, unused envelopes and notebooks.

'What sort of man is this Bauer?' Killigrew asked Brunel.

'Hard to say. He was a difficult man to get to know. Always played his cards close to his chest. And even after he'd been living over here for three years, his English was never very good.'

Napier picked up a small framed picture and peered at it. 'Is he married?'

'Not that I'm aware of. He never mentioned a wife to me. Why do you ask?'

'Sweetheart, then, perhaps?' Napier showed the picture to Killigrew. It was a likeness of an attractive, dark-haired young woman in a white dress.

'Anzhelika Orlova,' said Killigrew.

'Ye ken the lassie?' Napier asked in astonishment.

'Not personally. She's the *prima ballerina* of the Mariinsky Ballet Company. I saw her dance at Covent Garden a couple of years ago . . . quite exquisite. They say she's the new Taglioni.'

'So Bauer's an aficionado of ballet,' grunted Napier. 'I hardly ken how that helps; unless you intend tae go tae the Bolshoi-Petrovsky Theatre every night in the hope that he shows up.'

'That would be rather futile, given that the Bolshoi-Petrovsky burned down two years ago,' said Killigrew. 'I admit I don't know where the Mariinsky Ballet's based these days, but it must be somewhere in St Petersburg: they've not toured since the war began.'

'So there are limits tae your expertise!' Napier snorted irritably.

'Nobody's perfect,' Killigrew said easily. 'Fortunately, I do know a little about photography – the difference between a daguerreotype and a calotype, for instance. And that likeness you're holding is a daguerreotype.'

'Why dae I get the feeling you're aboot tae tell me why that's important?'

Killigrew smiled. 'Once a calotype has been taken, the image can be reproduced an infinite number of times; or at least until the negative wears out or fades with age, I suppose. That's why they're replacing daguerreotypes as the most popular form of photography.

You see, a daguerreotype cannot be reproduced: each likeness is unique.'

'So?'

'Bauer would have been here in London when the Mariinsky last danced at Covent Garden,' explained Killigrew. 'To get his hands on a daguerreotype of Anzhelika Orlova, the chances are he must have met her himself. And if he admired her sufficiently to keep a portrait of her in his office, the chances are he'll have sought to renew their acquaintance shortly after his arrival in St Petersburg.'

'And this is how you're going tae track doon Bauer and the *Sea Devil*, is it?' snorted Napier. 'By chasing after some bonny lassie?'

'It's a dirty job, but someone's got to do it.' Killigrew put on a suitably noble expression. 'For Queen and country, sir.'

Napier shook his head despairingly.

# IX

# Welcome to St Petersburg

---

'The name's Bryce,' Killigrew told the customs officer in French. 'John Bryce.' He proffered the forged passport.

'You are a citizen of the United States of America?'

'That's right.'

'What is your business in St Petersburg?'

'I'm a reporter for the *New York Herald*, here to report on the war with Britain and France from the Russian point of view.'

The customs officer nodded approvingly, and handed back the passport. 'That seems to be in order. Anything to declare?'

'There's a couple of boxes of cheroots in my bag. They're for my own personal use.'

The customs officer motioned for Killigrew to put the holdall on the table between them. The commander complied, and the customs officer opened the holdall to reveal a Colt revolver lying on top of the boxes of cheroots and the clothes neatly folded inside. 'What's this?'

'My handgun, sir. The right to bear arms is enshrined in the constitution of the United States of America.' Killigrew avoided looking at the man wearing a fur hat who stood against the wall nearby, his hands thrust deep in the pockets of his black leather greatcoat as he scrutinised Killigrew curiously.

'You are not in America now, M'sieur Bryce,' the customs officer told him. 'It will have to be confiscated.'

'Then you'd better give me a receipt.'

'As you will.'

It took them ten minutes to fill out the necessary paperwork; most of it in Russian, which Killigrew could barely read. His lessons from the Finnish pilot on board the *Ramillies*, who had given him his first grounding in Russian, had been entirely oral, and he had only begun studying the Cyrillic alphabet since he had accepted this mission.

Getting to St Petersburg had been surprisingly easy, considering there was a war on. He had travelled back through France and Germany by the same route he had travelled from Finland a few months earlier, albeit in reverse, before taking the steam-packet from Danzig. Passing through the Allied blockade in the Gulf of Finland, the steamer had been overhauled and stopped by the screw frigate HMS *Arrogant*. Killigrew had been forced to confine himself to his cabin in case he was recognised by any of the British officers who came on board to search for contraband of war: the steamer itself was registered in Stockholm, a neutral port, and so had been allowed to continue on its way once the boarding party had contented itself she was not carrying contraband of war.

After all the paperwork was complete, the customs officer searched the rest of the holdall. Killigrew felt the sweat dripping from his armpits as he waited for the man to discover the secret compartment containing the Lefacheaux revolver.

Finally, the officer snapped the holdall shut and handed it back. 'Enjoy your stay in Russia, M'sieur Bryce.'

Killigrew walked out of the custom house and paused on the Point, at the east end of Vasilyevsky Island: just one of the islands in the delta of the River Neva on which St Petersburg had been built. It was a bright, sunny day in the middle of July, the light glittering on the river where it branched into two channels – the Bolshaya Neva and the Malaya Neva – passing on either side of the island to empty into the Gulf of Finland. A short distance upstream he could see the imposing bastions of the Petropavlovsky Fortress on the north side of the river – housing the Imperial Mint as well as the 'secret house' where political dissidents were incarcerated without trial – while to his right he could see the impressive waterfront of the mainland, dominated by the façades of the Winter Palace and the Admiralty building with its golden spire.

A rank of hackney drozhkies stood nearby: odd little four-wheeled carriages drawn by two horses, with a seat at the front for the driver and room for only one passenger, who sat partly in it and partly astride it. Killigrew climbed astride the first. 'Dussot's Hotel, *pozhaluista*.'

The driver grunted, chucked the reins, and the drozhky pulled away from the pavement.

Killigrew took out his cheroot case and held it up. In the reflection of its polished tin surface, he could see the man in the fur hat and black greatcoat flag down another drozhky, driven by an identically clad fellow. They pulled out into the street behind Killigrew's drozhky, following at a distance. Nothing to worry about, he told himself: any English or French-speaking visitors to Russia would be of special interest to the spies of the Third Section.

Well, he was in harm's way, now: if not in the heart of the Russian Empire, then certainly at its head. Despite his outward display of nonchalance during his interview by the customs officer, his heart had been racing, and it had still not slowed. One mistake, one false step, and it would all be over. There would be no trial, and certainly no handing him back to his own people in exchange for a captured Russian officer: a brutal, drawn-out interrogation in the cellars of the Kochubey Mansion was the best he could hope for, and in the unlikely event of his surviving that, he would be put up against a wall and shot. He had been in more dangerous situations than this, but usually with at least a shipmate or two to watch his back.

Sweating and looking pale was only going to draw attention to him too. He forced himself to put thoughts of capture, torture and execution from his mind. Back in London, his performances in plays to raise money for charity had been praised for their naturalness, which he achieved by making himself believe – for a couple of hours, at least – that he *was* the character he was playing. Only now he had to carry off his performance as an American journalist not just for a couple of hours but for days if not weeks.

The drozhky crossed the Bolshaya Neva on a pontoon bridge, passing between the Winter Palace and the Admiralty before heading up the Nevsky Prospect – three miles long, nowhere less than eighty feet in width – with its fine palaces, shops and apartment buildings, crossing two of the many waterways that laced the city. Most of the buildings were designed on elegant, classical lines, with few of the onion domes that Killigrew associated with Russia. But then, St Petersburg had been founded by Peter the Great, who had wanted to westernise the country, and Killigrew had read somewhere that St Petersburg was no more typical of Russia than New York City was of the United States. There could be no denying that St Petersburg was a fine-looking city, perhaps the most beautiful Killigrew had ever visited; but then, he had never been to Italy.

If the city looked beautiful, it was marred by the stench in the sultry summer air. He recognised the stink rising from the canals because it was little different from the stink from the Thames when he had left London: the stink of effluent. It assailed his nostrils the moment he reached the Petersburg side of the Bolshaya Neva, and stayed in them, making him gag. Small wonder the Tsar and his family preferred to spend the summer months at the summer palace in Tsarskoye Selo.

The driver reined in the horses outside Dussot's Hotel. As Killigrew paid him, he saw the drozhky bearing the two men in greatcoats and fur hats park outside the town hall on the opposite side of the street. He had a feeling they were going to be his companions throughout his stay in St Petersburg, and he christened them Tweedledum and Tweedledee, after two characters in a John Byrom satire.

He took his holdall and entered the hotel. 'I'd like a room for one, please,' he told the *concierge* in French. He had not bothered to send a telegram ahead to reserve a room: most of the St Petersburg aristocracy moved into their country dachas during the summer months, and the city was relatively quiet at this time of year.

'I'll need to take your passport, sir.'

Killigrew handed it over: that was the way they did things in Russia, and there was no point drawing attention to himself by making a fuss; besides, he had a feeling that when he left he would do so in a hurry, without going through official channels.

'How long will you be staying, M'sieur Bryce?'

Killigrew smiled ruefully. 'Indefinitely.'

'That is no problem at all, M'sieur. If you'd care to sign the register?'

Killigrew was careful not to sign his real name out of force of habit. The Latin Letters looked strange and out of place amongst all the names written in the Cyrillic alphabet, although he noticed there were a few other Western Europeans staying at the hotel.

'Could you check to see if there are any messages for me?' Killigrew was not expecting any this early in his visit, but while the *concierge* had turned his back to check the pigeonholes, it gave him a chance to riffle through the preceding pages of the register. No sign of a Wilhelm Bauer, though – not that Killigrew had expected it to be that easy.

The *concierge* turned back. 'Here's your key: room two hundred and twelve. Do you need any help with your bags?'

'Thank you, I can manage.'

A pretty chambermaid showed him upstairs. The room was generously proportioned and comfortably furnished, with an icon of St

Christopher on the wall above the bed. Killigrew crossed to the window and glanced out: Tweedledum sat on the drozhky parked across the street, but there was no sign of Tweedledee.

He gave the room a cursory search for bugs, but as far as he could see it was free of cockroaches, bed-lice, silverfish and other nasty creepy-crawlies.

'This will do nicely,' he said, tipping the chambermaid generously.

'If there is anything else I can do for you, just give the bell rope a tug.'

'I'll let you know if anything comes up,' he assured her.

She left him to his unpacking. He stripped to the waist and scrubbed himself at the washstand, before changing into his evening clothes: a black swallowtail coat and matching trousers. Taking his revolver from the secret compartment at the bottom of his holdall, he slipped it into the inside pocket of the coat, before studying the cut in front of the cheval glass. Once Killigrew had explained his requirements, Henry Poole of Savile Row had been very accommodating in that respect: there was no trace of a bulge. He did not expect to need the gun so soon, but doubtless the agents of the Third Section would give his holdall a more thorough search than the one it had received at the custom house, along with the rest of the room, in his absence.

He put on his greatcoat, buttoning it up to the throat to cover the white muslin cravat so Tweedledum and Tweedledee would not realise he was in evening clothes, and after putting a little talcum powder on the catches of his holdall and a hair across the doors of the wardrobe, he locked the door of his room behind him and made his way downstairs, carrying his wideawake.

Tweedledee sat on a couch in the entrance hall, pretending to read a newspaper. Ignoring him, Killigrew handed his key back to the *concierge* and stepped outside. He paused to put his hat on at a jaunty angle and lit another cheroot before he set off, walking east along the Nevsky Prospect.

He had walked ten yards down the boulevard before a couple of gendarmes descended on him. His legs turned to water as one of them laid a truncheon across his chest.

'And what do you think you're doing?'

Killigrew felt nauseous, wondering what fatal mistake he could have made so swiftly. It did not matter: it had been foolish of him to think he could pull this off. Still, there was nothing for it but to bluff it out to the last.

'Just going for a walk,' he said, his heart pounding. 'There's no law against that, is there?'

'Perhaps not.' The gendarme indicated the cheroot between Killigrew's fingers with his truncheon. 'But there *is* a law against smoking in public on the streets of St Petersburg.'

Killigrew's astonishment managed to overwhelm the feeling of relief that coursed through his veins, making every nerve in his body tingle. 'You're joking!'

The policeman narrowed his eyes. 'You're not from around here, are you?'

'No, I'm an American.'

'Ah! American, eh? Well, you're not in the land of liberty any more, sir. I'm afraid we must ask you to accompany us to the superintendent's bureau.'

'You're arresting me for *smoking*?'

'The law is the law.'

Killigrew dropped his cheroot on the cobbles and crushed it beneath the toe of a half-boot. 'Perhaps an on-the-spot fine would clear the matter up?' he suggested, passing them both a few kopecks.

The two gendarmes exchanged glances. 'Well, maybe we can overlook this matter just this once, seeing that you are a foreigner,' said one, slipping the coins in his pocket. 'But don't let us catch you doing it again.' He touched his truncheon to the peak of his cap. 'Mind how you go, sir.'

'Thank you.'

Killigrew hurried on his way, wondering what kind of despotic, paternalist society outlawed smoking on the streets. Banning smoking in restaurants he could understand – not that he knew any restaurants where smoking *was* banned – but in the open air? What deranged lunatic had thought up that one?

Still, the encounter had reminded him of one important fact: it was not as if he was trying to pass himself off as a native. Ignorance of the local laws could be excused, up to a point. Even in Russia, they had to give foreigners some leeway.

He continued east along the Nevsky Prospect, crossing the Fontanka Canal via the Anichkoff Bridge. He had a knack for visually memorising any map he studied for a minute or two, and had looked at a map of the city – hopefully not too out of date – on the journey from Britain.

There was a constant stream of speeding carriages on the boulevard, and he took his life in his own hands just by trying to cross. He smiled:

it would be ironic to have come all the way to St Petersburg, risking torture and execution at the hands of the Third Section, only to be killed trying to cross the street. But that was life: it might as easily be ended by a speeding carriage or the cholera as by the enemies of his country, so there was no point worrying and playing it safe; life was too short to be spent fretting about the prospect of death. He would worry about it when it happened; for all he knew, it might turn out there was nothing to worry about anyway.

He managed to negotiate the traffic without any accidents. At the junction of Nevsky and Liteiny Prospects men sat on stools to be shaved by itinerant barbers, while porters and craftsmen touted for business. Killigrew threaded his way through this lively throng and turned right down Vladimirsky Prospect as far as Kuznichsky Street, where he entered a covered market.

The market bustled with shoppers, mostly the wives of the middling sort or the servants of the great houses in the city, purchasing food for their masters; evidently the poorer folk did their shopping elsewhere. The place was noisy with stallholders calling out their wares and thick with the delicious odours of smoked sausages, fish and freshly baked bread. Killigrew pretended to browse amongst the stalls, noting that Tweedledum had followed him inside; presumably it was Tweedledee's turn to wait outside with the drozhky.

Killigrew doubled back on himself. Seeing him approach, Tweedledum turned away hurriedly and pretended an interest in some sausages hanging from a butcher's stall. Killigrew walked straight past him; as soon as he had gone by, Tweedledum followed quickly. Killigrew turned left, and then doubled-back again. Again Tweedledum was forced to come to an abrupt halt and studied some *matryoshka* dolls on a toy maker's stall as if he had never seen such a thing before.

Killigrew smiled, reassured that the Third Section did not know who he really was or what he was doing in St Petersburg; if they had, they would certainly have assigned someone other than this buffoon to follow him. He made a sharp about-face and Tweedledum, who had been hurrying up behind him with the ends of his unfastened belt trailing, snatched a colander from an ironmonger's stall and inspected it with a critical eye. Killigrew made as if to walk straight past, and then stopped right next to him. To avoid meeting Killigrew's eye, Tweedledum turned his back to him and held up the colander, peering at it as if making sure the holes went all the way through.

Killigrew glanced down at the trailing buckle on the belt of

Tweedledum's greatcoat. Next to his hand, a saucepan hung from one of several nails hammered into the wooden strut supporting one corner of the stall's awning. He took the saucepan off the nail, turned it this way and that as if thinking of making a purchase, and then put the pan down on top of a casserole dish on the main display.

He looked at the people around them. The ironmonger running the stall was haggling with a woman over the price of a kettle. The other shoppers were too intent on making their own purchases to pay any attention to Killigrew and his shadow. The commander hooked the buckle of Tweedledum's belt over the nail, then turned and walked briskly towards the rear of the market.

Tweedledum hurried after him, but before he had taken two steps his belt brought him up short. Caught off guard, his legs kept walking while the shoulders of his coat pulled the top half of him backwards. He went over, the weight of his body pulling the prop out from the table of the stall. The whole lot went over, burying Tweedledum in a clattering avalanche of pots and pans. He tried to pull himself up by grabbing hold of another shelf, but that too broke away and more pots crashed down on him. Mindful that his quarry was going to get away, he struggled to his feet only to be seized by the irate ironmonger.

Killigrew slipped out at the back of the market and into a bookshop on the opposite side of the street. He took down a book from one of the shelves and leafed through it, peering out through the books displayed on the shelves in the window to where Tweedledum emerged from the market at a run, looking up and down in agitation. Tweedledee followed him out a moment later. The two of them had an angry exchange, and then ran off in opposite directions. Killigrew waited a minute or two before replacing the book on the shelf and emerging from the shop to cross back over the street into the covered market.

He made his way back to Nevsky Prospect, where he flagged down a drozhky to take him to Senate Square. He was driven as far as the Stroganoff Palace, where they turned left on to the embankment of the Moika – not another of St Petersburg's canals, as some thought, but a river, for all that her waters flowed sluggishly between her built-up banks. They followed the Moika as far as Vosnesensky Prospect, which crossed the river at the Blue Bridge between the Mariinsky Palace and the scaffolding-covered edifice of the new cathedral – clearly modelled after St Paul's in London – overlooking St Isaac's Square.

According to one of the guide books Killigrew had read on the journey from London, it was the widest bridge in the world: with a breadth of 320 feet and a span of 135, it was almost three times wider than it was long. Here the agents of aristocrats and landowners haggled with serf dealers over the price of huddled groups of wretched-looking folk dressed in rags. Killigrew had seen slave markets on the Guinea Coast, and that had been quite repulsive enough; yet somehow the spectacle of men dealing in the lives of their fellow human beings – men, women and children – as if they were cattle was even more shocking when you stumbled across it in a beautiful and supposedly civilised city like St Petersburg. It was a reminder that even if he did not agree with his government's motives in fighting this war, Tsarist Russia needed a spectacular military defeat to make her realise just how out of step with the rest of civilisation she was. One of the serf dealers was positively whipping some of his 'merchandise' right there on the bridge, and Killigrew wondered what kind of society banned smoking on the streets, but still permitted flogging slaves.

Senate Square was on the other side of the cathedral. There Falconet's equestrian statue of Peter I – made infamous as 'The Bronze Horseman' of Pushkin's poem – glowered from atop its granite plinth over the ornamental garden at the west end of the Admiralty building. Here the Decembrists had tried to stage their abortive coup thirty years earlier, in a doomed attempt to force the new Tsar to initiate a programme of reform to drag Russia kicking and screaming into the nineteenth century. Ironically, the failed uprising had had the opposite effect, and Nicholas I had become one of the most ruthless and reactionary of tsars . . . and that was saying something. Now that Nicholas was dead, it remained to be seen whether or not his son, Alexander II, turned out the same way.

Killigrew dismounted from the drozhky and paid the driver, before making his way to the address Napier had given him, one of the fine mansions overlooking the Neva on the Angliiskaya Embankment. He pulled on the doorbell and it was answered almost at once by a footman in knee-breeches and a powdered wig, a tough-looking customer with a scarred face.

'*Da?*'

'I'm a friend of Chekalinsky.' Killigrew had no idea who Chekalinsky was, only that his name was the shibboleth that would let him into Wojtkiewicz's house as surely as 'open sesame' let Ali Baba into the forty thieves' cave.

The footman did not raise an eyebrow at a stranger turning up on the doorstep and claiming to be a friend of Chekalinsky, but took a step back and ushered Killigrew inside. 'This way, *m'sieur*.' Apparently, Wojtkiewicz kept open house.

Killigrew stepped into a large, high-ceilinged hallway with a grandiose staircase leading up from the middle of the floor to the landing above.

'May I take your coat and hat, *m'sieur*?'

Killigrew shrugged off his greatcoat and wideawake hat, and the footman took them and hung them up in a walk-in closet off to one side.

'If you'll follow me, *m'sieur* . . .' The footman led the way across the marble floor with a measured tread. Killigrew followed him up the staircase. At the top, the footman opened a pair of double doors, and ushered the commander into the ante-room beyond. The footman closed the doors behind them, and Killigrew crossed to pause in the middle of the empty room, taking in the portraits of rosy-cheeked noblewomen in satin gowns and moustachioed officers in eighteenth-century uniforms, which hung on the rococo-panelled walls. A hubbub of voices came from the double doors on the far side of the room, and the footman walked past him to open them. The sound of voices instantly became louder, and a haze of tobacco smoke issued into the ante-room. The footman ushered him through.

Killigrew stepped into a large, plush salon where various ladies and gentlemen sat around on velvet-covered sofas, eating ices and smoking pipes respectively. Most of the men present were in various gaudy uniforms bedecked with gold braid. Clearly it was the done thing to wear full-dress uniform to purely social occasions here in St Petersburg, and there were few enough men in civilian garb to make him feel a little self-conscious in his evening clothes.

No sooner had the footman retreated, closing the doors after him, than another approached carrying crystal flutes of champagne on a silver salver. Killigrew helped himself to a glass and sipped it, sauntering through the crowded room. The walls were papered in a rather garish shade of purple, with matching drapes covering the windows. A number of doors led off the salon: through one, he could see generals and privy counsellors playing whist, while the unmistakable click and clatter of a roulette wheel emanated from another. A number of footmen stood at strategic points wherever he looked; if most people who employed footmen chose them on the basis of height, Wojtkiewicz clearly looked for width; in the shoulders rather than the girth.

'I don't believe I've had the pleasure, *m'sieur* . . .?'

Killigrew turned to see an alluring woman of thirty or thereabouts, dressed in an off-the-shoulder gown of scarlet tarlatan, lavishly trimmed with ribbons, lace and artificial flowers, yet not so elegantly cut that it did not display a modicum of cleavage. Her hair – somewhere between dark brown and brunette, but with auburn highlights where it caught the warm glow of the chandeliers – was in ringlets, so she was probably unmarried.

'Bryce,' he told her. 'John Bryce.'

She arched an eyebrow. 'An Englishman?'

'An American.' He told himself to relax. His Yankee accent was pretty good, just wasted on most Russians.

'Ah. An *American*.' She looked at him through eyes that were large and brown, but intelligent rather than vacuous, and an amused smile played on her sensuous lips. She held up a gloved hand for him to kiss. 'Permit me to introduce myself. I am the Countess Apollónia Vásáry.'

He bowed, and kissed her hand. '*Enchanté, madame*. Vásáry . . . that's not a Russian name, is it?'

She shook her head. 'Hungarian. But what brings an American to St Petersburg at this time, M'sieur Bryce?'

'Oh, I'm a reporter for the *New York Herald*. I'm, er . . . looking for a story. And yourself?'

She looked him up and down. 'I'm just looking. Do you think me dreadfully forward, introducing myself to a complete stranger?'

He smiled. 'Forward, certainly, ma'am; but not dreadfully so.'

'I travel around a good deal. Life is so short, and it is my ambition to see every part of this world before I die. But it is also good to make new friends, and when one has so little time one cannot always afford to wait for an introduction.'

'Couldn't agree more.'

'And what do you make of our host?'

'M'sieur Wojtkiewicz? I can't say I've met him . . . although I do feel I ought to pay my respects. Is he in here?'

She shook her head, making her ringlets dance prettily. 'He'll be upstairs, playing faro. Come on, I'll introduce you to him.'

He followed her out through a door beneath a painting of a tiger, and she led the way up a flight of stairs. Puzzled, Killigrew frowned before following, his nerves on edge.

At the top of the stairs they entered another salon, this one thick with

146

cigar smoke, inhabited exclusively by men, most of them above forty. The man who sat dealing cards at the head of the table was one of the few dressed in plain evening clothes, like Killigrew's, and every bit as exquisitely cut. His hair and neatly trimmed beard had long since turned white, although his moustache was salt-and-pepper and his eyebrows remained thick and black. He turned the cards out with practised dexterity, and the punters' arms darted back and forth across the table, rearranging their counters on the faro table while the case-keeper's hands fluttered over the beads in the case, nimbly keeping track of which cards had been played.

Killigrew did not gamble, except for pennies at whist to be sociable – ironically, his calotypic memory made him a dab hand at the game – but he had seen faro played often enough to know the rules. He saw at once there were some obvious differences in the way the game was played in Russia. For one thing, the banker sat at the head of the table instead of in the middle of one side, while the case-keeper stood at the opposite end of the table, allowing places for the punters on both sides. Instead of a faro box, which showed the uppermost card in the deck, the banker was dealing from a baccarat shoe, piling them alternately to the left and to the right.

'M'sieur Wojtkiewicz?' said the countess. 'May I introduce M'sieur John Bryce? He's a reporter from the *New York Herald*.'

The banker glanced up, studying Killigrew with hard, brown eyes. 'I understand they call faro "bucking the tiger" in your country, M'sieur Bryce. Do you play?'

'No.'

'Then you have no business in the faro room.' Wojtkiewicz went on dealing cards unconcernedly.

The countess smiled. 'I'll leave the two of you to get to know one another,' she told Killigrew. 'I can see you're going to hit it off!' She slipped outside again, closing the door behind her.

'Make a place for M'sieur Bryce, Hordienko,' Wojtkiewicz grunted without looking up from his dealing. One of the men stood up from his place at the table and gestured for Killigrew to be seated.

The commander sat down on Wojtkiewicz's left, hitching up the knees of his trousers at he did so. Someone put some counters and a game card and pencil-stub on the table in front of him. 'I'll stake you one hundred roubles to begin with,' said Wojtkiewicz. 'I trust you're good for it?'

Killigrew inclined his head, although it was going to make a nasty dent in the expense money he had been provided with if he lost that much.

The rules of faro were really rather simple. It was purely a game of chance, more like roulette than a card game. The punters did not touch the cards themselves. The banker dealt two cards at a time from the box; as it was played in England, the first card dealt 'lost' while the one showing face-up in the box 'won'. In the middle of the baize-covered table were pictures of a full suit of cards – spades, but suits did not matter in this game. Punters put money on one of the pictures, to bet on the value of the card, from ace to king. If the punter bet on the queen, for example, then if the next queen to turn out 'won', then so did the punter; if it lost, then the banker took the punter's money. If both cards were of the same value, then it was a 'split', and the banker took all wagers placed on that card. Punters could also 'copper' their bet by putting a penny – or a kopeck – on top of their wager, to denote that they were betting on that card to lose. It was one of the few gambling games where the odds were almost even, but if you got carried away the stakes could rise swiftly: wealthy aristocrats had been reduced to paupers on a turn of the cards at faro.

'Which part of the United States do you hail from, M'sieur Bryce?' asked Wojtkiewicz, pulling the cards from the shoe.

'New England, originally,' Killigrew said absently, his eyes on the game. It did not take him long to work out that the way they played it in Russia, it was the cards dealt on the left that won, while those on the right lost. 'Though I moved to the big city as soon as I finished school.'

'New York?' asked Wojtkiewicz.

'Where else?' Killigrew moved all his counters on to the three. In for a kopeck, in for a hundred roubles, he told himself. The game was already halfway through, but punters could enter the game or cash in their counters at any point, without waiting for the banker to reach the end of the deck.

Wojtkiewicz flipped the next two cards out of the shoe, putting the ten of diamonds on the right and the nine of hearts on the left.

Another player rearranged his counters on the layout. The next turn brought out the two of diamonds and the knave of clubs. A man who had bet on the knave saw his counters doubled. '*Paix*,' he said.

'Count Orloff always bets on the knave,' Wojtkiewicz remarked to Killigrew with a smile.

'I wish the knaves showed the same loyalty to me that I do to them,' grunted Orloff.

148

A chill ran down Killigrew's spine as he looked at the count, a man with close-cropped hair and a wen in the middle of his forehead. He knew the name well enough: Count Orloff was the head of the Third Section. Could his presence at the table be a nasty coincidence? He did not seem to be paying excessive attention to Killigrew, but that could mean anything or nothing.

Two more cards emerged from the shoe: the four of hearts and the trey of clubs. 'You have beginner's luck, Mr Bryce,' Wojtkiewicz remarked, as a footman acting as the croupier put another ten counters on the layout next to Killigrew's stake.

'I've a feeling I'm going to need it.' Killigrew knew the sensible thing to do was to walk away from the table, while he was a hundred roubles up; but if he did that he would have lost his chance to sound out Wojtkiewicz. A glance at the case told him there were no more treys left in the deck, so he moved his counters to the seven.

The next two turns brought out no sevens, but he won again on the third. Now he had four hundred roubles' worth of counters on the seven. He moved them to the queen.

'I see you're familiar with the works of Pushkin!' said Wojtkiewicz.

Killigrew smiled. On the journey from London he had been reading Russian literature, including 'The Queen of Spades', to brush up on his familiarity with the Cyrillic alphabet and to try to get a feel for Russian society. 'Let's just say I don't want to make the same mistake as Herr Herman.'

'As you will.'

Killigrew glanced at the case: there were two queens left in the deck, but the next three turns brought out none of them. The third showed he had been right to move his counters off the seven, however: it produced a split, and if there had been any money riding on the seven it would have gone to Wojtkiewicz.

The ace of hearts won on the next turn; if Killigrew had played the cards in the order recommended by the old countess in 'The Queen of Spades' – the order that had cost Herman so much money – he would have had eight hundred roubles by now.

Wojtkiewicz flipped out the next two cards: this time, it was the turn of the ace of diamonds to win. Killigrew wondered if Wojtkiewicz was toying with him. He had heard that there were 'gaffed' faro boxes, which could 'skin' the cards – bring them out in an order dictated by the banker – although he could not imagine how it was done. He would have to ask Molineaux: the petty officer was a master of prestidigitation, and there was no way of cheating at cards that he could not spot. Still, if it was possible for a faro box, it must have been possible for a baccarat shoe; if anything, the fact that cards remained invisible until they were taken out made it easier.

He wished Molineaux were at his side now.

Wojtkiewicz extracted the next two cards: the queen of hearts and the queen of spades. If the latter had mocked Herman at the climax of Pushkin's short story, the effect on Killigrew was doubled now, even if the money he had lost was nowhere near as disastrous.

Wojtkiewicz smirked. 'Bad luck, old boy. Have you had enough for one night, or would you like a chance to win back your money?'

Killigrew cursed himself inwardly. This was exactly the reason he never gambled for significant money. He had allowed himself to be suckered in . . . and now Wojtkiewicz was giving him a chance to get suckered in even deeper. The sensible thing to do was to walk away from the table; but he already owed Wojtkiewicz eight hundred roubles, which was rather more money than he could afford; and Killigrew suspected that Wojtkiewicz was not the sort of man who took kindly to those who could not pay their debts of honour. More importantly than that, he had been beaten, and Killigrew did not like to be beaten. Wojtkiewicz's smirk goaded him; doubtless it was intended to do exactly that.

Killigrew took out his cheroot case and lit one to buy himself a few more seconds to think. Was it a gaffed box? Even if it was not, the odds were still stacked in the banker's favour, even if only marginally.

*The devil take it*, thought Killigrew. 'Will you stake me another one hundred roubles, M'sieur Wojtkiewicz?'

'I assume you're good for it?'

'I'm good for it.' If the worst came to the worst, Killigrew could always telegraph Napier for more money in the morning, although the admiral would tear several strips off him when he learned why he had needed it, and he would end up paying it back out of his salary.

According to the case, there were only five cards left in the shoe. Killigrew bet half the money the Pole staked him on the three, coppering it to lose.

Wojtkiewicz turned the next two cards: the six of hearts and the two of clubs. Killigrew's fifty roubles stayed where they were.

'Let's make this interesting,' said Wojtkiewicz. 'I'll wipe the slate clean if you can call the turn.'

'And if I can't?'

150

Wojtkiewicz smiled. 'You'll owe me thirty-two hundred roubles.'

If it was a gaffed box, the banker could beat him whatever he called. But Wojtkiewicz clearly liked to play. He would not be interested in hanging Killigrew out to dry so quickly . . . would he? He wanted to sucker him in even deeper: another win to buoy up his confidence, trick him into thinking the game was not rigged, build the stake up even higher. How much money did Wojtkiewicz think an American journalist could be taken for?

Killigrew glanced at the case: the three cards remaining in the deck were a three, a four and a nine. He licked parched lips. 'Four, three, nine.'

Wojtkiewicz flipped out the first card: the four of clubs. Killigrew was still in the game, but it all depended upon the next card. Wojtkiewicz waited with all the skill of a showman, dragging it out before turning the penultimate card . . .

The three of diamonds.

Killigrew exhaled as a feeling of almost overwhelming relief surged through him.

A professional gambler, Wojtkiewicz took out the last card, the 'hock' as it was called, just in case the case-keeper had not kept an accurate track of which cards had been played, but it was the nine of clubs. Killigrew's knees would not get broken tonight.

Assuming he walked out now.

But he would be walking out empty-handed, and he did not want that. He wanted to wipe the smile off Wojtkiewicz's face.

The Pole shuffled the cards and reinserted them in the shoe. 'Another game, gentlemen?'

Killigrew shook his head. 'I've had quite enough excitement for one night, thank you. To tell you the truth, "Go Johnny Go-Go-Go-Go" is more my game.'

Wojtkiewicz blinked. ' "Go Johnny—" ' . . . what did you say?'

' "Go Johnny Go-Go-Go-Go",' Killigrew repeated, offhand.

'Never heard of it,' growled one of the other punters.

'No?' Killigrew feigned surprise. 'It's all the rage in the States.'

'How do you play?' asked Wojtkiewicz.

Killigrew regarded him in disbelief. 'Don't you know how to play "Go Johnny Go-Go-Go-Go"? I thought *everyone* knew how to play "Go Johnny Go-Go-Go-Go"!' He picked up the deck of cards, and shuffled it. 'It's perfectly simple: knaves are worth ten, kings are worth three . . . apart from one-eyed jacks, which are wild cards, but I'll come

151

to those in a minute. In round one you get a hand of nine, in round two a hand of seven. Deuces are wild cards as well, apart from diamonds, which retain their face value; apart from the king of diamonds, obviously. We play in sequence, unless you can match a pair or play a card in ascending or descending order. If you can, that's a "Go Johnny Go-Go-Go-Go". You stand up, pick up all the cards on the table, and shout "Go, Johnny, go-go-go-go!" The winner is the man with the most tricks after fifteen hands.' He began to deal out the cards. 'You'll pick up the rest as we go along . . .'

# X

# Countess Vásáry

---

Killigrew narrowed his eyes at Wojtkiewicz across the top of the baize table. 'That's very good, *m'sieur*. A full house . . . Are you quite certain you've never played this game before?'

Wojtkiewicz threw down his cards and picked up his pencil, toying with it. He did not scowl at Killigrew, but he looked as if he very much wanted to. 'Never,' he growled.

'If I didn't know better, I'd say you were trying to sharp me,' Killigrew chided him. 'But, the proof of the pudding is in the eating, as they say. I'm afraid even a full house doesn't beat a three-card trick with aces high in "Go Johnny Go-Go-Go-Go". Which leaves me the winner, I think.'

The pencil snapped in Wojtkiewicz's hands. 'How much do I owe you?'

'One moment, let me just work it out.' Killigrew scribbled some figures at random on the back of a game card. 'Nine out of fifteen tricks at fifty roubles a trick, plus thirteen for the queen of spades, multiplied by the number of players and divided by the number I first thought of . . . let's see . . . that comes to . . . seven hundred and ninety-eight roubles and thirteen kopecks. You know, I much prefer round numbers. Shall we call it eight hundred? It seems petty to quibble over a few kopecks.'

Wojtkiewicz raised a hand, and one of his flunkeys standing behind him put a chequebook and pen it in. He started to write out a cheque. 'Payable to John Bryce esquire, I presume?'

'I'd prefer cash,' said Killigrew.

Wojtkiewicz tore up the half-written cheque. 'Then my secretary will present you with the money at the door. Good evening to you, Mr Bryce. I dare say we'll meet again before you leave St Petersburg.'

'I'm counting on it.' Killigrew rose to his feet. 'Thank you for such a sterling service,' he said, tipping the case-keeper generously, and nodded to the other punters sitting at the table. 'Gentlemen . . .'

He made his way downstairs to the salon. There was no sign of Countess Vásáry. He helped himself to another glass of champagne as he passed, carrying it downstairs to the entrance hall and sipping it while he waited for his winnings. He had to wait the best part of ten minutes before a handsome young man with something of the air of a dandy about him – as far as his plain black frock-coat would allow – arrived. 'M'sieur Bryce?'

'That's me.'

'I'm Czcibor Jedraszczyk, M'sieur Wojtkiewicz's secretary.' Despite the elegant cut of his clothes, there was a hardness in Jedraszczyk's eyes that suggested the duties he was accustomed to carrying out for his employer extended beyond taking letters for him.

He handed Killigrew a bulky manila envelope. This was not the time or the place to take the money out and count it. Killigrew stuffed the envelope in one of the pockets of his swallowtail coat and tossed the empty champagne flute to a footman standing nearby. The flunkey caught it awkwardly, and another appeared with the commander's greatcoat and hat. He helped the commander shrug it on, and Killigrew gave the brim of his wideawake a snap before stepping through the door the flunkey held open for him.

Darkness had fallen, yet although the white nights of St Petersburg had ended a couple of weeks earlier, the city was close enough to the Arctic Circle for some ambient light to remain on the northern horizon even at midnight. Even though it was nearly eleven o'clock, it was still twilight, the sky above the rooftops a warm orange shading through pastel pink to a deep purple in the velvet firmament above. As much as Killigrew loved the Tropics, you could not beat the northern latitudes for long evenings with beautiful sunsets; it was so lovely, one could almost turn a blocked nostril to the stench of the canals. The lights of Vasilyevsky Island were reflected on the cold, black waters of the Neva, and a chill wind blew in from the Gulf of Finland. It stung his face, helping to clear his head after the champagne he had drunk and the stuffy atmosphere of the faro room. That was just as well: he was expecting trouble.

It did not take long to find him either, even if the form it came in did not immediately appear to be directed at him. He had not gone a hundred yards up the embankment before a woman's scream shattered the quiet of the night somewhere off to his right.

The mouth of an alleyway was just up ahead. He ran around a corner to see a woman in a fur coat backed against the wall in the shadows, while a man menaced her with a knife.

Killigrew smelled a rat the way a man with a piece of Limburger stuck up one nostril could smell cheese. He glanced over his shoulder, but there was no one behind him. Thrusting his hands in his pocket, he sauntered unhurriedly over to where the man had the woman backed against the wall. He took his time, so that the man seemed to run out of things to do, except flourish the knife repeatedly in the woman's face.

'Dear, oh dear, oh dear!' said Killigrew. 'Extemporisation obviously not your strong suit, is it?'

The man whirled, jabbing his knife towards Killigrew. Countess Vásáry – for the woman was none other – had a perfect opportunity to whack the knife-man around the head with her reticule, but she did not. Somehow Killigrew suspected it was not feminine frailty that caused her to hold back.

'Stand back!' snarled the man. 'Or I'll cut her!'

'Now, we both know that's a lie, don't we?' said Killigrew. 'We also know that after a vicious scuffle, I'm going to disarm you and you're going to run off into the night. The only problem is that these clothes I'm wearing are bound to get damaged in the fight, and since they cost me sixty dollars, I'd prefer it all round if we could forgo that particular formality.'

Bewildered, the man looked to the countess for a lead. She rolled her eyes in exasperation.

'Oh dear,' said Killigrew. 'You really aren't much good at this, are you?' He tapped the man on the jaw with his fist.

The man fell down obligingly. Killigrew kicked the knife from his hand, then grabbed him by the lapels and hoisted him to his feet. Before the man had a chance to realise what was going on, Killigrew spun him around and gave him a kick up the backside. The man staggered a short distance down the alleyway. He decided it was time to get out while the going, if not good, was a lot better than it might have turned out. Picking up his heels, he fled from the alley.

Killigrew dusted his hands off and turned to the countess. 'Was he the best you could get at such short notice?'

'I don't know what you're talking about, I'm sure!'

'*I'm* sure you do,' Killigrew said sourly. 'Never mind, have it your way. What happens now? I walk you back to where you're staying, and you invite me inside so you can look at my cuts and bruises?'

'I suppose it's the least I can do.'

'Sorry to disappoint you, ma'am. I haven't got any cuts or bruises. Still, we can't stand here talking all night. There are all kinds of suspicious characters about on a night like this. Next time we might run into some genuine cutthroats.' He gestured back down the alleyway.

'It's this way.' She indicated the other direction.

'Lead on.'

As she started walking, Killigrew took out his revolver and thumbed back the hammer. She jumped, startled by the sound, and eyed the gun unhappily.

'If this is a trap, you'll be the first to die,' he told her.

She shook her head. 'You wouldn't kill a woman. You couldn't.'

'Let's find out, shall we?' He followed her through the alley, keeping eyes and ears open in case any of her confederates tried to leap out at him.

'I suppose Wojtkiewicz's ruffians are waiting for us at your house?'

'Wojtkiewicz? You think I work for him?'

'Are you trying to tell me you don't?'

She shrugged. 'You seem to have your own ideas about who I am and what I want to achieve. Far be it from me to contradict you.'

Killigrew frowned. Either she had suddenly learned how to act, or this time she was telling the truth.

It was a five-minute walk through the unlit streets to the house. If not on the same scale as Wojtkiewicz's, it was still fairly grand. 'Your house?' asked Killigrew.

She shook her head. 'Prince Polyansky's. I'm just borrowing it while he's with his regiment in the Crimea.'

'Does he know that?'

She did not deign to reply, but led the way up the steps to the imposing portico, where she took out a bunch of keys and unlocked the door. He followed her inside. The gas lamps in the hallway were on, but turned down low.

'No butler?'

'I gave the servants the night off.'

'How very convenient!'

'For you or for me?'

'That all depends on what you were planning to do with me once you'd got me in your clutches.'

She smiled archly. 'You may never know now you've decided to take things into your own hands.' She started to ascend the staircase, leaving him gaping in astonishment below her.

He recovered himself with a shake of the head and bounded up the stairs after her, catching up with her just as she was about to open one of the doors on the landing. He caught her by the wrist with his left hand and twisted her arm up into the small of her back, pressing the muzzle of the revolver to her temple with his right.

'Ow! You're hurting me!'

'Just remember what I told you earlier. If this is a trap . . .' he hissed in her ear. 'Now, open the door.'

She reached out and turned the handle, pushing the door open to reveal an opulently appointed withdrawing room. He marched her into the room ahead of him. A fire crackled in the hearth, and a bottle of champagne stood in an ice bucket on a silver salver on one of the tables, next to a couple of crystal flutes. There were no assassins hiding behind the drapes or under the chaise longue.

'Do you treat all ladies this way?' she demanded.

'You're no lady.' Kicking the door shut behind him with a heel, he spun her around and pushed her into one of the plush easy chairs. She glowered up at him angrily.

'Whoever trained you didn't do a very good job, I'm afraid. In polite society, a lady always goes *behind* a man going up stairs, never in front of him. Even a Hungarian countess. Now who are you, and what do you want?'

She sighed. 'All right. My name isn't Apollónia, it's Ilonka. I changed it when I went on the stage.'

'Ilonka?'

She smiled wanly. 'Now, can you really blame me for changing it?'

He did not return her smile.

'But I truly am a countess, even if I wasn't brought up as one!' she insisted. 'I had an affair with Count Vásáry; he fell in love with me. After his first wife died of consumption, we waited a year, and then got married.' She smiled at the recollection. 'All of Budapest society was scandalised by the match. The scion of one of the noblest families in Hungary marrying an actress? But he did. And now I am Countess Vásáry.'

157

It sounded convincing enough. 'Oh-kay. That's who you are. But it doesn't explain what you're doing in St Petersburg; nor why you tried to waylay me in a dark alley with a fake assault.'

'When the Hungarians rebelled against the Habsburgs, my husband supported Louis Kossuth's Liberal parliament. He fought in many battles against the Austrians and we won many victories, as I'm sure you know.' A bitter tone entered her voice as she continued. 'But then Tsar Nicholas sent his troops to support the Habsburg monarchy. We could not hold out against the Austrians and the Russians. When General Görgey surrendered to the Austrians at Vilagos, Kossuth fled to Turkey. My husband refused to leave the country of his birth. He was arrested by the Austrian secret police and executed for treason. I was sent into exile.'

Killigrew nodded. Araminta and he had attended a public meeting addressed by Kossuth at Copenhagen Fields in Islington, and they had both been impressed by the Hungarian's oratory, as well as by the justice of his cause, and the injustice of its cruel repression. But one part of the countess's story did not ring true. 'So, you came to Russia: the country that helped the Habsburgs destroy the Hungarian Republic?'

'Not everyone in Russia supported the Tsar's actions; nor do they support them now, in this war with Britain, France and Turkey.'

'The serfs?'

She laughed. 'The serfs are like cattle. They will put up with any amount of oppression their masters choose to cram down their throats. Not that they are less than the men of any other country in the world; but centuries of brutal treatment have cowed them. Have you ever been south of the Mason-Dixon line in your own country, M'sieur Bryce? I think you will find the blacks raised in slavery are little different.' She indicated the bottle of champagne. 'Would you?'

He eased the cork out of the bottle with the aid of a napkin while she continued.

'If Hungary is to be free, then Russia must be freed first; and in Russia, revolution must come from the top. Tsar Nicholas crushed many members of the liberal aristocracy when he smashed the Decembrist uprising on his accession; but there remain a few powerful and influential people in St Petersburg who are working behind the scenes to make Russia a more liberal country, in spite of the efforts of men like Count Orloff, and the Third Section.'

Killigrew poured them each a glass of champagne. 'But Nicholas died five months ago. Isn't Tsar Alexander supposed to be more liberal than his father was?'

'Yes . . . but he is a young man, unprepared for the responsibilities of being the ruler of such a vast empire. He leans heavily on the men who advised his father.'

He handed her one of the flutes. 'Reactionaries like Count Orloff, you mean.'

She nodded, putting the glass to one side while she continued to speak passionately. 'It is not too late for Russia, but we must act quickly, while the government's attention is focused on the war with Britain and France.'

Killigrew took a sip of champagne. 'Exactly what is it you're planning to do?'

'You think I would tell you? For all I know, you could be an agent of the Third Section.'

'Do I look like an agent of the Third Section?'

'No . . . but then you do not look much like my idea of an American reporter, either.'

'And what does your idea of an American reporter look like?'

'Fat, self-satisfied . . . besides, how many reporters carry guns, M'sieur Bryce?'

'In America? All of us!'

She thought about that, and nodded.

He took another sip of champagne. 'Oh-kay, so you know what I am, and I know what you are. Where does that leave us? Where do I fit into your plans . . . if at all?'

'As an American newspaperman, you must hold a considerable amount of influence in your own country. In Hungary I learned the hard way that carrying out a bloodless revolution is one thing; maintaining it is another matter altogether. A new government will need the support of other nations. The United States is still a young country, but she is growing fast. Already she is stronger than many people in Europe are prepared to give her credit for.'

'You figure our President Pierce would be ready to go to war in Europe to support a *coup d'état* in Russia?'

'I know there is a great deal of sympathy in the States for Kossuth's cause. The same could be true of the cause here in Russia, if the Americans perceived that the new Russia was to be based on the same principles of your own founding fathers. Were Congress to announce its support for the new regime at an early stage, then war might not be necessary. None of us wants a bloodbath; but if the reactionaries prove harder to dislodge than we hope, that's just what we might have.'

'President Pierce don't always listen to what the *New York Herald* says. Heck – pardon my French, ma'am – but Mr Bennett – that's my editor – he don't often listen to what *I* tell him.'

'You can try, can't you?'

'It'd be my pleasure, ma'am. But there's still one thing you ain't explained to me. If all you wanted was to ask me that, why the charade in the alleyway, with that phoney robbery? Why not just ask me?'

'You think the Third Section would approve of my speaking of such things to a member of the American fourth estate? They have spies everywhere, M'sieur Bryce. It was necessary to make it look as if your coming to this house was entirely innocent.'

He drained his glass and put it down on the table. 'Entirely innocent, huh?'

Smiling, she rose to her feet and slipped her arms around his neck. 'That depends, M'sieur Bryce, on how you feel about mixing business with pleasure.'

He grinned. 'When a feller like me gets to interview a woman as lovely as yourself, ma'am, business *is* a pleasure.'

She kissed him, and he parted his lips to feel her tongue slip between them. He allowed himself to enjoy it at first, but then memories of Araminta flooded into his brain, and he felt suddenly ashamed that he could have forgotten her so quickly, even if only for a few seconds. It was not that he had consciously sworn a private vow of celibacy until he had avenged her. But he did not want to cheapen her memory by jumping into bed with the first attractive woman who made advances towards him. Besides, she thought he was an American journalist; she did not even know his real name. He had never seduced a woman under false pretences, and he was in no hurry to start now.

He felt a wave of dizziness sweep him, and for a moment he thought his old sickness had come back to haunt him, but it passed. *A little too much champagne*, he told himself.

He pushed her away.

'I'm sorry,' she said.

'No,' he said quickly. 'It ain't you. It's me. I . . . I guess I ain't used to having Hungarian countesses . . . I mean to say, I just ain't used to it, that's all.'

She smiled. 'Does my nobility offend your republican sentiments, M'sieur Bryce?'

'Let's just say I ain't used to my interviews going in this particular direction.'

'Interview . . .' she mused. 'I had not thought of it like that. Do you think this has been a satisfactorily penetrating interview, M'sieur Bryce?'

'I don't know. I figure I could go a heap deeper. Depends how much more you've got to reveal.'

She looked up at him, her eyes and moist lips shining in the firelight. 'Surely you want to cover the story properly?'

'Come at it from every conceivable angle, you mean?'

'You should really get to grips with your subject matter.'

Killigrew was starting to feel light-headed. *The devil take it*, he decided. Araminta would have wanted him to get on with his life, to live every moment of it and not waste a single minute. Perhaps a year's mourning was appropriate for some people, but the countess might not be available in seven months' time. Hell, *he* might not be around in seven months' time. Tomorrow he might be in front of a firing squad.

Lips locked together, the two of them sank on to the chaise longue. The next few minutes were spent kissing and caressing, until Killigrew had forgotten all about Araminta. Barely able to contain himself, he struggled with the fastening at the back of the countess's gown, until at last she pushed him back down and stood up, patting her tousled hair back into place.

He looked up at her, wondering if he had done something wrong.

She smiled at him. 'Wait here. I'll be two minutes.' She left the room.

Killigrew braced himself for what he suspected were going to be two of the longest minutes of his life. He clapped a hand to his forehead and blew his cheeks out. He was feeling dizzy . . . damn, that woman could kiss!

He needed to cool off a little, and glanced across to where his empty glass stood on the table next to the bottle in the ice bucket. He stood up, intending to cross the room to refill it, but the room really was spinning round him now. He must have had more to drink than he had realised. He managed to lurch as far as the next armchair, but then his legs crumpled beneath him and he sank to his knees. He tried to focus on the carriage clock on the mantelpiece, and saw two of them.

A couple of glasses of champagne did not do this to him. Even as he felt his own brain turn to mush, some part of him still had sense enough to realise he had been drugged. The hoariest trick in the book, and he had fallen for it like rain falling in a monsoon. Before long he would be helpless, alone in the house of a woman he should have known he could not trust . . .

Soon . . . but not yet. With a supreme effort of will, he managed to force himself to his feet and staggered across to the table where the butler had left the ice bucket. Sober, he would have needed a second or two to brace himself, but with fear joining forces with the drug coursing through his veins now, the imperative to clear his head overruled any hesitation. He doused his face until he could hardly breathe. It helped a little. He picked up the bucket and tipped it over his head, with scant regard for Prince Polyansky's Persian rug. That helped even more. Blinking through the icy water running down from his hairline, he staggered across to the door. It was tricky, as he could see two of them, but after much fumbling he managed to find the right one and get it open.

He stumbled out on to the landing, leaning on to the banister, and managed to grope his way to the top of the stairs. There was no sign of Countess Vásáry, or whoever the deuce she was. All he had to do was get out of the house . . .

He stared down the stairs. They swayed from side to side like a rope bridge across a yawning chasm. He put one foot out, missed the step, and tumbled head over heels to the bottom.

He sprawled on the marble floor for a moment, wondering if he was dead. How many bones had he broken in that fall? The easiest way to find out seemed to be to get up and walk to the door. As ideas went, that one was a non-starter: his limbs would not obey him, his bones, far from being broken, seemed to have turned to India rubber. But by dint of experimentation he managed to crawl on his hands and knees. The unforgiving marble floor hurt his knees, but he liked the pain; it was like a stinging slap to his brain, keeping unconsciousness at bay for a few precious seconds longer.

He was moving . . . but where to? Door, door, get to the door! Got to get *out*! He squinted at the door ahead of him, a few feet away . . . a few feet that looked like a hundred miles. There were three doors now. He squeezed his eyes shut. They were deceiving him, it was best not to trust them.

He knew he was pointed in the right direction. He crawled on until his groping hands reached something cylindrical and rough . . . it felt like an elephant's foot. Not that Killigrew had ever touched an elephant's foot, but he had a pretty clear idea that this was what an elephant's foot felt like. Why in the world was there an elephant in Prince Polyansky's hallway? (Not enough room for it in the pantry, ha ha ha.)

Umbrella stand! And . . . yes . . . there, next to it, an iron doorstop. He must be getting close now. A few more feet, and he banged his head against something. Soft wood after cold plaster . . . the door! He groped for the handle. He could hear a voice in the house behind him now, footsteps thundering down the stairs, just when he was so close to getting outside. He grasped the handle and turned it, but the door would not open. Raging, he tugged on it in vain, but the door was jammed.

Bolt! The countess would have bolted the door. He found the bolt, snicked it, heaved on the doorknob one more time, and it swung inwards until his knees were in the way.

The footsteps were on the floor behind him, getting louder and louder. Somehow he managed to twist his body to one side so he could open the door a couple more feet. The cold night air slapped him in the face, granting him a few more seconds of consciousness. He opened his eyes. It seemed to be very foggy all of a sudden, and the dark street spun around him. He flopped out on to the stone steps, and was aware of shouts, and footsteps pounding up the steps towards him. He felt hands lifting him, more voices . . . talking in Russian? Even if they had spoken English, he would not have understood a word of it. All he was aware of now was . . .

. . . nothing.

Killigrew had never been drugged before, but he had been knocked over the head a few times, so he was not entirely unused to waking up in unfamiliar and potentially dangerous territory. The throbbing in his skull, the churning in his guts, the dry sensation in his mouth as if his tongue had turned to cotton wool and swollen . . . yes, he had been here before.

At first he lay still, keeping his eyes shut – wanting to put off as long as possible the moment when stinging light invaded his aching head – but also straining to listen past the Anvil Chorus in his brain to try to work out if there was anyone else in the room with him. The only sounds were hoofs on cobbles, and someone shouting orders in a foreign language, but both were so muffled that they hardly troubled him.

He lay on something soft too, and a pillow cushioned his head. He moved his arms experimentally, as if stirring in his sleep, and was surprised to find they were not bound behind his back. Given how

163

foolish he had been in gulping down the countess's champagne like that, he knew he could count himself lucky to be waking up at all.

The moment could not be put off any longer. He opened his eyes. There was a slight twinge, but nothing a glass of Dr James's Powders – or whatever the Russian equivalent was – would not cure. He opened his eyes wider and found himself staring across a dimly lit room towards some plush velvet curtains.

He lay in a four-poster bed. When he thought of some of the rude awakenings he had suffered over the years, this one could only be described as the epitome of courtesy. Wherever he was, it was not a cell in the dungeons of the Kochubey Mansion: that was some consolation. All that was lacking was for a dulcet-toned flunkey to enter bearing a bowl of scented rosewater and to murmur that the sun awaited his pleasure.

But the dulcet-toned flunkey did not seem to be in any hurry. Killigrew, on the other hand, knew he was running out of time to find the *Sea Devil*, if time had not run out already. It was bad enough to be working to a deadline at the end of which hundreds of sailors might die, worse when he had no clue when that deadline was due. But one thing he did know: he did not have time to be lying in bed all morning.

He eased himself up into sitting position and pressed a palm to his forehead with a low groan. After a few moments the pain subsided sufficiently for him to find the strength to swing his legs out of bed so that his bare feet touched the rug. He fumbled for his fob watch, but it was not there. In fact, neither was his fob pocket, or the rest of the waistcoat, or any of the clothes he had been wearing. Now he was dressed in a cotton nightshirt: not his own, yet a good enough fit that it might have been bought for him.

Using one of the bedposts for support, he pulled himself on to his feet. His most pressing concern was for a chamber pot, and he found one under the bed. Having used it, he made his way groggily to the window, drawing aside the curtains to let sunlight flood into the room, making him wince. The barred window looked out over a courtyard in the middle of the building where he could see some men loading barrels into a dray-cart several floors below. There was no getting out that way, and no shouting for help either; although, if the room had looked out on to one of St Petersburg's streets, he would have been forced to reserve judgement on the advisability of that course of action, given some of the questions he might have been expected to answer if such cries had, by some miracle, brought help from the local gendarmerie.

He tested the bars anyway, largely as a reflex action. They were solid. Still, stone walls did not a prison make, nor iron bars a cage. He was about to try the door when he heard footsteps outside, and a moment later the door opened for him. Or rather, for a pretty blonde maid who had brought him a glass of something effervescent. On reflection, she was more welcome than a dulcet-toned flunkey with a bowl of rosewater; only the burly ruffian who stood on guard in the doorway while she was in the room marred the moment. He wore the black frock-coat and black-and-yellow-striped waistcoat of a butler, but he had the cauliflower ears and scarred knuckles of a pugilist.

'*Vvpeite*,' the maid urged him, smiling.

'What is it?' he asked her, remembering to use his Yankee accent. 'Dr Jamesky's Powders, or just good old-fashioned hemlock?'

She just smiled at him, not understanding.

Reasoning that if his captors wanted him dead, they would simply have poisoned him rather than go to the trouble of drugging him, bringing him here, taking his evening clothes off and dressing him in a nightshirt first, he took a tentative sip of the liquid. It certainly tasted as foul as Dr James's Powders. Best to knock it back in one go, he told himself; the craving to replenish the fluids in his dehydrated body would not be denied.

He gasped once it was all down, and put the empty glass back on the tray. She retreated, still smiling, and the burly ruffian motioned with a pistol for him to come out of the bedroom. Killigrew did not bother to ask where he was, or who his hosts were: doubtless he would be taken to learn for himself presently. Besides, the ruffian did not strike him as the chatty type.

Killigrew gestured at the nightshirt. 'Shouldn't I get dressed first?'

The ruffian shook his head, and gestured with the pistol again.

Killigrew stepped out of the bedroom, and the ruffian motioned for him to precede him. He padded barefoot along the carpeted corridor. It was another grand house, as far as he could tell; or an unfamiliar part of one of the grand houses he had already visited.

The ruffian gestured to a door. Killigrew opened it and stepped into a small, bare room with a tiled floor and a wooden bench with clothes piled on it.

'*Razden'te*!' ordered the ruffian.

165

Killigrew searched his groggy mind to remember what that meant, and was shocked when it came to him. 'Now hold your hosses, pardner! I ain't getting undressed in front of you—'

The ruffian pulled back the hammer of the pistol and levelled it at his head. '*Razden'te!*'

'Oh-kay, oh-kay!' Killigrew conceded. 'But no funny stuff, understand?' He pulled the nightshirt off over his head and stood there with his hands on his hips.

The ruffian gestured through the other door.

Killigrew opened it. A cloud of hot, dry steam hit him in the face.

'Well, don't just stand there with the door open!' a half-remembered voice called to him – in English, but with a Scots burr. 'You're letting the steam out!'

Killigrew closed the door behind him and peered through the mist to see Mscislaw Wojtkiewicz sitting in the middle of some tiered wooden benches. He was as naked as Killigrew. So was the blonde woman who sat behind him, her thighs straddling his hips as she massaged his shoulders. Her physique was . . . well, suffice to say that, given how vulnerable his modesty was at that moment, he was grateful that Wojtkiewicz's torso concealed the more distracting parts of her anatomy from him.

'Sit down, Mr Bryce.' Wojtkiewicz gestured to the benches opposite. 'If that is your real name, which I very much doubt. Oh, you can speak freely: Jadwiga here doesn't speak a word of English.'

'May I compliment you on yours?'

'When I was four years old, I watched as my parents were slaughtered by Cossacks when the Russians put down the Polish insurrection. After that I was adopted by a Scottish merchant who had known my parents well. I was raised in Edinburgh until I was fifteen.'

'That explains the slight accent.'

'Aye, people often wonder about that.'

'You're a very trusting man, if I may say so, Mr Wojtkiewicz,' said Killigrew.

'What makes you say that?'

'You don't know me – and I know you don't trust me – yet you're prepared to sit in here with me, naked and unarmed.'

'As are you. That's why I like to do business in my steam bath: no concealed weapons.'

'Yes, but . . . I do have the advantage of youth on my side.'

'You think so?' Wojtkiewicz grinned. 'You're welcome to try to kill

166

me, if that's why you're here. I'll pit my age and experience against your youth any day of the week.'

Looking at the Pole's body – in the presence of the blonde lovely massaging him, it helped to avert any embarrassing tumescence on Killigrew's part – he could well believe it. Wojtkiewicz was in good shape for a man of his years. The most recent Polish insurrection Killigrew knew of had been a quarter of a century ago; if Wojtkiewicz had been four at the time, it would have made him even younger than Killigrew. More likely the Pole was referring to the insurrection of 1794, which would have made him sixty-five now; but he had the body of a forty-year-old, and a fairly fit forty-year-old at that.

'I'd rather not,' he told Wojtkiewicz. 'It's far too early in the morning to be killing anyone.'

'And I thought the British always attacked at dawn?'

'I'm an American,' Killigrew reminded him.

Wojtkiewicz grinned. 'Yes, I must compliment you on your Yankee accent. Most Englishmen trying to pass themselves off as Americans try for a nondescript transatlantic twang, but I'd say you've got the New England accent off pat.'

'I should do: I was raised there.'

'And I'm Richard the Lionheart!' snorted Wojtkiewicz. 'Stand up and turn to face the wall. Well, go on, man! What, you think I'm going to creep up behind you and hit you?'

'The thought had occurred to me.'

'Relax, boy. If I wanted you dead, you'd be at the bottom of the Neva already.'

Killigrew stood up and turned to face the wall.

'Uh-huh,' said Wojtkiewicz, and Jadwiga asked something in Polish, giggling.

Killigrew turned back to face them. 'Seen everything you want to see?'

'More than enough. Jadwiga here wants to know how you got those five parallel scars on your shoulder blade. Souvenir of a jealous woman?'

'Yes . . . but I haven't turned my back on one since.'

'I seem to have heard that one somewhere before,' Wojtkiewicz said drily. 'If you got those scars from a jealous lover, my advice is to stop sleeping with polar bears and stick to women in future, Commander Killigrew.'

When Killigrew opened his mouth to protest, Wojtkiewicz raised a hand to silence him. 'Don't insult my intelligence by denying it. I've got a complete set of the *Illustrated London News* downstairs, and one of them has a good likeness of you in it. You'd better hope the Third Section doesn't have a copy of the same edition. They don't take kindly to British spies.'

In a way, Killigrew was relieved. And at least he could drop the accent.

'Naval officer, Arctic explorer, and now a spy,' mused Wojtkiewicz. 'You're a man of many parts, Mr Killigrew.'

'Jack of all trades, master of none. So now what? You're going to turn me in?'

'Don't think I'm not tempted. I know Count Orloff regards me with suspicion. In fact, the only reason he hasn't had me in the cellars of the Kochubey Mansion already is that some of my business contacts are . . . shall we say, useful to him? If I were to give him a British spy, it might allay some of his suspicions.'

'Then why don't you?'

'My sons. One of them killed fighting in Chechnya, one executed for refusing to fight against the Hungarians, and the third murdered by his fellow soldiers in an act of senseless, drunken brutality. Then there's the small matter of the years I spent in a Siberian salt mine after the second insurrection, and the wife I buried out there. I have no reason to love the Russians.' He grinned again. 'Besides, you still owe me eight hundred roubles, Mr Killigrew, and I have every intention of collecting. "Go Johnny Go-Go-Go-Go" indeed!'

Killigrew coughed awkwardly: that was a subject he preferred to skirt around, for now.

'Come on,' said Wojtkiewicz. 'I think we've broiled long enough.'

They left the sauna and entered the next room, where they were able to continue talking while dousing themselves in a couple of shower baths that stood side by side, working the pedals up and down with their feet to keep the stinging cold water squirting over their heads.

'For a man who doesn't like the Russians, Mr Wojtkiewicz, you have an interesting choice of address.'

'You think I should live in Poland? There is no Poland, Mr Killigrew. It was torn apart by the Russians and the Prussians. These days, a Pole is safer living in St Petersburg than he is in Warsaw.'

'You mean, it's easier for a Tsar to order brutality against his own subject peoples in towns and cities that are hundreds – if not thousands – of miles away.'

Wojtkiewicz nodded. 'They don't like to see it on their own doorstep: it reminds them of what they really are. Besides, I'm a businessman, and in a country as backwards as Russia – where the telegraph lines are still optical, and there are only two railway lines – a good businessman needs to be close to the seat of government. For now, my country is ruled from St Petersburg. But mark my words, Mr Killigrew: Poland will rise again.'

'Easier to undermine the tsarist government from the heart of the empire, you mean? No wonder you make common cause with the Countess Vásáry.'

Wojtkiewicz stopped pumping for a moment to stare at him, and then laughed. 'You think I'd trust that slippery bitch any further than I could throw her?'

'You didn't have any qualms about using her to trap me.'

'Using her to trap you? You *idiot*!' Wojtkiewicz started pumping again. 'That drugged champagne you drank was meant for her, not you! My men work quickly, but you don't think they could have drugged a bottle of champagne and broken into Prince Polyansky's house to plant it there in the fifteen minutes between you leaving the faro table and arriving at the house with the countess?'

Killigrew shrugged.

'No,' continued Wojtkiewicz. 'Capturing you was ... well, it was something I meant to do anyhow. But I knew I'd catch up with you sooner or later. St Petersburg is a small city, and I have friends in all kinds of interesting places. But it was the so-called countess I was after ... and thanks to you, she was able to escape! I suppose she told you that fairy tale about how she used to be an actress in Budapest? How she married a Magyar nobleman who fought for Kossuth's Hungarian Republic before being executed by the Austrians? That she's come to St Petersburg to make common cause with the surviving members of the liberal aristocracy?'

'She did mention something of that,' Killigrew admitted cautiously, reluctant to admit he had been completely taken in.

'I have contacts in Budapest who were kind enough to make some enquiries for me shortly after the countess turned up here. No one there has ever heard of a Count Vásáry. And I also know some of the liberal aristocrats who are trying to ensure Tsar Alexander follows a programme of reform. It's true this so-called countess has approached a few of them, but fortunately they were wise enough not to trust her. She's certainly not a member of their inner circle, if that's what you think.'

They stepped out of their shower baths and a couple of flunkeys stepped forward to pass them warm towels. After they had dried off, Killigrew followed Wojtkiewicz into the next room, where he found his evening clothes had been laundered, pressed and laid out for him.

'If she's *not* the Countess Vásáry,' Killigrew mused as they got dressed, 'and she's not working for you . . . then who *is* she, and – more to the point – who is she working for?'

'That's what I'd like to know,' growled Wojtkiewicz. 'And I might know by now, if it hadn't been for your blundering!'

Combing his hair in front of the mirror over the washstand, Killigrew flushed.

'My guess is she's an *agent provocateur*, working for the Third Section,' continued Wojtkiewicz, tying his bootlaces. 'It's lucky for you that you woke up at my house, rather than in the dungeons of the Kochubey Mansion! Does she know you're a British spy?'

Killigrew shook his head. 'No, I thought it best to keep that from her.'

'That's something, at least.'

They left the dressing room, and Wojtkiewicz led the way to his library, gesturing to a plush leather armchair in front of his desk. 'Sit down, Mr Killigrew.' He took a bottle of vodka from a desk drawer and a couple of tumblers, pouring them each a measure before sitting on the edge of his desk to hand one of the glasses to Killigrew. 'My own label,' he explained.

'It's a little early in the day for me . . .'

'Sun not over the foreyard, you mean? Drink, Mr Killigrew! You look as though you could do with the hair of the dog, as you say in your country. Down the hatch!'

'*Na zdrowie!*' responded Killigrew; it was the only Polish he knew. He knocked the contents of his glass back in one and it brought tears to his eyes. 'Whew!'

Wojtkiewicz laughed. 'That's real Polish vodka, Mr Killigrew: none of the imitation filth the Russians are starting to make for themselves.' He gestured vaguely with his tumbler. 'When I was a boy, distilling vodka was what you'd call a cottage industry: my father used to keep a still in the cellar. Nowadays everything must be . . . *manufactured*. All Polish vodka comes from a few large distilleries. When I had served my time in the Siberian salt mines, I had to operate on the same scale if I was to be able to compete. Now my ships export vodka all over the world.'

'Just vodka?'

Wojtkiewicz smiled. 'Amongst other things. I'm not what you'd call an educated man, Mr Killigrew . . .'

Killigrew gestured around the luxuriously appointed library. There were titles in English, French, German, Russian, and some other languages Killigrew did not recognise. The books looked tarnished enough to have been actually read, rather than simply bought for show. 'It doesn't seem to have done you any harm.'

'Self-educated, perhaps . . . I left school when I was thirteen and tried my hand at a number of different jobs: milkman, bricklayer, even a coffin polisher! For a time I served as a powder monkey in your Royal Navy, but when I was fourteen I lied about my age to join Napoleon's Polish Legion. I always was a big lad.'

'You served at Austerlitz?'

'Aye; and in the invasion of Russia, and the retreat from Moscow. After the Congress of Vienna partitioned Poland, I settled in Warsaw and with a few friends I was able to raise enough capital to build my first distillery. I would have been about the same age you are now when I got married. Ten years later came the second Polish insurrection. I should have known better, but I allowed myself to be drawn into the fighting, to think that finally Poland had a chance to establish itself as an independent country.'

'The Russians exiled you to Siberia.'

Wojtkiewicz nodded. 'When I returned, my sons were conscripted into the army and I resolved to be a loyal subject of the tsar. I started to rebuild my distilling company into what it is today. But as the years went by and I lost one son after another in pointless little wars on the fringes of the Russian Empire, I had to face what I had known in my heart all along: there can be no compromise with despotism. So! Now you know all about me.'

'Perhaps not everything,' Killigrew said with a smile. 'But enough to be going on with.'

'And now, will you tell me what it is that brings a British spy to St Petersburg?'

'Perhaps the less you know, the better.'

Wojtkiewicz laughed. 'That is good! You should not trust me; or anyone else in St Petersburg. Nor should I trust you. You too could be an *agent provocateur*.'

'As could you.'

'As could we both.'

Killigrew laughed. 'That would be embarrassing, wouldn't it? If we both hauled one another into the Kochubey Mansion, each claiming to have caught a dangerous dissident?'

'Aye! We might even end up provoking each other into carrying out some act of sabotage against the state!'

Killigrew shook his head ruefully. 'How do you live in a country like this? The injustice, the repression, the need for constant paranoia just to stay alive?'

'I understand how strange it must seem to you. But you get used to it. After you have lived in Russia for a few years, suspicion and double-dealing come as second nature. It would have been wiser for your masters to send someone raised here in Russia in your place. How long have you been in St Petersburg? Twenty-four hours?'

'Less.'

'I'm amazed you've survived this long.' Wojtkiewicz drained the last of his vodka, and sat down behind the desk. He took a box from one of the drawers of his desk and handed it to Killigrew. 'Your things.'

Opening the box, Killigrew found it contained his revolver, pocket book, watch, cheroot case, matches and loose change. He began tucking it all back in his various pockets.

'Let's get down to business,' said Wojtkiewicz. 'What can Mscislaw Wojtkiewicz do for a British spy?'

'I'm looking for a man named Wilhelm Bauer, a Bavarian engineer.'

Wojtkiewicz frowned. 'I don't know the name. I'll make some discreet enquiries on your behalf, but I can't make any promises. There's no shortage of Germans living and working in St Petersburg.'

'He's tall, aged about thirty-three, with dark hair and a moustache.'

'I'm honoured with the acquaintance of another German engineer, Professor Moritz Jacobi, who designed the infernal machines. If anyone is likely to know the whereabouts of this man Bauer, it's Jacobi. Where are you staying?'

'Dussot's.'

'Good. I'll try not to contact you there unless I have to. There's a *salon de thé* in the arcade at number forty-eight, Nevsky Prospect. Take tea there at four o'clock each day; if I have news, that's where I'll get word to you. Is there anything else I can do for you?'

'Yes. While I'm in St Petersburg, it would be a shame not to see the Mariinsky Ballet Company perform. Do you think you could get me a ticket to their latest production?'

Wojtkiewicz nodded. 'That shouldn't present any difficulties.

Ah . . . you do know where they've been performing since the Bolshoi-Petrovsky burned down, don't you?'

Killigrew shook his head.

'The Imperial Theatre. You know – in the Winter Palace?'

'The Winter Palace?' Killigrew swallowed, then gave a shrug: even if the Imperial family was in attendance the night he went to the ballet, it was hardly likely that any of them would recognise him. 'Ah, well, *"Vestigia retrorsum nulla"*!'

'Eh?'

'Horace: "No footprints backwards." From the lion's den, that is.'

# XI

## A Night at the Ballet

---

Killigrew returned to his hotel to find Tweedledum and Tweedledee waiting for him. Their relief was evident as they pretended to ignore him. He made his way up to his room, where the dislodged hair on the wardrobe door and the smudged powder on the catches of his holdall brought a smile to his lips. After changing into less formal day-wear, he made his way down to the dining room for a hearty dinner.

That afternoon he went to the Admiralty where, in his guise as an American journalist, he tried to get an interview with Admiral Rykord: not that he expected Rykord to tell him where he could find Bauer, but if he was going to convince the Third Section he was just an American reporter going about his business, he had to do something journalistic; and there was always the slim hope that Rykord would let something of interest slip. In the event, an official kept him waiting for two hours before telling him that the admiral was too busy to receive him, but if he left his card, it would be passed on.

He returned to the Nevsky Prospect at a quarter to four and found the arcade containing the *salon de thé* Wojtkiewicz had told him about. Reminiscent of the shopping arcades Killigrew had seen in Paris, the arcade itself was almost two hundred yards long, well lit by daylight flooding through a double-glazed atrium high overhead. Milliners, tailors, upholsterers, corsetières, haberdashers and countless other upmarket shops ranged down both sides. There were three restaurants, as well as pastry shops and cafés. In the *salon de thé* elegant samovars steamed on the marble counter. He sat down at one of the tables and ordered a pot of coffee from a waiter. Tweedledum sat down at one of the other tables and pretended to read a newspaper. The waiter had just brought Killigrew his coffee when a man approached his table and said something in Russian. The commander looked up and saw Jedraszczyk, Wojtkiewicz's secretary, standing over him.

Killigrew was careful not to let any recognition show on his face. '*Parlez-vous français?* I'm afraid my Russian's not too good.'

'Do you mind if I share your table, *m'sieur*?'

'By all means.'

'Thank you.' Jedraszczyk sat down, but said nothing more, engaging his attention in his own newspaper, the St Petersburg *Senatskiye Vedomosti*. When he got up to leave, however, he left the newspaper behind. Killigrew drank another cup of coffee before departing, picking up the newspaper on the way out.

When he returned to his hotel, a couple of gendarmes were waiting for him. 'M'sieur Bryce?'

'Yes?'

'Would you come with us, please?'

'Where are we going?'

'Superintendent Voronin wishes to speak with you.'

'Superintendent Voronin?'

'Our superior. It is purely a formality. Please come. Superintendent Voronin does not like to be kept waiting.'

'Do I have any choice?'

'It is purely a formality.'

*The devil it is*, Killigrew thought sourly as he accompanied the gendarmes outside, hoping they could not hear the thunderous pounding of his heart. His hands were wet with sweat where they gripped the newspaper. He made an effort to stay calm: in a country like Russia, perhaps being hauled in to be interrogated by a captain of the gendarmerie *was* a formality. And the gendarmes wore the black uniforms of the regular police rather than the sky blue of the Third Section. But then, perhaps the Third Section police sometimes wore the black uniforms from time to time to lull their victims into a false sense of security.

To Killigrew's relief, there was no closed *telezhka* waiting outside: that suggested they were not going far. The superintendent's bureau was in a tenement block otherwise occupied by private apartments, up four narrow flights of stairs, which saw an unceasing traffic of people of all classes who had police business: summonses, complaints against neighbours, complaints against shopkeepers, bad debts ...

Killigrew was willing to lay odds he was the only spy there that afternoon.

At the top of the stairs he was escorted by the two gendarmes through a succession of small, low-ceilinged annexes where crowds of people – in those rooms, four or five people became a crowd – waited to see the superintendent. Some of the commoner ones made comments as he was led past. Killigrew was getting so used to hearing Russian spoken, he was amazed by how easily he understood them without having to strain, or their speaking slowly and clearly for his benefit.

'Who's he, that gets to jump the queue?'

'Foreigner by the look of him.'

'Typical! Foreigners go straight through, while decent, law-abiding subjects of the Tsar are made to wait!'

'If you are law-abiding, Dusya Ivanovich, then I'm the King of England!' one of the gendarmes retorted good-naturedly.

'I heard that! That's slander, that is! Ooh, the shame of it!'

The gendarme knocked on the door to the next room. 'Come in!' a voice barked from the other side.

*This is it*, thought Killigrew. *Stay calm. Remember: you're an American journalist working for the* New York Herald. *You're a citizen of the United States and you've not done anything wrong. Kit Killigrew? Never heard of him. You can do this: you've been posing as an officer and a gentleman for the past seventeen years, so the imposture of a Yankee reporter shouldn't give you any trouble.*

The gendarme opened the door to reveal a spud-faced man with bags under his eyes in a plain frock-coat seated behind a desk, while an inky-fingered clerk stood to attention before him.

'The American journalist, sir,' said the gendarme.

The spud-faced man glanced at Killigrew, and nodded. Picking up a file from his desk, he handed it to the clerk. 'We will discuss this further tomorrow.'

'Yes, sir.' The clerk bustled from the room with the file.

'Come in, come in.' The spud-faced man motioned Killigrew through the door, and the gendarme closed it behind him, leaving the two of them alone. That was a good sign, Killigrew told himself.

The spud-faced man rose to his feet and offered Killigrew his hand. The commander was glad he was wearing kid-gloves: it disguised how damp his palms were.

'Superintendent Porfiry Petrovich Voronin,' the spud-faced man

176

introduced himself. He sat down, gesturing to the chair on the other side of the desk.

Killigrew hitched up the knees of his trousers and lowered himself into the chair. The furniture in the cramped office was not only old enough to have dated back to the Great War with France, but looked as though it had been involved in some of the fighting. He removed his wideawake and dropped it on to one knee.

'Forgive the summary way in which you were brought here,' said Voronin. 'I know it is not the way you do things in America, but . . .' He smiled. 'I'm sure you know we have our own customs here in Russia.'

There was too much intelligence in those eyes for Voronin to be an ordinary copper, Killigrew thought to himself. This man was Third Section.

'I must ask you some questions,' said Voronin. 'Purely a formality, you understand.'

'So the gendarmes who brought me here kept insisting,' said Killigrew. 'Let's get straight to the point, Superintendent. Am I here on any charge? Am I guilty of some crime?'

'Are you?' There was a mocking tone in Voronin's voice. 'You tell me.'

Yes, there was no doubt in Killigrew's mind: Third Section. He told himself that was nothing to worry about. Even if his claim to be an American journalist was still believed, they would nevertheless send a Third Section officer to interview any foreigner.

Voronin smiled, and gestured to the notes on the sheet in front of him. 'I must ask you questions. The sooner you answer them, the sooner you can be on your way and about your business. May I see your passport?' He held out his hand.

'The *concierge* at the hotel took my passport. I understood that was the way you did things here?'

'Sorry; a case of the left hand not being told what the right hand is doing. Your name is Bryce?'

'John Bryce, yes.'

'You are a citizen of the United States?'

'You know I am.'

'And your profession is that of journalist. Place of birth?'

'New Bedford. That's in Massachusetts.'

'Age?'

'Thirty.'

'And your current place of residence?'

'New York City. When I'm not working abroad, which is most of the time.'

'For which newspaper do you write, M'sieur Bryce?'

'The *New York Herald*.' *This is it*, thought Killigrew. *This is where it turns out there's another reporter from the* New York Herald *in St Petersburg, who's already been interviewed and was rather shocked to hear that another journalist he'd never heard of was claiming to be the St Petersburg correspondent.*

But Voronin merely made a note of it on the sheet in front of him.

'What brings you to St Petersburg?'

'I'm trying to cover the war from the Russian point of view.'

'Do you have an opinion about the war?'

'No.'

Voronin looked up at him in surprise. 'Surely you must have some opinion?'

'I have lots of opinions. What do you mean? Do I think it's justified? Do I think it's being fought well? Who do I think will win? Define "justified". Define "fought well". It's all a matter of point of view. I'm a reporter, Superintendent. My business is facts, not opinions.'

Voronin pursed his lips and nodded approvingly. 'I only wish all journalists shared your attitude, M'sieur Bryce. When will you be leaving Russia?'

'I hadn't decided yet. It all depends upon which way the war goes. Could be I'm here for the duration. Why? Are you in a hurry to see the back of me?'

Voronin smiled. 'No.'

'I'll be frank with you, Superintendent. My editor sent me here in case the British attack St Petersburg. That's not his opinion of what *will* happen; he's sent one of my colleagues to England in case you attack London.'

Voronin checked his notes. 'You arrived in St Petersburg yesterday.'

'That's right.'

'And last night you went to Mscislaw Wojtkiewicz's house on the Angliiskaya Embankment.'

'Sure.' There was no point in denying it: Count Orloff himself had seen him there.

'How do you know M'sieur Wojtkiewicz?'

'I don't. At least, I didn't; until last night.'

'Then what took you to his house?'

'I like gambling. That isn't a crime in Russia, is it?'

178

Voronin shook his head. 'But I am curious enough to know how you found your way to Wojtkiewicz's house so swiftly. He does not, shall we say, advertise?'

'That omission doesn't seem to do his trade any harm.'

'Tee-hee! No, indeed! But you must confess, it was fast work on your part to surmount that obstacle. I suppose you asked the *concierge* at your hotel where you could ... what do you Americans call it, "bucking the tiger"?'

It was clumsily done; perhaps this fellow was not so bright after all. But this was not the time to start underestimating him. 'No, as a matter of fact a colleague of mine in New York told me before I left. I knew he'd worked in St Petersburg in the past, I wanted to know what he could tell me about Russian customs, things I should be aware of. He works for a rival paper, but in our profession we like to help one another – until one of us gets the scent of a scoop. Then it's every man for himself.'

'And he told you about Wojtkiewicz's house?'

'That's right.'

'Have you ever met the Countess Vásáry?'

Killigrew frowned. 'The name rings a bell ... wait a minute, there was an aristocratic lady at Wojtkiewicz's house, she had a foreign name or something. I think she said she was the Countess Vásáry. Or something like that. Come to think of it, she was the one who introduced me to Wojtkiewicz.'

'Have you seen her since?'

Killigrew knew the art of lying lay in sticking as closely as possible to the truth, especially about things that could easily be checked on; once you started to embellish, you laid yourself open to all sorts of traps. But he could not tell Voronin about how he had 'rescued' the 'countess' later that night, because then he would have to explain why he had gone to Prince Polyansky's house, how he had been drugged, and how he had woken up back at Wojtkiewicz's house. It was a risk, nevertheless. Suppose the 'countess' was really an *agent provocateur* for the Third Section? They might be asking about her to lull him into thinking that she was not one of them; all he had to do was get caught lying about one little thing, and the whole imposture would collapse around him like a house of cards. Even if the 'countess' was not working for the Third Section, what about the man she had hired to 'attack' her? Could he have talked to the wrong people?

He realised he had hesitated too long before answering; Voronin was bound to have noticed.

'No,' he said. That was true enough: Voronin had asked if he had seen her since, which implied: 'since that night'. Besides, if they told him they knew he had gone back to Polyansky's house, he could always claim he had lied to protect her reputation. He was just an innocent American journalist: how was he to know she did not have a reputation worth defending?

Voronin made a brief note. Apparently he had not noticed Killigrew's hesitation. But perhaps he was a good actor too?

The superintendent put down his pen. 'Fine. Well, I do not think I need to keep you any longer.'

Killigrew struggled to keep the surprise out of his voice. 'You . . . does that mean I can go?'

'Certainly. Of course, I may call you back for further questioning. But for now, you are free to go.' He rose to his feet, and Killigrew did likewise. The two of them shook hands.

'I hope I've been of some help, although I can't imagine how,' said Killigrew.

Voronin smiled. 'Well, let us just say you have been very patient and co-operative, and leave it at that, shall we?'

Killigrew put his hat back on, turned to the door, laid his hand on the knob—

'Oh, just one other thing . . .' said Voronin.

Killigrew's heart lurched in his throat. Struggling to control his breathing, he turned back to face the superintendent.

Voronin was hunched over the papers on his desk, scribbling away furiously. 'You did not give me the name of your colleague in America who told you about Wojtkiewicz's house,' he said without looking up.

'No, I didn't.'

Voronin looked up at him quizzically.

'A good journalist always protects his sources.'

'Meaning?'

'I like to play faro. My colleague . . . well, I'm sure you know gaming isn't the only entertainment provided at Wojtkiewicz's house. And my colleague is a married man.'

'Fair enough. Goodbye, Mr Killigrew.'

For a split second, Killigrew thought he was going to have a stroke. There was no time to draw breath . . .

'I beg your pardon?'

. . . this was a test, the oldest one in the book, and the speed of Killigrew's reaction was as crucial as the reaction itself.

Voronin looked up at him innocently. 'Sorry?'

Killigrew's expression was equally innocent. 'I thought you called me . . . what was it, "Killigrew"?'

Voronin smiled. He even looked relieved. 'Sorry. My mind is on other things. Goodbye, M'sieur Bryce.'

'Superintendent.' Killigrew tipped his hat and left the office.

On the other side of the door, he resisted the temptation to lean back against it, sobbing for breath. He was not out of the lion's den yet, and for all the clerk at the desk outside was hunched over his desk, Killigrew knew he would be watching him out of the corner of his eye. Briskly but unhurriedly, he squeezed out through the succession of crowded rooms and began to descend the stairs, his heart and mind racing.

Killigrew. Voronin had called him Killigrew.

They *knew*.

No. If they knew, they would have arrested him by now. They *suspected*, but they did not *know*.

Still, it was enough of a shock that they suspected: the only thing keeping them from arresting him was the thought that he might really be who he claimed to be, and the last thing their Foreign Office wanted at the moment was the United States consul hammering on the door.

Or perhaps they were just trying to lull him into a false sense of security, get him to think they were only letting him go. Perhaps a closed *telezhka* waited on the street outside, to whip him off to the cellars of the Kochubey Mansion for the real interrogation.

Killigrew's legs felt watery: he was having trouble negotiating the stairs. *Stay calm*, he told himself. *Your name's John Bryce, you're an American citizen, and you haven't done anything wrong. Funny the way that superintendent called you by the wrong name as you were leaving. What was the name? You've forgotten already.*

But the blood still pounded in his ears.

He stepped outside into the bright sunlight. There was no *telezhka* waiting for him, only Tweedledum and Tweedledee on the other side of the street, pretending to read newspapers as they sat astride their drozhky. Killigrew remembered he was still holding the newspaper Jedraszczyk had given him. Was there a message hidden inside? Jesus, suppose Voronin had thought to examine it? But he had not.

Killigrew tucked the folded newspaper under one arm. What he needed was a cheroot to calm his nerves. He had taken his cheroot case

181

out and had almost put one in his mouth when he remembered the ridiculous public ordinance forbidding smoking on the streets. He tucked the case out of sight and was about to start walking when he realised he had no idea where in St Petersburg he was. He had been so worried about his imminent interview on the way there, it had not occurred to him to keep track of the route the gendarmes had taken to bring him here.

He took a deep breath. He had got away with it . . . so far. That was all that mattered. 'Goodbye, Mr Killigrew' – Jesus, did the bastards really think he'd fall for that one? He was tempted to walk straight across the street, right up to Tweedledum and Tweedledee, watch them squirm as he asked for directions back to his hotel. But that was exactly what Kit Killigrew would have done; he was just an American journalist. Now was not the time to get overconfident. Looking about, he saw a broad, busy thoroughfare at the end of the street, and headed towards it. It proved to be the Nevsky Prospect, and from there he had no trouble finding his way back to the hotel.

He stopped in the bathroom on the third floor and vomited into one of the earth closets. He wiped his mouth on a fistful of oakum, went to his room and gargled with whisky to take away the taste of bile, tap water in this city being just about the easiest way for a man to die of cholera.

He sat down on the edge of the bed, lit a cheroot with trembling fingers, and lay back with his head on the pillow to smoke it. By the time he stubbed it out in the ashtray, his heartbeat was approaching normal.

He sat up and opened the newspaper Jedraszczyk had given him. A pasteboard card fell out on to the floor. He stooped and picked it up, turning it over in his hands. It was a ticket to the ballet *The Star of Granada*, to be performed at the theatre in the Winter Palace that night.

'I wonder what would happen,' Killigrew murmured, 'if I were to draw my revolver and empty it into the Tsar's chest?'

Wojtkiewicz looked at him. 'Don't tell me you brought your revolver!' he hissed incredulously.

'No well-dressed man about town should be without one.'

Wojtkiewicz glanced across to where the young Tsar sat between his brother and the Tsarina. 'Well, you'd almost certainly kill him at this range. But I doubt you'd make your escape. If one of the cuirassiers didn't cut you down at once, they'd put you in the Petropavlovsky

Fortress and execute you at the first opportunity. The Third Section would torture you into admitting you were a British agent, your government would be embarrassed, and the war would go on exactly the same as before. In fact, I'd say there'd be even less chance of an early peace than if you let him live.'

'If I thought it would stop the war,' said Killigrew, 'I'd've pulled the trigger already.'

Wojtkiewicz gave him a sidelong glance. 'You would have done too, wouldn't you?' He shook his head in disbelief.

Killigrew raised his opera glasses to his eyes and gazed across the semi-circular neoclassical auditorium of the Imperial Theatre. The walls and columns were decorated with imitation marble, and statues of the nine Muses stood in niches, with bas-relief portraits of famous musicians and poets above them. The huge chandelier overhead was dimmed, most of the illumination in the auditorium coming from the limelight focused on the stage.

Military fashions were all the rage in St Petersburg that year, if the largely aristocratic audience was anything to go by. The young Tsar wore enough gold braid to rig an entire fleet of ships, and his brother – the Grand Duke Konstantin – wore the uniform of the admiral-general of the Imperial Russian Navy. The militarist theme was continued by the white-uniformed cuirassiers of the Imperial bodyguard, ranged around the outside of the auditorium, in case some madman took it into his head to make an attempt on the Tsar's life.

Count Orloff was there, in the sky-blue uniform of the Third Section. There was no sign of Colonel Nekrasoff, Killigrew noted with relief: the last thing he needed was to be recognised tonight as an officer of the Royal Navy. Besides, it was just as well: if Nekrasoff had been there – and if he had not spotted and recognised Killigrew before the final curtain – the commander would almost certainly have forgotten about his mission in order to trail and assassinate the colonel. There was a score to be settled there, and Killigrew would have no qualms about snuffing Nekrasoff's life out in cold blood.

There were members of the upper middling sort present in the audience too, although few of them wore evening clothes or had their stovepipe hats and gloves resting on their laps as Killigrew did: there was no shortage of sinecures in the Russian bureaucracy, and each one of them entitled the holder to wear a uniform, amongst other privileges.

He turned his attention back to the stage as the *corps de ballet* danced off and Anzhelika Orlova danced on for the *pas de deux* with

Marius Petipa, the Mariinsky Theatre Company's new *premier danseur*. Mademoiselle Orlova was in her late twenties, a petite, graceful young woman with a rosebud mouth, dark hair pulled back in a chignon and wide, dark eyes contrasting with the porcelain-doll complexion of her heart-shaped face: undoubtedly beautiful, yet with an air of the gamine about her that added to her elfin, fairy-like loveliness. Her costume consisted of an off-the-shoulder bodice and a gauzy skirt through which Killigrew could clearly see her legs all the way up to her slender hips, covered only by white, gauzy tights.

'You're sure your plan's going to work?' asked Wojtkiewicz.

'It can't fail,' Killigrew told him. 'I used it in Liverpool eight years ago to inveigle myself with the master of a slave ship. It's the same trick the Countess Vásáry tried to use to inveigle herself with me last night, except that where she took the role of damsel in distress, I take the role of the knight in shining armour.'

Wojtkiewicz gave him another sidelong glance. 'Knight in evening clothes, at any rate. You saw through the countess's act easily enough. What makes you think Mam'selle Orlova won't see through yours?'

'I'm a spy in a hostile country; it's my job to be suspicious of everyone I meet. She's an innocent young ballet dancer.'

Wojtkiewicz chuckled softly.

'What's so amusing?'

'Oh, nothing. It's just I never thought I'd live to hear the word "innocent" used in the same sentence as the phrase "ballet dancer".'

'Her morals may or may not be everyone's notion of purity. My point is, there's no reason why she shouldn't take me at face value. I just hope you made it clear to Casimir and Stanislas to go easy.' Casimir was Wojtkiewicz's butler – the broken-nosed ruffian who had escorted Killigrew to the Pole's steam bath the previous morning – and Stanislas was his coachman, a stocky fellow with a mop of black, curly hair.

'As soon as this act's finished, I'll go and make sure they're in position,' Wojtkiewicz told Killigrew. 'Does this have something to do with finding this man Bauer, or is your interest in Mam'selle Orlova purely . . . ah . . . artistic?'

'She may know where Bauer is.'

'You're going to a lot of trouble to find this fellow. What's so important about him, that you had to come to St Petersburg to find him?'

'Would you believe me if I told you he stole Prince Albert's snuff-box?'

'No, I would not!' Wojtkiewicz glowered at Killigrew, who just smiled.

The stage lights were dimmed to allow the stage-hands to change the scenery. Wojtkiewicz rose from his seat and left the auditorium.

Killigrew stayed until the final curtain. The ballet itself was not much to write home about, but Mademoiselle Orlova's exquisite dancing was more than compensation enough. When the *corps de ballet* had taken their final curtain call, the Imperial family left the auditorium to cross the arch into the main part of the Winter Palace, and Killigrew followed the other patrons out on to Millionaires' Street.

While the rest of the crowd dispersed, he made his way along the side of the Winter Canal to the Dvortsovaya Embankment, overlooking the Neva at the back of the theatre. Killigrew took up position in the shadows and waited. A number of people emerged and climbed into waiting carriages, and he recognised a few of the ballet dancers who emerged in a group, laughing gaily as they set off into the city. He hoped Anzhelika Orlova did not come out as part of a group: if she did, everything would be ruined.

When she finally did come out, Killigrew almost failed to recognise her, dressed as she was in a battered-looking greatcoat and a broad-brimmed wideawake. But there was no mistaking her petite figure and the grace with which she moved, even when walking with her hands in her coat pockets and her narrow shoulders hunched against the wind that blew up the Neva.

The two bulky figures that weaved drunkenly along the embankment had timed it to perfection. A bottle of vodka passed back and forth between them as they took turns taking a swig. With her eyes cast down, she did not see them until she had almost bumped into them. She looked up, startled, and tried to sidestep them, but one of them reached out and caught her by the arm.

'Hullo! What have we got here?' he slurred.

'Please, let me go,' said Mademoiselle Orlova.

'Have a drink with us.'

'No, thank you. I'm not thirsty.'

'Wassamarrer? We're not good enough for the likes of you, eh? We're good enough to die for you in your wars, but you won't even stop to acknowledge us in the street.'

Killigrew was impressed. Had he not known they were two of Wojtkiewicz's men, he would never have recognised them in those old soldier's greatcoats and false beards, and the way they staggered and slurred their words . . . consummate actors who were wasted as Wojtkiewicz's hired ruffians. He hoped they could sham-fight as convincingly.

One of them had pushed Mademoiselle Orlova back against the wall of the theatre and she struggled to break free as he tried to thrust the neck of the bottle between her lips. It was time to intervene.

Killigrew stepped out of the shadows. 'Unhand that woman, you scallawags!'

The two men turned to look at him. '*Tebya ne ebut, it ne podmakhivai!*' snarled one.

It was at that moment Killigrew realised that they were not Wojtkiewicz's men at all, but were in fact a couple of genuine drunks.

Before he could draw his gun one of them threw the vodka bottle at him. It bounced off his head to smash against the cobbles. He staggered and felt his legs turn to jelly beneath him. He sank to his hands and knees, and the two drunks closed in on him, kicking him viciously. He rolled up into a ball, wondering where the hell Wojtkiewicz's men were. He tried to protect his head with one arm while he reached for his revolver with the other, and then hesitated, realising that if Mademoiselle Orlova saw it, she would be suspicious immediately; if he did not draw it, on the other hand, he was going to get his skull kicked in . . .

Then one of the drunks sank to his knees, his face twisted in agony, one hand clutching his crotch. Someone jumped on to his shoulders and used them as a launch pad to leap into the air, delivering a kick to the other drunk's face as she flew past. He sprawled on his back, and as booted feet hurried across the cobbles to the fracas, he scrambled to his feet and ran off into the night. Suddenly there were three more men there. They grabbed the first drunk, but he had recovered sufficiently from the kick in the groin to break free of their grip and run off after his companion.

All Killigrew could see through swimming eyes was four pairs of feet, including one pair that could only belong to Mademoiselle Orlova. 'What happened?' a voice Killigrew did not recognise asked in Russian.

'It's nothing, it's all right,' a woman replied. 'Just couple of veterans who'd had too much to drink, that's all.'

'What about this one? Is he one of them?'

'He tried to help me.' She crouched over Killigrew. 'Are you all right? How many fingers am I holding up?'

He squinted at her hand. 'Seven?'

'Sounds like a foreigner to me,' said one of the men.

'That is a nasty bruise on his head.'

'Help me get him to the carriage.'

He felt himself lifted up and carried across the embankment. They manhandled him through the door of a carriage and put him down on one of the seats. The carriage rocked on its springs as two men climbed out and someone else climbed in there with him, and a moment later a cold, damp cloth was pressed soothingly to his forehead.

The carriage door was slammed shut, he heard her shouting instructions to the driver, and they rattled off over the cobbles.

Killigrew struggled to maintain his grip on his consciousness, then decided the game was not worth the candle and passed out.

# XII

# Pas de Deux

---

'It says here his name is Yown Vya'useh.'

'Yown Vya'useh? What kind of name is that?'

'It's an English one. And it's pronounced "John Bryce".'

'John – that's the English equivalent of "Ivan".'

Four different women were speaking, in French, but with delicious Russian accents, husky yet lilting. Lying on the chaise longue with his skull aching, Killigrew decided he was content to remain with his eyes closed for now, listening to their voices.

'I prefer "John",' said one. 'It sounds . . . ooh, exotic. "John Bryce".' The way she pronounced it, Killigrew decided he preferred it, too, and decided he envied this John Bryce fellow, whoever he was.

'Is he English, then?'

'It says here he's an American journalist.'

'American? That explains the gun.'

Killigrew reached for his own gun instinctively, wondering why it was important, and then it all came flooding back to him: his mission, his cover, the *Sea Devil*, the fight on the Dvortsovaya Embankment . . .

He realised he was going to have to open his eyes.

He was not looking forward to it. He was already imagining the way the light would lance in through his eyeballs to send blinding agony stabbing up into his skull, adding a fanfare of pain to the throbbing timpani that was already there in spite of the cold compress resting soothingly on his brow. Best to take it slowly, he told himself, opening only one eye to begin with, and that in no great hurry.

Except when he saw the four women standing over the chaise longue, he forgot all about his headache. He had already seen that Anzhelika Orlova was one of the most beautiful women he had ever encountered, but she hardly stood out in her present company.

She turned to one of them. 'He's awake.'

'Make him a cup of tea, Pola.'

'Why should I be the one who has to make the tea?'

'I'll do it,' offered the fourth woman, hurrying away from the side of the chaise longue.

'How are you feeling?' asked Mademoiselle Orlova.

'Absolutely wonderful,' he told her, without irony, remembering just in time to speak with an American accent. 'My name's Bryce, by the way – John Bryce.'

'I am Anzhelika Orlova,' she told him. 'This is Pola and Tanya.' She gestured to her two remaining companions. 'And that is Glazovoi,' she added, gesturing past the end of the chaise longue. 'He carried you up here.'

Killigrew had to twist his head to take in Glazovoi, who stood by the door with his brawny arms folded. Although Glazovoi wore a coachman's cloak and broad-brimmed hat on his bald head, he had the broad shoulders and short legs of a man who had spent much of his life pushing at the bars of a capstan. He was not smiling: his pock-marked face was not really designed for that.

'You can go now,' Anzhelika told Glazovoi.

The coachman shook his head. 'While he stays, I stay,' he growled.

She grimaced. 'You must forgive Glazovoi,' she told Killigrew. 'He can be somewhat overprotective of my virtue.'

'Doesn't he take orders from his mistress?'

'I am not his mistress. Glazovoi is Admiral Zhirinovsky's coachman.'

'And Admiral Zhirinovsky is . . .?'

'My patron.'

'Ah.' Killigrew put a world of meaning into that single word.

'It is not what you think. If it were, I would not be living in a dreary apartment block. But a ballerina must have a patron at court, yes?' She spoke in English now; a language Glazovoi did not understand, Killigrew suspected. 'I am indebted to you, M'sieur Bryce.'

'What for?' he asked.

'Coming to my aid.'

'Much good I did,' he said ruefully. 'If there's any thanks owing, it's from me to you for looking after me.'

She smiled. 'You diverted them long enough for me to break free and drive them off.'

'Yeah. Where did you learn to roughhouse like that?'

'That was not "roughhousing"; that was ballet.'

'Seems like your Russian ballet is kinda different from the way we do it in the States.'

'You have ballet in the United States?' asked Pola. 'I had thought America was a cultural desert.'

Killigrew smiled. 'We ain't all slave drivers and bushwhackers, ma'am.' He turned back to Mademoiselle Orlova. 'I go to the ballet in New York a heap, but I don't recollect seeing anyone get kicked in face like that.' He thought for a moment. ' 'Cept in one production of *La Sylphide*, but that was when Bill the Butcher and his Nativists got on stage and set about the *corps de ballet* for being foreigners.'

She grinned impishly. 'You should come to rehearsals.'

'I might just take you up on that,' he replied with a smile.

The fourth woman emerged from the kitchen with a cup of tea. 'I'm Natalya,' she said.

'Pleased to make your acquaintance, ma'am,' Killigrew told her, and she giggled.

He sipped the tea and cast an eye over the room. He lay on one of four beds, and from the way the furniture was arranged in the limited space available he guessed that this room was bedroom, parlour and drawing room for all four women. Now that he looked, he recognised Natalya as having danced in the *corps de ballet* earlier that night, so he guessed Pola and Tanya were dancers too. The rooms were little different from the shared lodgings of some of the opera dancers he had dallied with in London, but he could not help thinking that the *prima ballerina* of the Mariinsky Ballet might expect to be housed rather more comfortably.

'You all four live here?' he asked, making no attempt to keep the surprise from his voice.

The point was not lost on Anzhelika, and she grimaced. 'Ballet dancers are not held in the same esteem here in Russia as they are in the West, M'sieur Bryce. Like most ballet dancers, our parents are servants in the households of wealthy aristocrats. We are the lucky ones: we auditioned for Imperial Ballet School and won places. We are paid, but . . .'

'Why not emigrate to the West?' suggested Killigrew. 'You'd be paid better in London or Paris.'

190

All four women looked around nervously, as if he had blasphemed and could expect to be struck down for his pains at any moment. 'It is not permitted,' explained Anzhelika.

'I guess that's one way to stop talent from leaving the country.'

'At least it is our home,' said Natalya. 'In here we can do as we please, come and go as we please, beholden to no one.' She shot a glare up at Glazovoi.

Killigrew drained his cup of tea and laid it to one side, rising to his feet. 'Well, I reckon I've taken up enough of your time. People will talk . . .'

Anzhelika smiled sadly. 'I told you, M'sieur Bryce, we are considered little better than serfs. Our reputations are considered of no account.'

Killigrew jerked a thumb at Glazovoi. 'He don't seem to reckon so.'

'Are you quite sure you are well enough to leave?'

He nodded.

'Glazovoi will drive you back to your hotel. I'll show you to the door.'

'I'll come with you,' offered Natalya, but Tanya caught her by the arm and shook her head when Natalya looked at her enquiringly. Natalya shrugged, and remained in the apartment with the others while Anzhelika showed Killigrew out into the corridor and down the stairs, Glazovoi's ponderous footsteps following them down.

When they emerged from the building, Killigrew saw Tweedledum and Tweedledee sitting on their drozhky further up the street. They must have followed him from the Dvortsovaya Embankment. They pretended not to be interested in Killigrew, and he returned the favour.

'I still feel indebted to you,' he told Mademoiselle Orlova.

'Please, call me "Lika".'

'There must be some way I can pay you back for taking care of me, but I'm loath to be so crass as to offer you money . . .'

'Oh, I do not mind,' she replied brightly.

He pursed his lips, nodded, and took a few roubles from his pocket book. 'Will that cover it?'

She shook her head. 'It is too much.'

'Keep it. It's only money.'

She regarded him with one eyebrow arched. 'Are you sure you're American?'

'A quarter Irish on my maternal grandmother's side. Perhaps we can talk again before I return to the States, Lika?'

'Perhaps,' she said, without much enthusiasm. Or was it a lack of hope?

He took her hand and bowed to kiss it. '*Au revoir, Mam'selle.*'

She managed a smile. '*Au revoir, M'sieur Bryce.*'

Glazovoi opened the door of the monogrammed carriage standing nearby and gestured for Killigrew to get inside. He was not the sort of fellow one disobeyed without a very good reason. Killigrew climbed in the back, and as Glazovoi slammed the door shut and climbed on to the driving seat, the commander looked out of the window to see Lika standing on the threshold of the apartment block. She waved him goodbye, and as the carriage clattered away over the cobbles she retreated inside, closing the door behind her.

'Where to?' Glazovoi growled in Russian. It was a good language for growling in.

'Dussot's.'

They headed back to the Nevsky Prospect.

'You call this a backdrop?' the ballet master snarled at one of the scenery painters. 'What scene is it intended to represent? I cannot recall any scenes in this ballet which call for the set dressing "a foggy day in hell".'

'It's supposed to be impressionistic,' the scene painter said defensively.

'Impressionistic? Oh, it is. Why, just looking at it, I get a distinct impression. The impression that you have the artistic ability of a drunken Cossack! I could eat five bowls of borsch and *vomit* better scenery.'

The scene inside the Winter Palace Theatre that afternoon was familiar to Killigrew from his dabbling in amateur dramatics for charity. Anzhelika Orlova was on stage, practising arabesques, oblivious to the falling piece of unfinished scenery that would have swatted her like a fly had it not been for a quick-witted and nimble stage hand; a gnomish young man extemporised at the pianoforte in the orchestra pit; the ballet master's assistant – an attractive, bespectacled blonde – discussed lighting set-ups with a lighting engineer; four more stage hands sat on boxes playing cards; and two dwarfs juggled burning brands.

'Perhaps we'd better come back later,' Wojtkiewicz suggested as he entered the auditorium with Killigrew.

'You haven't spent much time at a theatre during rehearsals, have you?' Killigrew said with a smile. He was carrying a bunch of red roses, like any stage-door johnny. 'It doesn't get any better than this. Don't worry. They have a saying in the theatre: it'll be all right on the night.'

'It's not opening night I'm worried about, it's this afternoon that concerns me.' Wojtkiewicz shrugged and advanced down the aisle towards the stage.

A man in a black leather greatcoat sat in the front row, looking thoroughly bored as he switched his attention between the ballet master and Anzhelika. He could have been first cousin to Tweedledum and Tweedledee, and Wojtkiewicz nudged Killigrew and muttered: 'Third Section.'

Killigrew wondered what the Third Section agent was doing at the theatre – he did not look like an aficionado of the ballet – but Wojtkiewicz did not explain further.

The ballet master became aware of Killigrew and Wojtkiewicz and broke off from haranguing the scene painter to face them. 'Can I help you?' he demanded, in a tone that boded no good for anyone foolish enough to ask for help, or indeed to do anything but retreat from the auditorium with a muttered apology. He produced a lorgnette to regard the two intruders with practised disdain, but when he recognised Wojtkiewicz the change in his expression suggested that the Pole was a generous patron of the arts. '*Mscislaw, mon cher!* Where *have* you been hiding yourself these past few months? And who is your handsome young friend with the lamentable taste in waistcoats?'

'M'sieur Perrot, may I present M'sieur John Bryce? John, this is M'sieur Jules Perrot.'

That explained the presence of the watcher from the Third Section. Jules Perrot – once one of the most famous ballet dancers in the world, who had partnered Marie Taglioni for a while – was a Frenchman, and Russia was at war with France as well as Britain and Turkey. Only in a society as paranoid as Russia's would the secret police have had a watching brief on a ballet master of Perrot's stature.

Killigrew shook his hand. 'It's an honour, sir. It goes without saying that your fame has stretched as far as the United States.'

Perrot looked disappointed. 'Oh. An American. Oh, well, nobody's perfect. What brings you to St Petersburg, M'sieur Bryce?'

'I'm a reporter for the *New York Herald*.'

'A reporter . . . how unfortunate. If you've come for an interview, I never speak to the press—'

'I'm not a theatre critic,' Killigrew reassured him. 'I'm here to report on the war with Britain, France and Turkey. I only accepted M'sieur Wojtkiewicz's invitation to watch your rehearsals because I happen to be an aficionado of the ballet in my spare time. Say, come to think of it, I reckon it might be kind of interesting to write an article on how life in St Petersburg is carrying on as normal, in spite of the war. Perhaps a few words on that subject . . .?'

'I'm sorry, M'sieur Bryce, but as I said before, I never give interviews. Now, if you'll excuse me, I have work to do.' Perrot turned away and mounted the stage.

Killigrew spoke to his assistant. 'Would it be possible to have a brief word with Mam'selle Orlova?'

She looked Killigrew up and down, and then called over her shoulder: 'Lika! Your latest beau is here.'

Anzhelika looked down from the stage and saw Killigrew. 'M'sieur Bryce!'

He grinned and tipped his hat to her. 'You did say I should come and watch rehearsals.'

'I was joking,' she said, but she said it with a smile. 'Wait there, I shall just be one moment.' She ran off the stage.

The assistant turned her attention to the bouquet Killigrew was holding. 'Twelve?'

'I'm a stickler for tradition.'

'In Russia, it is unlucky to give someone an even number of flowers.'

'Oh! That would explain why the girl at the florist's made such a fuss. In that case . . .' He plucked one of the roses from the bunch and handed it to her, before proffering the remaining eleven to Anzhelika, who returned wearing a dressing gown over her costume, and tripped down the steps to greet him.

'Thank you, they're lovely. Anya, could you put these in water?' Anzhelika handed her roses to the assistant. 'How is your head this morning?' she asked Killigrew.

'Much improved, thank you kindly, ma'am.'

Perrot looked from Anzhelika to Killigrew and back again in astonishment. 'You know this fellow, Lika?'

She blushed. 'I told you I was assaulted by two drunkards last night; this is the man who tried to come to my rescue.'

Perrot arched one eyebrow. 'I've heard of a knight in shining armour, but a knight in a tartan waistcoat . . .? Forgive me, Lika, but we are supposed to be going through the steps of the *pas de deux* in act two. Where's Marius?'

'That's what I've been trying to tell you,' Perrot's assistant called up. 'M'sieur Petipa is indisposed. Food poisoning – some bad oysters he ate last night, the doctor says.'

Perrot looked as though he was going to explode. 'Food poisoning? *Food poisoning*? How dare he? On *my* time! How are we supposed to rehearse the *pas de deux* with our *premier danseur* indisposed?'

'Perhaps you can stand in for him, M'sieur Perrot?' Anzhelika suggested innocently.

'With my knees? Besides, I'm supposed to be the choreographer. I can hardly judge the effectiveness of the steps while I'm up here on stage. It's no good, you'll just have to do it on your own.'

'It is a *pas de deux*, not a *pas d'une*.'

'This is the theatre, *chérie*. We improvise. Suppose it were opening night, with the Tsar and Tsarina watching, and you had no *premier danseur*? You wouldn't expect me to call the whole thing off, would you? Let us face facts: you do all the work in this number. You just need someone to dance around. Why, I dare say even Count Orloff's greatcoated ape sitting in the front row would suffice. What do you say, M'sieur *le agent secret*? Do you think you could stand in for M'sieur Petipa?'

Tweedledumber looked panic-stricken, and glanced over his shoulder as if hoping in vain that Perrot addressed some other Third Section agent sitting behind him.

'Oh, well, perhaps not,' sniffed Perrot.

Killigrew knew an opportunity when he saw one. He rose to his feet. 'Perhaps I could be of service, sir?'

Perrot flicked his lorgnette open and peered at him. 'In what respect?'

'I took a few dancing lessons when I was a kid. It's been a while, and though I'm sure I'm no substitute for M'sieur Petipa, reckon I know the difference between a *pas de bourrée* and a *gargouillade*.'

'You do, do you? This is ballet, M'sieur Bryce, not baseball. A few lessons? It takes years of constant practice and training to make a *premier danseur*.'

'You think a guy learns how to play baseball overnight? Maybe I'll never make the *corps de ballet*, but if all you need is someone to stand around while Mam'selle Orlova goes through her steps, I've had plenty of practice of standing around on third base.' Killigrew had no idea what third base was, but he had an idea it was something baseball players spent a lot of time standing around on.

'Ballet as baseball,' sneered Perrot. 'This I have to see. Batter up,

195

M'sieur Bryce! Someone fetch him a pair of shoes and tights.'

'M'sieur Bryce!' Anzhelika protested in horror as Killigrew divested himself of his coat and half-boots. 'What are you doing?'

'You wanted a partner for the *pas de deux*,' said Perrot. 'Here he is. Or would you prefer my pet policeman there?'

'I would prefer not to do it at all.'

'So would I; except that we open this ballet in two weeks and we still haven't perfected the steps in this number. So be so good as to humour me, *n'est-ce pas*?'

'Very well. But no lifts!'

'What are you worried about? I'm sure M'sieur Bryce will have no difficulty catching you; provided he has remembered to bring his ... what is it called, a "baseball mitten"?'

Someone provided some ballet shoes and tights, and after getting changed Killigrew practised the basic five positions, feeling extremely self-conscious. When he had been a boy, his tutor had taught him a few basic ballet steps, telling him that if he wanted to excel as a swordsman he had to be nimble on his feet, and for that there was no better training than ballet. Killigrew had hated the lessons at the time; only years later, watching the ballet at Covent Garden in wonderment, had he occasionally wished he had applied himself more diligently to his dance lessons as a boy.

Not that Killigrew genuinely regretted the path his career had chosen: nimble on his feet he might be, but he had always known he would never be good enough to become a *premier danseur* of any standing. Nevertheless, he knew that the time he danced a *pas de deux* with the *prima ballerina* of the Mariinsky Ballet while posing as an American journalist on a spying mission to discover the whereabouts of a submersible boat would be a story he would one day tell his grandchildren ... assuming he lived long enough to have any. Even if he made a fool of himself, it would be worth it just so he could say he had done it.

'When you're ready, M'sieur Bryce?' Perrot called from the auditorium, singularly unimpressed with Killigrew's lesson one exercises.

'Just stand centre stage, and follow my lead,' Anzhelika suggested.

'This is the seduction scene,' Perrot explained to Killigrew. 'You are Prince Yuri, who has disguised himself as a stable boy to win the heart of the Princess Olga.'

'You're Princess Olga?' Killigrew asked Anzhelika.

'No, I am the Fairy Enchantress Lyudmila. I have fallen in love with the stable boy Grigory, not realising he is actually a prince.'

'Why would a prince disguise himself as a stable boy to win the heart of a princess?'

She smiled. 'It's just ballet, M'sieur Bryce.'

Perrot exploded. 'Just ballet? *Just* ballet? Ballet is not *just* anything, Lika! How many times must I tell you? You may dance like an angel, but if you want them to remember you, you must play your roles with utter conviction! *Be* the Enchantress Lyudmila . . . and enchant him.'

'I'm afraid I'm enchanted already,' Killigrew said with a smile.

She gave him a funny look.

'*You* just stand there,' Perrot told him. 'And try to look like a prince.'

'Disguised as a stable boy,' said Killigrew, 'wearing tights.'

'And try to put some passion in it, this time, Lika!' said Perrot. 'Remember, you're supposed to be in love with him. Difficult in his case, I know, but that's just one of the many challenges of ballet. Remember, love is blind. Even in the matter of waistcoats. Music please, M'sieur Balakireff! *Da capo!*'

The pianist played the introductory notes, and Anzhelika started with an arabesque before launching into a series of steps and leaps, dancing *en pointe*. Killigrew could only stand there and marvel at her grace as she glided about the stage as if walking on air, now fairy-like and delicate, now sinuous and sensuous, all the time drawing closer to him as she circled.

Finally, she stopped in front of him and a little to the left, and leaned over backwards – how she kept her balance was nothing short of a miracle – and elegantly extended an arm towards him.

'Now you take her by the arm, and the two of you *promenade*,' said Perrot. 'That's it, good.'

'Just like a quadrille,' remarked Killigrew, sorry that his appreciation of her exquisite movements had to end when he was brought into the dance.

Perrot rolled his eyes. 'Yes, M'sieur Bryce, just like a quadrille. I think we shall pass over the *grand jeté attitude croisé en arriére* that M'sieur Petipa would undertake here and move quickly to the *porté*. Now you break away, Lika, leaving M'sieur Bryce yearning . . . yearning, M'sieur Bryce, not dazed-looking . . . into the *soubresaut*, Lika, good, now the *ecarté* . . . very good. And now, together again. You put your arm around her waist and draw her close to your side . . .'

'Pardon the familiarity, ma'am.'

197

She smiled. 'Do not concern yourself, M'sieur Bryce. I have danced with far less agreeable partners.'

Killigrew drew her in close.

'*Promenade en manège* . . . *eh, bien*! Very good, M'sieur Bryce. Another nineteen years of rigorous training, we shall make a ballet dancer of you yet! Now you part, you take her by the hand, she pirouettes . . . magnificent!'

'You are getting the hang of it, M'sieur Bryce,' murmured Anzhelika. 'Just relax yourself, and go where the music takes you.'

'Now in close again, you put an arm around her waist . . . *other* arm, M'sieur Bryce . . .'

'Sorry!'

'. . . and you waltz *en manège*, she breaks away . . .'

Anzhelika launched into a series of *fouettés*, and Killigrew was so entranced that when she came back at him he was caught off guard, and it was luck rather than judgement that enabled him to catch her. He supported her with one arm about her waist as she bent over backwards, her bodice straining, their hips pressed together. He pulled her up sharply, drawing her in close, and looked down into her dark, wide eyes, her lips parted, and they spun around, foreheads and noses pressed together, her breath hot and sweet on his face. She brought up one thigh, hooking it around his leg, drawing the sole of one foot up the back of his calf, then the other, and her thighs were scissored around his hips, her hands clasped behind the back of his neck as they twirled.

Killigrew forgot all about their audience, about the submersible boat and the agonising torture and inevitable death that awaited him if the Third Section caught him. For now, all that mattered was the music, and the lovely woman in his arms. She jumped off him and landed neatly *en pointe*, they spun apart, caught each other by the hands and came in close again, whirling, and he took her face in his hands, and wondered what she would do if he kissed her, and she looked as though she were wondering the same thing, and then – thank Heavens! – the moment passed, and she broke away, spinning. From another pirouette she launched into a series of *sautés*, and the regret at the passing of that moment was only slightly mitigated by the beauty of her movement. He stood and watched her, feeling like a spare part once more, and wishing he had spent the past twenty years training to be a ballet dancer so he could dance with her properly, and . . .

She was coming towards him again.

Surely she didn't mean to . . . ?

Not with an untrained partner . . .?

She did!

She launched into a *grand jeté*, flying right at him. There was no time to panic, he just braced himself. As she passed over his head he caught her, his left hand against her bodice, his right on the inside of her thigh, and then for no reason other than that it seemed like the natural thing to do, he lifted her high over his head – she was as light as a feather – and she flung out her arms and threw her head back.

Killigrew was now faced with the problem of how to get her back down again, but she solved it by flicking a thigh past his face, and the next thing he knew he was lowering her to the stage, her hands on his shoulders, his hands on her hips. He lowered her slowly, wanting the moment to last for ever as their bodies touched, and she melted in his arms, her legs entwined with his, their arms about one another. How they got down on the stage was a mystery, but they did, Anzhelika dying in his arms with a shuddering sigh, her supple limbs splayed languorously, her back arched, breasts heaving as she gasped for breath, her face beaded with sweat. He bent over her, one hand gently caressing her cheek, the other on her thigh. Her lips were parted and he was desperately trying to think of a reason not to kiss her and drawing blanks, when he remembered they were not alone: the audience of Jules Perrot and his assistant, Wojtkiewicz, the pianist, the stage hands and the juggling dwarfs were all gaping at them, open-mouthed, as if Killigrew and Anzhelika had just had carnal intercourse on the stage right there in front of them. Killigrew could not say with any conviction that was not what had happened.

'*C'est magnifique*,' muttered Perrot's assistant, '*mais ce n'est pas le ballet.*'

'Um . . . perhaps a little *less* passion next time, Anzhelika,' suggested Perrot.

Killigrew heard someone clapping, and glanced towards the back of the auditorium to see a man dressed in the black-green uniform of a Russian admiral walking down the aisle towards them. He was a stocky man in his mid-forties with a neatly trimmed beard encircling a wide, hard mouth.

'Magnificent!' he enthused, although Killigrew thought he detected a mocking note in his voice. 'Encore, encore!'

Anzhelika hurriedly squirmed out from beneath Killigrew and stood up, dusting down the sides of her skirts. 'Samya!'

The man ascended the stage, took her hand in one of his, and bowed low to kiss it. 'Lika, *golubushka*! That was wonderful! If you dance half as well on opening night, it will be the triumph of the decade.'

'Unless the Tsarina has seizure in shock,' muttered Perrot's assistant.

The newcomer turned to Killigrew, who had risen to his feet. 'And you must be M'sieur Petipa?'

Anzhelika flushed crimson. 'This is not Marius, Samya.'

The man regarded Killigrew with renewed curiosity. 'No? Then who . . .?'

'Samya, may I present M'sieur John Bryce of the *New York Herald*? M'sieur Bryce, this is my patron, Admiral Prince Samoyla Iakovlevich Zhirinovsky. M'sieur Bryce kindly volunteered to stand in for Marius, who is indisposed.'

Admiral Zhirinovsky was amused. 'An American journalist? You are wasted as a reporter, my friend. If I were you, Perrot, I should sign this fellow up to your *corps de ballet*, before the Italians snap him up!' He clapped Killigrew on the shoulder. Still dizzy and breathless from the dance, Killigrew staggered under the force of the blow and almost fell into the orchestra pit. 'Tell me, Mr Bryce: where does an American journalist learn to dance like that?'

'My old fencing master insisted I learn ballet when I was a boy.'

'You fence? I did not know journalists fenced.'

'No, well, I . . . uh . . . you'd be amazed how many people take exception to the truth, Your Highness. A good reporter is well advised to learn how to defend himself in a duel.'

Zhirinovsky laughed. 'I can imagine. But I thought the handgun was the American weapon of choice?'

'It is. But I'm a European correspondent.'

'Of course! How silly of me.'

'M'sieur Bryce is the man who saved me from those two drunks last night,' added Anzhelika.

Zhirinovsky regarded Killigrew with renewed interest. 'Then I am in your debt,' he said, and took out his pocket book. 'What do I owe you for your trouble?'

'No reward is necessary, I assure you, highness.'

Zhirinovsky looked surprised, but returned the pocket book inside his coat. 'You must let me repay you somehow. I have it! I am having a ball on board my yacht – *Letayushchaya Tarelka* – tomorrow afternoon. You must join us.'

# XIII

# Novaya Gollandia

The *Letayushchaya Tarelka* turned out to be a paddle-steamer, which proved that not all Russian admirals were dead set against anything newfangled. She was a handsome vessel, about a hundred feet from knight-heads to taffrail, with an elegant sheer to her bulwarks and smoke rising from the slender funnel between her two rakish masts.

Killigrew arrived at the harbour on Vasilyevsky Island the following afternoon to find the yacht moored at one of the jetties. A couple of smart but burly sailors at the foot of the gangplank checked his name – or rather, Bryce's – on the guest list, and he made his way up on deck. A ten-piece band played a waltz on the forecastle, but no one was dancing yet: instead the guests stood around, chatting gaily. Most of the men wore uniforms of some description – naval and army – but there were also several civilians present. Killigrew looked, but could not see any that answered Bauer's description; but there were still more guests arriving. If the Bavarian had been invited to this ball, he might yet turn up; Killigrew hoped he would recognise him if he did.

There were plenty of women also, most of them too young and pretty to be the wives of the officers present, and wearing too much make-up to be their daughters. Evidently this was the sort of social gathering where one invited one's mistress. Helping himself to a champagne flute from the tray of a passing flunkey, Killigrew looked for Anzhelika, but if she was on board she was certainly not on deck. Perhaps a prince having the *prima ballerina* as a mistress was too scandalous for Zhirinovsky to parade her before St Petersburg society,

201

but Killigrew doubted it: he could see the admiral was in full-dress uniform, his breast bedecked with numerous decorations, and he suspected Zhirinovsky would wear a mistress like Anzhelika on his arm with just as much pride.

A steam whistle blasted, momentarily drowning out the band and causing several people to spill their champagne and raise hands to their hearts to check they were still beating. The two sailors who had been guarding the foot of the gangplank now came on board, dragging it up after them, and the mooring lines were cast off. Feeling the deck throb underfoot as the engine started up, Killigrew glanced over the rail to see Tweedledum and Tweedledee watching forlornly as the yacht moved away from the quayside towards the harbour mouth.

Zhirinovsky stood to one side, talking to a couple of civilians. Killigrew thought he caught a hint of a German accent from one of them, an elderly, bearded fellow with a pair of spectacles pushed back on his high-domed forehead and receding grey hair. It was not Bauer – the Bavarian was supposed to be much younger, with dark hair and Vandyke beard – but Killigrew was intrigued nonetheless. He moved the long way around the deck so he could approach from behind Zhirinovsky.

'. . . I suppose he's getting all the funding now?' the German was commenting bitterly, nodding to the other civilian, a tall, thickset, square-jawed man in his fifties. 'Why, his infernal machines don't even sink the enemy's ships when they explode right against their hulls!'

'At least my machines explode, Professor Jacobi!' retorted the square-jawed man. From his accent, he was either Swedish or Finnish. 'I too find myself a victim of—'

'Mr Bryce?' a woman said behind him.

Killigrew turned, his annoyance at the distraction from what promised to be a very interesting conversation indeed turning to the hope that it could only be Anzhelika.

He was in for a nasty surprise when he saw who it was, however.

'Fancy meeting you here!' she said.

'Likewise, Countess,' Killigrew said coldly. 'It's only fair to warn you that the Third Section hauled me in for questioning the other day—'

'Really? And you can still walk? Remarkable!'

'They were very curious about you. So am I, to tell the truth. Oh, and thank you for leaving me in the lurch at Prince Polyansky's house the other evening.'

She shrugged indifferently. 'I managed to get out of there. I assumed you could too.'

'It would have been easier if the champagne hadn't been drugged.'

'Yes, I rather thought it might be. I hadn't left Gustav with any instructions to leave a bottle of champagne out for me, and it isn't like him to use his initiative.'

'You might have warned me. Supposing it had been the Third Section?'

'The Third Section just break down the door: they don't go to a lot of trouble to drug you first. Wojtkiewicz?'

Killigrew nodded.

'But he let you go. Seriously, M'sieur Bryce, I am glad to see you hale and hearty.'

'Certainly hale. I'm not sure about hearty.'

'What did Wojtkiewicz want to know about me?'

'What makes you think he was interested in you?'

'Pffh! I am not a fool, M'sieur Bryce. The champagne was clearly intended for me.'

'Since you ask, he thought you might be an *agent provocateur*.'

'An *agent provocateur*.' She rolled the phrase around her mouth as if she were savouring a fine wine. 'Yes, I think I like that description. Do you find me provocative, M'sieur Bryce?'

' "Trying" would be nearer the mark.'

'Ah, but you know I am no agent for the Third Section.'

'I'm not sure I know anything of the kind.'

'Then why would the Third Section ask you questions about me, if I was one of their own?'

'To make me think you weren't.'

'Let's say I am an *agent provocateur*, working for the Third Section. Why would we want you to think otherwise? Unless you had something to hide.'

Killigrew smiled. 'We all have something to hide . . . "Countess". I could denounce you, you know.'

'You could, but what good would that do?'

'It might get the Third Section off my back.'

'Ah, but if you were to denounce me, I could just denounce you right back . . . Commander Killigrew.'

His stomach lurched, and not because the yacht emerged from the harbour at that moment, entering the choppier waters of the Gulf of Finland. Was there anyone in St Petersburg who *didn't* know who he was?

'Oh, yes, I've read all about your exploits in the *Illustrated London News*.' The countess smiled. 'Don't look so worried, Commander: your secret is safe with me.'

He looked around surreptitiously, but she had kept her voice low and there was no one else in earshot. 'My friends call me "Kit",' he told her, raising his champagne flute to his lips. 'And your secret . . .?'

'Is also safe with me. But if I were you I should tell your Admiral Napier that celebrities don't make the best spies. What good is a secret agent if, everywhere he goes, he is recognised?'

'I've managed to hold my own so far.'

She leaned forward to murmur in his ear. 'Don't worry. One day you'll meet the right girl, and you won't have to any longer.' Moving closer to him also gave her the chance to pat him on the crotch without anyone else seeing.

Unused to being groped in public, Killigrew started, spilling his champagne. He scowled at her, but she merely grinned impishly.

'Just who the devil are you?'

She glanced past his left ear. 'Haven't you heard?' she asked, moving past him, and he turned to see her link her arm through that of an elderly Russian admiral. 'I'm Admiral Rykord's niece.'

Beaming like the cat that got the cream, the admiral patted her hand and turned his attention disdainfully on Killigrew. 'And who is this, *golubushka*?'

'Oh, just some dreary little Yankee scribe.' Wiggling her fingers at Killigrew in a mocking wave, she led Rykord over to the other side of the deck.

Killigrew heard someone chuckling. He turned to see a dark-haired young man standing at the bulwark with a glass of champagne in one hand, watching the countess (or whoever the deuce she was) start to dance a waltz with Rykord. For one panicky moment, Killigrew wondered how much the young man had overhead, and then he relaxed: the young man had not needed to hear a word, the tableau had told its own story.

'Well, I'm glad one of us can find something to laugh at!' Killigrew said sourly.

The young man grinned. 'I'm sorry, that was rude of me.' He was another Swede – or a Finn – by his accent. 'I meant no offence.'

Killigrew waved dismissively. 'None taken. I guess that was kinda funny, seen through anyone's eyes but mine.'

'You'll have to forgive me. These days it is so hard to find anything to laugh at; when I do I have to seize the opportunity in both hands.'

'Woman trouble, eh?'

'Hm?' The young man chuckled again. 'No, nothing like that. I'll leave that to you,' he added with a smile. 'No, I'm just sick of this damned war. Can you tell me what it's about? If you can, you'll be the first.'

'Something to do with the Eastern Question, I think.'

'I hear Lord Palmerston says only three men have ever understood the Eastern Question. He says one's dead, one went mad, and he's the third!'

'That sounds like Pam,' admitted Killigrew.

'You know what I'd like to do?' asked the young man. 'I'd like to build a weapon so terrible, so destructive, it could destroy a whole city and wipe out everyone in it, just like that.' He snapped his fingers under Killigrew's nose. 'And then I'd give the secret – not sell it, mind you, but give it – to every government in the world.'

'In the hope they'd all blow each other up? It's a prime notion, don't get me wrong, but don't you figure there's a danger they might slaughter the rest of us in the process?'

'But don't you see?' the young man asked eagerly. 'If every nation had a weapon of such awesome power, they'd be too frightened to use it, for fear the country they were at war with would use their own weapon in retaliation. Maybe then we'd see an end to war.'

'Wouldn't work,' said Killigrew. 'They might be too afraid to use it, but it wouldn't stop them from using conventional weapons, so wars would go on just the same. Governments would just agree not to use your secret weapon. You'd be amazed at what agreements governments can reach when they're supposed to be at war with one another. In fact, if anything, it would make war more likely.'

The young man frowned. 'What makes you say that?'

'Well, look at the world as it is without your weapon. Each time the French build a man o' war, the Limeys have to build a bigger, better one. So then the French have to build two that are even bigger and better than that . . . and so on *ad infinitum*. And once you've got all these warships in the world, the governments that control them start feeling they have to use them. Do you really figure it would be any different with your secret weapon?'

'I hadn't thought of it like that.'

'You've got to understand the military mind. Besides, imagine a

205

world full of weapons like that. Sooner or later, one would be used. Even if it were an accident, the consequences would be appalling. And just look at the poltroons who comprise our governments. Would you trust those idiots with decisions of that magnitude?'

The young man held up his hands in defeat. 'All right, all right, perhaps it's not such a good notion. What would you do?'

'Me? About what?'

'To put an end to war.'

'I don't reckon you can. I'm sorry to have to say it, but I think it's in our nature. People say that we're somehow superior to all the other animals in creation because of what mankind has achieved, but what *have* we achieved? I mean, really? You don't see animals making war on each other, do you? Oh-kay, a lion may slaughter a wildebeest, but that's just nature for you, red in tooth and claw. They have to do it, to survive. But war . . . where's the benefit in that? If you want my opinion, we're the dumbest animals in creation. With all the technology we've developed, we could have it all, but instead we choose to make life difficult for each other at every opportunity; which is effectively the same as making life difficult for ourselves. And that makes no sense at all.'

The young man laughed. 'You sound like a nihilist!'

Smiling, Killigrew shook his head. 'No, just a cynic.'

'Scratch a cynic, you'll always find an idealist underneath.'

'Maybe.'

'Come on, there must be something we can do. Even if we can't put an end to war for all time, there must at least be a way to make people realise there's nothing glorious about it. It's just brutal, nasty and messy.'

'I figure it's the culture we live in. You just said it yourself: we glorify war. We need to change people's attitudes. Take a walk around any city in the modern world. Who do we put statues up to? The poets, the artists, the composers, who enrich our lives with their art? No. We raise statues to the statesmen who start wars, and the generals and admirals who fight them.'

'Sometimes I wonder if the artists are as much to blame as the statesmen and the generals and admirals. There are plenty of poets out there who glorify war. Look at Tennyson.'

'Sure, but they're just mutton-heads.'

The young man knitted his brow. 'Still, I think you might be on to something there. Perhaps we should work to create a society in which

206

the peacemakers are celebrated, and the warmongers are treated as the poltroons they are.'

'Instead of giving medals to soldiers, give them to peacemakers instead?'

'Something like that.'

Killigrew shook his head. 'Medals wouldn't be enough. Soldiers and sailors may treasure the medals they get, but that ain't what they fight for.'

'Then what do they fight for? Love of country?'

'Cold hard cash.'

'Ah, that cynical veneer of yours is showing again!' the young man said with a smile.

'Practical,' Killigrew said defensively. 'I'm just being practical. If you were to offer a cash prize with your medals for . . . for services towards world peace, you might be on to something.'

'Well, I suppose I'm in the right line of work to raise the money.'

'Oh? What is it you do, exactly?'

'I'm an armaments manufacturer.'

Laughing, Killigrew almost choked on his champagne.

'It's true,' insisted the young man.

'Forgive me for saying so, but ain't that kind of an odd line of work for a guy who hates war so passionately?'

The young man shrugged. 'Family business. See that fellow over there?' He nodded towards the square-jawed man in the fur coat who had been talking to Zhirinovsky and Professor Jacobi earlier. 'That's my father. Armaments manufacturer to the Tsar, no less. If it were up to me, I'd be a writer.'

'What kind of armaments does your father manufacture?'

'Oh, secret weapons,' the young man said airily.

'Really? I don't suppose he knows where I could find an underwater boat, does he?' Killigrew muttered into his champagne.

The young man shook his head. 'We only build infernal machines. If it's an underwater boat you're interested in, you'd have to speak to Herr Bauer.'

It took a conscious effort on Killigrew's part not to let the champagne flute slip from his fingers to shatter against the deck. 'Wilhelm Bauer?' he said, slowly and carefully.

The young man nodded. 'The *Khimera* is supposed to be a big military secret, but everyone in St Petersburg knows what he's been up to in that shed at the Duke of Leuchtenburg's shipyard. They moved it

207

to the testing pool in Novaya Gollandia last week, so I suppose it must be finished now.'

Killigrew guessed that the *Khimera* was the name the Russians had given the submersible: evidently someone at the Russian Admiralty did not have a very high opinion of the contraption's feasibility.

'Anyhow, now you know my dirty secret, what's yours?' asked the young Swede.

'Eh?'

'What do you do for a living? You're not a military man, and you're not a scientist or an engineer: if you were, we'd have met before now. And you're clearly not a politician.'

'Kind of you to say so. Funnily enough, I'm a writer. Well, a journalist, anyhow.' He proffered his hand. 'John Bryce, of the *New York Herald*.'

'Alfred Nobel of Nobel and Sons, at your—' the young man began automatically, and then he blanched and stared at Killigrew in horror.

'Whatever's the matter?'

'You . . . you're a *reporter*?' Nobel raised a hand to his mouth as if to stifle his own words, but that was bolting the proverbial stable door.

'I'm sorry, I guess I should have warned you. If you're embarrassed to be seen in my company, I can always move over to the other side of the deck. I won't take it personal.'

'But . . . I just told you all about Herr Bauer's secret weapon . . .'

'Don't worry,' Killigrew assured him. 'I won't tell anyone.'

'You won't tell anyone?' Nobel was incredulous. 'But . . . you're a *reporter*! And it's got to be the story of the century!'

'Sure, but who'd believe it in New York? If I put that in my next dispatch, you know what the telegram I'd get back from my editor would say? Just nine words: "Ha ha ha ha ha stop. You're sacked. Ends." Which reminds me, have you heard the one about the alsatian that goes into a post office to send a telegram?'

'Eh?'

'It takes a form, picks up a pencil in its paw, writes, and hands the form to the clerk. The clerk looks at it, and sees it's written: "Woof woof woof woof woof woof woof woof woof." So he says to the alsatian, "That's only nine woofs. For the same cost you could send another woof." And the alsatian gives him a funny look and says, "Yes, but that would be silly." '

Nobel stared at him, and then shook his head with a wry chuckle. 'Do you promise you won't tell anyone about the underwater boat?'

'You have my word of honour,' Killigrew assured him. *I might go to Novaya Gollandia tomorrow night and blow it up*, he thought to himself, *but I won't tell anyone*. 'Besides, you said it yourself: everyone knows already.'

'That's true.'

'Everyone knows what already?' asked Zhirinovsky, stepping up behind him and startling him.

Killigrew recovered himself quickly. 'Oh, the one about the alsatian who goes to a post office to send a telegram. Everyone's heard it.'

'Woof woof woof woof woof,' grinned Nobel.

Clearly at least one person in St Petersburg did not know it: Zhirinovsky looked from Killigrew to Nobel and back again as if they were both barking mad. 'If I could just tear you away from young Master Nobel's company for five minutes,' he said at last, 'there are certain matters I should like to discuss with you.'

Killigrew smelled something nasty, and it was not the canals. He feigned nonchalance. 'Be my guest.'

'Not here.' Zhirinovsky gestured around the upper deck. 'In my stateroom.'

'Uh-huh.' Killigrew gestured for the admiral to lead the way, and turned back to Nobel before following. 'I'll leave you to design your peace medals.'

Nobel nodded and raised his champagne glass. 'And the cash prize! Don't forget the cash prize!'

'Peace medals?' echoed Zhirinovsky as Killigrew followed him down the hatch to the lower deck. 'Cash prize? What was all that about?'

Killigrew looked him up and down. 'You wouldn't understand,' he said with a smile.

On the lower deck, Zhirinovsky turned at the bottom of the companion ladder, blocking the way aft to where his stateroom presumably was, and gestured down the next hatch. Common sense dictated that if Killigrew was going to make a break for it, now was the time to do it, when he only had Zhirinovsky to deal with. Except he was on a yacht a mile out from St Petersburg: there was nowhere to make a break to. This was one little drama he was going to have to play out to its conclusion.

He preceded Zhirinovsky down the next companion way, passing through the next door into the gloomy hold, lit only by a couple of lanthorns that swung from the deck head, casting eerie shadows across the crates and barrels stowed there.

He had hardly stepped across the threshold when something slammed into his stomach, driving the wind from him. He sank to his knees, and something was smashed across the back of his neck. Retching, he collapsed on to his hands and knees, but then felt himself grabbed by the arms and hoisted to his feet. Through eyes that watered with pain, he saw Zhirinovsky's coachman, Glazovoi, standing in front of him, patting a cant hook against the palm of one hand while two burly sailors with close-cropped hair held him firmly between them.

Zhirinovsky moved past them to stand where Killigrew could see him in the hellish glow of the lanthorns. 'I'll keep this short if by no means sweet: Mam'selle Orlova is mine. Do you understand?'

'Really?' Killigrew glowered at him. 'We don't hold with slavery north of the Mason-Dixon line.'

'You are not in your United States now, M'sieur Bryce. But I think Glazovoi can explain it better than I can – explain it in a way that will help you to remember if you should chance to run into Mam'selle Orlova again.' Zhirinovsky turned to the coachman. 'Keep M'sieur Bryce entertained while I attend to my other guests.'

Grinning, Glazovoi nodded, and waited for Zhirinovsky to go out. Once the door had closed behind him, the coachman rammed the butt of the cant hook into Killigrew's guts. The commander doubled up in agony, his legs crumpling beneath him so that the two men on either side of him supported his weight.

Glazovoi moved behind them, out of Killigrew's line of sight. The commander braced himself, but nothing could have prepared him for the searing agony of the cant hook being slashed across his kidneys. The two men holding him let go, and he staggered forward to slump against a stack of crates. As Glazovoi came at him again, Killigrew grasped one of the cargo battens holding the crates in place and tried to pull himself up, but the batten broke free of the beams. The cant hook swept over his head to bury its point in one of the crates as Killigrew sprawled on his back in the bilges.

Glazovoi stood over Killigrew, trying to pull the cant hook free. Realising he still held the cargo batten in his hands, the commander pushed himself to his feet and swung it back over his shoulder. Glazovoi let go of the hook and raised his arms to protect his head. The batten smashed against one of his wrists, and he stepped back with a yelp, nursing his arm.

Killigrew swung the batten again. There was not enough room between the crates to get a good swing up, but the tip of the batten whipped Glazovoi across the face, drawing blood and snapping his head around.

As Glazovoi retreated, the two sailors squeezed past him into the gangway between the crates to come at Killigrew again. He grabbed hold of a couple of battens overhead and pulled himself up between them, lashing out with both feet to catch the first in the chest and send him staggering back into his shipmate. Killigrew clambered up between the crates – not that there was much space overhead – and braced himself in position, his head twisted at an angle, his shoulders hard against the deck head. He pulled another batten free to jab one end of it at one of the sailors who tried to clamber up after him. He caught him in the throat and the man fell to the deck. As the other sailor tried to follow him, Killigrew pulled one of the crates over so that it toppled down into the gangway, knocking the man to the deck and pinning him there.

Killigrew dropped down on to the crate – the sailor beneath it groaning pitifully at the additional weight – and jumped over the other sailor who lay unconscious on the deck to confront Glazovoi, who had pulled the cant hook free and now held it in his good right hand as he stood at the mouth of the gangway, blocking Killigrew's escape. The commander snatched up one of the fallen battens and raised it to parry as the coachman swung the cant hook at his head. The wooden batten splintered easily, and Killigrew scarcely managed to duck before the hook connected with his ear. But Glazovoi had put too much strength behind the blow and he staggered, twisting, leaving himself wide open. Killigrew stabbed him in the face with the splintered end of the batten. The coachman dropped the cant hook with a grunt and raised a hand to his bloody cheek. Killigrew caught him by the arm – intentionally taking him by the broken wrist; this was neither the time nor the place for chivalry – and twisted it up into the small of his back. Glazovoi screamed in agony, and Killigrew drove him down the gangway, ramming him head first into the crates stowed on the other side of the main aisle. He lifted a knee into the coachman's crotch from behind, and as the coachman sank to his knees Killigrew seized his head in both hands and threw it against the side of a crate, splintering the wood.

Glazovoi sank to the deck and lay still.

Killigrew stood for a moment with his hands on his knees, gasping. He had not killed any of them – thank God! The last thing he needed was to get embroiled in a murder investigation – but they would not be in a hurry to tackle him again. When he had caught his breath, he brushed his hair back into place with his fingers, shot his cuffs, readjusted his cravat, and dusted himself off.

There was only one place on board where he would be safe until they returned to the quay: he made his way back up to the upper deck.

The guests still stood around talking or waltzing to the music of the band. Zhirinovsky was laughing at some joke Nobel *père* had told him, although the grin was quickly wiped off his face when he saw Killigrew emerge from the hatch. Smiling – it was an effort, but he managed it – the commander took a champagne flute from the tray of a passing flunkey and raised it in a mocking toast to the admiral.

Zhirinovsky remained where he was, listening to Nobel *père*, but from the way he kept glancing in Killigrew's direction it was clear to the commander that the admiral's mind was elsewhere.

A short while later one of the sailors Killigrew had beaten in the hold came on deck, looking very battered. Glaring at Killigrew, he crossed the deck to where Zhirinovsky stood, but before he could say anything Zhirinovsky signalled for silence, and made his excuses to Nobel before steering the sailor to a spot on the deck that was free of potential eavesdroppers. The sailor spoke at length, shooting the occasional scowl at Killigrew, while Zhirinovsky listened patiently. When the sailor had finished, Zhirinovsky spoke to him in low, urgent tones. The sailor nodded and went below once more.

Killigrew positioned himself with his back to his starboard bulwark. Zhirinovsky was not going to try anything in front of his guests. But the admiral had something on his mind, that much was obvious; and if trouble was on its way, Killigrew wanted to see it coming.

A few of the other guests came over to make small talk with him but, like Zhirinovsky, his mind was on other things, and he learned nothing of any import. What mattered was that thanks to Nobel *fils* he now knew where Bauer was testing the *Sea Devil*; whether he would live long enough to use that information remained to be seen. He cursed himself for a fool, for jeopardising his mission by becoming involved with a woman.

An hour later the yacht's engines started up once more, and they turned and headed back to Vasilyevsky Island. Killigrew checked his watch, wondering if Zhirinovsky had decided to bring the ball to a premature conclusion, but Glazovoi had smashed the watch with the first blow of the cant hook. He sighed and tucked it back in the fob pocket of his waistcoat.

The yacht entered the harbour, and he watched as they drew near the quayside. Already he could smell the sewage in the canals; while in the city, it was amazing how quickly one's nose grew accustomed to the stench, so that after a while one barely noticed it; but after getting a whiff of the fresh sea breezes in his nostrils, now the stink of the canals seemed stronger than ever.

The yacht manoeuvred into position alongside one of the jetties and sailors threw mooring ropes to the waiting dock workers. Once the yacht was moored, the gangplank was lowered, and Zhirinovsky stood at the entry port to accept his guests' thanks as they filed down. Two of the sailors took up position on either side of the entry port, watching Killigrew with narrowed eyes. This was going to get ugly. Unless . . .

Killigrew handed his empty champagne flute to a flunkey, grabbed hold of one of the stays supporting the foremast, and swung himself up on to the bulwark. From there he scrambled up on to one of the paddle-boxes and leaped for the jetty.

It was a drop of some twenty feet: he hit the planks and rolled over, before picking himself up and dusting himself off as casually as if that was the way everyone disembarked from a ship. Walking past the foot of the gangplank, he looked up to where Zhirinovsky stood at the entry port, glowering down at him. Killigrew smiled and waved up at him. One of the sailors asked Zhirinovsky a question, but he just shook his head without taking his hate-filled eyes off the commander.

Killigrew slipped out of the back door of his hotel that evening and made his way to Wojtkiewicz's house. The Pole had a large dining room with a long mahogany table, but the butler showed the commander to a room in the kitchens, where Killigrew was astonished to find Wojtkiewicz finishing supper with Anzhelika Orlova in a smaller, cosier room.

As soon as she saw Killigrew standing on the threshold, however, she rose from her seat with a smile of delight and ran across to embrace him. 'John!'

'Lika! What the Sam Hill are you doing here?'

'Looking for you,' grated Wojtkiewicz, his expression torn between amusement and annoyance.

'You are not pleased to see me?' she asked Killigrew.

'Delighted,' he assured her. 'It's just . . . unexpected, that's all. You know, your fancy man warned me to keep away from you today.'

She flushed. 'He is not my fancy man! He thinks because he is my

213

sponsor, that makes me his serf . . . but when he touches me, I feel sick.'

'Then why not find a new sponsor?'

'It is not so easy, in Russia. Besides, Zhirinovsky would never let me go. That is why I must leave the country. There is nothing to keep me here in St Petersburg.'

'Leave the country! Where will you go?'

'France. I have friends at the Paris Opera.' She looked hopefully from Killigrew to Wojtkiewicz and back to the commander again. 'You will help me?'

'What makes you think we can help you?' demanded Wojtkiewicz.

She looked crestfallen. 'You . . . you must have friends? Know people . . .?'

The Pole sighed. 'I'll make enquires, see what I can do for you. But I'm not making any promises, do you understand?'

She nodded gravely.

Wojtkiewicz checked his watch. 'And now it's getting late. I'll have Casimir show you to your room.'

After Anzhelika had left the kitchen, Wojtkiewicz poured out two glasses of vodka and handed one to Killigrew.

'She's staying here?' the commander asked him.

'She hasn't given me much choice!' scowled the Pole. 'She says she's frightened to go back to her lodgings. You know, if I had one scrap of sense, I should kill you both and dump your bodies a very long way from here. For all I know, you could both be *agents provocateurs* for the Third Section.'

'Hm. I don't suppose you could just dump our bodies a very long way from here – preferably in the vicinity of Danzig – and forget about the killing part of it altogether?'

'Get you out of the country, you mean? It would certainly be in my best interests to get you away from me, before you destroy yourself and drag me down with you. I've got a cargo of vodka sailing for Danzig tomorrow morning. The master of the ship carrying it owes me a favour. If we move quickly, I can probably have you both smuggled on board—'

'Ah. No can do, I'm afraid. There's somewhere I've got to be tomorrow night.'

Wojtkiewicz closed his eyes. His lips did not move, but Killigrew guessed he was counting to *dziesiec* in an effort to contain his temper. 'If you don't go tomorrow, you'll have to wait until Monday morning.'

214

'So be it.'

'Dare I ask what new mayhem you're planning to brew up tomorrow night?'

Killigrew sighed. It was about time he took Wojtkiewicz into his confidence; if the Pole had intended to betray him, he would have done it long before now. 'I'm looking for Bauer because we think he's built an underwater boat for the Russians. It's my job to find out more, and today I learned it's being tested at Novaya Gollandia.'

'Now you know where it is, why not head straight back to London to warn your Admiralty? Why wait until next week?'

'Because I mean to go to Novaya Gollandia to destroy it.'

Wojtkiewicz stared at him. 'I see.'

Killigrew smiled wanly. 'Aren't you going to tell me I must be out of my mind?'

'That goes without saying. But if you were the kind of man who gave up so easily when he was this close to achieving his goal, you'd never have come to St Petersburg in the first place.'

'Pity. I was rather hoping you were going to try to talk me out of it.'

Wojtkiewicz grinned. 'Oh, no! You don't get out of it that easily! Novaya Gollandia, eh? That's only a few streets from here, as it happens. It's an island in the middle of the city.'

'I thought this city was nothing but a mass of islands?'

'You're not far wrong. Novaya Gollandia is surrounded by water on three sides: the Admiralty Canal, the Kryukoff Canal, and the Moika.'

'And on the fourth side?'

'There is no fourth side: it's shaped like a right-angled triangle, with the Moika forming the longest side. And on the inner side of the canals, the perimeter is lined with rows of warehouses on all three sides, so that the centre of the island is all but hidden from the outside world. And believe you me, breaking in there is not going to be easy.'

'I dare say, but I must make the attempt nevertheless. Presumably there are bridges?'

'Aye; all heavily guarded, though.'

This all sounded very dispiriting, but Killigrew would not be put off so easily. 'I'd like to see for myself.'

'Be my guest. Tomorrow morning I'll take you for a walk around the outside.'

A grandfather clock tolled eleven in the hallway. 'It's getting late, and at my age I need my beauty sleep,' said Wojtkiewicz. 'I'll leave you

215

to tell Anzhelika the good news. Her door is on the left in the east wing. You know she's in love with you, don't you?'

Killigrew stared at him. 'That's ridiculous. She hardly knows me.'

'Who said love ever had to make sense? Be gentle with her, Killigrew. If you break her heart, I'll break your neck.'

Killigrew sensed Wojtkiewicz was not just saying it, either. He took his leave of the Pole and made his way upstairs, knocking on the door to Anzhelika's room. 'Who is it?' she called.

'Me.'

'John? Come in!'

He opened the door and stepped into an elegant bedroom dominated by a large four-poster bed. Anzhelika was sitting at the dresser, wearing a provocative nightdress that doubtless belonged to one of Wojtkiewicz's mistresses; Killigrew sensed the Pole had more than one. The commander was not shocked by her state of undress; before he had met Araminta, he had spent a lot of time in the company of opera dancers back in London, and he knew that theatrical women – used to sharing dressing rooms – were more relaxed about being seen *en déshabillé* than most ladies of his acquaintance.

As soon as he entered and closed the door behind him, however, she rose to her feet and turned to face him, toying with two silk ribbons that hung down from the bow tying the rather décolleté neckline of the nightgown.

'We can get you out of the country tomorrow morning,' Killigrew told her. 'If that's what you want.'

'Oh, John!' She ran across to him and flung her arms about his neck, planting kisses all over his face. Then she broke off and stepped back, frowning prettily. 'What about you?'

He shook his head. 'There's something I have to do before I can leave.'

'What?'

He smiled. 'Let's just say I've got a lead on an important news story.'

'When will you be leaving?'

'Monday morning.'

'Can I not wait until then, and travel with you?'

Killigrew grimaced. If what Wojtkiewicz had said was true – and from the way she looked at him, he had a feeling it might be – she was going to get a nasty surprise when she discovered who and what he really was. Yet he could not tell her the truth. Her desire to leave the country was motivated by her fear of Zhirinovsky, but that did not mean she did not love her country. What would she do if she found out why Killigrew was really in St Petersburg? Whatever his feelings for her, he could not afford to take the risk of finding out by telling her the truth. The whole business was starting to make him feel unclean. He sighed. What a lousy, filthy business espionage was! He desperately wanted to give her a scrap of truth, if only as a sop to his own conscience, but the best he could come up with was: 'All I can tell you is that I can't make any promises.'

She smiled. 'I trust you.'

He shook his head. 'There are a thousand and one things you don't know about me.'

'Why not explain them to me?'

'I wouldn't know where to begin.'

She pulled on the ribbons so that the bow came adrift, and with a shrug of her shoulders the nightgown slipped down to gather in a pool around her ankles. 'Start here,' she suggested.

# XIV

# Breaking and Entering

---

After returning to his hotel in the small hours of the morning, Killigrew got a couple of hours of much-needed sleep and went out again after breakfast. He gave Tweedledum and Tweedledee the slip in the crowds of shoppers beneath the arcades of the Gostiny Dvor, a huge complex of various shops all huddled together in one vast building. There he lost his pursuers without difficulty amongst the crowds emerging at the back of the complex and turning right on to Lomonosoff Street until he reached the Yekaterina Canal.

He followed the canal for over a mile, crossing from one embankment to the other each time he came to one of the many bridges that crossed it, even doubling back on himself just to make sure the Third Section had not got too clever and sent a second pair of agents to tail him. Once he was confident he had shaken off all his shadowers, he crossed the canal at the narrow Lions' Bridge, named after the pair of rampant cast-iron lions that supported the suspension chains. A short walk down the Officers' Street and left on to Glinki Street brought him to the Moika River, where Wojtkiewicz stood waiting for him on the Bridge of Kisses, muffled against the chill of the summer morning in an overcoat, comforter and fur hat. He leaned against the railing, gazing up the Moika to where the scaffold-covered dome of St Isaac's Cathedral rose above the rooftops. He did not look round as Killigrew walked past behind him and leaned against the railing half a dozen feet further on.

'You weren't followed?' the Pole asked without looking in Killigrew's direction.

'Only for a very small part of the way.'

Wojtkiewicz turned away from the railing and sauntered across the bridge. Killigrew fell into step beside him, and when the two of them turned the corner on to the embankment of the Kryukoff Canal, the island of Novaya Gollandia lay opposite them.

As they strolled north along the embankment, Killigrew was able to get a good look at the island; the outer face of it, at any rate. The canal was about twenty yards wide. Beyond that, a screen of birch trees growing from the grassy embankment partially screened the backs of the tall, red-brick warehouses beyond. There were no gaps between the warehouses, so that they presented an impenetrable screen around the centre of the island. There were windows, but none at ground level.

About two hundred yards along the canal – halfway up the east side of the island – they came to a gap in the warehouses where a channel led from the canal into the centre of the island, giving them a fleeting glimpse of the interior – more red-brick buildings – but the pathways on either side of the channel were heavily guarded by soldiers armed with muskets, and under the circumstances Killigrew thought better of craning his neck to get a better view.

At the north end of the Kryukoff Canal they came to the west end of Horse Guards' Boulevard, which led to the Admiralty Gardens about half a mile to the east. Here the channel turned left, around the north-east corner of the island, and became the Admiralty Canal. The canal was just as wide on the north side as it had been on the east, and the row of warehouses was unbroken. Killigrew glanced at the buildings on his right, overlooking the embankment: they seemed to be tenement blocks for the most part, four storeys high, although he doubted he would be able to see over the roofs of the warehouses even from one of the dormer windows at the top. About halfway along, he noticed one tenement with a sign in the window next to the door: 'Rooms to Let', printed in neat Cyrillic script.

At the north-west corner of the island, there was a bridge across the canal, and a gateway that led into a courtyard lying outside the enclosure created by the warehouses. Beyond, Killigrew could see what looked as if it might be an administrative block. Naturally, the gateway was guarded.

Killigrew and Wojtkiewicz crossed the bridge over the Moika to follow the far embankment of the river along the island's south-west side: the hypotenuse of the right-angled triangle. The river was nearly forty yards across, twice the width of the Kryukoff or the Admiralty

Canal. About two-thirds of the way back to the Bridge of Kisses, they passed another water gate into the heart of the island, this one topped by an imposing red-brick arch, flanked on either side by a brace of Doric columns of granite and high enough to accommodate masted boats.

They reached the graceful arc of the Red Bridge over the Kryukoff Canal at the south-eastern corner of the island, completing their circuit. All in all, the island of Novaya Gollandia resembled nothing so much as a castle: the two canals and the river forming its moat, the backs of the warehouses the curtain walls. Wojtkiewicz had not exaggerated the impregnability of the place.

'What do you think?' the Pole asked now, as they crossed the bridge.

'Tricky,' Killigrew admitted. 'But not impossible.'

'You actually think you can get inside?' Wojtkiewicz demanded incredulously.

'I think so, yes. The difficult part is going to be getting across the canal. It's not even twenty yards across on the east and north sides: easy enough to swim. Except that assuming if I managed to swim across without catching my death of cold or cholera, I'd still have to worry about leaving a trail of wet footprints for any patrolling guards to find.'

Wojtkiewicz nodded. 'You could always wait for the canals to freeze over in winter,' he suggested flippantly.

'I don't think I can afford to wait that long. If they've brought the *Sea Devil* here for testing, that means she's all but ready.'

'What about a boat?'

Killigrew shook his head. 'The guards would see me coming.' He took out his notebook and began scrawling in it with a pencil stub. 'I'll need a few bits and pieces.' He tore the page out and handed it to Wojtkiewicz, who goggled at it in disbelief.

He pointed to the last item on the list. 'Where do you expect me to find one of those? St Petersburg isn't a whaling port, you know.'

'Oh, I'm sure a man of your resources shouldn't have too much difficulty tracking one down. Did you see the building with rooms to let on the north side?'

'Yes, I noticed you noticed that.'

'Do you think you could have one of your men rent the top-floor garret for me?'

'Under an assumed name, of course?'

'Of course. Naturally, I'll reimburse you the first fortnight's rent and deposit. One of your men can slip me the key inside a newspaper at the *salon de thé* in the Passage. You can deliver the items on that list to the apartment overlooking the canal this evening. Just leave them inside.'

'Tonight!'

'I can't afford to wait.'

'You realise, of course, that if you're successful in breaking into Novaya Gollandia and destroy this underwater boat, it's going to be a good deal more difficult to smuggle Mam'selle Orlova – or anyone – out of the country afterwards than it would have been before? The Third Section will be watching the roads and the ports like hawks.'

'We'll think of something.'

The Pole nodded. 'Yes. It shouldn't be too much trouble for a man who can break in and out of Novaya Gollandia. The question is, are you that man?'

Killigrew grimaced. 'That remains to be seen. Oh, and I'll need a fireworks display in this vicinity. Shall we say, about midnight? It doesn't have to be a big one, just very noisy. Lasting about five minutes?'

Wojtkiewicz sighed. 'I'll see what I can do.'

They went their separate ways, Killigrew returning to the Gostiny Dvor and windowshopping until Tweedledum and Tweedledee were able to pick up his trail. He let them spend the rest of the day following him so they would have plenty to put in their reports to their superiors: one p.m., subject dined alone at a *traktir*; ate *seludka pod shuboi*. Two p.m., subject walked to the Tauride Gardens and spent an hour strolling about aimlessly. Four p.m., subject drank two cups of coffee at the *salon de thé* in the Passage at No. 48, Nevsky Prospect . . .

This time it was Wojtkiewicz's coachman, Stanislas, who was at the *salon de thé*. Killigrew sat at his table. Neither of them exchanged a word, but when Stanislas got up, he left his newspaper behind. Killigrew drank another cup of coffee and took the paper, leaving a couple of kopecks on the table as a tip before hurrying back to his hotel. In the privacy of his room, he opened the paper and a couple of keys linked by a ring fell out. A tag was attached to them bearing two words: 'Good luck.'

Tweedledum was sitting on a chair in the entrance hall when Killigrew finally emerged from the dining room after a leisurely supper. Ignoring the Third Section agent, Killigrew made his way up to his room and lay on the bed, smoking a cheroot. When he had finished, he rumpled the bedclothes so it would look as if he had slept there overnight. Then he changed into a dark pair of trousers, a black cable-knit sweater and a pea jacket. He thrust his clasp knife in one pocket along with his miniature telescope and a box of matches, and checked his revolver was primed and loaded before tucking it in the other.

It was half-past ten by the time he opened the door to his room and peered out. The corridor seemed deserted and he was about to step outside when a door opened further along. He quickly withdrew into the room, holding the door to, until a bickering couple had passed by.

He waited a few moments, then eased the door open a crack. Seeing the coast was clear, he stepped outside and made his way to the servants' stairs at the back of the building. On the ground floor, he could hear the staff clattering about in the kitchen. He tiptoed past the open door and made his way to the exit. The door opened into a yard at the back of the hotel. The sun had set an hour ago, but there was still plenty of light in the sky, and to make matters worse there was a full moon rising.

Emerging from the yard, he headed north-west, sticking to the back streets until he came to the Yekaterinsky Canal, where he followed the embankment back to the Nevsky Prospect and crossed at the Kazan Bridge. From there Kazan Street took him to Voznesensky Prospect, which he followed as far as the Blue Bridge. Beyond St Isaac's Cathedral, he turned left on to Horse Guards' Boulevard, walking down its length until he emerged on to the embankment of the Admiralty Canal at the north side of Novaya Gollandia.

The harsh glare of limelight lit up the air above the warehouses, and Killigrew could hear the hiss and clank of steam engines, the rattle of chains, and an occasional if incomprehensible order shouted in Russian. His hope that the staff of Novaya Gollandia would not be working this late on a Wednesday night had been in vain.

In the moonlight, he had no trouble relocating the house with the 'Rooms to Let' sign in the window. He tripped up the steps and tried one of the keys in the lock of the front door, but the lock would not turn. He tried the other key. That would not turn, either. Had he come to the wrong building? Worse still, had Wojtkiewicz's man rented the wrong set of rooms? Fighting off a rising sense of panic, he jiggled the key in the lock, until at last the mechanism surrendered with a click. He let himself in and gratefully locked the door behind him, hurrying up four flights of stairs to let himself into the garret at the front of the building.

He crossed to the window, drew the curtains, then struck a match and used its light to find an oil lamp standing on one of the tables. He lifted the glass flue long enough to apply the flame to the wick, and shook out the match, tossing it into the cold fireplace. As the dim yellow glow filled the room, he saw the place was clean if spartanly furnished. A large delivery crate dominated the room – someone must have had a devil of a job getting it up the stairs – and Killigrew was wondering how he was supposed to open it when he noticed that someone had thoughtfully left a pry-bar on the sideboard. He prised up the lid to reveal the bounties within: one satchel; two lengths of rope of Italian hemp, one 150-feet long, the other fifty feet; a grappling iron; a bull's-eye lantern; a ten-foot coil of Bickford's safety fuse; one snatch block; a roll of brown paper; a medium-sized paint brush; one small bottle of treacle; and a harpoon gun.

The harpoon gun was a shoulder gun, made by Robert Brown of Connecticut. It looked much like an ordinary shotgun, except it was made entirely of gunmetal – stock and all – and it had an unusually large bore of 1⅜" to accommodate the harpoon. Wojtkiewicz had generously included half a dozen of these: they were nearly three feet long, with swivel barbs on the head that folded back against the iron shank to aid penetration, but swivelled outwards for additional holding power when any tension was applied to withdraw the harpoon.

First he took the fifty-foot coil of rope and cut six feet off it, tying it into a harness that he fastened to the snatch block. He rove one end of the remaining forty-four feet through the eyelet in the shank of the grappling iron. Then he stuffed the bottle of treacle, paint brush and brown paper in the satchel, along with his revolver, cheroot case and miniature telescope: he did not want them falling out of his pockets in the course of the acrobatics he was about to attempt. The pry-bar did not fit in the satchel without sticking out from both ends, but by buckling the straps down tightly he hoped he could secure it against slipping out.

Turning his attention to the harpoon gun, Killigrew rove one end of the 150-foot line through the hole at the butt-end of the iron, then ran it along the shank and passed it through the two holes at the head, securing it with an eye-splice. Standing the gun itself on its stock, he measured three drams of gunpowder into the muzzle; the recoil would kick like a mule, but he did not want the iron to fall short for lack of a sufficient charge. He added a wad, and inserted the iron into the barrel, using the knob at the butt-end of the shank to ram home the wad against the powder, so that when he was finished both iron and line protruded from the muzzle.

223

A loud report outside startled him, followed by a crackling noise and the sheeting of sparks. Realising it was the fireworks display he had requested, Killigrew smiled; but he had to work fast now. He looked about the room until his eyes fell on the low beams overhead. There was so little headroom in the garret, he was able to make the other end of the line fast to one of the beams without having to stand on a chair. Then he placed a percussion cap on each of the two nipples at the gun's breech, and laid it down by the foot of the wall just beside the door.

He put out the oil lamp and crossed to the window in the darkness, drawing the curtains so he could gaze out. The rockets were shooting up from somewhere to the east of the island, exploding in showers of red, green and yellow sparks. Even when the fireworks were not bursting directly overhead, there was enough light from the full moon for him to see the warehouses on the other side of the Admiralty Canal clearly enough; if anything, it was a little too bright for his liking. He opened the window as wide as it would go.

Crossing to the far wall, Killigrew picked up the harpoon gun and stood with his back braced against the wall behind him, so the recoil would not knock him down. Raising the stock of the gun to his shoulder, he sighted down at the barrel at the trunk of one of the birch trees on the far side of the canal. He glanced down at the coil of rope in the middle of the floor, making sure there was nothing for it to catch on as it ran out through the window.

He sighted on the slender tree trunk once more, sliding his finger through the trigger guard. The range was about forty yards. He started to squeeze the trigger, then broke off to wipe sweat from his brow with his sleeve. *Take your time*, he told himself. *You've only got one shot at this.* True enough, he had five more irons, but only one line: if he missed, he would have to drag the iron back through the canal and across the street on the embankment below, and there was too great a chance the barbed head of the iron would snag on something. Besides, it was not as if he had all the time in the world. He had told Wojtkiewicz to make the fireworks display – which he hoped would cover the report of the harpoon gun – last five minutes. At least three minutes were past now.

Killigrew sighted at the tree, but his hands were shaking. He was painfully conscious of what a rotten shot he was. He took deep breaths, willing his heartbeat to slow down. *It doesn't matter*, he told himself. *If you miss, you'll just have to find some other way of getting on to that island. Or better yet, you can abandon this insane mission and return to London to report your findings to Lord Palmerston, which was all they asked.*

He drew a bead on the trunk and exhaled slowly, squeezing the trigger.

The report sounded deafening in the close confines of the garret, and the muzzle flash dazzled him as the stock slammed bruisingly into his shoulder. Had he not had his back braced against the wall, he would certainly have been bowled over by it. He was aware of the line whipping out through the window in the wake of the iron. Then the line ran straight from the beam to the window.

He crossed to the window and looked out, half expecting to see someone on the street below pointing up at him, but the embankment was deserted. He followed the rope across the canal with his eyes to see the iron embedded in the tree trunk: not dead centre, but almost to one side, so there was little more than the bark holding it in place.

Killigrew listened for a moment. Someone in the tenement block *must* have heard the report of the gun and realised it was much closer and louder than the fireworks that continued to pop and crackle in the sky overhead.

The fireworks stopped. In the ensuing silence he could hear nothing: no shouts, no footfalls on the staircase outside the door as someone from one of the rooms below came up to investigate. Exhaling a sigh of relief, he braced one foot against the window-sill and hauled on the line with all his might to test the iron's hold on the tree. The slender trunk bent a little, but the iron seemed secure enough. He crossed back to the beam, drawing in as much slack as he could before retying the line.

He looped the satchel over his head so it dangled from one shoulder, then tied one end of the forty-four-foot length of rope about his waist, before looping the remainder of the coil over his head so it was suspended from the other shoulder. The harness belayed to the block went over his head and under his arms, and he hooked the block over the rope. He lowered the trailing end of the forty-four-foot rope out of the window so the grappling iron dangled a few feet below him, cocked one leg over the window-sill, and then the other, so that he was perched there. A final check to make sure the sheave of the block rested squarely on the line, a deep breath, and he swung himself out into space.

The world seemed to spin around him as he twirled this way and that, the oscillation of the grappling iron below him exacerbating his own swinging. The chill night air stung his face. As the birch tree bent

225

under the strain, the line sagged, and gravity carried him to the middle of the line, so that he dangled nearly halfway across the canal, some forty feet below him. He felt horribly exposed in the moonlight. Off to his right he could see the two guards standing at the gate on the other side of the bridge leading over the canal. Either one of them had only to glance to his right, and he was bound to see the figure hanging over the canal scarcely a hundred yards away.

Killigrew waited for the gyrations of the harness to die down, then reached up to grasp the line above his head. He began to haul himself along it, hand over hand, until he was over the island's grassy embankment. When he reached the tree he wrapped his legs around the trunk to keep him in position and leave his hands free to work. Under his weight, the creaking birch swayed alarmingly. He was still twenty feet from the gable of the warehouse, and some twenty feet below its apex. Working the forty-four-foot coil of rope out from under the harness, he held it in one hand and played out about five feet through the other, letting the grappling iron dangle below him. He swung it back and forth, until the iron had enough centrifugal force for him to swing it in a circle, faster and faster, and then let fly. It arced up, landed on the roof of the warehouse and rolled down with a clatter into the gutter between two gables. He gathered it in, and hauled on it to test the hold. It came free, dropping down to land with a thud on the embankment at the foot of the wall.

He gathered the rope in, coiling it in his left hand, and tried again. This time the iron did not even clear the roof, but clanged off the bricks to fall to the ground once more. He glanced at the guards off to his right. Both of them had cigarettes out now and one of them cupped his hands to accept a light from the other: they had not heard the sound.

The iron cleared the roof on the third attempt, once more rolling down into the gutter between two gables. He gathered the rope in once more, expecting the iron to fall free again, except this time it caught on something out of sight. He hauled on it: it seemed fast, but could he trust his weight – his life – to it? Since he could not free it, it seemed he did not have much choice in the matter. There was no turning back now.

Killigrew shrugged himself out of the harness and swung away from the tree, hitting the wall at an angle with an impact that snatched the breath from his lungs and sent him spinning dizzyingly back out again, before gravity mastered the situation and swung him perilously close to a window. Bracing his feet against the bricks, he clambered up hand over hand until he was able to haul himself up on to the roof.

He crawled into the gutter between two gables, out of sight from the windows of the houses on the other side of the canal, and lay on his back on the tiles of the roof, panting. When he had caught his breath, he edged his way to the far end of the roof, and was able to look down into the space at the middle of the island.

The two channels that led between the warehouses joined in a single, large basin in the middle. The fronts of the inward-facing warehouses formed another triangle, more than three hundred yards down each side. Limelights floodlit the whole area, and Killigrew could see crew-cut *matrosy* – Russian sailors – in grey pea jackets and flat forage caps working on the docks around the basin, unloading naval stores from a fifty-foot pinnace on the far side of the basin. A funnel rising amidships betrayed the presence of a steam engine on board. It was unusual to see such a small craft with a steam engine: an experimental craft, Killigrew presumed. There was no sign of the *Sea Devil*, but a boat-house facing across the basin on the quay below him looked promising.

He retreated from the edge of the roof and looked around. As he had surmised, there was a skylight amongst the tiles. The pitch of the roof was not too steep, and he clambered up to it without difficulty. A grille of iron bars a foot apart protected the glass, which was grimy and covered with algae. The space below was in darkness. Killigrew took off his belt and tied it tightly around two of the bars, sliding the pry-bar through the loop and turning it. The belt was tightened against the bars, until they bent perceptibly. He went on turning the pry-bar, tightening the belt, until the two bars touched in the middle. Repeating the performance with the next two bars, he managed to create a gap two feet wide.

Next he took out the bottle of treacle and emptied it on to the skylight, smearing it all over the glass with the paintbrush until every inch had been covered. He unrolled the brown paper, laying it over the treacle-covered glass and fixing it there. Then he took the pry-bar and tapped the glass through the paper, increasing the force of each blow and hoping the sound of the men working in the middle of the island would mask the noise. At last the glass cracked, and he repeated the blow at the same strength all the way around the pane. He peeled back the brown paper carefully, bringing the shards of glass stuck to the underside with it, so that none dropped to the floor below to make a tinkling noise. It was amazing what you learned when you had a former burglar as a boatswain's mate on your ship.

Pulling the last shards of glass from the window-pane, he peered into the darkness below. He had the impression it was a long way down: all the way to the ground, in fact, which had to be at least fifty feet. He untied the rope from the grappling iron and belayed it around two of the bars that had been bent together. He tied a knot in the other end, a couple of feet from the bottom, so he would know when he was running out of rope, and dropped it through the skylight. Then he eased himself through, gripping the rope tightly, and shinned down into the darkness.

There was still some light from the moon coming through the skylights and the windows, and his eyes quickly adjusted to the gloom. Tall spars were stacked around the sides of the warehouse, standing on their ends so they would dry out more quickly, but most of the floor seemed to be covered in some strange, circular objects that he could not quite make out.

Killigrew was still a few feet off the ground when the soles of his half-boots touched the knot at the end of the rope. He looked at the strange objects below him. There were dozens of them, all cones; about two foot tall, their bases about fifteen inches in diameter.

Infernal machines: he had seen a diagram of one in the *Illustrated London News* shortly before leaving England.

He muttered a word that a gentleman like himself only knew from spending so much time in the company of coarse-mouthed sailors.

The devices were packed so closely together that their rims touched, and any spaces between them had the explosion-triggering horns projecting into them.

He lowered himself a couple more feet, and then unfolded one leg until the sole of his boot rested on the mooring ring, now at the apex of the cone. He wondered how much weight one of the zinc cones could bear. Perhaps if he divided his weight between two of them . . .? Slowly, he relaxed his arms until the two cones took most of his weight. Still holding on to the rope, he straightened, trying to balance on the cones.

To get to the clear floor space just inside the door, he would have to move from cone to cone, and taking his foot off one would leave all his weight on the other. Still keeping his hands on the rope so he could haul himself up the moment he felt the cone start to buckle under his weight, he lifted one foot and put it down on top of the next cone.

It did not crumple or explode. He lifted his foot from it, and put it down on the next.

So far, so good.

Now he had to let go of the rope if he was to make any further progress towards safety. Balancing awkwardly on the two cones, he lifted one leg and put his foot on the next cone. When he lifted the other foot, however, he felt himself teetering. He flailed his arms wildly in an effort to keep his balance, see-sawing his body back and forth. Best to keep moving, he told himself, and put his foot on the next cone. Arms spread like a tightrope walker – *let's see M'sieur Blondin try this one!* he thought wryly to himself – he picked his way across the cones. He had almost made it when he felt one of the cones start to crumple beneath his foot. He quickly lifted his leg and transferred his weight to the apex of another cone, but now his legs were spread so far apart it was almost impossible to keep his balance. He straightened and stepped on to the next cone. Feeling himself falling forwards, he kept moving in that direction, struggling to keep his feet below his centre of gravity, until he was able to leap from the last of the cones and roll over on the dusty flagstones beyond.

He glanced back at the partially crumpled cone, and scrambled back against the doors of the warehouse, throwing his arms up to protect his face from the blast. If the glass ampoule within had been cracked, he had only a few seconds before the acid ignited the powder. Eight pounds was not a big charge by any means, but it was enough to set off the mines surrounding it, and they would be enough to set off the mines surrounding them: a wave of explosions, spreading outwards through the infernal machines stored there. The zinc casings of the cones would be shredded like paper, the jagged pieces of metal hurled in all directions like shrapnel. Throwing his arms up to protect his head was a futile gesture. At least his death would be relatively swift and painless . . .

How long had passed since the cone had begun to crumple? Ten seconds? Fifteen? From what he had heard, the infernal machines that had detonated under the *Merlin*'s hull must have exploded more or less simultaneously. With growing confidence, he permitted himself to believe the device would not explode after all.

Picking himself up and dusting himself down, he turned his attention to the huge door. There was a Judas gate, and he opened it a crack to peer out. Two stacks of timber were arranged on the quayside before him, and through the gap between them he could see the *matrosy* unloading the naval stores from the pinnace in the glare of the limelight: kegs, casks, crates and bundles. Were they going to work all night?

Limelight or no, Killigrew knew that sooner or later he was going to have go out through that door. But to delay the moment as long as possible, he turned his attention back to the infernal machines and the rope that dangled from the skylight above them. He might have to leave in a hurry – assuming he got the chance to leave at all – and he did not want to play tiptoe over the infernal machines again. He started to move them, one at a time, clearing a path through to the bottom of the rope.

He crossed back to the Judas gate and peered out again. The *matrosy* working on the quayside gave no indication that they were nearing the end of their task; fortunately none was looking in the direction of the warehouse. Killigrew slipped out, crouching low, and dashed across the cobbles to duck down behind one of the stacks of timber. Glancing back at the warehouses behind him, he saw each had a number painted on the doors in large, white Arabic numerals. The one he had just emerged from bore a '13'. *My lucky number*, he thought ruefully.

He peered around the stacked timber. No one had seen him emerge from the warehouse. The large wooden doors at the front of the boat-house were shut, but he could not see anywhere else in the shipyard where the *Sea Devil* might be stored. Creeping from timberstack to timberstack, he made his way around the back of the quayside, working his way towards the boat-house. At least the bright limelights cast the shadows into relative darkness.

There was a door at the rear of the boat-house, but it was padlocked. There was a small window beside it. He opened his clasp-knife and inserted the blade between the frames of the sash, sliding the catch open. He pushed the window up and dragged himself inside, rolling on the flagstone floor within. Gasping for breath, he sat up. The only light within filtered through the grimy window behind him and through the water beneath the gate at the front of the boat-house.

As his eyes adjusted to the gloom, he realised there was a figure standing against the wall a few yards away. Killigrew froze, waiting for the other man to speak first, but the figure remained motionless. Had he not even seen him climb in through the window?

Killigrew spent what seemed like an eternity waiting for the other man to speak or move, but the man remained as motionless as a tailor's mannequin. Slowly, moving an inch at a time, Killigrew reached inside his satchel until his fingers closed around the comforting grip of his revolver.

He whipped it out and levelled it at the man.

Who still did not stir.

Killigrew picked himself up and walked towards the man, keeping the gun aimed at his chest. As he drew nearer, he realised what he was looking at. He raised the gun and tapped the muzzle gently against the glass plate in the front of the brass helmet. The diving suit was empty, of course.

He tucked the revolver in his pocket and took out the bull's-eye, opening the front to light the wick inside with a match. He closed the front once more, shaking out the match, and cast the beam about the interior of the boat-house, taking care not to let the light shine against the gap in the gate or the windows.

A dock some seventy feet long ran in from the front, with a slipway at one end and a winch for hauling boats out of the water. In addition to the diving suit, there was an air pump, workbenches, and racks of various tools.

But no iron cylinder fifty-two feet long and twelve feet wide. Nothing of any description that might be an underwater boat, for that matter. He crossed to the dock and aimed the bull's-eye's beam into the gently lapping water. The beam picked out the concrete bottom of the dock.

No *Sea Devil*.

He felt the cold steel of a pistol muzzle touch him behind one ear. 'Don't move! Turn around . . . very slowly.'

Killigrew turned around . . . very quickly. With his left hand he batted the arm holding the pistol aside, while with his right he thrust the bull's-eye's light into the moustachioed face of his opponent, a pigeon-breasted young man in the uniform of a *michmani* in the Imperial Russian Navy. Killigrew barely had time to register that the *michmani* was alone, and then agony exploded through his loins as a knee was lifted into his crotch. Even as he doubled up in pain, he instinctively seized the *michmani*'s right hand in his left, holding the gun aside, and clapped a hand over his mouth to prevent him from crying out. The two of them fell to the flagstones, grappling. Killigrew reached for the *michmani*'s throat, missed, and clutched at the young man's bosom instead.

His soft, yielding, decidedly *feminine* bosom.

The bull's-eye had fallen on the flagstones beside her head, the light shining through its cracked lens to reveal the false moustache was coming adrift.

'A woman!' Killigrew hissed in astonishment.

'Get your hands off me!'

231

She punched him in the jaw, snapping his head around, and drew her legs up between them, kicking him off her. Writhing in the agony of his throbbing scrotum, he fumbled in his pocket and managed to pull the revolver out. She kicked it from his wrist and he heard it clatter in the shadows off to his left. Then she had picked up the bull's-eye, and its dazzling light shone in his tear-filled eyes.

'You!' she exclaimed. 'I might have known!'

'Do I know you?' he gasped.

She turned the light on her own face, pulling off the moustache with her other hand. He squinted up at her to see her cap had fallen off in the struggle, her brunette hair spilling down in ringlets on either side of her face. There was no mistaking those large, dark eyes or the cheekbones that flanked her amused smile.

'Countess Vásáry,' he groaned, shifting himself into a sitting position and massaging his aching crotch. 'Or whatever your real name is.'

'Plessier,' she told him. 'Aurélie Plessier.'

'French?' he asked.

She nodded.

'What are you doing here?'

'The same as you, I should imagine: trying to destroy the underwater boat your government so carelessly lost to the Russians.'

'A lady spy?'

She grinned. 'Do not be fooled, *mon brave*: as you yourself observed, I'm no lady!'

'Yes, but . . . even so . . . espionage is no job for a woman.'

'Was not Delilah a woman? I have managed very well so far; is it not so?'

'You've been lucky so far, I'll grant you, but this is a job for a man.'

'Lucky *mon cul*! I'm doing better than you, at least!'

'And just how do you come to that conclusion?'

'I'm not the one sitting on his backside clutching his testicles.'

Still wincing in pain, Killigrew realised he was not keeping the British end up. He forced himself to his feet, although he could barely stand straight. 'The *Sea Devil* isn't here.'

'Your powers of observation do you credit. They must have moved it.'

'Any idea where to?'

'If I knew that, would I be standing here now?'

Before Killigrew could think of a suitable retort, light flooded the boat-house as the door was opened and a soldier stood silhouetted on the threshold. Seeing Killigrew and Aurélie, he shouted '*Stoi!*' and started to unsling his musket.

Forgetting all about his pain, Killigrew dived across the room to where his revolver had fallen. He snatched it up and raised it in one hand, squeezing off a couple of shots. One of them hit the soldier in the chest and he slumped back against the open door, dropping the musket as he crumpled to the flagstones.

'Bravo!' Aurélie said scathingly. 'Why not simply send calling cards to the Russians announcing our presence?'

'And just what would you have done?' demanded Killigrew.

'This!' As another soldier stepped through the doorway, she whirled and produced a stiletto from her sleeve, flinging it across the boat-house. It took the soldier in the throat, and he crumpled with blood jetting on either side of the haft.

The two of them ran across to the door. As Aurélie retrieved the stiletto, wiping the blade clean on the dead soldier's greatcoat, Killigrew looked out to see six more soldiers charging across the quayside towards the boat-house. He brought up his revolver and squeezed off a couple more shots, missing all six of them but making them dive to the cobbles or scatter for cover, at least. It would not be long before they rallied, however, and more and more soldiers seemed to be emerging on to the quayside. He slammed the door.

'Now listen to me,' he told Aurélie firmly. 'If we work together, and you do exactly as I tell you, we might just have a chance of getting out of here alive . . .'

'*Mon cul!* Every woman for herself!' She sprinted across the boat-house, diving head first into the dock. She cleft the water like a knife and swam out under the gate.

Killigrew was still staring after her in astonishment when the door shuddered as one of the soldiers outside started throwing his shoulder against it. Killigrew fired twice, splintering holes through the planks. The shuddering stopped and there was the sound of a body hitting the ground immediately outside. A moment later the window shattered as something smashed through to land at Killigrew's feet: a grenade with the fuse sputtering. He took the brass helmet from the diving suit and dropped it over the grenade. It exploded, the helmet shooting up on a column of flame to smash a hole through the roof. It smashed a second hole on the way down before splashing into the dock.

Three more grenades came flying through the window. Killigrew thought about kicking them into the dock to extinguish their fuses, but there was not time to get all three: he took a deep breath and threw himself into the dock instead. The surface lit up above him as the grenades exploded, the water pounding his ears. He swam out under the gate into the basin outside, surfacing amongst the shadows in the lee of the quayside. There was no sign of Aurélie. Glancing back towards the boat-house, Killigrew saw the Russians were being very cautious before entering the building, even though the explosion had blown all the windows out. He took another deep breath and duck-tailed under the water once more, swimming across to where a set of stone steps were cut in the side of the quay. He hauled himself out of the water and peered over the top of the steps to see Aurélie standing with her palms pressed against the side of a stack of timbers while two Russian soldiers levelled their muskets at her and a third frisked her under the watchful eye of a burly NCO.

They were so intent on Aurélie, none of them was looking for Killigrew. Perhaps they thought she had been acting alone. The next stack of timbers was only a few yards away, and he reckoned he could reach it without being spotted. From there, it was only a short distance to the door of warehouse number thirteen.

He sighed, and snapped open the frame of his revolver, tipping out the spent cartridges and replacing them with fresh rounds from his satchel. Her creed might be 'every woman for herself', but Killigrew lived by a different code altogether: one that would not permit him to turn and run, abandoning a woman to the cellars of the Kochubey Mansion; even if she was the sort of woman who unhesitatingly left a chap to die and used expressions like '*mon cul*'! He stood up and stepped on to the quayside, levelling his revolver as he advanced on the four soldiers.

'Let her go!' he commanded in Russian.

The NCO turned to regard him with amusement. 'It's all right, lads,' he told his men. 'That gun's no good to him with wet powder.'

Killigrew aimed at the NCO – always start with their leaders, he told himself – and opened fire. His first shot splintered one of the timbers behind the NCO's head. Then the other soldiers were unslinging their muskets, and there was no time to pick his targets. All he could do was blaze away, aiming for the relatively large targets of their chests. Fortunately they were bunched close together, and his only concern was that he might hit Aurélie.

She proved to be perfectly capable of looking after herself, however, snatching a four-by-two from the pile and swinging it at the head of the soldier who had been frisking her, laying him out. Next she turned on the NCO and swung the plank at his head, but he caught it and tore it from her grip. Showing no reluctance about striking a woman, he swung it back over his shoulder. Aurélie had no reluctance about striking a man, for that matter, and she moved in close, butting him on the bridge of the nose. He staggered back against the stack of timbers, and she turned and ran. Killigrew was about to finish the NCO off with his final shot when he realised that the only other Russian still standing was levelling his musket at him. Killigrew swung the revolver round and shot him first, hitting him in the chest.

And then it was just Killigrew and the NCO.

Killigrew drew a bead on his chest and squeezed the trigger. The hammer fell on a spent cartridge: even M'sieur Lefacheaux could not invent a revolver that carried more than six bullets.

Realising he was not dead after all, the NCO grinned wolfishly and charged, swinging the four-by-two at Killigrew's head. The commander ducked beneath it and the plank connected with nothing except air, but that did not stop the NCO's onrush. He crashed into Killigrew, bowling him over, and the two of them grappled on the quayside. Killigrew tried to swing the grip of the revolver at his opponent's head, but the NCO caught him by the wrist and rolled on top, smashing his hand repeatedly against the cobbles until the revolver flew from his fingers. Taking the four-by-two in both hands, the NCO pressed it against Killigrew's throat, choking him. Then the NCO's whole body seemed to shudder, and his eyes crossed and glazed over. Killigrew threw him off to reveal Aurélie standing over him.

Killigrew rubbed his neck gingerly. 'What happened?'

'I kicked him in the balalaikas,' she explained, clasping his hand and hauling him to his feet.

He snatched up his revolver and tucked it back inside his pocket. 'I thought you said every woman for herself?'

'I decided I owed you one. Besides, I need you to show me a way out of here.'

'What's wrong with the way you came in?'

'They're between me and it.' She pointed to where three dozen more soldiers were charging on to the quayside from the direction of the main gate.

'Warehouse thirteen,' he told her, pointing in the opposite direction.

She needed no further bidding, but sprinted across the cobbles so fast that Killigrew struggled to keep up. She got the Judas gate open and disappeared inside. He stumbled in after her, closing the door behind them, and the two of them lifted the bar and slotted it across the gate.

'I'll tie the rope around you, climb up first, then pull you up after me,' he told Aurélie. 'You'll be quite safe, I assure you—'

He turned to see she was already shinning up the rope perfectly nimbly without any assistance from him.

The Judas gate shuddered as the Russians outside started to batter at it. The bar would not hold for ever, but it would keep them at bay for a couple of minutes, and a couple of minutes was all Killigrew needed to get clear. Seized by a momentary inspiration, he picked up one of the infernal machines and put it down just inside the door, with one of its horns pointing towards the planks.

Aurélie was already scrambling up through the skylight above. Killigrew shinned up after her. This time, at least, she had the grace to wait and help him squeeze through at the top, but she did it with the air of a younger partner whose style was being cramped by grampa.

Once on the roof of the warehouse, Killigrew ran to the outer edge and gazed down to where the line still ran from the birch tree to the window of the tenement on the street on the other side of the embankment. 'Bring the rope and the grappling iron,' he told Aurélie over his shoulder.

'The rope I just dropped back down into the warehouse so the Russians cannot climb up after us, you mean?'

'Yes, that one,' he agreed sourly.

She joined him at the edge of the roof and followed his gaze down to the birch tree, twenty feet out from the back of the warehouse. Realising her error, she looked up at him with a sheepish, impish grin. 'Oops?'

# XV

# A Pleasant Cruise Through St Petersburg

The soldiers were still battering at the door of the warehouse; and from the sound of splintering wood, the bar on the door was going to give way at any moment. On the roof of the warehouse, Killigrew seized Aurélie by the hand and dragged her on to the next roof, leading her up the sloping tiles to the apex.

No sooner were they running down the other side than a succession of explosions shattered the night, growing louder and overlapping as Killigrew's impromptu booby-trap exceeded his wildest expectations. He glanced over his shoulder to see the shattered tiles from the roof of the warehouse borne up into the night sky by a billowing cloud of flame. The roof beneath their feet shuddered and a great wave of hot air slapped into their backs, throwing them down into the gutter between the next two gables.

Aurélie picked herself up. 'Now what?' she asked.

'How should I know?' he retorted.

'I thought you had a plan!'

'I did!' he reminded her. 'Right up to the moment where you threw the rope away.'

They continued running over the gables, up one side and down the other, again and again and again. It was remarkably like trying to move on a violently pitching deck, Killigrew was surprised to find. They rounded the angle at the north-east corner of the island and made their way down the east side, crossing a dozen more gables. The next warehouse's gable ran longitudinally rather than transversally, and they jumped down on to it from the eaves. Killigrew landed awkwardly on the tiles and yelled in alarm as he tumbled over the edge. He managed to catch hold of the guttering, and dangled helplessly with his feet scrabbling against the brickwork before Aurélie appeared above him.

'Where would you be without me to look after you?' she demanded, clasping his free hand to help him haul himself back to safety.

'About thirty feet below where I am now,' he admitted, 'but spread over a wider area.'

They edged along the side of the roof to the gable end, where the way was blocked by the gap for the channel running from the central basin into the Kryukoff Canal. It was fifty yards to the continuation of the roof on the other side of the channel, and thirty feet to the cobbles below.

Killigrew and Aurélie peered over the edge. 'How do we get down?' she asked.

'I'm open to suggestions.'

'We jump!'

'Sensible suggestions, I meant.' Killigrew took another look over the edge. There was a ledge a couple of feet below him, and a few more feet below that a series of brickwork buttresses supported the gable-end of the warehouse: although steeply pitched, the buttresses were not sheer, and there was a good chance he and Aurélie could climb down.

Squirming on his belly, Killigrew eased his legs out over the edge until his feet touched the ledge. He eased himself down from that until his legs touched the top of a buttress, and from there he could see there were a number of windows looking out across the gap. Straining to reach from his precarious perch, he managed to push up one of the sashes, and looked up at Aurélie on the ledge above him.

'Do you think you can—' he started.

She looked at him as if butter would not melt in her mouth, inviting him to continue with only a hint of a smirk on her lips.

'Oh, never mind,' he sighed. 'Just follow me.'

He lowered himself from the top of the buttress and dangled from one hand until he could hook the other over the window-ledge and swing himself across. The toes of his half-boots scrabbling against the brickwork below, he boosted himself up and through the window to tumble on the bare floorboards within. Aurélie landed on top of him barely seconds later. As annoying as she was, Killigrew had to admit it was a good thing she was every bit as nimble as he was, otherwise they would never have got this far.

'Are you all right?' she asked. 'You look . . . *derangé. Pardonnez-moi,*' she added, squirming on top of him.

'My pleasure, mam'selle,' he assured her.

She grimaced, and pushed herself up by putting a hand against his face and thrusting his head down. Once she had climbed off him, he picked himself up and followed her down the corridor to the flight of stairs at the end.

Three flights below they reached a hallway with a stout door at the far side. Killigrew tried the handle: it was unlocked. Opening it a crack, he peered out across the quayside. No one was rushing towards them: he could hear shouts from somewhere off to the right, out of his line of vision, but the only Russians he could see were the *matrosy* working on board the steam pinnace tied up at the quay on the far side of the channel, now loading it with more infernal machines from one of the warehouses. Smoke issued from the pinnace's funnel, and there was a glow from the furnace on deck. It was impossible to tell if the engine had sufficient pressure up, but Killigrew could only hope. There was a drawbridge across the channel separating them from the quay, but it was down, thank heavens.

Aurélie tugged at his sleeve. 'We're still on the island,' she reminded him.

'It's all right. I think I've just found a way out of here.'

'Oh?' She sounded sceptical, so he opened the door a couple of inches further so she could see for herself. 'But no! You are not serious?'

'But yes,' he retorted, throwing the door open. '*Après vous, ma petite barbouze.*' He ushered her outside.

There was no need to tell her not to run. The two of them crossed the drawbridge at a steady walking pace. Off to their right, the boat-house was a smoking ruin, and soldiers were carrying away the wounded men scattered before the shattered remains of warehouse number thirteen.

'How's your helmsmanship?' he asked her in a low voice as they approached the steam pinnace.

'My what?'

'Do you know how to steer a boat?'

She shook her head.

'Never mind. When we get on board, you cast off the mooring ropes and I'll take the helm. You do know how to cast off mooring ropes, don't you?'

She scowled at him. 'What about those men on board?'

239

'After we've dealt with them, I meant. We could take them with us, but I doubt we'd relish their company. They don't look like witty and amusing companions to me.'

'Will two of us be enough to crew her?'

'More than enough,' he assured her. 'It's not as if we're planning a six-month cruise on the open sea.'

'I hope you know what you're doing!'

'Trust me.'

'You sound like a politician.'

He looked hurt. 'I say, that was a low blow! Bow-fast first.'

'*Pardon?*'

'The one at the front. Er . . . that's the pointy end.'

She nodded, glowering at him, and continued along the quayside while Killigrew dropped down into the stern of the pinnace. '*Dobryi vecher, mouzhiki,*' he told the *matrosy*.

'*Dobryi vecher, szr,*' they replied, bowing and scraping at the accent of an officer without looking at him properly.

Aurélie unlooped the bow-fast from its mooring bollard, and crossed to where the stern-fast was tied. Seeing what she had done, one of the *matrosy* ran to the gunwale to stop her, protesting. Reaching the gunwale, he looked up at her, and gaped in astonishment when he realised she was a woman. She kicked him in the head.

With a shout of alarm, another *matros* ran to his shipmate's aid. Killigrew tripped him up, sending him flying headlong across the deck to crack his head against the engine casing. A third stared at Killigrew in amazement, and got a fist in his jaw for his pains, tumbling him back over the gunwale. Aurélie cast off the stern-fast, and jumped down into the stern. She picked up a shovel and used it to whack the stoker in the face, flipping him back over the gunwale into the basin.

The soldiers on the opposite quay had seen what was going on by now, and levelled their muskets, but at that range their aim with the antiquated weapons was erratic at best, not so much a danger as a distraction.

Killigrew waved Aurélie across to join him by the engine, and showed her two levers, tapping one. 'Push this one forward when I say, "Turn ahead, half," and both of them when I say, "Turn ahead, full". Pull them back for "turn astern". Got it?'

'I think I can remember that,' she said drily.

'You'll have to stoke the furnace, I'm afraid,' he told her, moving aft to take up position at the tiller. 'Keep an eye on the pressure gauge:

if it goes into the red, stop shovelling. If it falls, start shovelling again.'

The soldiers had reloaded, and were running around the quayside now. 'Turn ahead, full!' Killigrew shouted as one of them dropped to one knee and levelled his musket, sending a bullet close enough to smash splinters from the taffrail.

Aurélie pushed both levers forward and the deck throbbed beneath their feet as the engine shuddered into life, the screw-propeller churning the water astern into a millrace. Killigrew adjusted the tiller, turning the bow away from the quayside, and as the propeller blades bit at the water the pinnace surged forwards. He aimed the prow at the channel leading out of the basin into the Moika River, beneath the great arch between the warehouses on that side.

'How come you know so much about the engine on a Russian steam pinnace?' demanded Aurélie.

'Check the name-plate on the boiler!' he called to her.

' "Seaward and Capel, Millwall, eighteen fifty-three".'

He nodded. 'Great Britain, arms manufacturer to the world!'

'That must make you very proud,' she said, deadpan.

'Anything but,' he assured her.

As the pinnace approached the channel leading beneath the arch, soldiers converged on from both sides of the quay. The first to reach it started to winch down the drawbridge to block their escape.

'We'll never make it!' Aurélie yelled at Killigrew.

'Of course we will,' he shouted back. 'Although having said that, you might like to duck your head.'

She threw herself down on the deck between the engine and the gunwale, and Killigrew crouched at the tiller. The soldiers lining the side of the channel fired down into the boat, their bullets splintering the woodwork or spanging off the iron frame of the engine.

The drawbridge was at forty-five degrees when the pinnace's prow passed beneath it. There was plenty of clearance.

Except for the mast, of course. It bent forwards as the bridge pressed against the forestays on the starboard side, and then the stays snapped and the mast whipped back, rocking the whole boat. Then it whipped forward again, so it was moving at more than twice the pinnace's accelerating speed when it struck the bridge. There was a splintering crash, and the mast went by the board while the bridge itself was ripped off its hinges to flop down across the gunwale, where it caught on the transom. The pinnace slewed around to starboard, and Killigrew adjusted the tiller to compensate, the whole vessel groaning in protest. It started to heel over, and for one heart-stopping moment he was sure they would turn turtle. Then the wrecked bridge slid off the transom and crashed sideways into the water.

The impact had all but stopped the pinnace, and even though the propeller drove them on as soon as they were clear of the obstruction, it was still slowed down sufficiently for half a dozen of the soldiers on the quayside to risk trying to jump down on her deck. Three of them even made it, two sprawling on the deck boards while the third managed to hook his hands over the gunwale. One of them lunged at Killigrew with his bayonet. With the far side of the Moika River looming up, the commander did not dare release his grip on the tiller even for a second, but the soldier was struggling to keep his balance on the rolling deck. Killigrew kicked him in the chest and threw him back against the port gunwale, while Aurélie laid the other low with her shovel. As they passed beneath the arch, Killigrew jinked the tiller to port, scraping off the man who clung there so that he fell into the water with a scream. Then they had emerged into the Moika and Killigrew pushed the tiller to starboard, making a sharp left.

'No!' Aurélie shouted in panic. 'Turn right!'

It was too late, however, even if Killigrew had been inclined to follow her advice. There was hardly any room to manoeuvre in the narrow confines of the river. The tight turn was enough to heel the pinnace over to port, catching the man with the bayonet off guard and throwing him over the gunwale.

Once they were in midstream, heading up-river, Killigrew brought the tiller back amidships. 'Told you we'd make it,' he shouted to Aurélie, who was busy pushing the unconscious man over the side.

'But there's no way out this way!' she wailed.

'There's no way out whichever way we go,' he called back mildly. 'The best we can hope to do is put enough distance between them and us to give them the slip.'

'The bridge!' she yelled.

They rounded the south-east corner of Novaya Gollandia, and the graceful arc of the Bridge of Kisses loomed up ahead.

'Plenty of clearance,' Killigrew assured her.

'Even for that?' She indicated the slim funnel that rose above the engine amidships.

'Ah, that. Yes, I'm afraid we're going to have to lose that.' Killigrew took out his clasp knife and tossed it to her. 'Cut through the stays supporting it, or it'll pull us over when it goes by the board!'

She opened the knife and sliced through the stays. Already the pinnace's prow was under the bridge. 'That's good!' Killigrew called to her. 'Now get as far for'ard as you can!'

As she scrambled to the bow, Killigrew jinked the tiller to port, slewing the pinnace's stern around to starboard. He wanted to hit the bridge at a slight angle: what he did not want was for it to fall back and land on his head.

The funnel hit the side of the bridge with a resounding clang and the whole vessel shuddered and yawed in the water, threatening to capsize. There was an eldritch sound of rending metal, and the funnel toppled like a felled tree, smashing down on the port gunwale and bouncing into the river where it landed in the water with a terrific splash. The pinnace rolled sickeningly, but Killigrew pushed the tiller to starboard, straightening her out. A sooty downdraught of smoke from the truncated funnel blinded him as they passed under the bridge, but then they were through and steaming down the river on the other side. Killigrew whooped in exultation.

Beyond the Bridge of Kisses, the Moika ran more or less straight as far as he could see in the half-light of the summer's night. As a getaway vehicle, he might have wished for something slightly less conspicuous, but they were clipping along at a good seven knots, the small boats moored at the embankments on either side dancing in their wake.

Aurélie had stopped shovelling. 'How's the pressure?' called Killigrew.

'Nearly in the red!'

'All right, that should give us enough steam to get us away from here.'

'They'll be coming after us,' she warned him. 'We should turn off: try to lose them.'

'If you see any turnings, be sure to point them out to me!' he retorted. From his recollection of the map of St Petersburg, the Moika ran all the way to the Fontanka Canal, a mile and a half away. The only turn off was the Winter Canal, and that was on the other side of the Nevsky Prospect; and he intended to ditch the pinnace long before they reached the busy intersection at the Police Bridge.

The next bridge loomed up at them out of the darkness, a narrow suspension bridge for pedestrians. The truncated funnel scraped sparks from the underside, but otherwise they passed beneath it without a hitch. Half a minute later, Killigrew saw a bend in the river about fifty yards ahead. He was getting ready to make the turn – the clumsy pinnace was a swine to handle in the narrow canal – when Aurélie glanced astern.

'We've got company!'

Killigrew looked over his shoulder to see a troop of horsemen cantering past the suspension bridge on the embankment, just over a hundred yards behind them.

'Well, I certainly didn't invite them!' he retorted with mock petulance.

The appearance of that many horsemen could be no coincidence. From the way they rode in formation they had to be soldiers, although it was difficult to make out more than that in the half-light. Killigrew turned the pinnace around the bend, and they lost sight of the horsemen, but for less than half a minute. They were scarcely ninety yards astern, and gaining on the pinnace, when they reappeared.

'Can't you make this thing go any faster?' demanded Aurélie.

Killigrew shook his head. 'We're flat out as it is.'

Another bridge loomed out of the darkness, less than a hundred yards ahead. They would reach it ahead of the horsemen, but then what? Sooner or later the cavalrymen were going to pass them on the embankment, and then they would take up position on the next bridge and shoot down into the pinnace as it passed beneath; and at that range, even Russian soldiers would not be able to miss. Yet to jump ashore would only leave them on foot, to be ridden down by the horsemen. Killigrew looked for some kind of transport on the embankment – horses, a drozhky, anything – but in vain.

'How far to the Blue Bridge?' Aurélie asked suddenly.

'About two hundred and forty yards beyond the next bridge,' Killigrew told her.

'We'll lose them there,' she decided, and started to fiddle with one of the infernal machines stowed in the bow.

'What the devil are you playing at?' he demanded. 'I shouldn't monkey about with one of those if I were you: it's liable to blow up in your face!'

'I know what I'm doing,' she retorted.

'That's what Rear Admiral Seymour said!' Killigrew muttered under his breath.

He heard the crack of a carbine, and glanced over his shoulder to see the horsemen were less than sixty yards astern now, their muzzles flashing in the gloom as they shot from the saddle. The received wisdom was that a man could not shoot straight from the saddle, but someone had forgotten to tell these troopers. The bullets soughed through the air about the pinnace, kicking up spurts of water from the river up ahead, and one bullet splintered the gunwale alarmingly close to where Killigrew stood. He crouched beside the tiller.

'Better keep your head down!' he called to Aurélie.

'Thanks for the advice!' her voice came from somewhere forward of the engine.

Then they had passed under the next bridge, which hid them from the view of the horsemen for the next few seconds. They had covered less than fifty yards, however, when more shots sounded. Killigrew glanced astern to see the horsemen – dragoons, judging from their brass helmets – had passed the bridge and were continuing to gain on them. There was still no sign of the Blue Bridge up ahead.

Killigrew winced as a bullet ricocheted off the casing of the boiler: if the metal ruptured, the whole thing would burst and the Russians would kill two birds with one stone.

At last the Blue Bridge – where Killigrew had seen the serf-market four days earlier – appeared less than a hundred yards ahead. But the dragoons were barely two dozen yards behind the pinnace, and making more and more of their shots tell. The gunwale to Killigrew's left was starting to look like a piece of Swiss cheese. Judging from their relative speeds, pinnace and dragoons would reach the bridge at about the same time, but it was going to be a close-run thing.

The Blue Bridge was getting closer. It was so wide, it looked more like they were about to enter a tunnel than pass under a bridge. The dragoons would not have time to dismount and take up position at the near railing, so they would ride across to line the far railing, waiting for the pinnace to emerge at the other side. If Killigrew and Aurélie were going to give them the slip, it would have to be before then. Fortunately, nothing could have given them better cover than the Blue Bridge.

Killigrew looked around for a coil of rope so he could tie off the tiller. Beyond the bridge, he knew, the Moika continued straight for another five hundred yards or so before curving around to the left. If the dragoons saw the pinnace emerge on the other side, they might not realise the two saboteurs had abandoned ship and continue to pursue it upstream, giving Killigrew and Aurélie a chance to slip down one of the side streets leading off the embankment. He tweaked the tiller, edging them over to the right-hand embankment where there was less clearance between the truncated funnel and the underside of the bridge.

'Aurélie!' he called.

There was no reply at first, and for a moment he feared she had been struck by a bullet – a moment in which he ran the whole gamut of emotions from horror to self-recrimination – but then she called back.

'What?'

'I need some rope! Can you see a coil lying around up there, hanging from one of the pinrails perhaps?'

'One moment!'

The bridge was only fifty yards ahead, and the dragoons had almost drawn level. Killigrew ducked as more shots splintered the gunwale.

'We haven't got a moment!' he shouted back tersely.

Forty yards, thirty . . . what the hell was she playing at?

She crawled astern, keeping the engine between herself and the dragoons on the embankment. Fortunately the dragoons had left off shooting – saving their ammunition for a fusillade when the pinnace emerged from under the far side of the bridge – and they spurred their horses into a gallop.

Aurélie handed Killigrew the coil of rope. 'Get the anchor,' he told her, cutting the rope in two. He made a final adjustment to the tiller before tying it off with the smaller length, then Aurélie returned with the small, four-fluked anchor from the bow and handed it to him.

The dragoons had reached the bridge seconds ahead of them and disappeared from view as they galloped across to the far railing. Killigrew rove the longer length of rope to the anchor and dangled it over the starboard gunwale. 'Stand on my left!' he told Aurélie.

He began to swing the anchor, forwards and back, parallel with the side of the pinnace. The prow had already passed under the bridge. Killigrew twirled the anchor in a circle, like a leadsman preparing to swing the lead. When the bridge was only a few yards away, he released one end of the rope, and the anchor snaked up over the blue-painted railing above. He hauled in the slack until the flukes caught against the railings, making it fast around his torso. He could only hope the dragoons on the bridge would be engrossed in reloading their carbines and waiting for the pinnace to emerge below them.

'Put your arms around my neck!'

She complied, and he lifted her up in his arms, stepping on to the transom and swinging from the stern as the pinnace moved out from beneath them. In the shadows below the bridge, he could just make out a faint glow of light at the far side, silhouetting the pinnace as it chugged on, leaving the two of them swinging over the water.

Pleasant though it was to have Aurélie's arms around his neck, her body pressed against his and her face inches from his own, Killigrew now faced the prospect of hauling both his own weight and hers up to the railings above. Without any prompting from him, however, she climbed up him, grabbing the rope above him and stepping on his head to boost herself up. When she was level with the surface of the bridge, she raised her head slowly and peered through the railings; the coast must have been relatively clear, for she scrambled over the railing and turned back to reach for him.

He hauled himself up. Through the railings, he could see the dragoons a hundred yards away. They had dismounted from their horses, leaving a few of their number to hold the bridles while the rest crowded at the far rail, their carbines levelled at the water below. Aurélie clasped Killigrew's hand and helped him up over the railing.

He had barely got his feet back on solid ground when one of the dragoons holding the horses glanced across the bridge and saw them. He shouted a warning to his comrades, and several of them whirled, levelling their carbines. Aurélie was already dashing across the embankment to the corner of the Mariinsky Palace, but Killigrew felt like a rabbit caught in the gig-lamps of a pony-chaise speeding down a country lane. At that range, there was a chance that in the poor light *most* of them would miss with their carbines . . .

Smoke billowed up from under the bridge as the pinnace emerged, and the dragoons froze, torn between shooting at the man frozen against the far railing or pouring a hail of lead down into the boat. In the event they did not get the chance to do either, for a terrific explosion tore the night apart, hurling up flames that silhouetted the dragoons and tossed the ones standing at the rail to the cobbles, while the horses reared in terror.

The blast snapped Killigrew out of his daze, and he turned and sprinted after Aurélie. He reached the side of the Mariinsky Palace and found himself gazing down the Vosnesensky Prospect, but Aurélie was nowhere to be seen. He cursed. A bullet chipped the masonry a few inches from his hand and, hearing booted feet clatter across the cobbles behind him, he did not bother to waste time glancing over his shoulder, but stumbled headlong down the boulevard.

He had scarcely covered more than fifty yards when a handful of the dragoons rounded the corner of the palace and sent more bullets buzzing past his head. Cursing Aurélie for leaving him high and dry, he threw himself back and forth across the empty street in a series of zigzags to throw the dragoons' aim off, at the same time well aware he was only putting off the inevitable moment when one of them mounted his horse and rode him down. He dashed for the mouth of the Officers' Street, only to see a drozhky rattling towards him. He started to veer away, looking for another bolt-hole, when the driver of the drozhky called out to him.

It was Aurélie: she reined in across his path, the wheels of the drozhky skidding on the dew-slick cobbles. 'Get on!'

Killigrew needed no second bidding; he had not really needed the first. He climbed on to the back of the drozhky, she flicked her whip across the horse's back, and they clattered off. The dragoons continued to shoot after them until she made a sharp left on to Kazansky Street, followed by a right at the next junction. There was no sign of their pursuers by the time they reached the embankment of the Yekaterinsky Canal 350 yards further on. Aurélie turned the drozhky left, and at the next bridge they crossed the canal to reach Sennaya Square, where she parked the drozhky behind one of the stacks of covered hay bales in the market place.

The two of them slipped down an alleyway, hurrying through the shadows until they came to a courtyard where they could pause for breath. Abruptly, Aurélie pushed him against a wall and kissed him passionately. He was so caught off guard, by the time he had relaxed sufficiently to enjoy it and give her his full attention, the two patrolling gendarmes were past them and she broke off the kiss. Killigrew gazed after them in disappointment.

Aurélie was already hurrying on. Killigrew made to follow her, and had almost caught up with her when a shadowy figure burst out of the doorway of one of the ramshackle apartment blocks and crashed into her. The two of them staggered, and Killigrew interposed himself, but the shadowy figure – a wild-eyed, pale-faced student clutching an axe – seemed even more frightened than they did. He backed off, muttering to himself, then turned and dashed into the night.

'Clumsy idiot!' Aurélie shouted after him in gutter-Russian. 'Look where you're going!'

'Are you all right?' Killigrew asked her in a low voice.

'Of course! You?'

'I'll be glad of a chance to change out of these wet clothes.'

'Me too.'

'You know, we make rather a good team, you and I.'

'Yes,' she agreed drily. 'It's a pity we didn't find the *Sea Devil.*'

'Perhaps if we worked together . . .'

'Team up, you mean?'

'Worked cheek by jowl . . .'

She grinned impishly. 'Sorry; I work alone. And you'd best get back to your hotel. I've a feeling the Third Section will be on their way now to find out whether or not you're tucked up in bed.' She turned on her heel, skipped away from him, and then the darkness swallowed her up and she was gone.

He sighed, and headed off in a direction he hoped would take him back to the Nevsky Prospect.

# XVI

# From Russia With Love

---

The sound of the first explosion echoed across the rooftops of St Petersburg. Working late in his office, Superintendent Voronin threw down his pen and stood up, moving around his desk to open the door to the annex outside his office.

'What was that?' he demanded of the clerk at the desk.

'I don't know, sir.'

'Find out. And have Sergeant Astapchyonok bring my carriage around the front with two gendarmes standing by.'

'Yes, sir.' The clerk hurried out of the room and Voronin retreated to his office to put on his greatcoat and a wideawake. He made his way through a maze of corridors until he came to a door that most people in the building walked straight past, thinking it was nothing more than a closet. In fact, it opened into a stairway leading up to the roof, and Voronin was one of the few people who had the key. He made his way up on to the roof, where there was a walkway behind the balustrade.

Voronin liked to come up here when he needed to think and the hubbub of the office was too distracting. It was nice and quiet up there, and even during the day the sounds of the streets below were little more than a droning in the background. He looked around, scanning the horizon in all directions until he saw the pall of smoke off to the south-west: over Novaya Gollandia, by the look of it. The navy was working on some kind of top secret experiment there; he wondered if it had gone wrong.

The second explosion that shattered the stillness of the night was closer, about halfway between Novaya Gollandia and the roof where

Voronin stood, but even so there seemed to be a delay between the blossoming of yellow flame that rose over the Moika Canal and the crack of thunder that followed. Voronin gripped the balustrade and stared as a second cloud of smoke mushroomed up.

He snapped out of it and ran back downstairs. Sergeant Astapchyonok was waiting for him outside where two gendarmes – Evdokinchik and Chorny – sat on the driving board of a carriage.

'Did you hear the second one, sir?' the sergeant asked him, wide-eyed.

Voronin nodded. 'Between St Isaac's Cathedral and Mariinsky Palace.'

'Should we go there now?'

Voronin shook his head. 'Whatever happened, whoever was responsible will be long gone by the time we get there. In fact, it would not surprise me if he was long gone already. Take me to Dussot's: with luck we'll get there in time to catch him sneaking in the back door.'

They climbed in the carriage and drove down the Nevsky Prospect, pulling up outside Dussot's Hotel. Voronin jumped out.

'Evdokinchik, stay here with the carriage and guard the front door,' he ordered. 'I want to know who comes and who goes. Check their papers; and if they have no papers, arrest them. Chorny, you go round the back and do same at the back door. Both of you be on the lookout for M'sieur Bryce. Astapchyonok, you come with me.'

As Chorny hurried off down the alley at the side of the hotel, Voronin and Astapchyonok approached the front door. It was locked, so the sergeant hammered on it until it was answered by a sleepy-eyed night porter. Voronin forestalled any grumbling about the lateness of the hour by flashing his warrant card.

'Has anyone come in during the past half-hour?' he demanded.

'No one's come in for the past three hours.'

The two of them hustled the night porter back inside. 'Give me the key to M'sieur Bryce's room,' ordered Voronin.

The night porter glanced at the pigeonholes behind the reception desk. 'M'sieur Bryce's key isn't here. He must be in his room.'

'We'll see about that. Give me the spare.'

Voronin took the key and the two of them dashed up the stairs to Bryce's room. Astapchyonok hammered on the door. 'Open up, M'sieur Bryce. This is the police.'

There was no reply. Voronin and Astapchyonok exchanged glances, and the sergeant hammered again, but all was still on the other side of the door. Voronin unlocked it and threw it open. There was no sign of Bryce. The bed was dishevelled.

Astapchyonok laid a hand on the mattress. 'Cold.'

Voronin nodded. 'We've got the *drachevo* now.'

'Which *drachevo* would that be, Superintendent?'

Voronin and Astapchyonok turned to see Bryce standing on the threshold, dressed only in a vest and drawers, barefoot, a glass of water in one hand.

'Where have you been?' demanded Voronin.

Bryce raised the glass. 'I went to the kitchens to get a glass of water. Why? Surely that's no crime? Even in this cockamamie country.'

'Why not ring for the chambermaid to bring you a glass?' demanded Astapchyonok.

Bryce grimaced. 'We don't hold with having servants waiting on us hand and foot where I come from. I knew the way to the kitchens; didn't see the point of getting someone else out of bed at this time of night to do it for me.'

'Your clothes are damp,' observed Voronin. 'How did that happen?'

Bryce grinned ruefully. 'Had an accident with the pump in the kitchens. Ain't you people ever heard of faucets?'

'And you've been in bed all night,' said Voronin. It was a statement rather than a question, because he knew what the answer was going to be and he knew it would be a lie.

'Sure. Look, what's all this about, Superintendent? Has this got something to do with those two explosions I heard a while back?'

There was a knock on the open door. Voronin glanced up to see Evdokinchik standing there. 'I thought I told you to guard the front entrance?' he told the gendarme angrily.

Evdokinchik saluted smartly. 'Yes, sir. But I was ordered to bring you this.' He handed Voronin a note.

The superintendent read it through twice before tucking it inside his glove. 'Come on,' he told Astapchyonok. 'Let's go.'

'Does that mean I can get some peace now?' demanded Bryce.

Voronin rounded on him. 'Don't think about trying to leave the country, M'sieur Bryce. I'm not finished with you yet.'

'You got an accusation to make against me, Superintendent, I suggest you have some proof. The United States' State Department don't take kindly to having its citizens' rights trampled all over.'

'We'll see.' Voronin marched from the room and was followed downstairs by Astapchyonok and Evdokinchik.

'Guilty as hell,' opined the sergeant. 'I still don't know what he's guilty of, but I'll wager my last kopeck he's guilty of it. And you're just going to let him go, sir?'

'For now. Orders from Kochubey Mansion: Bryce is "hands off".'

'What does he have to do for us to be allowed to arrest him? Assassinate the Tsar?'

'I don't know. But I mean to ask the man who ordered the "hands off" notice before this night is out.'

A second carriage awaited them outside, parked behind the one that had brought them from the office. Voronin crossed to speak to the man who sat in the shadows behind the windows, a thin-faced fellow with a cane.

'Superintendent Voronin?'

Voronin nodded.

The thin-faced man showed him his own credentials, which established him as Lieutenant Kizheh of the Third Section. 'Admiral Zhirinovsky would like a word with you.'

Voronin turned back to Astapchyonok. 'Get Chorny and head back to the bureau,' he told him, before climbing in the second carriage with Kizheh. There was no point telling Astapchyonok when he would be back, because where the Third Section was concerned you could never be sure of anything.

Which meant Voronin could not be sure if he would ever be returning to the office.

He was driven up the Nevsky Prospect and along Horse Guards' Boulevard to Novaya Gollandia, where the guards on the bridge over the Admiralty Canal stopped them. Quite a lot of guards, Voronin noted: the navy, closing the stable door after the horse had bolted. Kizheh showed their NCO his credentials and the carriage was waved through without further questions.

Once on the island, the carriage pulled up outside one of the administrative blocks and Kizheh led the way through a door and up a flight of stairs to one of the offices, leaning heavily on his cane. A stocky, bearded man in an admiral's uniform sat behind the desk.

'Admiral Zhirinovsky?' asked Voronin.

The admiral nodded and regarded him coolly. 'And you are?'

'Police Superintendent Voronin. I was told you wanted to see me?'

'Indeed I do, Superintendent. I understand you are aware of the identity of the saboteurs who attacked this place earlier tonight?'

'I think I may know who one of them was, yes: a man calling

himself John Bryce, posing as an American journalist. But he bears a remarkable resemblance to Commander Christopher Killigrew of the British navy.'

'I know this Bryce. He's staying at Dussot's. I suggest you go there at once and arrest him, Superintendent.'

Voronin stared at the admiral in astonishment. 'Arrest him! I was just about to arrest him when I received a note telling me Bryce was "hands off", and ordering me to report to you.'

'No one's going to arrest Bryce,' said a new voice.

Voronin turned to see Nekrasoff enter. The colonel took out a silver cigarette case, extracted a cigarette, tapped it twice against the case and plugged it in the corner of his mouth. Kizheh struck a match to light it for him.

'What do you mean, no one's going to arrest Bryce?' spluttered Zhirinovsky.

'Because Superintendent Voronin is quite right, Admiral: Bryce is indeed Commander Killigrew, a British spy.'

'Tonight he broke into this shipyard, blew up a warehouse full of Professor Nobel's mines, stole an experimental steam pinnace and blew it up on the Moika Canal before making his escape,' Zhirinovsky fumed. 'May I ask what else he has to do before you order his arrest?'

'Killigrew is *not* going to be arrested because he is working for me.' Nekrasoff took a drag on his cigarette, puffed a long stream of blue-tinged smoke into the air, and smiled broadly. 'He just doesn't know it yet.'

'You've had a busy night,' Wojtkiewicz remarked when Killigrew arrived at his house the following morning. 'Explosions at Novaya Gollandia, gun battles in the streets . . . your handiwork, I take it?'

'I had a little help,' Killigrew admitted modestly as the two of them crossed the hall.

'That's the end of the *Sea Devil*, then?'

'Unfortunately not. It wasn't there. They must have moved it.'

'Where to?'

'I wish I knew.'

'So it's back to the drawing board?'

'I'm afraid so,' Killigrew agreed as they ascended the stairs. 'I'll just have to keep looking, that's all.'

'Keep looking! Are you insane? Face facts, Killigrew: your mission is a failure. You've got to get out of the country as soon as possible. It's only a matter of time before the Third Section hauls you off to the Kochubey Mansion for questioning.'

'They came to my hotel last night. I think I managed to throw them off the scent.'

'You went back to your hotel?' Wojtkiewicz shook his head in disbelief. 'You are totally insane; you know that, don't you?'

Killigrew managed a wan smile. 'I've long had my suspicions . . .'

Wojtkiewicz sighed and shook his head again.

They reached the top of the stairs. 'Where's Lika?' asked Killigrew.

'In the ballroom. You know the way?'

'Yes. I'd like to speak to her in private, if I may.'

'Unchaperoned, eh? Oh, to be young and in love! I'll be in the library.'

Killigrew made his way to the ballroom, where he found Anzhelika practising arabesques. She broke off as soon as she saw him and ran across to embrace him, but he caught her by the wrists and slammed her back against one of the walls. There was pain and confusion in her eyes as she looked up into his tight-lipped face.

'Where's Bauer?' he demanded.

'Who?'

'Wilhelm Bauer. A Bavarian engineer. You met him when you danced at Covent Garden four years ago. You gave him a daguerreotype of yourself. If you'd given him a calotype, well . . . I dare say calotypes of Anzhelika Orlova are ten a penny. But daguerreotypes? I'll lay odds you remember each and every one you've ever given to someone. Bauer's in Russia now; probably somewhere in this city. In fact, I suspect he's been here weeks. Do you mean to tell me he hasn't sought to renew your acquaintance? Or do you have so many lovers you find it difficult to keep track?'

She struggled, wanting to slap him, but he held both of her wrists tight. So she kicked him in the crotch instead. He gasped in agony and released her, staggering across to collapse in one of the chairs, clutching at himself.

'Yes, I knew Willy,' she admitted. 'Yes, we met in London four years ago. And yes, we were lovers – not that it is any business of yours. You knew I was not a virgin. Did you expect me to give you a full list of my past lovers? I do not remember you offering me the same courtesy when we became lovers; though I will wager your list is ten times as long as mine.'

'It's probably not as long as you think,' he said hoarsely.

She ignored him. 'It is a strange double standard in our society, do you not think? A man can have as many lovers as he pleases and everyone thinks he is a big man; but if a woman does not save her maidenhood for the marriage bed, she is called a slut.'

'I never called you a slut.'

'Then what is your interest in Bauer?'

'He's invented a secret weapon. My job is to find it and destroy it, before the Russians use it to kill hundreds of my countrymen.'

'Your countrymen?' She finally noticed that he had stopped using an American accent. 'You are an Englishman! An English spy!'

He nodded. 'What I told you before still stands: Wojtkiewicz and I can get you out of the country, and I know a ballerina of your calibre will have no difficulty in getting work at the Paris Opera.'

'You were never interested in me, were you?' Her tone was bitter. 'It was Bauer all along. You have just been using me to find him. And I thought you loved me!'

'I *do* love you. Christ! How could I not?'

'You would say that. You will forget all about me when you have got what you want.'

Killigrew shook his head. 'If I've been remiss in telling you how I feel about you, it's because I'm conscious of how many men have used those words in the past without meaning them. But I've also got a job to do, and I need your help. So I'll ask you once again: where's Bauer?'

'You would have me betray my country?'

'Do you know what this secret weapon Bauer's invented is?'

She shook her head tearfully.

'It's a boat that sails underwater, Lika. It can attach an explosive to the hull of a ship without anyone on board even knowing it. Men die in war, Lika. I've served in the Royal Navy long enough to know that. But at least until now they've been given a fighting chance. Bauer's machine will give them no chance at all. I'll admit my heart hasn't been in this war. But I do know I can't stand back and let the Russians use Bauer's machine to kill men in that way. There are eleven hundred men on the British flagship, and if Bauer sinks it then most of them will die by drowning.

'Do you know what it's like to drown, Lika? I do; thanks to a session in a torture chamber courtesy of the Third Section of your Tsar's Imperial Chancery. They say drowning is a pleasant way to die – that you just slip under the waves and then you're gone – but you can take it from me, it isn't like that at all. You feel your lungs fill with water. You gasp for air, but there's no air to be had. There's a tightness across your chest like an iron band that grows ever tighter, until you stop struggling and pray for death because you know it's the only chance you've got to escape the agony...'

Anzhelika hung her head. 'Helsingfors. Willy has gone to Helsingfors.'

Wojtkiewicz took Killigrew and Anzhelika in his carriage as far as Kabalovka, a small town just north of St Petersburg on the road to the Finnish border. Jedraszczyk was waiting for them with a couple of horses at one of the town's many inns; not the main coaching inn on the high street, which the Third Section kept under observation, but a smaller place at the edge of town.

Anzhelika was wearing clothes given to her by Wojtkiewicz; left behind at the mansion by one of the Pole's former lovers, Killigrew guessed: mink hat, coat, and a matching fur muff suspended from her neck to hang across her bosom.

He took Killigrew to one side while she swung herself into the saddle. 'Are you sure about taking her? It would be better if I put her on one of my ships. I could smuggle her as far as Danzig; perhaps even deliver her to your fleet in the Gulf.'

Killigrew shook his head. 'Abandon a lady on her own in a strange city? Worse still, leave her on a ship crewed by licentious sailors? Perish the thought! Besides, she insisted on coming with me. She's been an absolute brick about all this so far; and frankly, I'm going to need all the help I can get when I get to Helsingfors.'

'Yes, I've been thinking about that. Do you have any idea how you're going to get her out of the country? Assuming that by some miracle you survive this lunatic mission of yours to find and destroy the *Sea Devil*.'

'I thought perhaps I could bribe the skipper of a fishing boat to take us out to the British fleet.'

'Risky. The Finns have no love for the Royal Navy since your comrades started cutting out their merchant ships and burning their fishing boats and maritime stores. Identify yourself to the skipper of a Finnish fishing boat, and he and his crew might just be tempted to hand you over to the Russians; if they don't prefer to slit your throat for themselves.'

'You have a better suggestion?'

257

Wojtkiewicz nodded. 'There's a secret organisation in Finland called the Wolves of Suomi, much like the Carbonari in Italy. They're dedicated to fighting for Finnish independence from Russia. Before the war they contented themselves with trying to stir up anti-Russian sentiment amongst their countrymen by distributing seditious leaflets and daubing nationalist slogans on the walls of public buildings. More recently they've been giving the Russian troops stationed in Finland merry hell: blowing up ammunition stores, robbing army payrolls, you name it. They've no love for the British either, but . . . well, they may just realise that their enemy's enemy is a potential friend. You could do worse than persuade your War Office to have modern arms shipped to them. I've done them a few favours in the past, so they owe me. Drop my name, and it should stand you in good stead with them.'

'I'll do that,' agreed Killigrew. 'How do I contact them?'

'With difficulty! Usually they prefer to contact you.'

'And if they're not looking for me?'

'There's a professor of geology at the University of Helsingfors who may be able to put you in touch with them. His name's Rasmus Forselius: he was sent to Siberia when he was a student for advocating Finnish independence. That's where I met him. He's not an active member of the Wolves of Suomi – the Third Section keep a close watch on him still – but I think he knows who they are.'

'If the Third Section suspects him of being involved with these Wolves of Suomi, I wonder they haven't arrested him to torture some names out of him.'

Wojtkiewicz grinned. 'I'm sure they'd like to. But Finland isn't Russia, Killigrew: it's a constitutional duchy within the Russian Empire, and the Finns guard their separate rights jealously. Even the Third Section has to treat them with kid gloves. Now you'd best be on your way: it's a four-day ride to Helsingfors, and with the Third Section out looking for you, you'll have to avoid the main roads. There are plenty of hunting lodges in the forests of Finland – they're free to use for anyone who finds them – so you can avoid the inns on your journey.'

'I've put food in the saddle bags,' put in Jedraszczyk. 'Rye bread, cheese, smoked sausage, a few apples, and some coffee . . . it's not much, but it should keep you going until Helsingfors.'

Killigrew thanked him.

'You've got a compass?' asked Wojtkiewicz. 'Those endless forests and lakes can get confusing.'

'I can navigate using my—' Patting the fob pocket in his waistcoat, Killigrew broke off. 'Damn!'

'What's wrong?'

'My watch – Zhirinovsky's coachman broke it. It's useless.'

Wojtkiewicz sighed and pulled his own fob watch out by its chain. 'Here – take mine.'

Killigrew held it in the palm of his hand. It was gold, made by Moulinie Frères of Geneva. 'I can't accept this! I owe you enough money as it is.'

'It's a gift,' growled Wojtkiewicz, 'so don't insult me by refusing it – or talking about money.'

Killigrew tucked the watch in his pocket and looped the chain through one of the buttonholes of his waistcoat. Then he embraced the Pole. 'I don't know how I can ever repay you for all your help.'

Wojtkiewicz grinned. 'Just be sure that when you get to Sveaborg, you do unto the Russians as they've being doing unto my people since time immemorial.' He mimed grabbing someone by the scrotum and giving it a good wrench. 'Hit the bastards where it'll bring tears to their eyes!'

Killigrew and Anzhelika covered two score miles before sundown that afternoon, riding through a landscape of pine forests interspersed with long, thin lakes. They did not talk much: Killigrew sensed that Anzhelika was sulking because he had not told her the truth about who he was and what he was doing in St Petersburg until he had been forced to. Well, he could hardly blame her for that; only pray that she would eventually realise he had had little choice.

They headed roughly north-west. Killigrew had no compass, but he had Wojtkiewicz's watch, which, he guessed, kept excellent time.

When dusk came on they were still more than fifty miles from the Finnish border by his reckoning, so they stopped for the night at a barn on the outskirts of a small village, dining on the food Jedraszczyk had packed for them, curling up to sleep in the hayloft afterwards.

They were roused at dawn by the moaning of a rising wind, and after breakfast emerged from the barn to find a gale brewing up. The sky was gravid, but Killigrew insisted they pushed on regardless, determined to reach Helsingfors as soon as possible. The most recent reports in the Russian press had put the Allied fleet off Nargen, on the Estonian coast, but that had been two days ago; by now it could be anywhere in the Gulf of Finland.

The wind gusted through the forests, making the trees groan and sway, and the foliage below danced as if every bush and clump of bracken were alive. It stung their cheeks and brought tears to their eyes. Even if Anzhelika had been in a conversational mood, shouting above the howling of the wind took too much effort to be worthwhile. The sky remained overcast all day, occasionally sending down patters of fat droplets of rain without ever really summoning the enthusiasm for a full-blown shower. They skirted the Gulf of Vyborg in the afternoon, giving the port itself a wide berth, and when darkness came on they could find no shelter but were forced to huddle in a hollow in the forest.

The gale continued unabated the following day but they rode on nonetheless. Killigrew reckoned they must have crossed the border an hour or two after starting out, not that there was any marker in the forests: the landscape of pines and lakes was the same in Finland as it had been in Russia. They skirted the town of Hamina late in the afternoon, and when they stumbled across a hunting lodge an hour afterwards Killigrew decided it was time to stop for the day.

A hunting lodge – that was what Wojtkiewicz had called them, at any rate. Killigrew's experience of hunting lodges was limited to the one on the Duke of Hartcliffe's Scottish estate; he did not expect that anything quite so grand was provided *gratis* for the common folk of Finland, which was just as well otherwise he would have been severely disappointed by the small, one-room log cabin they found. From the look on Anzhelika's face as she surveyed the Spartan interior, her own hopes had not been so modest.

'It could be worse,' he told her. 'Four walls, a roof over our heads, running water . . .' He gestured to the small stream that ran through the forest nearby. 'What more can you ask for?'

'A bed and somewhere I can my powder nose,' she replied acerbically.

'I think those furs are what pass for the bed . . .'

'From the look of them, they are inhabited already!'

'. . . And as for a necessary, you'll just have to go around the back.' She sighed. 'You want me to make a fire, I suppose?'

'Thanks, but the last time I asked a woman to get a fire going, I almost burned to death.' That had been Araminta, trying to make a pot of coffee in the galley of Hartcliffe's yacht at Cowes Regatta the day he first met her. He felt a pang at the memory: they had been able to laugh about it afterwards, and remembering that he would never laugh about anything with her again filled him with pain.

'What's wrong?' asked Anzhelika.

'Nothing. I just thought of something, that's all.'

'What?'

He put on a smile to reassure her. 'Nothing for you to worry about.'

They dined on sausage, cheese, bread and apples and afterwards Anzhelika arranged the furs into two piles . . . on opposite sides of the cabin. *Well, that speaks for itself,* Killigrew thought ruefully. He wrapped himself up in his share of the furs and snuggled down to sleep, listening to the ululating threnody of the wind as it gusted around the eaves of the cabin. He must have fallen asleep almost at once, for the next thing he knew the fire had burned down to its embers, and he awoke to find Anzhelika snuggling against him.

He turned to face her. 'I thought you were sulking?' he whispered.

'I was.'

'Then why the sudden change of heart?'

'I thought, why punish myself?'

She kissed him, and he drew her closer to him, the two of them making gentle yet passionate love in front of the fire.

In spite of his nocturnal exertions, he woke early the following morning, roused by the sound of the birds twittering in the trees. It took Killigrew a moment to realise that the gale must have finally blown itself out. Leaving Anzhelika to sleep a little longer, he rebuilt the fire so he could brew some fresh coffee, and stepped outside to relieve himself against the back of the cabin before fetching some water from the stream. A fine mist hung amidst the boughs of the trees, but there was a fresh, earthy scent in the air.

He went back inside and brewed the coffee over the fire. When she smelled it, she opened her eyes and smiled across at him.

'Time to go,' he told her.

'Must we?' she mumbled sleepily. 'Could we not stay and live here for all time?'

' "Come live with me and be my love",' he quoted. 'It's a tempting proposition. But I've got a job to do.'

'And if you had to choose between me and your job, which would it be?'

'If you love me as much as you expect me to love you, that's a question you won't press me for an answer to,' he replied. 'If the Russians succeed in sinking the *Duke of Wellington* and the Allied fleet withdraws – which it almost certainly will, with an old woman like Dundas in charge – then the war will just be dragged out a few more months. It's not just the men on the *Duke* I've got to worry about; it's the thousands more who will die if this war can't be brought to a swift conclusion.'

'What makes you sure the *Sea Devil* will be used to attack the *Duke of Wellington*?'

'I'm not. But it's the logical thing to do. It's the most powerful ship in the Allied fleet – in the world, for that matter – and it's the British flagship. She's the pride of the Royal Navy, and the Royal Navy is the pride of Britain. Sink her and the damage to morale both in the navy and at home will be incalculable.'

After a swift breakfast of bread and cheese, they went outside and were about to mount up when they heard hoof beats. Hundreds of hoof beats, the jingle of harness, booted feet marching more or less in time, and the rumble of wheels over a rutted track.

Killigrew and Anzhelika exchanged glances. Even as they listened, the sound grew louder.

'They're coming for us!' she whispered.

'If they are, they've sent a whole army after us. Wait here a moment.'

'Where are you going?'

'Not far.'

He moved quickly through the bracken, his eyes straining to see through the mist and the trees for the source of the sound. The Russian soldiers materialised out of the mist so suddenly he almost ran into them. He ducked down behind a clump of ferns to watch as they marched past on the road below. There were hundreds of them: a squadron of hussars leading the way, followed by a whole regiment of fusiliers, horse-artillery, a ponderous baggage train of ox carts and another squadron of hussars bringing up the rear. Killigrew reached for his revolver, not that it would be much use to him against an entire army.

Once the soldiers had all marched past, he retreated to where Anzhelika waited. She looked relieved to see him.

'Russian soldiers,' he told her curtly, helping her into the saddle. 'Marching west, towards Helsingfors.'

'The same way we're headed,' she said.

He nodded, and swung himself up on to his own horse. 'They're not moving fast. We'll leave them behind us soon enough if we skirt around to the north.'

The mist faded, but the sky became gravid until finally the heavens opened an hour and a half before noon, slashing through the boughs overhead to drip on Killigrew and Anzhelika as they continued on their journey, drenching them. The rain continued on and off until two o'clock, when the sun broke out and chased away the clouds. It soon grew warm enough for Killigrew and Anzhelika to ride with their coats rolled on the backs of their saddles, and even beneath the forest canopy the sun soon dried them out. Thousands of birds sang in the boughs overhead, and occasionally they caught a glimpse of an elk through the trees. The only people they saw were a woodsman cutting logs and a party of huntsmen. They waved to both from a distance and received waves in return. In spite of the soldiers they had seen that morning, it was easy to forget there was a war on and they were fugitives in enemy territory.

They chatted as they rode. Killigrew did not like talking about himself, but he was content to listen to her prattle on about her childhood: growing up as the child of servants in the household of a Russian count, her subsequent training at the Imperial School of Ballet, and anecdotes from the time she had spent touring Europe and the eastern seaboard of America with the Mariinsky Ballet.

As the afternoon wore on they found another hunting lodge, so identical to the last one that for a moment Killigrew wondered if they were going around in circles. By his reckoning they could not be more than thirty miles from Helsingfors and would reach it the following afternoon. They dined on the last of the sausage, bread and apples, washed down with a cup of water from a nearby stream, and afterwards they sat on the porch, Killigrew keeping the mosquitoes at bay with a cheroot while the two of them watched the sky turn from pink to purple via orange and crimson. That night their lovemaking was more frenzied than usual, as if they both knew they were running out of time in more ways than one.

As they rode on the next day, it became increasingly difficult to avoid the roads converging on Helsingfors, until finally they gave it up altogether and followed the main road. The first people they passed were a well-to-do family in a coach and four rattling along the dusty track as if all the demons in hell were on their tail. Killigrew thought little of it until they passed several more such carriages, all heading away from Helsingfors. Then they saw the horse-drawn wagon, piled high with household goods: chairs, tables, paintings, even a grandfather clock that clanked and bonged with every rut in the road.

'Looks like someone's moving house,' Killigrew remarked.

263

More carriages passed them, and more furniture-laden wagons, and then he knew something was amiss. Within half a mile the traffic had become a steady stream of humanity: long-faced men, frightened-looking women and bawling children accompanying wagons and dog-carts piled high with all the valuables they could carry. A plump housewife chided a freckle-faced little girl for clutching a kitten instead of helping her father and brothers push a wagon.

Killigrew reined in his horse to address one of the refugees in Swedish. 'What's going on?'

'Haven't you heard? The enemy fleet's anchored off Helsingfors!'

# XVII

# Geology

 

'How long has it been there?' Killigrew asked the refugee urgently.

'Since yesterday afternoon.'

'Has it started bombarding?' As soon as Killigrew asked it, he realised it was a stupid question: they were close enough to the city to have heard if a bombardment had commenced.

'No, but it's only a matter of time!'

There were a dozen more questions Killigrew wanted to ask, but he knew they would only be answered when they reached the city. He rode back to where Anzhelika waited and told her what he had learned.

'What now?' she asked.

'We go on as before. And pray we're not too late.'

'But what if the Allies bombard the city?'

'They won't do that,' Killigrew told her. He was fairly sure that was true. 'Why bombard civilians when they've got Sveaborg to fire on?'

There was too much traffic coming out of Helsingfors for them to make any headway on the road, so they skirted the adjoining fields until they were on the heights overlooking the city, where they were brought up short by the sight of an entire army on parade: cuirassiers in gleaming breastplates; hussars wearing fat busbies; plumed lancers; dragoons with crested brass helmets; tall, moustachioed grenadiers; fusiliers, *jägers*, and artillerymen; all neatly arrayed in serried ranks upon the heights. Squadrons of horsemen galloped back and forth, teams of horses thundered past, drawing field guns and limbers, bugles blared, drums rattled, non-commissioned officers barked crisp commands, palms slapped against musket-stocks, bands played and regimental colours fluttered in the breeze. By Killigrew's reckoning there had to be at least ten thousand men there.

One of the officers reviewing his company glanced curiously at Killigrew and Anzhelika as they rode past less than a hundred yards away, but all he saw was a couple of civilians approaching Helsingfors.

'Just keep riding,' Killigrew murmured to Anzhelika.

From the heights they had a fair view of the rooftops of the city below, standing on a peninsular jutting out into the Gulf of Finland with two bays enclosed by islands on either side. Four miles off – less than three miles from the southern tip of the peninsular – Killigrew could just make out the ships of the Allied fleet, anchored on the glittering waters of the gulf. The ships were too far out for him to be able to see if the *Duke of Wellington* still floated.

'Do they mean to land soldiers?' asked Anzhelika.

Killigrew shook his head. 'No troopships with the Allied fleet this year.' He knew that between them, the ships of the British contingent could muster a force of some six thousand marines, and he did not doubt they were a match for the Russian troops parading on the heights; but such a victory would be won at a high cost in terms of human life, and to no advantage. Even if the British fleet could capture Helsingfors, it could not hold it. Besides, even if Dundas had been fool enough to attempt a landing – which a younger Napier might have done – the sight of all those troops would have discouraged him, which was doubtless why the Russians had paraded their garrison there.

The fleet could have come for one purpose and one purpose only: the bombardment of Sveaborg.

Leaving the Russian army behind them, Killigrew and Anzhelika rode down towards the city and found a livery stable on the outskirts. A bearded old man leaning against the door watched them approach.

'Give you two hundred marks for the pair,' he said before either of them could dismount.

Killigrew blinked at him. 'Two hundred marks?'

'All right, make it three. But that's my final offer.'

'Three hundred seems a little steep to me for a couple of old screws.'

'I can make it less, if you want. But I can sell them on for five.'

Killigrew smiled. 'If you can sell them on for five, what's to stop me from doing likewise?'

'A man's got to make a profit, hasn't he? Besides, you don't know the people I know. I'll make it four hundred . . . but that's my final offer.'

266

'Done.'

The two of them shook on it and the man scurried inside and emerged within a minute carrying a wad of notes. Killigrew handed him the bridles and counted the cash. 'Why the high price of horseflesh?'

'Everyone wants draught animals so they can get their property out of town. Draught horses, oxen, dogs, screws – folk are desperate enough to take whatever I can give them.'

Killigrew tucked the money in various pockets about his person and he and Anzhelika continued into the city. Laid out on an orderly grid pattern, Helsingfors was small and relatively young as cities went. There were fine town houses and neoclassical buildings painted in pastel shades of pink, brown, blue and yellow, with white pilasters and window frames. The high green dome of the Lutheran cathedral dominated the city skyline, with four smaller domes at each corner of the building.

As Killigrew and Anzhelika walked to the centre of town, it soon became clear that the owner of the livery stables had been exaggerating: not everyone in the city was convinced the Allies would bombard it, if the numbers of shops that had disdained to put up shutters and close until further notice was anything to go by, even if the streets did seem to be sparsely populated for a Tuesday lunchtime.

It was nearly two years since Killigrew had last visited Helsingfors. He led the way to the South Harbour, where the fish market bustled in front of the Imperial Palace, the residence of the governor-general of the duchy. They made their way along the promenade on the side of the harbour until they emerged from the south side of the city on the downs at the tip of the peninsular, where the government observatory and optical telegraph station stood on a hill. From there it was less than half a mile to West Svarto, the nearest of the islands that made up the Sveaborg cluster.

They saw at once why the city was so quiet: if half the population had fled in fear of the supposedly imminent bombardment, then the other half had come to the downs to view the fleet. Well-to-do families sat in their landaus and victorias, feasting from picnic hampers, smiling and laughing beneath the warm summer sun, women flirted beneath twirling parasols, and a brass band played cheerful tunes. Some enterprising folk had set up barbeques and were selling cuts of meat and sausages, or dispensing beer from kegs; all for inflated prices, naturally. There was a distinct carnival atmosphere. After forty years of peace in Europe, war had become entertainment.

Plenty of the sightseers had brought telescopes and opera glasses – a few more enterprising souls were renting out their own, and charging by the minute – so Killigrew felt no qualms about taking out his miniature telescope to view the fleet for himself. The ships had anchored about two and a half miles south of Helsingfors, beyond the reach of Sveaborg's guns. He quickly picked out the *Duke of Wellington*, the largest of them all, riding at the centre of a cluster of warships at anchor. And there was the *Ramillies*. It was just past four o'clock – eight bells in the afternoon watch – and by now the crew would be clearing the deck.

'Twenty mortar vessels,' he counted under his breath, 'nineteen gunboats, six steam frigates, six support vessels, five ships of the line, four blockships, three paddle-sloops, two corvettes . . .'

'And a partridge in a pear tree,' concluded Anzhelika. He glanced at her, and she grinned.

'Well, the *Duke*'s still there,' he told her. 'All present and correct, as far as I can see.'

'If the fleet arrived yesterday afternoon, surely this underwater boat has had plenty of time to make an attack?'

'Maybe it already did, and failed. Or maybe the Russians were caught by surprise. Perhaps the *Sea Devil* isn't ready yet. Or perhaps the Russians aren't in any hurry.'

'But you cannot count on that.'

'No,' he agreed. 'I can't.'

His gaze fell upon a small islet about a mile and a half to the south, where he could see French marines setting up a battery of five brass thirteen-inch mortars. There could be no doubt about it: Dundas had finally screwed his courage to the sticking place and the Allies' preparations for the bombardment of Sveaborg were in earnest.

Killigrew turned his attention to the maritime fortress. A neo-gothic castle perched on a crag overlooking the Rhine might look more impregnable, but such a castle would only last about half an hour under a sustained bombardment from the shell-guns of a single decker. No, a gothic castle was all very picturesque, but the days of castles had died with chivalry and knights in shining armour. For true menace – for a sight that filled your heart with a foreboding sense of impregnability – you needed a modern fortress: squat, ugly, and indomitable.

A complex spread across five of the low-lying islands off the Finnish coast, Sveaborg had first been built in the previous century by Finland's

Swedish overlords, in a style of which Vauban would have approved: all casements, ravelins and glacis to deflect the round shot of attacking men o' war. But the fortress had been strengthened and modernised when the duchy had become part of Russia; and according to the latest reconnaissance reports from the fleet that Killigrew had seen back in London, now it was in the process of being modernised yet again in preparation for the British attack that everyone anticipated. Bunkers were being strengthened against mortars, new forts built, extra artillery batteries added.

The five islands – Vargon, Gustafvard and East, West and Little Svarto – clustered close together, four of them linked by bridges built across the narrow channels that separated them. Barracks, dockyards, gunboat sheds, factories, foundries, administrative buildings, an arsenal, a magazine, a hospital and a church were all housed within the crenellated granite walls that frowned over the rocky outer shores of the complex. There was even a mill for grinding the fortress's copious supplies of grain into flour. A complete and self-contained community, the complex could hold out for weeks if not months in the event of a siege. A year ago, the incomplete fortress of Bomarsund had fallen to the Allies in a matter of days; but they would find Sveaborg an altogether tougher nut to crack.

'What are those boats doing?' asked Anzhelika.

Killigrew trained his telescope to where she pointed, at the sea between the fleet and the fortress. There were dozens of launches, pinnaces, cutters and dinghies from the fleet, moving slowly about the water in fits and starts. At first he could not work out what they were doing: they seemed to be working in pairs, dredging lines between them. Finally, it hit him. 'They must be sweeping the sea for infernal machines,' he explained. 'That's where the fleet will probably take up position for the bombardment: Dundas won't send the gunboats and mortar vessels in until the area's been thoroughly surveyed for hazards.'

'How long will that take?'

'A day or two. They don't seem to be in any hurry.' *But why should they be?* he asked himself. The only Russian ships in the vicinity rode at anchor in the bay behind Sveaborg, protected by its batteries, and they were outnumbered and outgunned by the Allied fleet. The Russians would have to be mad to sally out, and Dundas and Seymour knew it. So they could take as much time as they wanted to prepare the bombardment.

Killigrew and Anzhelika had missed dinner, but since he was feeling flush after his transaction with the owner of the livery stables, he stumped up for a couple of smoked sausages, and rolls to wrap them in. He handed one to Anzhelika, and the two of them munched on the snacks as he led the way back into the city. When they had finished, Killigrew produced a linen handkerchief so they could wipe the grease from their fingers and chins.

'What do we do now?' Anzhelika asked as they walked back along the promenade. 'Try to steal a boat to get to the fleet, to warn them about the *Sea Devil*?'

'Not much point,' Killigrew told her. 'Admiral Seymour wouldn't believe me. Dundas might, but if he did he'd just call off the attack. And that would be almost as disastrous as if the *Sea Devil* did sink the flagship.' The result would be the same: no Allied ship of the line would dare go within range of a Russian port for fear of the *Sea Devil*, and the blockade of Russia's Baltic ports would be broken.

'So what *do* we do?'

'I'm not sure what can be done,' said Killigrew. It was a white lie: he had a very good idea of what he had to do, but it was not a prospect that he cared for, and he certainly did not want to worry her. 'We have to try to contact the Wolves of Suomi and find out how much help they'll be prepared to give us . . . if any. But first, we need to set up a base of operations.'

An elegant four-poster bed dominated the middle of the bridal suite, and there was even a separate but en suite room for their own private bath, with running water (cold *and* hot) and one of the latest flushing water closets.

There had been no baggage to carry for the chambermaid who had shown them up to the room, but Killigrew tipped her generously from the wad of notes the owner of the livery stables had paid him.

'Thank you!' She curtsied and hurried out, closing the door behind her.

Anzhelika leaned her back against the wall behind her and folded her arms. 'So, this is your notion of a base of operations,' she remarked drily.

He shrugged, grinning. 'If you've got to go, you might as well go in style. Besides, after four nights of living rough we both deserve to enjoy rather more salubrious surroundings.'

Booking into Helsingfors' finest hotel was a calculated risk, but one

270

Killigrew thought they could afford to take: Third Section surveillance was not as intensive in this city as it was in the Russian capital, and if their agents were trying to identify the Wolves of Suomi they would be more interested in locals than in a Swedish merchant and his Russian wife. Killigrew's greatest fear was that someone was going to recognise Anzhelika as the *prima ballerina* of the Mariinsky Ballet. She insisted she had never danced in Helsingfors, but Killigrew knew it was not improbable that more than one resident of the city might have seen her dance on a visit to St Petersburg.

He divided the wad of notes into two, and handed half to her. 'You'll need some new clothes; head up to the end of the promenade by the fish market and turn left, you'll find plenty of dressmakers' shops on the esplanade.'

'How much should I spend?'

'As much as you like.'

'Why, Herre Johansson! I think you must be the perfect husband!'

He chuckled. 'You're too kind, Fru Johansson! Get me something while you're about it.' He gave her his measurements: it would have to be off the peg, but there was no time to wait around for a tailor's fitting.

'What are you going to do?'

'I'm going to the university.'

He walked with her as far as the fish market, and while she turned left on to the esplanade he cut through a side street into Senate Square. The ground sloped up to the north, where the cathedral stood at the top of a broad flight of stairs; the senate building was over on his right, and the university on his left. There was a notice board inside the hallway with various notices tacked to it. A number of public lectures had had the word 'cancelled' scrawled over them – due to academic nervousness about the intentions of the Allied fleet, no doubt – but there were more that were still on for that night. Fleet or no fleet, it was largely business as usual in Helsingfors that day.

One notice in particular caught Killigrew's eye:

Professor Rasmus Forselius
(University of Helsingfors Department of Geology)
will give a public lecture in
Subaqueous Deposits
at 8 p.m. on Tuesday 7 August
Lecture Theatre 1
Price of Admission: One Mark

271

'. . . The abundance of carbonate of lime produced by springs in regions where volcanic eruptions or earthquakes prevail is explained by the solvent power of carbonic acid. As the acidulous waters percolate calcareous strata, they hold a quantity of lime in suspension and carry it up to the surface where, under diminished pressure in the atmosphere, it may be deposited or, being absorbed by animals or vegetables, may be secreted by them. Which point brings my lecture to a conclusion.'

The audience rose for a rapturous standing ovation; even Killigrew, who cried out 'Encore! Encore!' until Anzhelika pulled him back down into his seat.

'What?' he asked her. 'I enjoyed it. Fascinating stuff.'

'Really?'

'No. Actually, I didn't understand a word of it.'

'Then why draw attention to yourself?'

'Imagine you're a Third Section informer on the lookout for a British spy in a university lecture hall. Who's the most likely candidate? The chap standing up at the end and shouting "Encore!", or the fellow sitting quietly at the back?'

'They teach you this in spy school back in England, do they?'

'Lor', no. I'm making it up as I go along.'

The rest of the audience had risen to its feet and was filing out of the lecture theatre. On the stage, Professor Rasmus Forselius gathered up his notes and tucked them in a satchel. Killigrew had been expecting someone older, perhaps bald-headed with a goatee beard: in fact Forselius was about forty; not tall, but well built, with a clean-shaven jaw and rather long blond hair.

As some of the people filing out of the university into Senate Square set off walking, others waited for their carriages or flagged down cabriolets. Killigrew bagged a cabriolet while there was still one spare, asking the driver to wait: he did not know whether the professor would be leaving in a carriage or on foot.

He looked at Anzhelika, her dark eyes peeping at him over the muffler wrapped over her nose and mouth. Wrapped up in her warm clothes, she looked even more vulnerable than ever. 'Perhaps you should go on to Åbo ahead of me,' he suggested. 'Try to find a boat and get out of the country as soon as you can.'

She shook her head. 'Oh, no you don't. I'm staying right here with you.'

'I'd feel a lot happier if you went. Please, Lika, for your own safety.'

272

'I can look after myself . . .' She pressed a hand to the back of her forehead.

'Are you all right?'

'A bit of a headache, that's all. Perhaps I should go back to the hotel and lie down.'

'I'll come with you.'

'You're supposed to meet the professor, remember? Do not concern yourself, I'll be all right.'

Killigrew glanced around the square. He was starting to wonder if perhaps Forselius had gone out some back way when he saw the professor emerge from the building and set off walking, one hand in the pocket of his frock coat, the other swinging his satchel as he whistled jauntily to himself. He did not make for any of the waiting carriages: Killigrew guessed he lived nearby. 'At least take the cabriolet,' he told Anzhelika, helping her up. 'Are you sure you'll be all right?'

She nodded. 'I've some powders back at the hotel; I'll be all right in an hour or two. Will you be long?'

'That depends on how co-operative the professor is willing to be. I'll try to join you for supper.'

She smiled. 'I'll have them put some champagne on ice.'

'Make it the 'forty-six, if they have any left.'

She gave the cabbie the name of the hotel, and Killigrew watched her depart before looking around for Forselius. The professor was already a hundred yards away, and Killigrew had to walk briskly to narrow the gap.

He followed him up the street between the university library building and the cathedral, into the smart residential area to the north of the city. The professor passed through the front door of a fine-looking town house – a butler appeared, to let him in – and Killigrew continued towards the end of the street. Then he doubled-back, making sure that no one had been following him while he had followed the professor, and pulled on the doorbell.

The butler answered the door. '*Ja?*'

'Is this the home of Professor Rasmus Forselius?' Killigrew asked in Swedish, a language in which he was a good deal more fluent than Russian.

'Indeed it is, sir.'

'My apologies to the professor – I appreciate the hour is unsocial – but I wonder if I might have a word with him?'

'Do you have a card?'

Killigrew shook his head. 'Just tell him Colonel Nekrasoff of the Third Section is here to see him.'

Scarcely a muscle flickered in the butler's face. 'Very good, sir. If you'll wait here I'll see if the professor is in.' He withdrew and closed the door behind him.

Killigrew did not wait for him to return, but casually made his way to the alley at the back of the house. Even as he arrived, the kitchen door opened and the professor emerged, struggling to pull on his overcoat while transferring his satchel from one hand to the other. He ran straight into Killigrew and would have fallen to the cobbles if the commander had not caught him.

'Excuse me,' he muttered, and tried to brush past, but Killigrew held him fast.

'You're in a hurry, aren't you? What does a loyal subject of the Tsar have to fear from an agent of the Third Section?'

Forselius stared at Killigrew. In the light from the back of the house, the commander saw the professor's shoulders slump and the colour drain from his face.

'It's a nice night,' said Killigrew. 'What say you and I go for a little walk?' Keeping a firm grip on the professor's arm, he steered him towards the end of the alley.

'What do you want with me? I've done nothing wrong.'

'I'm glad to hear it. Tell me, Professor Forselius, does the name Wojtkiewicz mean anything to you? Mscislaw Wojtkiewicz?'

'I don't know that name.'

'That's funny. He knows yours. He tells me he met you in Siberia.'

'He might have done,' Forselius admitted truculently. 'I met a lot of people in Siberia. You can't expect me to remember all their names.'

'He tells me you might be able to put me in touch with the Wolves of Suomi.'

'I don't know anything about that.'

'Oh, but I think you do.'

'Look, what's all this about? What do you want with me?'

'I need your help.'

'*You* need *my* help!' Forselius peered at Killigrew. 'You're not an officer of the Third Section!' he decided accusingly.

'Perish the thought! I'm a British spy.'

'British!' Forselius scowled. 'And why should a Finn want to help an Englishman?'

'Because we have an enemy in common.'

'The Russians?'

Killigrew nodded. 'With the help of the Wolves of Suomi, I can hit the Russians where it hurts. Will you take me to them?'

'I told you, I don't know any of the Wolves of Suomi.'

'You still don't trust me?'

'Well, now that you mention it . . .' sneered Forselius.

Killigrew sighed. 'Just tell them I'm staying at the Grand Hotel under the name of Herre Johansson, and if they'll contact me I have a proposition for them which may be to our mutual advantage.'

Anzhelika collected the key to her room from the reception desk and made her way upstairs. Unlocking the door, she stepped into the darkened room. She was reaching for a box of matches to light the oil-lamp on the bedside cabinet when someone grabbed her from behind, clamping a mouth over her hand.

She sank her teeth into it. The man muffled a yell, and she rammed an elbow into his ribs, breaking free.

'Lika, it's me!' gasped her assailant. 'Kit!'

Recognising his voice, she relaxed and struck a match. 'What devil do you mean by it, hiding in the dark and frightening the living daylights out of me?' She lifted the glass flue from the oil-lamp and applied the match to the wick.

'*I* frightened the living daylights out of *you*?' he retorted angrily. 'You told me you were coming straight back here. What was I supposed to think when I returned and found no sign of you? I thought you'd been picked up by the Third Section.'

'I went for a walk, that's all.'

'A walk?'

'Yes, a walk. I thought it would help to clear my head.'

'And did it?'

'It had, until you grabbed me like that.'

'Sorry. You might have left me a note to let me know where you'd gone. For all I knew, you were being tortured in a dungeon somewhere.'

Her glowering expression turned to one of delight. 'You were worried about me!'

'Of course!'

She reached out to touch his cheek tenderly. 'I am sorry. You are right; I should have left a note. It was thoughtless of me not to.'

He removed his glove: her teeth had torn the kid leather, but the skin beneath, although marked, was not broken. He massaged his palm ruefully. 'You were right about one thing, at any rate: you *do* know how to look after yourself.'

She took off her coat and hung it in the wardrobe. 'Did you speak to Professor Forselius?'

Killigrew nodded. 'Wojtkiewicz's hunch was right: he *is* a member of the Wolves of Suomi; or connected to them somehow, at least. Not that I could get him to admit as much straight out, even after I'd told him who I was.'

'He probably thought you were a Third Section agent, trying to trap him. What makes you so sure *he* is not working for Third Section?'

Killigrew grimaced. 'I doubt it, if he was sent to Siberia. Sometimes you have to take things on trust.'

'Not in this business.'

He looked at her, frowning. 'You're starting to sound like an expert in espionage.'

'I am a quick study.' She unpinned her hair and shook her head so that her long, chestnut locks spilled fetchingly across her shoulders.

The sound of a cannon shattered the quiet of the night. Killigrew dashed across to the window. His reasons for choosing the bridal suite of the finest hotel in Helsingfors as his base of operations were not entirely hedonistic: the window offered as good a view of Sveaborg as that in any hotel in the city.

He peered out in time to see more muzzle flashes from the Russian batteries in the distance, followed a couple of seconds later by their reports. He could not make out much else in the darkness.

'Put the light out!' he hissed at Anzhelika.

She turned the oil-lamp off. 'What is it? Has the bombardment started?'

He cupped a hand against the glass to peer out, but could see little in the darkness outside. The echoes of the last shot faded in the night, and were not replaced. 'Whatever it was, it's over now,' he told her. 'Only one of the Russian batteries firing, I think. Most likely a false alarm.'

In the faint moonlight coming through the window, he saw she was not convinced, but when another minute passed without any more shots being heard, she relaxed visibly. 'What now? Will Professor Forselius help you get in touch with the Wolves of Suomi?'

'He didn't say so, but I got the impression he'd try. Their curiosity's bound to be piqued by a man claiming to be a British spy. I told Forselius where we're staying. For now, the ball's very much in their court.'

276

'So now we wait.'

He nodded. 'Shall I order us some supper?'

'I'm not hungry. I thought the walk would help me work up an appetite, but it doesn't seem to have worked.'

Smiling, he took her in his arms. 'Well, perhaps we can find some other way for you to work up an appetite, Fru Johansson . . .'

Killigrew was awoken by a knock at the door to his hotel room. He reached under the pillow for his revolver. 'Who is it?'

'Chambermaid, *min herre*.'

'You couldn't come back in half an hour, could you?'

'Yes, *min herre*.' He heard her footsteps padding down the corridor to the next room.

He took Wojtkiewicz's fob watch from the bedside cabinet and flicked it open – nearly half-past ten, daylight was wasting – before turning to smile down at Anzhelika's sleeping head on the pillow beside him. He adored foreign women: most Englishwomen he knew were brought up by their mothers to believe that sex was something shameful, to be done only between husband and wife, and then only to be suffered by the woman as part of her marital duties. If Anzhelika was anything to go by, Russian women had a very different attitude to such things.

He crawled out of bed and washed and shaved himself thoroughly in cold water from the washstand, moving quietly so as not to disturb Anzhelika, but in vain.

'You're up,' she remarked sleepily.

'Good morning.'

'Good morning to you too.' She yawned and sat up on the edge of the bed.

He started to get dressed. 'I thought I'd go out and get some coffee at that café on the promenade. It's a glorious day, we could have breakfast on the terrace.'

'All right. Give me a chance to get dressed, and I will see you there.'

'By all means.'

He left the room and made his way downstairs, stopping at the reception on his way out of the hotel, but there were still no messages for Herre Johansson. Mildly disappointed, he left the hotel and strolled up the promenade in search of a newspaper vendor. Purchasing a Swedish-language newspaper, he took a table on the café's terrace and ordered a coffee from a waiter. He smoked a cheroot and read the paper while he waited. The news was all about the Allied fleet, which was

277

hardly news, and the price of herrings, which was certainly news to Killigrew, if not particularly interesting.

He glanced at the other people sitting at the tables around him. A young couple gazed adoringly into one another's eyes, a trio of young women gossiped, and at another table an elderly man with a military bearing and a bristling grey moustache sat with an intense-looking youth who wore a student's cap. Killigrew frowned: somehow they did not go together. The man with the moustache seemed too old to be the student's father, too young to be his grandfather. They sat there not talking, the military man placidly smoking a pipe and staring off into space while the student pored over a book; one might have thought they were strangers who had been obliged to share a table, but there were plenty of empty tables.

Killigrew shook his head. He told himself he was jumping at shadows. It was a beautiful day, and even with the Allied fleet anchored a couple of miles off the coast, the war seemed a long, long way away. All he could do for now was wait for the Wolves of Suomi to contact him. If he did not hear from them by nightfall, he was going to have to act alone: he could not be sure the Russians would hold off using the *Sea Devil* for a third night in a row. Even if they did contact him, there was no guarantee they would agree to help. He wondered if he could get away with stealing a rowboat after dark – or at least what passed for darkness in Helsingfors at the beginning of August – and trying to find out where they kept the *Sea Devil*. But if the worst came to the worst and he did not return, where would that leave Anzhelika? He shook his head: perhaps he could off-load her – albeit temporarily – into the care of the Wolves of Suomi. But in the meantime, there was no reason why he should not relax and enjoy himself, provided he did not let his guard drop too much.

He heard footsteps behind him and started to twist in his seat as Anzhelika bent to give him a peck on the cheek before sitting down opposite him. They ate a hearty breakfast, Killigrew paid, and then the two of them began walking along the promenade.

'Should we not go back inside?' Anzhelika asked him as they passed the hotel. 'If the Wolves of Suomi want to contact you . . .'

'If the Wolves of Suomi want to contact me, I think they'll manage to find me.'

They made their way back to the south downs. The crowds of the previous day were no longer there, although it was still early. Even so, there were a few people out: some come to view the fleet, others merely out for a morning's constitutional. Seeing several men there with telescopes and opera glasses (they were always men), Killigrew took out his own miniature telescope and gave the fleet the once-over. All ships were present and correct. Perhaps there was something wrong with the *Sea Devil*; perhaps there was no need for him to get into Sveaborg after all.

But he knew that if he gave up now, and that night the *Sea Devil* succeeded in sinking one of the Allied ships, he would not be able to live with himself. He had not come this far to quit now. Besides, the fleet was more than two and a half miles out from Sveaborg: that was a long way for a vessel travelling underwater, all but blind; and why should the Russians try it, when they knew that sooner or later the fleet would have to move in closer to get within range for the bombardment? Perhaps that was why the *Sea Devil* had not yet attacked; perhaps that was all the Russians were waiting for.

He turned his miniature telescope on Sveaborg once more, studying the defences, looking for a way in. The three outermost islands bristled with the guns of countless batteries, but perhaps there was a way in via one of the inner islands, Little Svarto or East Svarto. There was a small, rocky islet between the nearest island – West Svarto – and the shore below where he stood. Dredging his memory, he came up with its name: Langhorn. From the shore to Langhorn was a swim of about two hundred and fifty yards, and a similar distance on the other side to West Svarto, except that there he would be swimming beneath the guns of a Russian two-decker moored across the channel as a floating battery. If he made the crossing when the tide was on the turn, the current would not be too great; the tides in the Baltic were negligible anyway. Perhaps it could be done under cover of darkness; not that there was much in the way of darkness at this latitude at this time of year, and that did not last long. But assuming he managed to swim out to West Svarto and somehow creep past the shore batteries? There was a lot of ground to cover between the five islands. Although four of them were linked by bridges he was sure to bump into a patrol while he was searching, and with soaking wet clothes he would attract suspicion at once.

He realised he was already in danger of attracting suspicion: Sveaborg looked no different than it usually did, and everyone else on the downs that morning was staring at the Allied fleet. Realising he had been staring at the islands for too long, he turned away. There were plenty of other people in the park whose suspicions might have been aroused. The young man in a student cap who loitered nearby, his hands thrust deep in the pockets of his pea jacket . . .

279

The same student who had been sitting a couple of tables away from him at breakfast.

Killigrew looked around. Sure enough, there was the military man, smoking his pipe on a bench. There was such a thing as coincidence, but this was stretching it a little too far.

Anzhelika sensed the change in his mood. 'What is wrong?'

'Don't look now, but we've picked up a couple of shadows.' He started to walk unhurriedly back the way they had come, towards the city centre.

She had self-restraint enough not to look around. 'Third Section?' she whispered nervously.

'They don't look like Third Section agents.'

'Not all Third Section agents wear fur hats and leather greatcoats. They employ occasional spies who could be anyone: young, old, male, female, rich, poor. Anyone they can put pressure on to do their bidding. Besides, who else would they be?'

'Perhaps they're Wolves of Suomi.'

'Then why do they not approach you?'

'They're probably wondering if hordes of Third Section agents will manifest themselves the moment they do.'

She grimaced. 'I do not know about you, but all this tiptoeing around is starting to wear on my nerves.'

'Agreed. Keep walking back towards the city centre. I'll catch up with you in a moment.'

'Where are you going?'

'To stir things up a little.' He peeled away from her, cutting across the grass to intercept the military man, who just happened to be walking on a parallel path to theirs.

'Excuse me, sir?'

The military man seemed to snap out of a deep reverie. 'Yes?'

Killigrew produced a cheroot. 'I wonder if I might trouble you for a light?'

'Certainly.' The military man struck a match and Killigrew cupped his hands around the flame to light his cheroot.

'Much obliged. You wouldn't happen to be interested in geology, would you?'

The military man's reaction was interesting, but not in the way Killigrew had hoped it would be. 'So that's the signal you people are using these days, is it?'

Killigrew grinned uneasily. 'You tell me.'

'Filthy young pup! I don't care what your sort gets up to behind closed doors, but I wish you didn't insist on cruising for trade in public places. There are children present, for God's sake!'

'My apologies.' Killigrew backed off. 'I mistook you for someone else.'

'I'll say you did,' the military man snorted in disgust. 'Someone . . . or something.'

Killigrew hurried after Anzhelika and caught up with her on the road back into town. 'What was all that about?' she asked.

'Oh, just me making a fool of myself, as usual.'

They had not walked more than a hundred yards along the road when a carriage overhauled them and a rough-looking man jumped out in their path. He produced a pistol and waved it at them both.

'Get in.'

'Don't take this the wrong way, but you wouldn't happen to be interested in geology, would you?'

'Get a move on!' snarled the man.

# XVIII

# The Wolves of Suomi

Someone pulled a rough sack over Killigrew's head the moment he climbed inside the carriage. He heard Anzhelika cry out in alarm as she was subjected to the same indignity. Then the blinds on the windows were snapped down, and someone sat next to him, jabbing what felt suspiciously like the muzzle of a pistol in his side. The carriage door slammed, the man next to him shouted something to the driver and they jolted off over the rutted track. Killigrew was made to twist round, and his hands were grabbed and tied behind his back.

They must have been in the carriage for at least a quarter of an hour, but Killigrew sensed they were constantly doubling back on themselves to shake off any followers, so it seemed unlikely they could have gone more than a couple of miles. More to the point, he could hear the clop and rattle of other carriages, and the cries of street vendors proclaiming their wares, so he guessed they were still in Helsingfors.

When they pulled up the sounds of the streets were still audible, but muffled now, as if on the other side of some houses. He heard the door click open, and someone grabbed him by the shoulder.

'Out!'

With the muzzle of a pistol in the small of his back, he climbed out of the carriage. Unable to see, and with his hands bound, he stepped gingerly on what felt like cobbles. Impatiently, someone grabbed him by the shoulders from behind and turned him slightly, thrusting him forward. He tripped and stumbled over something – a threshold? – and then found himself being pushed up a flight of carpeted steps. A door was opened at the top, he was marched a short distance with someone's hand on his arm. Someone else rapped at a door.

'Come in!' a man's voice called in Swedish.

The door was opened, Killigrew was swung round by the hand on his arm, and he was pushed forward.

'Stand there!' another voice growled.

The door was closed behind them.

'Is this him?'

'Yes, *min herre.*'

'All right, let's have a look at them.'

The sack was whipped off Killigrew's head. He found himself standing in the middle of a comfortable-looking withdrawing room where a fire crackled in the hearth. A blond, square-jawed man in his mid-forties sat opposite him in an armchair, his fingers steepled, while the student and the gentleman with the military mustachios stood behind his chair, flanking him. The military gentleman had a revolver in his hand, and it was levelled at Killigrew. Anzhelika stood on Killigrew's right, a sack still over her head until the rough-looking fellow pulled it off from behind, leaving her standing there blinking, her dark hair tousled. He backed off and tugged a pistol from his belt, levelling it.

'The Wolves of Suomi, I presume?' Killigrew said in Swedish.

'We'll ask the questions here!' snarled the rough-looking man.

The seated man held up a hand for silence. 'Well, Nils?' he asked, without taking his eyes from Killigrew's face. 'Is it him?'

The student moved in front of the chair to peer at Killigrew's face more closely. 'It could be. If it is, he's fleshed out a bit since then, but that's to be expected. There's one way to be sure, though.'

'Oh?'

'He should have five parallel scars on his back.'

'Take a look, Hjorth.'

The rough-looking man handed his pistol to Nils and unbuttoned Killigrew's frock-coat, waistcoat and shirt. Moving behind him, he tugged his collar back and down roughly, exposing his back. Then he spun Killigrew around so they could see the scars on his back for themselves.

'It *is* him!' Nils exclaimed joyfully.

'Untie him,' ordered the man in the armchair.

Hjorth produced a large, wicked-looking knife and spun Killigrew around again, cutting through the bonds on his wrists.

'Lieutenant Christopher Killigrew of the Royal Navy,' remarked the man in the armchair.

Killigrew massaged his chafed wrists. 'My friends call me Kit. You have the advantage of me, *min herre.*'

'Forgive me.' The man rose to his feet and proffered a hand. 'I'm Friherre Per Stålberg. This is Major Lindström, Jost Hjorth and Nils Nordenskjöld.' He indicated the man with the military mustachios, the rough-looking fellow and the student in turn.

Killigrew shook hands with him. Stålberg's grip was firm and strong.

'It's lucky for you Nils is fascinated by Arctic exploration,' the *friherre* continued, indicating Nordenskjöld. 'He thought he recognised you at the café from your picture in the *Illustrated Helsingfors News.* The scars on your back clinch it.'

Anzhelika cleared her throat and twisted so they could see her hands, still bound behind her back. 'What about the woman?' asked Hjorth.

Friherre Stålberg turned his gaze on Killigrew, who was rearranging his clothing. 'Well? What about her?'

'It's all right, she's with me.' Killigrew finished buttoning his shirt, and quickly retied his cravat.

'We can see that,' growled Major Lindström. 'As to whether or not it's "all right" remains to be seen. Well, madam? Who are you?'

'Anzhelika. Anzhelika Orlova,' she told them.

Lindström's lantern jaw dropped. 'Not the Anzhelika Orlova of the Mariinsky Ballet . . .? Good God above, it *is* her! Hjorth, cut her bonds.' He tucked his revolver inside his jacket and stepped forward, proffering his hand. She took it in one of hers, which he raised to his lips to kiss, bowing and clicking his heels as he did so. 'Forgive me, mam'selle . . . I had no idea . . . permit me to introduce myself. I am Major Vidrik Lindström, formerly of the Swedish Army.'

'*Enchanté,*' she returned.

Stålberg smiled. 'We do seem to have some celebrated people with us today: a famous Arctic explorer, and the *prima ballerina* of the Mariinsky Ballet.' He turned to Killigrew. 'Do all British spies travel in company with famous ballerinas?'

'Oh, yes,' Killigrew returned glibly. 'They're standard issue. You'd be amazed how many society doors are opened for a chap when he has a famous ballerina on his arm. Damned useful in my current line of work.'

Lindström flushed, realising how much he had gushed when he had recognised her, and Anzhelika chuckled.

284

'I'm told you have a proposition that may be to our mutual advantage,' prompted Stålberg.

Killigrew nodded. 'I need two things. Firstly, I need to get Mam'selle Orlova here safely on board one of the British ships in the Gulf; and secondly, I need to get into Sveaborg as soon as possible.'

The Wolves of Suomi laughed as if Killigrew had suggested they help him get to the moon.

'Sveaborg!' exclaimed Stålberg. 'We've been trying to get into Sveaborg for months! Do you have any idea how much ammunition the Russians have in their arsenal there? If we could blow that place up, it would really make the Tsar sit up and take notice!'

'And don't the Russians know it!' growled Lindström. 'That place is more heavily guarded than the Winter Palace in St Petersburg.'

'I've been inside the Winter Palace,' Killigrew said evenly. 'Well, the Imperial Theatre, at any rate.'

'There's a difference.' Stålberg crossed to the sideboard and poured out a couple of glasses of brandy. 'They don't sell tickets to ballet performances on Sveaborg. What's your pressing need to get there? Would it have something to do with that huge cylinder they dragged here a week ago?'

'What huge cylinder?' Killigrew asked sharply.

'You tell me. All I know is, it took two hundred men to drag the wagon carrying it; and that must have been specially built to bear such a heavy burden.' Stålberg handed a glass of brandy each to Killigrew and Anzhelika. 'Came all the way from St Petersburg, they say. Covered over with a tarpaulin, so no one knew exactly what it was.'

'Would it have been about fifty feet long, twelve feet high and eleven feet wide?'

Stålberg and Lindström exchanged glances. 'Aye,' said the major. 'What do you know of it?'

'The *Sea Devil*,' Killigrew told them, sipping his brandy. 'It's an underwater boat—'

'A what?' interrupted Stålberg.

'An underwater boat. A boat that travels under water.'

Lindström threw back his head and laughed. 'Now I know you're lying. You're talking like a fool: without air, the crew would all asphyxiate. An underwater boat! There's no such thing.'

'There is now,' Killigrew told him. 'A Bavarian engineer named Wilhelm Bauer designed it for the Russians. Well, actually, he designed it for the British, but that's not important. What is important

285

is that I destroy it before the Russians use it to sink one of our ships.'

'Enough!' Lindström turned to Stålberg. 'Do we have to listen to these fairy tales, Friherre? The man's mad . . . or a liar.'

'Not so hasty, Major,' said the student, Nordenskjöld. 'I have heard of such things. I believe that the Americans built one in their War of Independence to sink a British battleship; it was not successful, but there have been others since . . . who knows? Perhaps the Russians *have* succeeded in developing a boat that sails under water.'

Stålberg rubbed his jaw. 'Whatever it is, it must be important for the Russians to drag it all the way here from St Petersburg.' He regarded Killigrew with a pair of penetrating blue eyes. 'So, you think this thing they took out to Sveaborg is your underwater boat, and you want us to help you get out there so you can destroy it?'

'That's the general idea.'

'Impossible,' said Stålberg. 'Sveaborg was heavily guarded as it was; since that thing arrived, they've doubled the guards. I don't have so many men I can afford to lose any in a futile attack on Sveaborg. Besides, why should we help the British, when all they've done in Finland since this war began is attack our fishing ports and burn our property?'

Killigrew grimaced. 'Sorry about that. Some of our boys in Admiral Plumridge's squadron getting a little too enthusiastic, I fear. They don't understand there's a difference between Finland and Russia.'

'That will be small consolation to the fishermen who've lost their livelihoods.' Hjorth's tone was bitter.

'All I can say is I'm sorry. And that if I get back to the fleet afterwards, it'll never happen again once I've spread the word about how the Finns helped me. I might even be able to arrange for us to smuggle some guns to your people to help you in your fight against the Russians.'

'You'd like that, wouldn't you?' sneered Lindström. 'Finns risking their necks fighting against the Russians, so British sailors don't have to.'

'We've got all the guns we need,' said Stålberg. 'Besides, I told you that getting you on to Sveaborg would be impossible. You *might* succeed – *if* you were lucky – and *if* God were on your side – in getting on the islands. But this much I guarantee: you wouldn't get off again. Well, not alive, certainly. So a promise from you about what you can arrange after you rejoin your fleet is worth as much to us as a castle in Spain.'

'So you won't help me?' asked Killigrew.

'No,' Stålberg told him flatly. 'Not that we wouldn't like to. Oh, I wouldn't mind if the Russians *did* sink one of your ships: perhaps then the rest of your fleet would be too scared to enter the Gulf of Finland, and Finnish fishermen and sailors could sleep soundly again at night. But anything that makes the Russians angry makes me happy, and I think destroying this secret weapon of theirs will make them very angry indeed. But it's in Sveaborg.'

'So?'

'Tell him, Major.'

'Sveaborg's impregnable,' said Lindström. 'It was impregnable when I was stationed there as a young ensign back in 1809, when we were fighting the Russians and our leaders shamefully betrayed us by handing the fortress over without a fight; and since that day the Russians have been busily engaged in making it even more impregnable. Especially this past winter. We've been watching from the shore.'

'Let me explain something to you, Herre Killigrew,' said Stålberg. 'How many members do you think the Wolves of Suomi have?'

'No more than a few dozen, I should think.'

'You're not far wrong. And do you know why we have so few members? Apart from the fact that we prefer to have a small, tight-knit organisation, with less chance of betrayal, of course. Do you know why so few Finns have rallied to our cause? Because the people of this duchy are afraid, Herre Killigrew: afraid of the Russians. And it's easy to understand. Look at a map of Finland and Russia. Russia, one of the most populous countries in the world, a country whose standard military tactic is to send its men towards the enemy as cannon fodder in a full-frontal attack, safe in the knowledge that no matter how many die, there will always be plenty more where they came from. Then look at Finland: not a small duchy, geographically, but sparsely populated. The Finns have no love for the Tsar, I promise you, but naturally they are nervous of trying to take on Russia. They are nervous because they don't know what I have learned in the ten years I've been fighting the Russians: the Russians are stupid.

'Oh, I don't believe they're born stupid. But from the day they're born, their landlords beat them into submission, teach them only to obey orders and punish them for having the temerity to think for themselves. Such men do not make outstanding soldiers: I believe that one free-born Finn is worth ten Russian *mouzhiki*. And that is why we fight the Russians: not because we're naïve enough to think our puny efforts will be enough to drive the Russians out of Finland, but in the hope that we will show our people that the Russians are not invincible. One day, I pray, our efforts will inspire our people to rise up against their oppressors, and establish an independent state. Perhaps not in my lifetime, but if by my death I can inspire my people to fight for what is rightfully theirs, I'll not think my sacrifice a vain one.

'And wouldn't we dearly love to strike a blow against Sveaborg? You know what the name means, don't you? "Fortress of the Swedes." Ironic, really, that a fortress built by the Swedes to defend us against the Russians should become a symbol of the Russian oppression of Finland. So if your Royal Navy can smash Sveaborg, perhaps I will find it in my heart to forgive your people – just a tiny bit – for the harm they have done to my countrymen since they started raiding our shores last spring. But it will be no small undertaking, even for a fleet as large as the Allied one in the Gulf of Finland at present. For a handful of us, armed with rifles and knives? The people of Finland would view us not as martyrs, but as fools bent on suicide.'

Killigrew smiled. 'It's often the man regarded as a fool bent on suicide in his own lifetime who is thought of as a great martyr after his death. I'm not asking any of you to come with me. Just help me get there.'

Stålberg frowned, and sighed. 'There may be a way,' he admitted with evident reluctance. 'There is some bigwig from St Petersburg arriving in Helsingfors today. Whoever it is, they are having a ball in his honour at the citadel on Vargon tonight. Mostly the guests will be the officers from the regiments garrisoned in and around the city, but a few of Helsingfors' most prominent citizens have been invited.'

'I don't suppose there's any chance of getting our hands on an invitation or two?' Killigrew asked without much hope.

Nordenskjöld laughed. 'There's every chance. The printer who's been ordered to make the invitations is the same man who prints our pamphlets for us.'

'The problem is, each invitation had the name of the invitee printed on it before it was sent out,' put in Stålberg. 'Oh, we can have a blank one printed and write a name of our own devising on it; the difficulty will be getting the same name on the guest list, because you can lay odds the Russians will have a copy of the guest list at every checkpoint between here and Sveaborg.'

'Could you get me a copy?' asked Killigrew.

Stålberg looked at Nordenskjöld. 'It shouldn't be too difficult,' the student told him.

'In the meantime, I need you to help me get Mam'selle Orlova out to the British fleet, where she'll be safe,' said Killigrew.

Anzhelika looked horrified. 'No! I want to stay with you, Kit! Besides, it will allay suspicion if you turn up at the ball with a woman on your arm.'

He shook his head firmly. 'And supposing the bigwig from St Petersburg recognises you? I'm sorry, Lika. It'll be too dangerous.' He turned to Stålberg. 'Can you help get her out to the fleet?'

The *friherre* and the major exchanged glances. 'It might be possible,' said Lindström. 'But it'll have to wait until after dark.'

Stålberg turned to Hjorth. 'Would your cousin be willing to help him?'

'I think so, for the right price.' Hjorth turned to Killigrew. 'I have a cousin who owns a fishing boat at Mattby; assuming the British haven't already destroyed it since I last heard from him,' he added sourly. 'He's not one of the Wolves of Suomi, but he does us the occasional favour when we need to get someone in or out of Finland without going through the usual channels, if you catch my drift. If we can convince him he'll be paid enough, he'll take Mam'selle Orlova out to your fleet.'

Killigrew nodded. 'I don't know how far the *Duke of Wellington*'s strongbox would stretch, but I'm sure Admiral Dundas can be persuaded to give your cousin a letter of protection ordering his boat to be spared if he ever gets stopped by the British or French.'

Hjorth laughed. 'If Dundas can give him that, he'll take Mam'selle Orlova to the Australias and back!' He turned and left the room.

'Until then you'd best stay here,' Stålberg told Killigrew and Anzhelika. 'I've a couple of guest bedrooms you can use if you need to clean up. Tonight we shall dine together, and with any luck by then Hjorth will have arranged your transport to the fleet.'

'I'll get started on that note to Dundas,' said Killigrew.

While Lindström showed Anzhelika upstairs, Stålberg took Killigrew to his library and gestured to the desk. 'There's notepaper in the drawer. Is there anything else I can get you?'

'A cup of coffee would be nice.'

Stålberg grinned. 'Coffee it is.'

As the *friherre* went out, Killigrew sat behind the desk and dipped a pen in the inkwell. He gnawed at the end of it: it had to be brief, yet convincing. He started scratching away. Stålberg returned with a cup of coffee, but Killigrew was so engrossed in his writing he did not look up, so the *friherre* left the cup and saucer on a coaster. When Killigrew had finished the note, he took the five blank sheets of paper that had been below the sheet he had been writing on – they bore an impression that could easily be read by anyone with a pencil – and the blotting paper he had used, and put them on the fire in the grate, making sure they were properly burning.

He emerged from the library to find Stålberg coming down the stairs. 'Here's the note,' he said.

The Finn grimaced. 'I'm afraid the situation has changed drastically since you started writing it.'

'What do you mean?'

'I think you'd better come and see for yourself.'

Bewildered, Killigrew followed Stålberg up two flights of stairs and into a loft. The Finn pulled down a ladder and climbed up it, pushing up the trap door at the top. Killigrew followed him up, and found himself standing on the roof of the house. Major Lindström was already there, standing next to Stålberg at the balustrade with a pair of opera glasses levelled towards Sveaborg. He proffered them to Killigrew, who raised them to his eyes.

'What am I looking for?'

'The flag they've just raised over the citadel on Vargon.'

Killigrew found it with the glasses: a white standard bearing an image of a double-headed eagle. 'The Imperial Standard.'

'That means that our bigwig from St Petersburg has arrived,' said Stålberg. 'And that he's a member of the Imperial Family. The Tsar himself, perhaps, or his brother the Grand Duke Konstantin.' He shook his head. 'He must be crazy to come to Sveaborg, now of all times!'

'Crazy, or very brave,' said Killigrew. 'He's probably come to boost the garrison's morale. Still, the Russians must have a lot of faith in their granite casemates if they're prepared to risk his life like that.'

'Either that, or they know something your Admiral Dundas doesn't,' growled Lindström. 'In any event, you can forget about getting on to Sveaborg tonight. If they doubled the guards when this German contraption arrived, they'll quadruple it now there's a member of the Imperial Family there.'

Realisation hit Killigrew like a mule's kick in the chest. 'It's the Grand Duke Konstantin,' he said.

'You can recognise him?' Lindström said incredulously. 'From here?'

Killigrew shook his head. 'He's come to see the *Sea Devil* in operation. That's why it hasn't attacked yet. He wanted to be here when the *Duke of Wellington* was sunk.' He handed the opera glasses back to Lindström and turned to Stålberg. 'You've got to help me get on that island. Now more than ever.'

'And I tell you it's impossible.'

'Nothing is impossible. There must be a way . . . there *must*.'

At the sound of a commotion in the street below, Lindström leaned over the balustrade and frowned. 'Ah . . . I don't want to worry you, Friherre, but we've got visitors.'

Killigrew and Stålberg joined him at the balustrade, looking over to see two dozen Russian infantrymen gathering at the front door below.

Lindström was already running across the roof to look down at the other side. 'They've got the back covered, too!' He pointed his revolver at Killigrew. 'It's him! He led them here! How else could they have found us?'

'Then why would he be so insistent that we take him to Sveaborg?' demanded Stålberg.

'So he could lead us into a trap!'

Stålberg knocked Lindström's gun aside impatiently. 'But we're already in a trap.' He crossed to the side of the house and picked up a ladder resting against the balustrade.

Killigrew helped him lower it across the gap so that the far end rested on the house on the other side of the alley. Stålberg smiled sadly. 'I always knew this day would come,' he explained.

'Lucky you were ready for it, then,' Killigrew said briskly. 'You and Lindström get across. I'll go downstairs and send Mam'selle Orlova up to you. Just get her to the British fleet. I'll try to hold them as long as I can.'

Stålberg turned to Lindström. 'You still think he is an agent of the Third Section?' Before the dumbfounded major could reply, the *friherre* was already striding across to the hatch.

Killigrew hurried after him. 'You're wasting time, Friherre. I'll hold them as long as I can, but—'

Stålberg put a hand on his shoulder. 'No, it is you who is wasting time. This is not your fight, Herre Killigrew. Go with God: I am sorry we could not help you.'

'You think I'm going to walk out on you now?'

Anzhelika climbed up through the hatch, followed by Nordenskjöld. 'Soldiers!' panted the student. 'They broke down the front door . . .'

Lindström clasped him by the shoulder. 'We know, lad.'

'Take these two and get them to safety,' Stålberg told Nordenskjöld, indicating Killigrew and Anzhelika. 'We'll hold the Russians as long as we can.'

Lindström was already descending the hatch. 'Take them to Fru Gyllenhammar's!' he called. Nordenskjöld nodded.

Stålberg was about to follow Lindström down when Killigrew caught him by the arm. 'I'm not running out on you. Perhaps I *am* responsible for leading them here . . .'

Stålberg indicated Anzhelika. 'She is your responsibility, now.' He tore his arm from the commander's grip, jumped down the hatch, and slammed it after him.

Killigrew tried to haul it open again, but Stålberg had bolted it from below.

'Quickly, *min herre!*' Nordenskjöld called from where the ladder was stretched between the two roofs.

Shots sounded in the house below, shouts and screams of pain. Killigrew swore and ran across to join Nordenskjöld and Anzhelika at the balustrade. The student jumped up and tripped across the ladder on to the far roof, turning and gesturing for them to follow.

'You next,' Killigrew told Anzhelika. 'I'll follow.'

She hesitated on the balustrade. 'I am scared of heights.'

'I'm scared of bullets,' Killigrew retorted, taking her by the hand. 'Go on, it's all right, I've got you. Just don't look down and you'll be all right.'

The two of them edged out on to the ladder. Nordenskjöld waited on the other side, ashen-faced, running his fingers through his hair in agitation. At last Anzhelika was close enough for the student to reach out and take her hand, and he hauled her to safety. Left on his own in the middle of the wobbling ladder, Killigrew teetered for a moment, but managed to regain his balance. He tripped the last few feet and dragged the plank across after them. Nordenskjöld was already hauling up a skylight, and the two of them lowered Anzhelika through it. The

292

trap door on the roof behind them splintered asunder, and the first of the soldiers emerged. Nordenskjöld dropped through the skylight and Killigrew jumped through after him a moment before the soldier fired.

He landed on a bed, the springy mattress catapulting him off and against the wall, where he slumped to the floor. Before he had even had a chance to get his bearings, Nordenskjöld had helped him to his feet and was ushering him out through the bedroom door after Anzhelika.

'Whose house is this?' she asked as the three of them hurried downstairs.

'I have no idea,' Nordenskjöld admitted cheerfully.

On the last flight, they met a butler coming upstairs. He stopped and stared in astonishment at the three complete strangers. 'Er . . . can I help you?' he stammered.

'It's all right, we'll find our own way out,' Killigrew assured him, patting him on the shoulder as they ran past.

They reached the servants' hall on the basement floor and Nordenskjöld led the way out of the kitchen door into the area, where a set of stone steps led up to the mews at the back of the house.

Nordenskjöld and Anzhelika were running for the street, but Killigrew managed to catch them both and laid hands on their shoulders to stop them. 'Walk, don't run!'

They slowed their pace and stepped out of the mews. There were soldiers everywhere, but whether they were searching for the three fugitives or merely running around like headless chickens was anyone's guess.

Nordenskjöld led Killigrew and Anzhelika out on to the waterfront in time to see a troop of Russian soldiers marching Stålberg and Lindström across a small stone bridge that led across the narrow channel separating the island of Skatudden from the mainland. That the two men had been taken alive was small consolation: if Killigrew had been in their place, he would have preferred a quick death from a bullet to torture at the hands of the Third Section. But in that instant, he and his companions could only think of themselves, and before they could be recognised they ducked down one of the aisles between the stalls of the fish market on the quayside.

They slipped down an alley at the side of the Imperial Palace and turned left into Senate Square. Nordenskjöld led them through a labyrinth of back streets and alleyways until they emerged on to a wide boulevard where a strip of parkland with trees and grass separated the north and south esplanades. A few blocks further along, Nordenskjöld

293

abruptly ducked sideways through the door of a dressmaker's shop, and Killigrew dragged Anzhelika in after him.

The young woman standing behind a counter where ribbons and artificial flowers were on display looked up in alarm at their pell-mell entrance. 'Fru Gyllenhammar!' she called.

A plump but elegantly dressed woman wearing just a little too much make-up to conceal the ravages of age emerged through the curtained doorway leading to the back of the shop.

'Trouble,' Nordenskjöld told her.

'It's all right, Helga,' Fru Gyllenhammar told the shop assistant, holding aside the curtain and waving Nordenskjöld, Anzhelika and Killigrew through.

In the back room, there was row upon row of ball gowns, and various hampers on castors. Nordenskjöld pulled one of the hampers aside to reveal a trap door below. He heaved it up to show a ladder leading down to the basement. Killigrew scrambled down, pausing at the bottom to help Anzhelika climb down after him before turning to take in their surroundings. They were in a cellar with whitewashed walls and a flagstone floor. There were several rows of shelves, each shelf bearing dozens of hatboxes. There were no windows, so Killigrew took out his matches and lit a brass oil-lamp hanging from a beam overhead while Nordenskjöld climbed down after them. The trap door was closed above his head.

'Now what?' asked Killigrew.

'I don't know!' Nordenskjöld protested in anguish. 'Let's wait here a bit, see if any of the others made it.'

'Did Hjorth get back from his cousin's house?'

Nordenskjöld shook his head.

'What about the other Wolves of Suomi?' asked Anzhelika.

'What other Wolves of Suomi?' retorted the student. 'There was only ever the six of us, unless you count Professor Forselius, and we can't drag him into this. He's already suffered more than his share for the cause.'

Anzhelika's jaw dropped. '*Six* of you? You mean to tell me there were only ever six Wolves of Suomi?'

Nordenskjöld nodded. 'Originally there were only five, until the professor introduced me to Stålberg. I managed to persuade him that I could be of some small use to the cause.'

'He wasn't exaggerating when he said he preferred a small, close-knit organisation, was he?' remarked Killigrew.

'The fewer of us there were, the less chance there was that someone might betray us.'

'Well, someone certainly betrayed you,' said a new voice.

Killigrew turned, and groaned when he saw who was climbing down the ladder from the shop above. 'You!'

Aurélie Plessier reached the foot of the ladder. She turned to face him with a smile. 'We meet again, Commander Killigrew.'

'You do have the habit of turning up in the most unexpected places,' he told her.

'As do you.'

'You heard what happened?' Nordenskjöld asked her anxiously.

'Stålberg and Lindström arrested?' She nodded. 'I guessed that if anyone got away you'd plan to rendezvous here. I was coming to the house when I saw the soldiers ahead of me. That Third Section officer with a limp was there.'

'Lieutenant Kizheh?' asked Killigrew.

'You know him?'

'I gave him the limp!' He looked from Aurélie to Nordenskjöld and back again. 'You two know each other, I take it?'

Aurélie smiled. 'We've been working with the Wolves of Suomi for months.'

' "We" being the French secret service, I suppose. You might have told us!' Killigrew added bitterly. 'We could have used their help.'

'Friherre Stålberg specifically asked us not to get the British involved,' Aurélie told him. 'I can't imagine why that should be, can you?'

Anzhelika was pawing at Killigrew's sleeve. 'Kit, who is this woman?'

He sighed. 'Lika, meet Aurélie Plessier of French military intelligence. Aurélie, this is Anzhelika Orlova—'

Aurélie nodded. '*Prima ballerina* of the Mariinsky Theatre, yes, I know. You have an interesting idea of working undercover, Commander: taking one of the most famous women in Russia with you wherever you go!'

'You were saying something about someone having betrayed us when you came in?' Killigrew reminded her.

'For seven years the Wolves of Suomi have evaded all attempts by the Third Section to trap them; and yet on the very day you and Mam'selle Orlova turn up on their doorstep, they are raided by the Third Section and Stålberg and Lindström are taken into custody. It is very curious, *n'est-ce pas*?'

Realising the import of her words, Nordenskjöld looked from Killigrew to Anzhelika with a hardening expression.

'Very curious,' agreed Killigrew. 'Are you suggesting I led them there?'

'Inadvertently, perhaps.'

Killigrew shook his head. 'They put our heads in a sack and drove us all around town before taking us to the house. There's no way Lika or I could have led them there.'

'Yes? And what about the scarf?'

Killigrew narrowed his eyes. 'Scarf? What scarf?'

'The scarf that was hanging from one of the second-floor windows.' Aurélie turned to Anzhelika. 'I suppose you hung it there? When did you agree with Colonel Nekrasoff that that would be the signal to let him know where the Wolves of Suomi were? Back in St Petersburg, or after you arrived here in Helsingfors?'

'You think I am the traitor?' spluttered Anzhelika. 'That is ridiculous! I'm a ballerina, not a spy for the Third Section! Kit, tell this woman she talks like a crazy person. She is the traitor!'

Killigrew felt only one emotion – rage – but the rage was torn between Anzhelika for fooling him and himself for being fooled. 'Is she?'

The colour drained from Anzhelika's face. 'But . . . even if this is true, surely I would let myself be taken by the soldiers who broke into the house, not escape with the rest of you.'

'Escape with the rest of us . . . in the hope we'd lead you straight to another cell of the Wolves of Suomi,' he said bitterly. 'How could I have been such a fool? All this time I thought I was leading the Third Section a merry dance, when in fact I've been dancing to their tune! They didn't need watchers to keep an eye on me, because they had you.'

'But . . . Kit! Was it not I who told you Bauer had gone to Helsingfors?'

'Yes, so I'd lead you and your Third Section pals straight to the Wolves of Suomi. How long have you been working for Nekrasoff, Lika? Did he contact you after we met outside the Winter Palace that night, or was it before that? Were you working for him when you seduced Bauer into defecting to Russia with the plans for the *Sea Devil*?' He advanced on her, not sure what he was going to do, only aware that for the first time in his life, he felt an urge to hurt a member of the fair sex; and not just hurt her, either, but kill her. It was only with difficulty he restrained himself from grabbing her by the throat and choking the life out of her.

She took a step back apprehensively, and suddenly pulled a tiny two-barrelled 'turn-over' pistol from inside her fur muff. Smiling now, she levelled it at his chest.

'You did not know I had this, did you?'

# XIX

# A Dirty, Filthy Business

---

'Hidden inside her muff?' Apparently unconcerned, Aurélie clucked her tongue mockingly. 'That was careless of you, Kit. I would have thought that would be the first place you looked!'

But if Aurélie was unconcerned by the gun in Anzhelika's hand, the ballerina was equally unconcerned by the Frenchwoman's insouciant tone. 'Yes, I've been working for Colonel Nekrasoff for over four years now,' she taunted Killigrew. 'He approached me back in 'fifty-one, when I danced at Covent Garden. He knew all about the *Sea Devil* even then: he was in London to persuade Bauer to defect to Russia with the plans. He gave me a chance to serve my country, and I was proud to accept. We did not succeed then, but the seeds were sown. Over the next few years, Bauer became increasingly convinced that Scott Russell was seeking to steal his plans. Finally he contacted Nekrasoff and sent him a copy of the outline he'd originally shown to Prince Albert. Nekrasoff went to London to arrange Bauer's defection, and while he was there he received a telegram telling him about how Jurgaitis stole the outline from the Admiralty, and Commander Kit Killigrew got the plans out of Finland . . .'

Killigrew nodded. 'So he sent Ryzhago to ambush me at Folkestone, and when that didn't work he turned up at my rooms in Paddington.' He frowned. 'But he must have guessed I'd go straight from London Bridge station to the Admiralty with the plans.'

Anzhelika's grin became fractionally broader. 'That's the most brilliant part of the plan. Nekrasoff knew it was too late to retrieve the plans, but he saw a way to cut his losses by learning the identities of Wolves of Suomi.'

298

'So he tortured Araminta because he thought I could tell him. But I couldn't, so he killed her. He gained nothing. I fail to see what's so brilliant about that, Lika.'

She laughed. 'Still you do not see it? Nekrasoff knew all along you knew nothing of the Wolves of Suomi. But he saw a way to make you lead us to them. That is why he went to your rooms: he knew if he killed Miss Maltravers, you would go crazy for revenge, no? And when your Admiralty saw the plans for the *Sea Devil*, they would send you to destroy it.'

Killigrew shook his head, unwilling to believe, even in the face of her admission, that she was a spy for the Third Section. 'No. You're lying. You must be. Nekrasoff framed me for murder; and then sent two assassins to kill me. Why would he do that, if he wanted me alive to come to Russia and lead him to the Wolves of Suomi?'

'Nekrasoff did not send the assassins; Tabard did. That is why Nekrasoff had Tabard killed; and made sure you had an alibi when it was done. He needed you to *think* he wanted you dead, but was careful to make sure your name was cleared.'

'And I played right into his hands,' Killigrew said bitterly.

She faced him with her hands on her hips and her eyes blazing defiance. 'So, now what? You're going to try to make me see the error of my ways? The great Kit Killigrew, such a passionate lover, no woman who has lain in his arms won't be converted to the cause of Queen Victoria and the British Empire!' She shook her head. 'You're good, but not that good. As a lover, I mean. As a spy, you are hopeless. You should have stayed on the quarterdeck of the *Ramillies*, where you belong. Nekrasoff was right about you: you were out of your depth from the beginning.'

He stared at her, shaking his head. 'I loved you.'

'No. You were using me . . . or rather, you thought you were. In reality, I was using you. It was not difficult.'

'Why?'

'Because I enjoy it. As a ballerina in Russia, I am treated like a serf, but as a spy? I get respect from men like Count Orloff and Colonel Nekrasoff. And I get to make fools of men like you, who would treat me like a plaything which serves no useful purpose but their amusement.'

'You enjoy lying to people, tricking them, using them?'

'Do you expect me to believe you have not enjoyed yourself over the past two weeks doing exactly the same thing?'

299

'What I've done, I did for Queen and country—'

'Do not lie to me! It is a game: you know that. Using people like chess pieces while they are still useful, disposing of them when they become expendable. It is like being God, is it not? Knowing things other people do not know, getting to decide who lives . . . and who dies. But do not dress it up by pretending you were forced to do it in a noble cause.'

'You make me sick,' he told her bitterly.

She laughed. 'Of course I do. Because you look at me and you see a reflection of yourself.'

He started to turn away, then swung back and caught her by the wrist, forcing the gun aside. She struggled like a wildcat, trying to claw at his face with her left hand while bringing the gun back to bear with her right. The two of them grappled, Killigrew's greater weight and strength pushing her back through the shelves behind with a crash. As the hat boxes cascaded down around them, she managed to break free. Killigrew looked up and found himself staring down the barrel of the pistol, and there was enough hatred in her eyes to convince him that she meant to pull the trigger.

And then the light went out in those eyes as blood squirted past his head, jetting from either side of the haft of one of Aurélie's knives where it was embedded in Anzhelika's throat. She crumpled to the flagstones.

Killigrew staggered back, staring in horror at her body where it lay amongst the debris of the shelves and crumpled hat boxes. Remembering all the hours they had shared in one another's arms, and looking down at the bloody corpse at his feet, he felt sick.

Aurélie put a hand on his shoulder. 'You are all right?'

He nodded. 'I think so.'

'*Nom d'un chien*! You really loved her?'

Killigrew shook his head. 'I fell into the same old trap.'

'Oh?' She crouched to retrieve the knife, wiping the blade clean on Anzhelika's fur coat before secreting it about her person once more. Her foot knocked against the turn-over pistol on the floor; she stooped to retrieve it, hitching up her skirts to tuck it into a garter.

'I fell in love with the idea of someone who looked like her.'

Aurélie sighed. 'You men! If a woman has a nice shape, you forget about the important part: what is up *here*.' She tapped her temple.

Killigrew slumped against the wall and sank down to sit on the cold floor, feeling sick at heart. A beautiful, graceful woman of incomparable

300

talent, whose life had been snuffed out as if it had been nothing. He wondered why he had really accepted this mission: to save lives, or for revenge? He remembered telling Strachan at Araminta's graveside that the Russians would need more than two graves to tidy up after he'd claimed his revenge, but the death of Anzhelika Orlova was one death too many, even if she was an enemy spy. In the end, he had become no better than the men who had murdered Araminta.

'She had to be killed,' said Aurélie, seeming to read Killigrew's mind. 'You would have tied her up until after you completed your mission, yes? And then what? You let her go? She goes straight to Nekrasoff and tells him about Nils, Hjorth and Fru Gyllenhammar, and he arrests them and executes them along with Stålberg and Lindström.'

'What mission?' Killigrew asked her bitterly. 'We're finished. Lindström was right: there's no way into Sveaborg. Now the Grand Duke is here, they'll send the *Sea Devil* out tonight, and his Imperial Highness can watch and applaud as the *Duke of Wellington* sinks and eleven hundred seamen are sent to a watery grave. The British fleet will probably withdraw, the war will drag on another year or two, and thousands more will die . . . all because I was foolish enough to think I could take on the Third Section and win.'

The trap door at the top of the ladder opened again. Killigrew, Nordenskjöld and Aurélie all looked up sharply, but it was only Hjorth. He took in the scene illuminated by the guttering flame in the oil lamp. 'What happened? There were soldiers at Stålberg's house when I got there. Lucky I saw them before they saw me.'

'They've arrested Stålberg and the major,' Nordenskjöld explained hoarsely. The light made his eyes look hollow. 'She betrayed us,' he added, indicating Anzhelika's bloody corpse.

Hjorth nodded. 'I guessed as much.'

'My own damned fault,' said Killigrew. 'I'm sorry.'

Hjorth shook his head. 'We all knew what we were getting into when we formed the Wolves of Suomi. Herre Stålberg and the major knew the risks. Who could have guessed that a ballerina of Mam'selle Orlova's stature would be working for the Third Section?'

'Wojtkiewicz warned me that anyone could be an informer for the Third Section; so did Mam'selle Orlova herself, come to think of it. I should have heeded them.'

'No use crying over spilled milk.' Hjorth sighed. 'Ah, well. It was fun while it lasted.' He gazed levelly at the corpse. 'We'll have to shift her,' he decided. 'Before she stinks up the place.' He climbed back up

301

through the trap door to reappear a moment later carrying a large roll of tissue paper. 'Help me wrap her in this so we don't get blood all over ourselves carrying her out of here,' he told Nordenskjöld. 'We'll take her to the forests outside the city and dump her body.'

Killigrew did not have the stomach to help as Hjorth and Nordenskjöld wrapped the corpse in paper and manhandled it up through the trap door. He heard wickerwork creak as it was dropped in one of the hampers.

Hjorth thrust his head through the open trap. 'You two wait here,' he told Killigrew and Aurélie. 'We'll be back in a couple of hours. There's nothing you can do now anyhow. When it gets dark, I'll take you to Mattby. My cousin's fishing boat is there, he can take you out to the fleet.'

Killigrew nodded wearily, and Hjorth closed the trap once more, leaving him alone with Aurélie. 'This is a dirty, filthy business,' he said, his voice full of self-loathing.

'Yes. But it is necessary.'

'Is it? Sometimes I wonder . . .'

'Sending wooden ships to attack granite batteries is folly,' Captain Sulivan began without preamble once the junior officers were seated in the great cabin of the *Duke of Wellington*. 'So said Nelson, and it would be a brave man who would disagreed with anything *he* had to say on the subject of naval tactics. And I have no pretensions to courage.'

The lieutenants smiled at Sulivan's self-deprecating humour. As captain of a surveying ship, he was certainly not in a position associated with great courage, except they all knew that he had taken considerable risks over the past few days in sounding the waters around Sveaborg in preparation for the forthcoming bombardment.

'However, I would ask you to put his comment in context,' Sulivan continued. 'Nelson lived in a time before steam engines and shell guns became commonplace and, mark my words, those change everything. That puts us in a challenging situation: we can no longer rely on the received wisdom, so that means we have to make up the rules as we go along.'

Lieutenant Adare glanced around the faces of the other junior officers who had assembled in the great cabin of the *Duke of Wellington* to be briefed on Captain Sulivan's plans for the forthcoming attack on Sveaborg. Until the previous evening, it had been anybody's guess which of the *Ramillies'* lieutenants would be put in charge of the blockship's tender, Her Majesty's gunboat *Swiper*, for the forthcoming attack. Of course, Adare had hoped and prayed it would be himself, but his wardroom colleagues must have done so too. During the past few weeks – pottering back and forth, up and down the Gulf of Finland, without ever really getting to grips with the enemy – Captain Crichton had allowed each of the *Ramillies'* lieutenants a chance to command the *Swiper*.

Not that commanding the *Swiper* had been much fun: far too much of the task seemed to involve passing on to Captain Crichton the engineer's excuses as to why the gunboat could not keep station with her mother ship. But they had all been aware that their captain's eyes had been upon them, as he tried to decide which of them would be best suited to her command when it really mattered, during the bombardment of Sveaborg; and if the engine had proved unreliable, at least it had done so without favour, embarrassing all five of the lieutenants equally.

Quite why Crichton had selected Adare was a mystery to the lieutenant himself. If he had not disgraced himself while commanding the *Swiper*, nor had he been able to excel himself any more than his colleagues. He had the feeling that Crichton had only made his mind up moments before he had called Adare to his day-room: the old man had been so brusque and curt about it – a long way from his usual, genial self – that Adare had been given the feeling he had decided to press ahead with telling the second lieutenant before he could change his mind again.

'Whether my thinking is correct will be up to yourselves – and the men under your command – to prove or disprove,' continued Sulivan, standing next to a blackboard on an easel on which he had sketched a map of Sveaborg and the proposed dispositions for the fleet. 'I most certainly hope it is the former.'

Although Sulivan was not a natural speaker, his tone had gained the smooth eloquence of a man giving the same speech to a different audience for the umpteenth time, without losing any of its customary intensity. Groups of junior officers who, like Adare, had been appointed to the command of the smaller vessels, had been going on board the *Duke* for these briefings since yesterday morning: first the officers commanding the mortar vessels, now the gunboat commanders.

'Our primary objective is to minimise the risk to the liners of the fleet, and consequently to the men on board them. The liners will maintain their current position here, east of Skogskar . . .' He indicated the spot at the bottom, left-hand corner of his plan. 'Your job will be to keep the batteries occupied while the mortar vessels concentrate on bombarding the rest of Sveaborg. I dare say you reckless young fools will all be pleased to hear that we're content to remain well out of range of the Russian batteries, and to leave the dangerous work to you.

'By now the last of the mortar vessels should be in place, in a crescent, here, facing Vargon and Gustafvard from a range of thirty-three hundred yards. They'll be firing at extreme range, and they've anchored hawsers fore and aft so they can haul themselves in or out of range as necessity demands. They'll be under the command of Captain Weymiss. *Euryalus*, *Dragon*, *Magicienne* and *Vulture* will act as supply ships, six hundred yards behind the line, making sure the mortar vessels are supplied with all the shells and powder they need.

'You will be forward of their position, at a range of twenty-four hundred yards, relying on your superior manoeuvrability to keep you out of trouble. Mr Moriarty and I have already surveyed this area: it's clear of infernal machines, and we've marked the location of the shoals on your charts, so pay particular attention to them. I do not – I repeat, do *not* – want any of you running aground. You'll form four flotillas: two to the north-west of Abramsholm and two to the south-east. *Magpie* and *Weasel* will be here, on the north-west flank, while *Badger*, *Biter*, *Pelter*, *Starling* and *Thistle* will be between them and Abramsholm, bombarding the western batteries. The rest of the gunboats will manoeuvre south-east of Abramsholm, except for *Stork* and *Snapper* on the south-eastern flank, north-east by north of the Laghara Shoal: they'll be supervised by Captain Hewlett, on account of his particular experience at firing Lancaster guns.

'Quite simply, you will play "Ring a Ring o' Roses", circling prow to stern, describing anticlockwise circles with a diameter of approximately five hundred yards. As your bows come to bear on the target, you will fire your primary ordnance; as you come broadside on to the target, you will fire your secondary ordnance. At six knots that will give you just under eight minutes to reload between shots: more than enough time, so there's no need for your gun crews to rush. We're relying on the higher trajectory of the mortars to do the most damage against the Russian bunkers. They'll be using incendiary shells. Your job will be to keep the Russians' heads down with a continuous rain of shells that will, we hope, frustrate their efforts to stop the fires from spreading. *Cornwallis*, *Hastings* and *Amphion*, meanwhile, will launch a diversionary attack against the south-east end of Sandhamn, while

304

*Arrogant*, *Cossack* and *Cruiser* will engage the Russian troops positioned on Drumsio Island.

'I expect the bombardment to commence tomorrow morning at seven o'clock sharp, gentlemen. The mortar vessels will start the shooting match and that will be the signal for the rest of you to join in. Yes, Mr . . .?' he added when someone raised a hand.

'Slater, sir, HMS *Gannet*. How long is the bombardment to last?'

'The intention is to maintain it for forty-eight hours,' Sulivan told him crisply.

The junior officers gasped.

Sulivan waved them to silence. 'The key to this plan is maintaining a heavy and *sustained* fire. By now you should all know how short Baltic summers are: whether or not we succeed in reducing Sveaborg, we won't have time for another major operation before autumn sets in, so we're putting all our efforts into this one. Yes, Mr . . .?'

'Adare, sir, HMS *Swiper*. With all due respect, it's a little unfair to ask our boys to work the guns continuously for that amount of time, and frankly I doubt even our own guns will be able to maintain that rate of fire for so long.'

Sulivan smiled. 'Thank you, Mr Adare, I was just coming to that point. The gunboats will be withdrawn some time tomorrow evening to give your crews a chance to rest; we'll be sending in a flotilla of boats equipped with Congreve rockets some time after dark to keep up the pressure on the Russians. If all goes well, your gunboats will resume their bombardment at first light on Friday. I know it's still going to be gruelling for you and your crews, and it's a good deal to ask, but then there's a great deal riding on this attack. If we can reduce Sveaborg, it will prove to the Tsar that even St Petersburg isn't safe behind the granite batteries of Kronstadt. If not, well . . . I think we'll be able to count ourselves lucky if the worst thing that happens is they throw rotten eggs at us when we sail back to Portsmouth . . .'

'How does a girl like you get to be a girl like you, anyhow?' Killigrew asked Aurélie while they waited in the cellar beneath Fru Gyllenhammar's shop for Hjorth and Nordenskjöld to return. The two of them sat side by side with their backs to the whitewashed wall. Killigrew could not bear the silence any longer; needed to listen to her talk to muffle the sound of the ghastly rattle in Anzhelika's throat as she had died, which still echoed in his ears.

'The same way that you got involved in this,' she replied.

'Oh?'

She smiled wistfully in the gloom. 'She falls in love.'

'Ah. And what sort of Adonis caught your eye, then?'

'A fisherman's son. I was living with my parents in Marseilles at the time; they were failed colonists; we'd just moved back from Algeria, where our farm had gone bankrupt. My father was unemployed for the rest of his life; he drank himself to death a few years ago. I shed no tears when I learned he was dead: he used to beat my mother. We were very poor. *Alors*, one day my Adonis of a fisherman's son was conscripted into the army. I was nineteen and in love, and distraught at the thought of being separated from my beloved. So I joined my lover's regiment as a *vivandière*. My parents did not object; my father scarcely knew what day of the week it was most of the time, let alone what his only daughter was up to, and my mother . . . she knew they needed what little money I could send back. Our regiment shipped out for Algeria, but I did not care, for I was with the man I loved, and I knew he was so courageous he would soon be promoted to *capitaine*, and we would never want for money again . . . Then one day he went out with a patrol, and they never came back. I had lived in Algeria for nine years, and even as a child I knew what Abd el-Qadir's men did to French soldiers when they captured them. So, I went crazy for revenge.' She tapped Killigrew on the arm. 'You see? I too have been where you are now.'

'And how does a pretty little *vivandière* get revenge against the army of Abd el-Qadir?'

'It started when we were posted to a fort in the desert. One day the Arabs attacked. We were almost overwhelmed . . . everyone was needed to man the walls, even *les invalos* from the infirmary. Naturally, I picked up a musket and began blazing away with *mes copains*; when it came to hand to hand fighting, I fixed the bayonet on my musket and fought with the others.'

Killigrew tried to imagine the pretty woman beside him at the parapet of a desert fort, thrusting her bayonet into the stomach of an Arab, and failed miserably.

'They tell me I fought like a wild animal that day; I can remember little of it. But afterwards my colonel commended my courage, and a few weeks later I was called into his office. He had found out I spoke Arabic – I had learned it as a child – and with my dark complexion – my mother was a Catalan: in the sun, my skin turns as brown as any Arab's – I could easily pass for an Arab woman. He wanted me to go

306

down the kasbah and pretend to be an Arab, to see what I could learn. Naturally, I agreed. I was still crazy for revenge.' She shrugged. 'Within six months, I was Abd el-Qadir's lover.'

If Killigrew had been sipping a drink, he would have sprayed it across the room then. 'No wonder the poor devil had to surrender back in 'forty-seven!' he gasped, staring at her in astonishment.

'I would like to think the intelligence I was able to pass back to headquarters contributed to our victory. Ah, but it was a bad war, that one. By the time it was over, I had learned not to hate the Arabs quite so much; our men were just as guilty of doing terrible things as they; and we were in their country; is it not so?'

'You're lucky you didn't get your throat slit!'

'It is true I was . . . what is the English expression? Ah, yes: "thrown in at the deep end"! But I learned fast. It seems I had an aptitude for dissimulation. And *mon chef* was sufficiently impressed with my work to ask me to work for military intelligence all the time.'

'And you accepted? In spite of your misgivings about the way the war was fought?'

'A good spy does not just win wars; she can sometimes prevent them too. Like the time your country and mine almost went to war back in eighteen fifty-two.'

'We didn't come that close to war, did we?'

She smiled slyly. 'How little you know. *Mon chef* saw to it that I learned many things. He taught me how to behave like a lady, so I could move freely in all the courts of the world, listening to the great statesmen of the world boast of the secrets they knew, little thinking that my pretty little head could do more than be impressed by them.'

'Pillow talk, eh?' grunted Killigrew, wondering if Aurélie was any better than Anzhelika; or if Anzhelika had been any worse than Aurélie.

She shook her head. 'A professional woman spy never gives herself to the men she wishes to spy on; *mon chef* taught me that.'

'Oh?'

'A man will say many things to impress a woman if he is fool enough to think she will give herself to him because of it; and most of them are. But once he has had his way with her? Poof! No longer is he interested, and she had thrown away her advantage.'

'So, what else did *votre chef* teach you?'

'I learned many languages – English, German, Italian, Hungarian, Russian – and how to use many different kinds of guns, how to write in codes and ciphers, how to pick locks and break open safes, how to pass messages without being seen, how to withstand interrogation and torture, how kill a man with my bare hands, how to break into houses, how to shake off a tail, or tail a man without being shaken off, how to throw knives . . . but I imagine your Admiral Napier saw to it you received the same kind of education?'

'You must be joking!'

'No? You are . . . what is the English expression? Ah, yes: "pulling my legs"!'

'God's truth. They just gave me a new revolver and wished me the best of British before packing me off to St Petersburg.'

'Ah, you English and your gentleman amateurs! It is a miracle you are still alive!'

He rubbed his face wearily. 'I have made rather a mess of things, haven't I? I dare say *votre chef* would not be impressed.'

'I dare say *mon chef* would have been taken in by Mam'selle Orlova just the same as you were. Even I did not realise she was working for Colonel Nekrasoff until it was too late.'

'You didn't spend as much time with her as I did.'

'*Tiens!* The more time you spent with her, the more you fell in love with her. Console yourself, my chicken . . . you have done well, considering. And you saw through me, did you not?' She pouted. 'Perhaps I am not as beautiful as Mam'selle Orlova was?'

'I wouldn't say that . . .' He leaned across to give her a peck on the cheek, but she placed a finger against his lips.

'Ah, no,' she told him with a smile. 'Have you not learned that in espionage, it is not good to fall in love?'

He grinned. 'Who said anything about falling in love?'

'Ah! You are starting to learn, I think. I wonder where the Third Section took Stålberg and Lindström?'

'Conversation deftly changed,' he acknowledged wryly. 'Nils and I saw them being taken across the bridge to Skatudden. I suppose they must have a gaol there or something.'

'On Skatudden? No. Third Section headquarters in Helsingfors is on Alexander Square; they must have been taking them to Sveaborg.'

'What makes you say that?'

'The ferry for Sveaborg leaves only from the naval base at Skatudden.' She sighed. 'It is for the best.'

'What do you mean?'

'In a day or two, our fleets will bombard Sveaborg. Stålberg and Lindström will most likely be killed in the bombardment, but better that than they are tortured to death by the Third Section.'

'For a moment there, I thought you were going to suggest we try to rescue them.'

'If they had been at Third Section headquarters, perhaps. But while they are in Sveaborg . . .? Impossible!'

Killigrew nodded, shifting uncomfortably on the cold flagstones. Realising he was sitting on something, he reached under himself to pull it out: a crushed hatbox. He prised off the lid and took out the battered bonnet within. Chuckling humourlessly to himself, he turned the crumpled thing over in his hands. A thought occurred to him, and he lifted his face to stare up at the underside of the ceiling.

'What is it?' asked Aurélie.

'I was just thinking . . .'

The trap door opened suddenly and Hjorth and Nordenskjöld climbed back down into the cellar. 'Well, that's that,' said Hjorth. 'By the time anyone finds her, the wolves will have picked her carcase clean. She'll be unidentifiable.'

'Hjorth!' Scowling at him, Aurélie jerked her head at Killigrew.

But the commander had leaped to his feet, throwing down the crushed bonnet. 'Nils, did you get that guest list for tonight's ball?'

'Yes, it's right here.' Nordenskjöld reached inside his jacket and pulled out several sheets of paper. 'Why?'

Instead of replying, Killigrew stood next to the student as his measuring himself against him. 'You're about my build, aren't you?'

'I suppose so . . .'

'I don't suppose you have such a thing as a tailcoat I could borrow?'

'You're not still thinking of going to the ball tonight, are you?' asked Hjorth. 'I told you, every invitation will be checked against the guest list: with the security they'll be lining up tonight, if your name doesn't tally they'll throw you in a cell before you can say "sparvagnsaktie-bolagsskensmutsskjutarefackforeningspersonalbekladnadsmag-asinsforradsforvaltaren".'

'That's easily solved,' said Killigrew. 'I've been to enough of these affairs to know there's always some goose there that no one else knows; some greasy-fingered merchant who wrangled his way on to the guest list in the hope of making some important business contacts.'

'So?'

'So all we've got to do is work out who it is.'

Nordenskjöld produced the guest list and the four of them gathered round to look at it. 'Most of the people on this list are Russian military

309

. . . a few Finnish senators and senior officers from the militia . . . all of these people will know one another.' He turned to the second page.

'How about the Lundqvists?' asked Hjorth, reading over his shoulder.

Nordenskjöld shook his head. 'He's a reservist. Colonel Dahlgren will know him, and you can be sure he'll be there tonight.' He ran his finger down the list of names. 'The Ögrens? How in the world did they manage to wangle an invitation?'

'Who are the Ögrens?' asked Hjorth.

'Exactly!'

Nordenskjöld and Hjorth turned to stare at one another, their faces cracking into triumphant grins. 'The Ögrens!'

Killigrew cleared his throat. 'Who are the Ögrens?'

Even as Ambrosius Ögren stood before the mirror above the mantelpiece in his parlour, retying his cravat with his corpulent fingers, he was in two minds about attending the ball on Sveaborg. The Russians might be maintaining their sang-froid in the face of the British fleet, but Ögren made no bones about admitting to himself that there was nothing *froid* about his *sang*. The Rosenbladhs had already abandoned their town house: even as Ögren glanced out of the window and across the street, he could see their servants loading a wagon with their most prized possessions preparatory to carting it all off to their summer house in the country. Ögren could not help thinking they had the right idea.

But it would be a shame not to go after he had lobbied so long and hard to get an invitation for himself and his wife. It was true, he would not know anyone there: he expected most of the other guests to be Russian military officers and a sprinkling of senior Finnish politicians, most of whom looked down at his kind with contempt, when they bothered to regard him at all. But this was a matter of business, not pleasure. His attempts to get an import permit for the new American rifles his company dealt in having failed through the usual channels, he had hoped to buttonhole a senior Russian military officer at the ball and persuade him to use his influence to pull a few strings at the necessary government office in St Petersburg. Russia needed modern arms, didn't it? That was why the Allies had not yet been beaten in the Crimea, despite the incompetence of the British generals. Ögren's business was small scale: there was no Finnish army as such, and the weapons he currently imported were hunting rifles for the private market. But if he could become a contractor to the Russian army – even if only supplying modern rifles to the newly formed Finnish *jäger* regiments – he'd be a millionaire.

*No*, he corrected himself: *a billionaire!*

Grimacing with impatience, he emerged from the parlour to stand in the hallway and called up the stairs. 'Are you nearly ready, Ottilia? The ball is supposed to start at eight!'

'I won't be long! Stop fretting! It's unfashionable to turn up on time to these things anyhow.' If Ottilia said that, then it had to be true, for she was an inveterate social climber who learned all the rules of aristocratic etiquette if only so she could mock the other ladies of her own circle when they failed to meet her exacting standards. She had been beside herself with glee when she had related to her husband how sick with envy her friends were when she told them she and her husband had been invited to this ball. Even if he had been able to make his mind up against attending, she would certainly not have permitted it anyway: if the entire French army had stood between her and a chance to rub shoulders with the Grand Duke Konstantin and Governor-General von Berg, she would not have let it get in her way.

*The Grand Duke Konstantin*, thought Ögren. There had been a rumour that some bigwig from St Petersburg would be attending, but when Ögren had acquired his ticket he had never hoped in his wildest dreams that it might be the Admiral-General of the Fleet. Fleets had marines, didn't they? And didn't marines need rifles? And the grand duke was supposed to be a very forward-thinking young man, not the sort to turn his nose up at the latest armaments at all.

Ögren toyed with the idea of taking a sample of his wares to the ball so he could demonstrate the new rifle's effectiveness. They were bound to have some kind of firing range somewhere in Sveaborg, and he was a pretty good shot even though he did say so himself, thanks to the hunting parties he frequently took potential clients on at his lodge in the country. But he decided against it: it probably was not the done thing to turn up to a ball carrying a rifle. Besides, Sveaborg being a military installation, there might be guards who would take a dim view of a man with a firearm trying to get in to a social event at which the Grand Duke would be present.

The bell of the front door jangled. Ögren frowned: he was not expecting anyone, and it was a little late in the day for callers. Hadn't Ottilia told *everyone* she knew that they would be going to the ball?

His butler appeared from below stairs. 'See who that is, Arvidsson, and tell them we're not at home,' Ögren told him as he headed for the front door. 'Once you've got rid of them, tell Wickmann to bring my carriage round to the front.'

'Very good, sir.'

It occurred to Ögren that if he were not going to take a sample of his wares, it would be remiss of him in the extreme to neglect to take a good supply of calling cards. He entered his library and took half a dozen from a stack in the drawer of his bureau. As an afterthought, he took the rest of the stack, distributing them in various pockets of his tailcoat, so there was no danger of running out.

He almost forgot the most important thing of all: the invitation! He scrabbled through the papers in the drawer, but there was no sign of it. Panic set in at once. What had he done with it? Of course, the mantelpiece! He hurried into the parlour and there it was, propped up behind the carriage clock.

He tucked it in an inside pocket and checked his fob watch against the clock. It was nearly half-past seven: they were going to miss the eight o'clock ferry from Skatudden if Ottilia did not get a move on. He took out a fat cigar and snipped off the end, lighting it and sticking it in his mouth. He knew he would not have time to finish it before they set off, and Ottilia always grumbled when he smoked in the carriage, but it was her own fault for keeping him waiting like this: he needed the rich tobacco to smooth his nerves.

'These people would like a word with you, sir,' Arvidsson said behind him.

'I thought I told you we weren't receiving?' snarled Ögren.

'I did tell them you weren't at home, sir, but they were most insistent.'

Ögren turned and saw that Arvidsson had his arms straight up in the air. There were three men and a woman standing behind him. The woman and one of the men looked pleasant enough – the woman was rather attractive, in fact – and both were in evening wear, the man in a chimney-pot hat, black tailcoat and white cravat and waistcoat, the woman wearing a *sortie de bal* over an off-the-shoulder ball gown of dark blue velvet.

It was the other two men who bothered Ögren: and Arvidsson too, to judge from the butler's ashen expression. Hardly surprising, really, since neither of these men was dressed for a ball; unless the latest fashion accessories from Paris included scarves tied over their mouths and noses, and double-barrelled shotguns.

'What the devil is going on?' demanded Ögren.

'My apologies for the inconvenience, Herre Ögren,' the man wearing

312

evening clothes said in excellent Swedish. He was thirty or thereabouts, dark-haired, with a saturnine complexion, carrying a black holdall in one hand. 'Do exactly as we tell you, and there'll be no need for anyone to get hurt.' To emphasise his point, he reached inside his tailcoat and pulled out a revolver, levelling it at the arms merchant.

Ögren liked guns. They had made him a comfortable living over the years, and he had every hope that they would make him an exceedingly rich man in the very near future. What he did not like was strangers bursting into his house and waving them in his face. Not that his brain – paralysed as it was with fear – was able to formulate the thought in any meaningful way, but his bladder made the point quite adeptly with an involuntary loosening. He reddened in humiliation as a puddle spread and soaked into the rug at his feet.

'I don't think this one will give us any trouble,' said the saturnine man. 'You two go and round up the servants,' he told the two masked men. They nodded and hurried from the room.

'I'll find Fru Ögren,' said the woman, following them out.

Ögren took out his pocket book and held it out to the saturnine man. 'Here: take it! My wife's jewellery is in a box on the dresser in her boudoir. Take anything you want, just please don't hurt me!'

The saturnine man waved the pocket book away impatiently. 'I don't want your money. All I'm after is your invitation to the ball in Sveaborg tonight.'

'That's all?' stammered Ögren, scarcely able to believe his luck. He took the invitation from his inside pocket and held it out to chimney-pot hat. 'Here, take the damned thing!'

'Much obliged.' Keeping his revolver levelled at Ögren, the man put down the holdall and took the invitation in his left hand, tucking it out of sight inside his tailcoat.

The two masked men returned with Wickmann. 'This is the only other servant we could find,' one of them told the saturnine man. 'He says he's the coachman. Says the rest of the servants have been given the night off.'

'Is this true?' asked the saturnine man.

Ögren nodded hurriedly.

The masked man who had spoken thrust the muzzles of his shotgun in Wickmann's chest. 'Take off your coat!'

Wickmann removed his greatcoat, and the other masked man took it from him, putting his shotgun aside – but taking care to lay it out of anyone else's reach – to shrug the coat over his threadbare frock-coat.

313

'And the hat,' the first masked man said, with an impatient gesture. Wickmann took off his round, black, broad-brimmed hat and handed it to the other, who put it on his head and picked up his shotgun again before glancing in the mirror to assess his appearance.

Ottilia entered with the young woman close behind her. 'Ambrosius!' she protested. 'What in the world is going on? Are we being robbed?'

'In a manner of speaking.' Now he knew they had not come here to murder and rob him, he was regaining some of his composure. 'Calm yourself, woman. They only want my invitation.'

'What? *Not* our invitation to the Grand Duke's ball?' She turned to the young woman behind her. 'No! You can't! You've no idea how long I've been looking forward to tonight. I've bought a new gown specially ... had my hair done ... I've told all my friends I'm to go ... I'll be humiliated! Ruined! I'll never be able to show my face in Helsingfors Society again!'

A revolver appeared in the young woman's hand as if by magic, and she pressed the muzzle to Ottilia's forehead. 'How very fortunate for Helsingfors Society!'

Ottilia turned crimson. 'Ambrosius! Are you going to stand there and let her speak to me that way?'

Ögren opened his mouth, but no sound came out when he felt the muzzles of one of the shotguns just behind his ear.

'Tell her "Yes",' the masked man holding the shotgun advised him.

'Yes,' Ögren told his wife in a very small voice.

The strangers marched the Ögrens and the two servants through to the dining room, where they ordered them to sit down at the table before producing several coils of rope and tying them securely in their chairs.

'Pardon me.' The saturnine man took Ögren's forgotten cigar from his unresisting fingers.

'What do you need to tie us up for?' Ögren demanded nervously.

'It may turn out that this ball is so wonderful that we simply can't tear ourselves away,' said the young woman. 'In which case, it would be so *very* disappointing if the *real* Ögrens turned up with a few gendarmes in tow to denounce us as impostors. So our associate there is going to stay with you for a few hours to keep you company.' She indicated the older of the two masked men. 'If you behave yourselves, you'll still be alive when he leaves at first light. I'm sure your servants will untie you when they arrive in the morning.' She glanced across at the saturnine man. 'You have the invitation?'

He patted the breast of his tailcoat. 'Cinderella, you *shall* go to the ball!'

'*Barrons-nous*. Don't wait up for us,' she added to the man staying behind. She went out, followed by the other two men.

The man who stayed behind waited until they heard the front door close behind them before sitting down facing his charges with the shotgun across his lap. Leaning back, he cast an unimpressed eye over the rococo moulding around the edges of the ceiling, and puffed out his cheeks. Then he lowered his gaze to take in his captives.

'All right, how about a game of charades to while away the hours?'

Ögren closed his eyes as if in pain.

# XX

# Sveaborg

---

Nordenskjöld had whipped off his mask by the time they reached the front door, and he climbed on to the driving board of the Ögrens' carriage, while Killigrew and Aurélie climbed in the back. Nordenskjöld whipped up the horses and they clattered off over the cobbles.

'What time is it?' asked Aurélie.

The sun was still sinking towards the horizon, so there was more than enough light for Killigrew to check his watch by. 'Five to.'

'We've missed the eight o'clock ferry, then.'

'We might have been on time if you hadn't spent so long deciding on that gown!'

'But there was such a choice! It's easy for you men, you all wear the same clothes: black tailcoat and trousers, white waistcoat and cravat . . .'

'There's still the little matters of cut and material,' he protested defensively. 'It doesn't matter; there's another ferry at nine. No one arrives at these balls on time anyhow.' He stood up to bang on the underside of the roof with his fist. 'Nils! Can you keep driving around for fifty minutes? It's going to look suspicious if we turn up at the naval base on Skatudden with an hour to spare before the next ferry.'

Nordenskjöld opened the hatch. 'In a city as small as Helsingfors, someone's going to notice a carriage driving around in circles.'

'All right, do you know a place where we can kill some time without drawing attention to ourselves?'

The young man thought for a moment. 'There's a glade in the forests just outside the city. It's hidden from the road, so no one will see us there.'

'Sounds good!'

It took them ten minutes to reach the spot, an idyllic hollow surrounded by pine trees. The only sound in the gathering twilight was the twittering of birds. Killigrew and Aurélie got out to stretch their legs. Nordenskjöld made himself comfortable on the driving board of the carriage and took out a small, well-thumbed book to read.

'We'll wait here for half an hour, then head back into town,' Killigrew decided, striking a match against the side of the carriage to relight Ögren's cigar, and then puffing away contentedly. 'What are you reading?' he asked Nordenskjöld.

The student held up the book so he could see the spine.

'*Principles of Mineralogy?*'

'It's what I studied for my Ph.D.'

'You're a Ph.D.?'

'Newly qualified.'

'What are you going to do now? Become a mining engineer?'

'A mineralogist, like my father.'

'Interesting work?'

He smiled. 'It is if you're interested in mineralogy. And you get to travel. I love travelling. What I'd really like to do is become an Arctic explorer like you.'

Killigrew shook his head. 'Take my advice, my lad: stick to being a revolutionary in a tyrannical empire. It's much safer!'

They waited until the sun had kissed the horizon, and then climbed back into the carriage. Nordenskjöld drove them back into Helsingfors through the dusk and they crossed the bridge into Skatudden. It was easy to find the naval base: the island was not large, and most of the buildings were the wooden shacks of the shanty town there, so the three-storey brick buildings of the naval barracks were visible all over the island.

Nordenskjöld opened the hatch in the ceiling. 'There's a queue of carriages trying to get into the yard,' he hissed out of the corner of his mouth. 'The guards are checking inside each one.'

'It's nothing to worry about,' Killigrew told him. 'No more than we expected. How fast are they going through?'

'They're keeping the carriages moving.'

Killigrew nodded, reassured. With scarcely ten hours before the bombardment started, they could not afford to waste another hour by missing the nine o'clock ferry.

Nordenskjöld reined in the horses when they reached the back of the

317

queue. They moved forwards in fits and starts as each carriage ahead of them was waved through, until finally they reached the gates and one of the guards – not one of the usual naval infantry in a dark green greatcoat, but a booted cuirassier in full dress, including brightly polished breastplate and helmet – came around to the window of the carriage. He saluted smartly and looked at Killigrew.

'*Inbjudningskort, min herre*?' he asked.

Killigrew's heart was pounding as he handed over the invitation for the guard's inspection: if the Ögrens had already escaped and informed the police of the theft of their invitations, this was the moment Killigrew, Aurélie and Nordenskjöld would find out about it.

The guard read the card out to a colleague. '*Gospodin i Gospoda Ambrosius Ögren!*'

There was a pause before the reply: one of the other guards no doubt checking the names against a guest list. The wait for the reply seemed inordinately long.

'*Da!*'

The first guard handed the card back to Killigrew and stepped away from the carriage, waving it through. Nordenskjöld flicked the reins across the horses' backs and they trundled through the gateway, rattling down the main thoroughfare of the naval base to the dockyard, which had been converted to a carriage park for the night. Nordenskjöld pulled up. Killigrew and Aurélie waited for him to jump down and open the doors for them: the immaculate cuirassiers on guard on the jetty would know enough of etiquette for their suspicions to be aroused if they had to open the doors for themselves.

But Nordenskjöld seemed to be in a world of his own. 'Nils!' hissed Killigrew. 'Get the door!'

'Oh! Sorry!' He jumped down, opening the door to hand Aurélie down from the carriage. Killigrew climbed out after her, straightening his tailcoat.

'You'd better take the carriage back to Ögren's house and see if Hjorth needs any help,' he told the student in a low voice.

'What about you?'

'We'll be all right. This is where we go our separate ways, Nils. I wish I could thank you and your associates properly for all you've done to help us.'

'If you can get Friherre Stålberg and Major Lindström free, that will be thanks enough.'

'We'll certainly try our best,' Killigrew promised him; although he knew they could not be sure that Stålberg and Lindström had not already been executed, or spirited off to the cellars of the Kochubey Mansion; and destroying the *Sea Devil* had to be their top priority.

'I wish I was coming with you,' said Nordenskjöld.

Killigrew shook his head. 'Not this time, Nils. Don't worry: one day you'll have some adventures of your own.' He smiled. 'As an Arctic explorer, perhaps.'

Nordenskjöld returned the smile. 'Perhaps.'

Killigrew and Aurélie stood back as the young man climbed on to the driving board and flicked the reins across the horses' backs. They watched him drive the carriage back up to the entrance to the naval yard, and then Killigrew proffered a crooked elbow to Aurélie. 'Shall we?'

She took his arm and the two of them walked across to the jetty.

It was five to nine and the ferry – a small paddle-steamer – already waited. More cuirassiers checked their invitation before they were allowed up the gangplank. The ferry's upper deck was crowded with men in tailcoats and sashes and women in ball gowns. The Russians had not thought to lay on any extra ferries tonight, as a result of which those not wishing to turn up only fifteen minutes after the ball had started (or, worse, forty-five minutes before) had been obliged to wait for this one.

The ferry's steam whistle sounded on the dot of nine, startling some of the ladies present, and the gangplank was brought in board while a couple of crewmen unfastened the mooring ropes from their bollards and jumped nimbly for the rail. As they scrambled to safety, the paddle-wheels plashed at the water and the ferry reversed away from the jetty. Once clear, the helmsman spun the wheel and the boat turned to face the Kronbergsfjärden – as the wide bay behind Sveaborg was called – before the order was given to stop the engines, then turn ahead.

The other guests crowding the upper deck smiled and laughed gaily, not in the least bit bothered by the Allied fleet on their doorstep. *Thus Nero fiddled while Rome burned*, thought Killigrew. As the ferry gathered way and rounded the headland at the east end of Skatudden, he glanced off to port to the anchorage in the middle of the Kronbergsfjärden. He counted six Russian ships of the line, a frigate, a brig, a corvette, and three paddle-sloops. There was no indication that they were readying themselves to sally out against the Allied fleet: they were outnumbered and outgunned anyway. But the day-to-day running of a fleet needed to be carried out, and boats and lighters moved

319

constantly between the anchored ships and the quayside, ferrying out men and supplies.

Turning away from the rail, he got a shock when he saw Lieutenant Kizheh standing on the other side of the deck.

Swearing under his breath, he turned his back immediately, but he had a feeling it was too late: he had caught Kizheh's eye, and the lieutenant had had enough time to get a fleeting glimpse of his face.

'D'you see that fellow standing on the other side of the deck, wearing a sky-blue uniform and leaning on a cane?' he muttered to Aurélie out of the corner of his mouth.

'No, but I see a fellow leaning on a cane and wearing a sky-blue uniform coming towards us.'

'Damn. Leave this one to me.' Leaving Aurélie at the rail, he started to push his way through the crowds to the fore hatch. There was no need to glance over his shoulder to see if Kizheh followed: the tap-tap-tap of his cane against the deck told its own story. Reaching the hatch, Killigrew lifted it up and descended the companion ladder below, only to run straight into a *matros* on the lower deck.

'I'm sorry, sir. Passengers aren't permitted below decks. This area is for the crew only.'

'Sorry, I was looking for the necessary.'

'There isn't one for passengers. We'll be arriving at East Svarto in less than ten minutes. You can—'

'*Matros!* Seize that man!' called Kizheh, coming down the companion ladder.

Killigrew tried to drive his knee into the *matros*'s crotch, but the Russian was fast: he twisted on his ankles to receive the blow against his thigh. When Killigrew tried to punch him in the face, the *matros* deflected the blow with an upraised arm and caught him by the wrist. Twisting Killigrew's arm up into the small of his back, he slammed him against a bulkhead and pinioned him there. An oil-lamp in a gimbal on the bulkhead inches from his face dazzled his eyes.

'Good work!' Kizheh came the rest of the way down the companion ladder and flashed his identification at the *matros*. 'Lieutenant Kizheh, Third Section. This man is a dangerous British spy!' Tucking his identification away, he produced a revolver and pressed the muzzle to Killigrew's forehead. 'What do you think, Commander? Should I take you to Sveaborg so Colonel Nekrasoff can put you in front of a firing squad? Or I should I just pull the trigger here and now, blow your brains out all over the bulwark? No . . . you don't deserve a quick death.' He

320

lowered the revolver until it was pointed at Killigrew's thigh. 'Perhaps I should make you suffer first, as you made me suffer when you shot me in the foot—'

'Er . . . excuse me?' interrupted a woman's voice as more footsteps sounded on the companion ladder. 'Is there somewhere on board I can powder my nose?'

Kizheh half turned away from Killigrew to address her over his shoulder. 'This is not a good time, Madame—'

Killigrew braced a foot against the bulkhead and threw himself backwards, slamming the *matros* against the bulkhead behind them and breaking free. He clasped Kizheh by the wrist, smashing his hand against the oil-lamp so that the broken glass lacerated his skin and the wick burned him. Kizheh cried out as his hand opened reflexively, allowing the revolver to fall to the deck. Killigrew seized the cane from his other hand, holding it against Kizheh's throat and forcing him back against the bulkhead, throttling him. Behind him, he heard the *matros*'s body fall to the deck with a thud.

Kizheh's struggles became weaker, until finally he became limp and the cane crushing his windpipe was the only thing holding him up. Killigrew gave the cane another push for good measure, and then let him drop to the deck. He backed away to see Aurélie kneeling over the *matros*'s corpse, wiping the blade of her throwing knife clean on his guernsey, taking fastidious care to make sure she did not get any of the blood on herself.

'I thought I told you to leave this one to me,' Killigrew said angrily.

'Oh, yes, because you were making such a fine job of it when I came down the hatch just now!'

'I could have handled them,' he said surlily, wondering if it was true.

As he stared down at the corpse at his feet, he felt himself trembling, nauseated. No matter how many times he killed, there was always something slightly sickening about it. He supposed that was something to be grateful for. He had promised himself that the day he started to enjoy it would be the day he resigned his commission.

Aurélie hitched up her skirts and petticoats to slide the knife back into the sheath strapped to one of her ankles. 'We'd better get them out of sight before someone else comes along,' she prompted, snapping him out of his reverie.

Killigrew glanced around and saw the door in the bulkhead behind her. 'Bow locker,' he grunted, grabbing the *matros* by the ankles and dragging him across the deck.

Aurélie took Kizheh's ankles. 'How is it I had to deal with the big, burly sailor while you got the skinny cripple?' she demanded.

'The skinny cripple had a gun,' Killigrew reminded her. 'Besides, that one was personal. Anyhow, you're the one who's always boasting you can look after yourself.'

He opened the door to the bow locker and between them they tossed the two bodies in there. Killigrew threw Kizheh's cane on top of them and dragged a tarpaulin over the corpses before closing the door once more.

As he stooped to pick up Kizheh's revolver, Killigrew saw there were a few shards of glass on the floor below the broken lamp. There was no time to look for a dustpan and brush, so he swept them against the foot of the bulkhead with the side of a half-boot so they would not crunch underfoot when anyone came down the passage.

'Is there any blood on me?' he asked Aurélie.

She looked him up and down. 'No. Plenty on the floor, though.'

He licked his fingertips and pinched out the still-burning flame of the oil-lamp, plunging the passageway into darkness. 'No one will notice it now.'

'A broken lamp, blood on the floor and two corpses in the bow locker . . . someone's going to notice this mess sooner or later.'

'Let's just pray it's later rather than sooner. We only need a couple of hours to rescue Stålberg and Lindström and destroy the *Sea Devil*.'

They went back up on deck. The scene was much the same as they left it – no one seemed to have any clue as to the drama that had been played out below – except that now it was almost dark, the night sky a rich shade of indigo, and the ferry was drawing close to Sveaborg.

The Kronbergsfjärden was undoubtedly a superb anchorage. Although shallow, the wide bay was sheltered from the gulf beyond by a chain of islands of which Sveaborg was only a part; yet the only channels deep enough to admit a ship of the line to the Kronbergsfjärden ran on either side of Sveaborg, right under the fortress's batteries. As the ferry approached the fortified islands, Killigrew saw the two-decker anchored across the channel between Langhorn and Little Svarto as a floating battery, and in the distance he could make out the masts of an even larger ship anchored where he guessed the second channel must lie.

The ferry passed Little Svarto – as its name implied, the smallest of the five islands, and the only one not connected to any of the others by a bridge – which was dominated by a single large fort. The ferry tied up at a landing stage at the north side of East Svarto, the largest of the islands. Killigrew and Aurélie had to queue to get ashore as more cuirassiers checked their invitations against the guest list as they disembarked, so the arriving guests were strung out in a long line as they set off into the island.

A single-storey red-brick barracks masked the rest of the island, although the white, onion-domed tower of a church rose up behind it. Half as high as the church tower, a three-storey tower with a belvedere on top rose up from the middle of the barracks, with an archway below. A string of paper lanterns guided the guests through the arch, so Killigrew and Aurélie followed them. On the other side the lanterns led the way down the side of a parade ground; the church stood to the right while on their left was another row of barracks, again built in red brick but three storeys high this time. On the far side of the parade ground the lanterns led them to the right, past another three-storey barrack-block and a 'C'-shaped red-brick building with the word 'Arsenal' on a sign above the door in Cyrillic script. Ahead and to their right, they could see a stretch of water – Artillery Bay, the channel between East Svarto and Vargon, narrowing to a width of about thirty yards where a wooden bridge spanned it up ahead.

'Gunboat sheds, off to your right,' muttered Aurélie.

Killigrew glanced that way and saw two sheds on the shore just over two hundred yards off, opening into Artillery Bay where it grew wider. Beyond there was a crossroad in the waterway where the channels between West Svarto, East Svarto, Little Svarto and Vargon met. If Killigrew was looking for the *Sea Devil*, then the gunboat sheds – about a hundred feet long and fifty feet high – warranted closer inspection, but there were too many guards around for him or Aurélie to break away from the other guests following the line of paper lanterns.

Once they had crossed the wooden footbridge they could hear the sound of a band playing a mazurka coming from up ahead. They followed the lanterns between two more buildings and emerged on another parade ground to see the citadel ahead of them, a large, star-shaped, casemated fort with bastions and ravelins.

The guests had to queue at the gateway formed by an arched tunnel beneath a crenellated tower. Here their invitations were taken to be checked against the guest list once again. In addition to the usual immaculate cuirassiers, Killigrew spotted a burly fellow with a lumpy face standing in the shadows of a corner. He wore a black leather greatcoat and a fur hat. Killigrew was tempted to mutter 'Third Section' under his breath to warn Aurélie, but saw no point in worrying her unnecessarily: it was not as if she would not already be on her guard.

As each couple went through, their names were passed to a magnificently dressed flunkey in a powdered wig and knee breeches, who announced their names to the gathering beyond.

'Herre and Fru Ambrosius Ögren!'

Killigrew was aware of all eyes turning to stare at them: there were plenty of grafs and grafinas, friherres and friherrinas, and even a couple of dukes and duchesses; but very few herres and frus. This was the real moment of danger, when someone was going to shout out: 'That's not Herre Ögren and his wife!' As he braced himself, he instinctively looked for a way out, but the place was a disaster if it was a quick exit you were after.

Their host for the night, Governor-General Friedrich von Berg, had decided to hold the ball in the compound of the citadel. It was certainly large enough – nearly two hundred and fifty yards across – and, with fairy lights hung from the granite walls or strung from lines stretched overhead, it looked lovely; and it was a suitably mild night for an open-air entertainment. But it was still a fortress, which meant there was only one way in or out – the heavily guarded gateway they had just come through – and there were more guards patrolling the battlements above the fairy lights.

Aurélie saw the problem too. With a broad smile fixed on her face, she hissed out of the corner of her mouth to Killigrew, 'We've just walked into a trap!'

He gave her arm what he hoped was a reassuring squeeze. Several seconds had passed, and no one had denounced them. In fact, most of the guests had returned to their conversations, pointedly ignoring the two bourgeois Helsingfors parvenus who had stumbled into their midst, although a few young military officers eyed Aurélie speculatively, wondering if she had her card marked for *every* dance. Most of the guests already there were army or navy officers, resplendent in bright uniforms with yards and yards of gold braid, although there were a few civilians in black alpaca tailcoats, who had arrived on the eight o'clock ferry.

'I need a drink,' muttered Aurélie.

'Why not?' said Killigrew, steering her to intercept a flunkey, who moved amongst the throng with a silver salver of champagne flutes.

The most dangerous moment was past, and while overconfidence now might yet prove fatal, he felt they could relax a little. They each took a glass of champagne and moved to stand across in a corner, watching the couples dancing in the middle of the compound. They were playing the awkward, out-of-place bourgeois couple to the hilt.

Killigrew cast an eye over the other people attending the ball. A thickset, bearded man in his late twenties wearing the full-dress uniform of the admiral-general of the Russian fleet had to be His Imperial Highness Grand Duke Konstantin Nikolaievich Romanoff, brother to the young Tsar. He stood with Governor-General von Berg and a man in the dark green uniform of a rear admiral of the Russian navy; Matyushkin, the naval officer commanding Sveaborg, Killigrew supposed. Inevitably, a crowd of fawning toadies surrounded them. Change the language and the uniforms, and this might have been an Admiralty levee back in London.

'Now what do we do?' asked Aurélie.

'We can't afford to bide our time,' mused Killigrew. 'They've let two nights slip by without using the *Sea Devil*; surely they won't miss a third. They might be preparing her to set out even as we speak.'

'We may even be too late,' said Aurélie.

'I haven't come this far to give up now. The first chance I get, I'll slip out of here and try to find the *Sea Devil*. I'll leave you to rescue Stålberg and Lindström.'

'All right. See if you can see a discreet way out of here.'

Killigrew looked up at the battlements above them. The guards were looking out to sea and only occasionally glanced into the compound below, but there was no way someone could climb up there and slip over the parapet without being noticed. The only other way out was the main gate. Gazing towards it, he noticed a man in the uniform of an artillery captain going out without being questioned.

'What I really need is a Russian naval officer's uniform,' he told Aurélie.

She cast an eye over the throng. 'Plenty to choose from. What about that fellow over there?' She nodded to a heavily built man in the green-so-dark-it-was-almost-black uniform of a naval lieutenant.

'Too big.'

'All right . . . how about that one?'

'Too small.'

'That one?'

'Too wide.'

325

'That one?'

'Too tall. You're not even trying!'

'Well, pardon me! Must you be so fussy?'

'With this many naval officers to choose from, we might as well make the effort to find one who's roughly my build. It's going to look damned suspicious if I try to march out with my sleeves flapping over my hands . . . wait!' He nodded to a naval captain-lieutenant standing on his own in one corner. 'Just right! Do you think you could lure him somewhere quiet and out of the way?'

'Luring men somewhere quiet and out of the way is my speciality!' she asserted, moving from his side to glide across to where the captain-lieutenant stood.

Killigrew watched as she started to address him. He glanced at her and flicked his eyes away with a bored expression, casting his gaze elsewhere. Aurélie persisted, putting a gloved hand on his arm and leaning forward slightly, the better to show off her cleavage, but for all the reaction she got from him he might as well have been made of stone. After a couple of minutes she gave up and walked back to where Killigrew stood.

'Not a glimmer,' she told him. 'He must be an auntie.'

'How can you tell?'

'If you were a man, would *you* be able to resist me?'

'Well, no, but I . . . wait a minute, what do you mean, *if* I was a man?'

'I'm teasing you. He's all yours, Casanova.'

Killigrew swallowed. 'Oh, the things I do for Queen and country!'

Aurélie watched as Killigrew walked up to the captain-lieutenant and introduced himself.

The Russian favoured him with a smile, which was more than he had deigned to give her; sometimes even a woman had her limitations. The two of them talked for a couple of minutes, and then the captain-lieutenant led Killigrew across to the door of one of the blockhouses surrounding the compound. Aurélie had to give credit where credit was due: the Englishman was a fast worker.

She was about to follow and give him a hand when the powdered flunkey's voice boomed from the gateway: 'His Highness Rear Admiral Prince Samoyla Iakovlevich Zhirinovsky!'

She swore under her breath. Quickening her pace towards the door Killigrew and the captain-lieutenant had just disappeared through, she had almost made it when a handsome man in an ornate sky-blue uniform stepped into her path.

'Forgive me, madame, but I don't believe I've had the pleasure . . .'

She resisted the temptation to brush him off with '. . . and I don't think you're likely to, either' and instead gave him her most dazzling smile.

'Nekrasoff,' he introduced himself. 'Colonel Radimir Fokavich Nekrasoff, at your service.' He bowed low, clicking his heels.

If her smile flickered, he showed no signs of noticing, although at the mention of his name she felt as though a fist of ice had punched through her stomach to clutch at her innards. '*Enchanté*, Colonel. I am Madame Ögren.'

'I wonder if I might be so bold as to ask for the pleasure of this dance?' he suggested as the band struck up a waltz.

She glanced around, trying to look casual, searching for Zhirinovsky, but he had disappeared into the throng. If she wanted to hide, there were probably few better places in the compound than amongst the crowd of dancing couples. Besides, instead of looking at Nekrasoff as a threat, it occurred to her that he also presented an opportunity: perhaps he could tell her where Stålberg and Lindström were being held. And Killigrew could look after himself for a few minutes.

She extended a hand to him. 'Why, Colonel, I'd be delighted.'

He slipped an arm around her waist and whirled her away with the throng. He was a good dancer. 'Is there a M'sieur Ögren?' he asked her.

'Oh, yes. He's here somewhere.'

'Would he have any objections to my dancing with his wife?'

'Most certainly! Ambrosius gets terribly jealous. I cannot think why,' she added archly, fluttering her eyelashes at him in mock-innocence.

Nekrasoff grinned. 'Should I be afraid of him?'

'He *is* a gun-dealer. But he's also a terrible shot. He takes his clients out on hunting trips sometimes. They shoot up the whole forest, but they rarely come back with any trophies.'

'These hunting trips are usually an excuse for men to get drunk together away from their wives,' snorted Nekrasoff.

'You do not hunt yourself, then?'

'Oh, I'm a hunter of a different sort. My quarry is men.'

'Isn't that illegal?'

'Not if you're an officer of the Third Section of His Imperial Majesty's Chancery.'

327

'You're an officer of the Third Section? That must be terribly exciting.'

'It has its moments . . .'

'Thank heavens I'm only a mere woman! I hardly think I should be able to cope with that much excitement.'

'You might be surprised. We employ all sorts of people in the Third Section.'

'Even women?'

'Women make the best spies of all. As a matter of fact, one of my most brilliant agents is a woman. She's just helped me to expose a nest of traitors right here in Helsingfors.'

'Really?' asked Aurélie, wide-eyed.

'Yes, as a matter of fact I've got two of them locked up here in Sveaborg—'

'Colonel Nekrasoff?' said a new voice.

They both turned, and Aurélie's heart leaped into her mouth.

It was Zhirinovsky.

# XXI

# The *Sea Devil*

Killigrew followed the captain-lieutenant into a latrine. The place was surprisingly clean for a latrine on a Russian military base; he supposed a squad of defaulters had been ordered to spend all day making it immaculate in preparation for tonight. Killigrew had attended enough supposedly sophisticated balls to know it would not stay in its pristine condition for long, but thankfully it was early yet and the place was still empty.

Smiling at Killigrew, the captain-lieutenant backed into one of the stalls. Killigrew followed him inside . . . and threw a fist into his Adam's apple.

Clutching at his throat, the captain-lieutenant collapsed on to the earth closet. He was trying to scream, but no sound would emerge from his crushed windpipe. Following him into the stall, Killigrew took off his chimney-pot hat, hung it from the hook on the back of the door, and replaced it with the peaked cap from the captain-lieutenant's head. Then he grabbed a fistful of his hair and hauled him up, spinning him around and encircling his neck with an arm. Placing his other hand against the back of the captain-lieutenant's head, he gave it a wrench, snapping his neck. The man's lifeless body crumpled to the floor.

Killigrew looked down at the corpse. After killing Kizheh, he scarcely had any self-loathing left in him for one night; but at least Kizheh had deserved to die. This poor devil's only crime had been sodomy; still a hanging offence in Britain, admittedly, except he had never seen anyone hanged for it, and he invariably turned a blind eye whenever he stumbled across it on board ship.

329

He stripped off his tailcoat, hung it up on the back of the door, and dragged the tunic off the dead man, shrugging it on. He hurriedly unfastened his trousers and pushed them down around his ankles, kneeling before the victim to take off his jackboots. He unbuckled the man's belt and unbuttoned his fly before rolling him over and dragging off his trousers.

'Disgusting!' a voice exclaimed behind him.

Startled, he twisted to see the door on the stall had swung open as far as the chimney-pot hat on the peg would allow, and now a major of grenadiers stood outside, glowering at him. 'Typical damned sailors! You should be ashamed of yourselves!'

'Don't criticise what you haven't tried,' Killigrew told him, pushing the door to and making sure it was bolted this time. He heard the major muttering under his breath as he relieved himself into the trough. *This never happened to the other feller!* Killigrew thought ruefully as he took off his own trousers and put the captain-lieutenant's on in their place. *And some people think espionage is glamorous!*

By the time he had completed his disguise, the major had gone and the latrine was deserted once more. Killigrew took Wojtkiewicz's fob watch from the pocket of the discarded waistcoat. It was nearly ten o'clock. The captain-lieutenant's uniform had no waistcoat, so he slipped the watch into his trouser pocket.

He climbed over the top of the stall door and dropped down on the flagstones outside. He had arranged it so it looked as though the stall was merely occupied.

There was a tarnished mirror on the wall above the washstands, and he checked his appearance in it before venturing outside. It felt good to be back in uniform, even if it was the uniform of the enemy, and he had to admit that the uniforms of Russian naval officers were rather dashing: a shade of green so dark it was almost black, with a double-breasted tunic, matching trousers, and patent leather jackboots. He set the officer's peaked cap on his head at a jaunty angle, and went outside.

The ball was in full swing now. Killigrew looked around for Aurélie and got a shock when he saw her talking to Nekrasoff and Zhirinovsky. Glancing past the admiral, she caught Killigrew's eye and gave him an infinitesimal shake of her head, as if to tell him she had the situation under control. She had never met Nekrasoff, of course, and as far as he was aware she had only met Zhirinovsky once, at his ball on board the *Letayushchaya Tarelka*. Perhaps he had not recognised her? One thing was certain: if either he or Nekrasoff had known she was a spy working for French military intelligence, they would not be standing around making polite small talk with her; a session in a cellar with thumbscrews and brass knuckles was more their style. Besides, there was nothing he could do: they might not recognise her, but at the first glimpse of him they would both be screaming for the guards to seize him. Trying to convince himself she would be all right, he headed for the gateway before either of them glanced in his direction.

No one tried to stop him as he passed through the gateway. He crossed the bridge back on to East Svarto, receiving the salutes of a handful of *matrosy* who passed him. Walking past the arsenal, he turned left before he reached the parade ground to follow the shore to where the gunboat sheds stood.

He approached the first. The windows were boarded up on the inside, but he could see light between the cracks. Now that Kizheh was dead and Nekrasoff and Zhirinovsky were back in the citadel, there seemed little danger of being recognised, so he adopted the bold approach, opening the door and marching straight inside.

A large dock running out below the gates at the far end of the shed dominated most of the floor, with a flagstone quay on three sides of it and a wrought-iron gantry running overhead. A gunboat eighty feet from stem to stern took up the entire length of the dock, its topmasts taken down to allow it to fit inside. The only people in the shed were four *matrosy*: stokers, by the look of their broad shoulders, grimy faces and vests covered in coal dust. They each sat on a wooden crate, arranged around a fifth crate that served as a card table between them, but as soon as Killigrew entered they leaped to their feet and formed a line, standing rigidly to attention and saluting.

Killigrew glanced at the gunboat. No smoke issued from the funnel, although there were vents in the roof above to allow it to escape so the boilers could be fired without filling the shed with smoke.

'Why in the devil's name aren't you getting steam up?' he demanded of the stokers.

'We've received no orders,' stammered one.

'What?' Killigrew exploded furiously. 'Admiral Matyushkin's orders to Captain Kovaleff were quite specific. Did he not pass them on?'

'N-no, sir. We don't know any Captain Kovaleff—'

'Whether or not you have Kovaleff's social acquaintance is no concern of mine, *matros*! The fact remains that this gunboat is due to be moved out at ten o'clock; and here we are at a quarter to, and the boilers are cold! This is a shambles! I'm going to have to report this to the admiral at once; but I shall be back in one hour. If you do not have a good head of steam up by then, your next posting will be to the Petropavlovsky Squadron! Do I make myself clear?'

'Yes, sir!' chorused the *matrosy*.

'Jump to it, then!'

The stokers raced one another to get on board the gunboat. Killigrew left them to it, slamming the door behind him. Unless some idiot came along to countermand his orders, they might be able to use the gunboat to escape once he had destroyed the *Sea Devil* and Aurélie had rescued Stålberg and Lindström.

He opened the door to the next gunboat shed and marched inside. The interior was the mirror image of the shed next door, except that instead of a gunboat in the dock he found what could only be the *Sea Devil* itself.

Having spent so long going over the plans with Brunel, there was no mistaking the fifty-two-foot-long, iron-black cylinder that floated low in the water in the dock. It looked like nothing so much as a big, black mechanical whale. There was a hatch on top, and a raised box at one end with three portholes in it.

To Killigrew's dismay, however, there were also nine *matrosy* in there, playing cards or dozing on the floor as they waited for orders. They scrambled to stand to attention at the sight of his uniform. So much for his hopes of being able simply to put a keg of gunpowder in the *Sea Devil* and light the fuse.

When the nine *matrosy* were standing in a line, Killigrew marched up and down in front of them, trying to put a swagger he did not feel into his step, although the dark-green uniform seemed to help. He inspected the *matrosy* with a critical eye.

'You are the crew?'

'Yes, sir!'

'Who is in charge here?'

'Lieutenant Fedorovich, sir,' said one of the men, a non-commissioned officer.

Killigrew looked around nervously for Fedorovich, but there was no sign of any officers.

'Lieutenant Fedorovich has been murdered,' he told them crisply.

The *matrosy* looked shocked enough to suggest Fedorovich was popular with the men assigned to serve under his command.

'Most likely by those swine, the Wolves of Suomi,' Killigrew continued, 'in revenge for arrest of their co-conspirators. I am ordered to take his place. I am Captain-Lieutenant Kovaleff, and I have orders to take the *Khimera* out at once.' He hesitating before continuing, watching their faces, but their expressions gave nothing away. They were probably expecting a speech, but he did not have time for one: Lieutenant Fedorovich might turn up at any moment and ruin everything.

'Our target is the *Duke of Wellington*,' he told them.

The *matrosy* huzza'd. Smiling indulgently, Killigrew waited for them to fall silent. 'That's the spirit, *mouzhiki*.' He indicated the *Sea Devil*. 'She is ready to go?'

'Ready and waiting, sir,' said the NCO.

Killigrew selected two of the *matrosy* at random. 'You and you: open the sea gates.'

'Yes, sir!'

'The rest of you board the *Khimera*. No, not you, Sergeant: I want a word with you first.'

'Sir?'

As one of the *matrosy* jumped on to the deck of the *Sea Devil* and opened the hatch, Killigrew took the NCO to one side and addressed him in a low tone. 'What is your name?'

'Zubakoff, sir.'

'I've done salvage work in my time, Sergeant Zubakoff, so I know my way around inside of a diving suit,' he confided. 'But I must confess this will be first time I've been in one of these contraptions. That means you're going to have to hold my hand. Can I count on you?'

'I shan't let you down, sir,' the sergeant said gravely.

Killigrew clasped him by the shoulder. 'Good man.'

The watergates were open now. The last two men stepped on board and descended the hatch, and Killigrew and Zubakoff climbed down after them.

The interior of the *Sea Devil* was dark and cramped with ten of them in there; one of the men lit the wick in a hurricane lamp. The iron sides reflected no light, and the interior felt dank and cold.

'You know anything at all about how these things work, sir?' asked Zubakoff.

'Herr Bauer briefed me on the principles while I was in St Petersburg, and I've studied the plans, but I'm unfamiliar with the controls.'

Zubakoff nodded. 'The treadmills control the screw propeller,' he explained, pointing to them. 'The helm controls the rudder, just like on an ordinary ship; this wheel here handles trim; and these valves control the ballast so we go up or down. Each of us knows our duties, sir. You just tell us what you want the *Khimera* to do, and we'll do it. Um . . . Lieutenant Fedorovich used to stand in the observation cupola to con the ship during trials.'

'Then I shall do likewise.' Killigrew made his way to the front of the vessel. A short ladder led to the box at the prow of the ship. He was about to ascend when he noticed another doorway leading forward, with a porthole set on it. 'What's through there?'

'Underwater hatch, sir,' Zubakoff told him. 'That's where Ustimovich will get out to fix the explosives to the *Duke of Wellington*'s hull. We'll have to be sitting on the bottom when he does, though: flooding the front compartment plays havoc with the *Khimera*'s trim.'

Killigrew peered though the porthole. The compartment was unlit, but he could just make out enough room for four men to stand, provided they were thin and not averse to intimacy, but not taking into account the space taken up by the diving suit hanging from one bulkhead and the coiled air-hose running from a valve in the bulkhead to the brass helmet.

He ascended the ladder to stand on the fourth rung, so his head and shoulders were in the observation cupola. Peering through the thick, salt-stained glass, he could see the interior of the boat-shed clearly enough.

He descended once more. 'Very well, then. Let's see how well you know the initial diving drill,' he told the *matrosy*.

Standing at the helm, Zubakoff grinned. 'You heard the captain-lieutenant, *mouzhiki*. Check the inner and outer underwater hatches are sealed, Volkoff.'

One of the *matrosy* squirmed through the watertight doorway below Killigrew into the chamber forward, and emerged a moment later, screwing the wheel on the inner doorway to seal it. 'Underwater hatches sealed.'

'Close the upper hatch, Yukhin.'

Another *matros* climbed the central ladder and closed the hatch above them. Killigrew knew the clang was the sound of his own tomb being sealed. He was sorry not to have a chance to rescue Stålberg and Lindström, or to avenge Araminta's death, but push had come to shove and he knew his personal desires had to take second place to his duty; and that was to destroy the *Sea Devil* and

334

save the lives of the men on board the *Duke of Wellington*, even at the cost of his own.

Yukhin screwed the hatch shut. 'Upper hatch sealed.'

'Commence air purification.'

Yukhin grasped a handle and pumped it. Water began to drip from dozens of tiny holes drilled through the pipes that ran along the ceiling of the contraption.

'Is that supposed to happen?' Killigrew asked dubiously.

Zubakoff grinned. 'Unnerving, isn't it, sir? Don't worry, that's just to purify the air.'

Killigrew glanced down. The water collected in the bilges below the iron grating that formed the deck, from where it was presumably pumped back into the pipes.

'The water's too shallow to submerge in the dock, sir. Lieutenant Fedorovich would take us out on the surface, and then submerge in Artillery Bay. We're ready to go when you are, sir.'

'Excellent. Take her out, Zubakoff.'

'Yes, sir! You heard him, *mouzhiki*: let's go!'

The men on the treadmills began to step, turning the wheels. Gears groaned eldritchly. Killigrew climbed back up to the observation cupola and peered out. The *Sea Devil* seemed to be motionless, but as the men on the treadmills gained momentum and the wheels turned faster, the strange contraption began to move forward, out of the gunboat-shed and into Artillery Bay. Killigrew could see some artillerymen working on the opposite embankment. Seeing the *Sea Devil* emerge, they cheered and threw their caps into the air, although Killigrew could scarcely hear their huzzas.

Even with the men on the treadmills going flat out, the *Sea Devil* did not move at more than two knots, and that was on the surface where the water resistance was at its lowest. This was going to take for ever. He caught himself, and smiled: was he really in such a hurry to die?

'Four points to starboard, Zubakoff,' he called down from the observation cupola.

'Four points to starboard it is, sir.' The sergeant spun the wheel, and the *Sea Devil* turned ponderously.

'Bring her amidships,' Killigrew ordered when the *Sea Devil* was pointed towards the crossroads where the four channels between Vargon and East, West and Little Svarto met.

' 'Midships. We can reach the open sea under the pontoon bridge

335

between Vargon and West Svarto, sir,' said Zubakoff. 'There's enough water, provided we stick to the middle of the channel and don't go below three fathoms.'

'Very well. We'll submerge as soon as we get to the middle of the roads. Steady as she goes.'

Below him, one of the *matros* burst spontaneously into song, and when Killigrew did not tell him to be quiet the others joined in:

> God save the noble Tsar!
> Long may he live, in power,
> In happiness,
> In peace to reign!
> Dread of his enemies,
> The Faith's sure defender,
> God save the Tsar!

Killigrew mouthed the words of 'Rule, Britannia!' Through one of the side portholes in the observation cupola, he could see a dinghy rowed after them by four *matrosy*, while a man in a lieutenant's uniform gestured frantically in the stern sheets. Lieutenant Fedorovich, he presumed: back too late to save his command. Fortunately, the nine *matrosy* working below him could see nothing of the dinghy.

'Zubakoff?' he called down.

'Sir?'

'Take her down: three fathoms.'

'Yes, sir. Flood ballast tanks!'

As one of the *matrosy* pumped water into the ballast tanks, the *Sea Devil* began to submerge. It was eerie to stand in the observation cupola as the water level rose on the other side of the portholes. Killigrew's heart beat frantically in his chest, until he forced himself to get a grip. This was no different from being in a diving suit. Besides, it was his plan to die, or at least death was likely to be the result of his plan. The water would be shallower here than he had originally intended, but he was not sure he could keep up the imposture much longer. The Russians would be able to salvage the *Sea Devil*, he had no doubt, but not before the Allied fleet had reduced Sveaborg to rubble. At this depth, he might yet be able to escape this iron coffin, but only to be caught by the Russians, and doubtless die a lingering death in the Kochubey Mansion; assuming Nekrasoff bothered to take him all the way back to St Petersburg.

'Depth: three fathoms,' reported Zubakoff. 'Maintain neutral buoyancy!'

'Hold it there.' Unseen by the men in the body of the underwater boat, Killigrew took his revolver from his holster and pressed the muzzle to the glass of one of the viewing ports. He took a deep breath: this was the point of no return. When he pulled the trigger, he would be condemning himself and the *Sea Devil*'s crew to a watery grave; but it would be worth it, to save the lives of the men on board the *Duke of Wellington*, and all the others who would die – British, French, Turkish and Russian – if the war was prolonged.

He pulled the trigger. The report was deafening in the confined space. As thick as the glass was, it was no match for a ·43" calibre slug travelling at 650 feet per second. The bullet punched a hole clean through, shattering the glass, and the water poured in.

The force of it caught Killigrew off guard, almost knocking him from his perch. He had to drop the revolver and hold on with both hands. Above the roar of the rushing torrent, he could hear the Russians shouting in panic below.

Only Zubakoff kept his head. 'One of the viewing ports must've shattered! Here, use this to try to fother it while we pump out the ballast!'

One of the matrosy appeared below Killigrew, clutching a great-coat as he looked up at the torrent. It was unlikely that a coat stuffed in the port was going to stem the flood, but Killigrew was determined to make sure the *Sea Devil* went down and stayed down. As the *matros* tried to climb up beside him, Killigrew kicked him in the face, and the man fell down with blood streaming from a smashed nose.

Another *matros* tried to grab Killigrew by the ankle. The commander aimed a kick at him, but the man managed to avoid it and hooked a hand over his belt, trying to drag him down. Killigrew's foot slipped on the wet rung and he fell. The two of them crashed to the deck, and the commander knocked the man out with a right cross.

The water level rose in the bilges beneath the grating that formed the deck. As it rose above the grating, Killigrew saw his revolver lying there, but Yukhin caught him from behind and held him in an arm lock before he could grab it.

'We're losing neutral buoyancy!' shouted someone. 'We're sinking!'

'Someone fother that port, for Christ's sake!'

Yukhin spun Killigrew around to face another *matros*, who punched him in the stomach. Judging from the force of the blow, the *matros* had overcome a lifetime of subservience to fulfil a lifelong dream: striking a superior officer. Killigrew kicked him in the crotch, and when the man doubled up he kneed him in the face, before bracing a foot against the side of one of the treadmills, launching himself backwards across the vessel so that Yukhin was slammed against the bulkhead. Killigrew felt the arms that gripped him loosen, and the sailor slipped down to the deck.

Zubakoff left the helm and charged towards Killigrew. The commander fumbled in the rising water for his revolver and grabbed it in time to bring the sergeant up short.

'The powder will be wet!' Zubakoff said uncertainly.

'Pinfire revolver,' Killigrew told him.

'Depth, four fathoms and sinking,' moaned the *matros* watching the bathometer.

Killigrew caught sight of a movement out of the corner of his eye as one of the other *matrosy* suddenly appeared from behind one of the treadmills. He spun round and pulled the trigger, but not before the *matros* got his hands on his wrist and forced the gun aside. The noise of the shot was deafening in the confined space, but not as bad as the whine of the bullet as it ricocheted off a dozen metallic surfaces, each ear-shattering clang merging with the echoes of the last.

And then the bullet hit Killigrew squarely in the forehead.

On board the *Duke of Wellington*, Captain Caldwell approached the marine on duty outside the door to the great cabin at twenty-five past ten. The marine saluted and knocked on the door for him.

'Who is it?' Rear Admiral Dundas called from within.

'Captain Caldwell to see you, sir.'

'Show him in.'

The marine opened the door and ushered Caldwell inside. The captain found Dundas sitting at the table with Commodore Pelham. The two of them were playing 'Old Maid' by the light of the oil-lamp hanging from the deck head.

Caldwell saluted. 'You asked me to remind you when it was coming up to half-past ten, sir.'

'So I did.' Dundas stared thoughtfully at the cards in his hand for several moments.

'Something wrong, sir?' Pelham prompted him.

Dundas shook his head. 'It's just I can't help thinking . . . it isn't too late to call off the attack . . .'

Pelham looked horror-stricken. 'You can't, sir! Everything's in place; everyone's just waiting for the word.'

'Yes, but I can't help thinking . . . what if something goes wrong? What if the place is more heavily defended than we realised?'

'The gunboats will be able to pull out quickly enough if that's that case. Please, sir, think of how the public will react back in Britain.'

'Public opinion, yes . . .' Dundas seemed to drift off into a reverie.

Caldwell still stood waiting on the threshold. 'Your orders, sir?'

Dundas took one of the cards from Pelham's hand: the ace of spades. That matched his ace of hearts, so he took them and laid them both aside. 'Send a general signal through the fleet: "Have steam up by three a.m." '

Pelham looked relieved.

Caldwell saluted. 'Aye, aye, sir!'


A young *michmani* in undress uniform weaved through the crowd of gaily dressed men and women in the citadel until he found Admiral Zhirinovsky, who still stood talking with Nekrasoff and Aurélie. He stood to attention and saluted.

'Sorry to disturb you, sir, but lookouts report steam rising from the funnels of the enemy steamers.'

'Keep your voice down!' Snarling, Zhirinovsky glanced nervously at the other guests nearby, but they were all too engrossed in their own conversations to have heard what the *michmani* had said. He pasted a phoney smile on his face in case anyone was watching. 'Do you want to spread fear and despondency? I'm sure it's nothing to worry about.'

The *michmani* flushed. 'Sorry, sir. Your orders?'

'My orders? Carry on, *michmani*. Those are my orders. Most likely the enemy are planning to steam away from here at dawn, just as they steamed away from Kronstadt and Reval!'

'Yes, sir!' The *michmani* saluted again and turned on his heel, marching away.

'Do you really believe that?' Nekrasoff asked quietly. 'The intelligence reports of my own department suggest Dundas will attack. Like all British admirals – like the British government – he is a slave to the beast with many heads. Napier was dismissed because he did not attack; Dundas knows from that example he has no choice.'

Zhirinovsky snorted. '*Our* intelligence reports suggest that neither

Dundas nor Seymour has the courage to risk any of their ships in an attack against granite batteries.'

'And what about Pénaud? Suppose he puts some backbone into them?'

'Then let them attack. Their shell guns and steam engines will be powerless against our defences!'

'Shouldn't we warn his Imperial Highness that an attack may be imminent?' said Nekrasoff.

'Do you want to be one to tell him we fear a British attack?' demanded Zhirinovsky. When Nekrasoff said nothing, he smiled triumphantly. 'Well, neither do I. Besides, I want him to be here to see with his own eyes when my *Khimera* sinks the *Duke of Wellington*.'

'When will it set out? If you're right about the Allies steaming away at dawn without firing a shot, isn't there a danger we'll miss our chance?'

Zhirinovsky smirked. 'The *Khimera* is already on its way to the Allied fleet. I gave Lieutenant Fedorovich orders to set out at half-past ten.' He took out his fob watch and glanced at it. 'By my calculations, it should be in position to attach explosives to the *Duke of Wellington*'s hull by one o'clock this morning. Even if the Allies are planning to attack at dawn, I think they'll soon change their minds when they see their flagship mysteriously blown out of the water!'

Nekrasoff shot a glance at Aurélie. 'Should we be discussing this in front of Madame Ögren?'

Zhirinovsky waved dismissively. 'Oh, it's all right. She doesn't speak a word of Russian. Do you, my little Finnish trollop?' he added to Aurélie, still speaking Russian.

She looked at him blankly. '*Pardon*?'

'You see? The silly bitch doesn't understand a word.'

A man in a black leather greatcoat and fur hat came through the crowd and stood to one side, trying to catch Nekrasoff's eye. 'Excuse me one moment,' Nekrasoff told Zhirinovsky and Aurélie, crossing to speak to the man. 'Yes?'

The man leaned forward to whisper in the colonel's ear. At first Nekrasoff looked horrified at what he was hearing, but as the man continued to whisper a smile spread across the colonel's face.

'Splendid, splendid! That's the best news I've had all year!' He crossed back to where Zhirinovsky and Aurélie stood. 'Madame Ögren, I fear I must take my leave of you for now. A matter demanding my immediate attention has been brought to my notice. If you'll excuse me?' He clicked his heels and bowed low to kiss her hand. Straightening once more, he turned to salute Zhirinovsky. 'Your Highness . . . you said the *Khimera* set out at half-past ten?'

'Those were my orders.'

Nekrasoff's grin became fractionally wider, if such a thing were possible. 'I'm sure your orders are *always* obeyed, Highness.' He saluted and clicked his heels again, marching towards the gate after the man in the greatcoat.

'What was all that about?' asked Aurélie.

'I don't know . . .' Zhirinovsky frowned. 'If I didn't know better I'd say that devil Nekrasoff is up to something,' he muttered to himself in Russian. 'Maybe I should check the *Khimera* did go out on time . . .'

'*Pardon*?'

'Oh, nothing, nothing,' he assured her. 'I was just thinking, I too may have to tear myself away from your delightful company.'

'Your Highness!' she protested. 'Surely you would not be so ungallant as to leave a young woman alone amongst a strange gathering?'

'What about your husband?'

'He seems to have disappeared.' More than an hour had passed since she had seen Killigrew slip out of the compound in the captain-lieutenant's uniform, but if she had been expecting to hear an explosion since then she had been disappointed. And she had not liked the look on Nekrasoff's face just before he left. When a man like Nekrasoff smiled, it boded no good for someone. She wondered if she should give Zhirinovsky the slip and try to find Killigrew to make sure he was all right. But while a man in the uniform of an officer could slip out of the compound without attracting attention to himself, a woman sneaking about the naval base in a ball gown was going to arouse the suspicions of everyone she passed. And besides, Killigrew was counting on her to rescue Stålberg and Lindström, and so far she had not even found out where Nekrasoff was holding them.

Zhirinovsky was looking at her with a thoughtful expression on his face. 'You know, you seem strangely familiar to me. I cannot help but think we have met before.'

'Now that you mention it, I've been thinking I've seen you some-where before too.' She frowned. 'Ambrosius took me with him on a business trip to St Petersburg last week . . . I remember going to a ball on a steam yacht with some of my husband's colleagues.'

'Ah, yes . . . you were with Admiral Rykord that day, I seem to recall.'

341

'He was kind enough to take me under his wing. Ambrosius could not come, he suffers terribly from *mal de mer*. He was even sick on the ferry that brought us out here tonight.'

'Have you been married long?' Zhirinovsky asked her.

'Oh, about two years. And four years before that, to my first husband.'

'Your first husband?'

She nodded. 'He died of cholera four years ago.' She knew it was dangerous to extemporise a back story for the identity she had assumed; but she felt she was on fairly safe ground here: everything would be over, one way or another, before Zhirinovsky had a chance to check her background. 'Ambrosius was very good to me in the difficult time that followed.'

'Ah . . . so that's why you married him.'

'I'm not sure I follow you.'

'You felt indebted to him.'

'Perhaps.'

'Do you have any children?'

She shook her head. 'So far, our union has not been blessed.'

Zhirinovsky laughed. 'Children are no blessing, believe me! I have two boys of my own, both grown up now. One of them is in Sevastopol, serving with Black Sea fleet.'

'So you are married too?'

'Alas, no. My own wife departed this life some years ago.'

She looked around the compound as if still searching for her husband. 'Oh, this is just too thoughtless of Ambrosius, wandering off and leaving me alone like this!' she protested, on the verge of tears.

'There, there, madame!' Zhirinovsky put a comforting arm around her shoulders. 'Console yourself. I'm sure he cannot have gone far. It seems he is not so attentive after all,' he could not resist adding.

She grimaced. 'I confess his tenderness to me waned soon after our marriage . . . but you don't want to hear of my troubles . . .'

'To the contrary, madame . . . may I call you Ottilia?'

'Please.'

'To the contrary, Ottilia; what kind of friend would I be, were I to refuse you a shoulder to cry on?'

'You are too kind, sir.'

'Please, call me Samya.'

'To tell the truth, I have . . . oh! I know it is wrong of me to even think it, and yet . . . I have doubts about my husband . . .'

'You think he is unfaithful to you?'

'Is it wrong of me to be so distrusting?'

'I'm sure you are mistaken, Madame. And yet . . .'

'What?'

'Nothing, nothing. Forget I spoke.'

'No, please, Highness . . . Samya . . . go on.'

'It is just . . . well, perhaps I am unduly cynical, yet if I am it is because I never cease to be amazed by how many men with perfectly beautiful wives like yourself can be tempted to stray from the path of propriety. And when Colonel Nekrasoff was here I thought I saw . . . but no, it is nothing. I'm sure it was perfectly innocent.'

'Samya, if you know something – and if you consider yourself my friend – then I demand that you tell me all!'

'It is nothing. I only saw the man you arrived with talking to Gravina Hornfeldt. I'm certain her reputation is wholly without foundation. You must know how disrespectfully men talk of beautiful young widows, I'm sure . . .'

Aurélie burst into tears and buried her head in Zhirinovsky's breast with a wail. 'Oh, I knew it! That beast! He cares nothing for me! I know he keeps at least one mistress, though he thinks I know nothing of it.'

Looking about, embarrassed at the stares they were getting from the people around them, Zhirinovsky steered Aurélie out of the citadel and gave her his silk handkerchief while she had a good snivel.

'Oh, look at me!' she said at last. 'Getting all histrionic again. I've made a proper spectacle of myself, haven't I?'

'Quite understandable, under the circumstances.'

'Oh, I must look an absolute fright, I know. Is there somewhere around here I can compose myself?'

'My quarters are not far from here . . .'

'Prince Zhirinovsky! Whatever can you be thinking?'

'Forgive me, madame. I was not thinking at all. You are right: it would be quite unseemly. The *matrosy*'s latrines are further away, but perhaps it would be more fitting . . . although I should warn you, the facilities there are somewhat, shall we say, basic?'

'*Matrosy*'s latrines? I'm not sure I care for the sound of that. I mean, it is not as if there is anyone around to see us; and you being an admiral – and a prince – even if they did, I'm sure no one would even *dream* of accusing a man as respectable as you of any impropriety.'

Smiling triumphantly, he led her across the bridge back to East

Svarto and they made their way to the small house he had been allocated as his residence while he was based at Sveaborg.

'My bedroom is upstairs,' he told her. 'You will find all you need to make your *toilette*, I think . . . I will make drinks for us. You look as though you could do with one.'

'Oh, Samya! You are such a gentleman!'

# XXII

# A Guest of the Tsar

---

Killigrew felt the stinging slap of water in his face and for a moment he was back on the *Sea Devil* with water slopping in around the rim of the hatch. Except there was an immense pain in his wrists and shoulders he could not account for. He was standing on his own two feet through no volition of his own; or rather, was hanging from his wrists with his feet resting on the ground. He tried to stand to take the pressure off his arms.

His skull throbbed, particularly in the forehead. He remembered something hitting him there when the bullet ricocheted all around the interior of the *Sea Devil*. He was trying to work out what had happened when it hit him with almost as much force as the bullet had.

He had contrived to shoot himself in the head.

And, apparently, lived to tell the tale.

How many times had the bullet spanged off the iron sides of the underwater boat? Enough to rob it of nearly all its impetus, so it had been all but spent by the time it struck him. A lucky escape, but the worst kind of luck: he had failed in his mission, and now he was a prisoner.

He opened his eyes to find Ryzhago standing over him with an empty bucket in one hand, dripping water. With the other meaty fist he punched Killigrew in the stomach.

It was a punch to make the commander wish he were still unconscious. He wanted to double up, to hug the pain within him as if it was a wounded wild animal squirming in his arms, but his chains prevented him. Looking up, he saw his wrists were manacled,

345

the chain between them looped over a hook dangling from a series of chains and pulleys suspended from the girders below the ceiling.

'Easy, Ryzhago!' an urbane, all-too-familiar voice chided the big man mockingly. 'After all, we owe Commander Killigrew our gratitude. It was thanks to him we were able to arrest the ringleaders of the Wolves of Suomi.'

Killigrew twisted his head to see Colonel Nekrasoff standing to his left, an amused smile playing on his face. 'Let me down and give me a gun,' Killigrew slurred thickly, 'and we'll call it quits.'

Nekrasoff chuckled. 'Still as flippant as ever, even at the end of it all. I would have expected nothing less. Although I must confess, you impressed even me with your resourcefulness this time. Successfully penetrating Sveaborg's defences, coming within an ace of sinking the *Sea Devil* . . . I'll admit, this time you have been most troublesome. But as I told you back in London, you were out of your depth – in over your head.'

Looking around the room he was in, Killigrew found himself back in the gunboat shed. The *Sea Devil* was in its dock, a couple of *matrosy* standing on its back working stirrup pumps to empty it of water. A naval lieutenant emerged from the hatch, followed by a civilian whom Killigrew recognised as Bauer from the magic-lantern portrait Brunel had shown him. Both of them were wet to the knees.

As the two of them approached, Nekrasoff turned to the civilian. 'Well, Herr Bauer?'

'We can have the water pumped out of her within the hour.'

Nekrasoff turned back to Killigrew. 'Sergeant Zubakoff was able to fother the viewing port long enough to get the *Khimera* back to the surface,' he explained triumphantly. 'You see, your efforts have been quite in vain—'

'Now hold on a minute!' protested the lieutenant. 'Pumping the water out of the *Khimera* is just the beginning. We've still got to replace the glass in the port.'

Killigrew grinned at Nekrasoff. 'You were saying?'

Ryzhago punched him in the stomach again. Through the waves of nausea that swamped him, he heard Nekrasoff tell Fedorovich curtly: 'Then replace it!'

'It isn't easy to cut glass of that thickness,' grated Bauer. 'It will take time.'

'How long?' Nekrasoff demanded impatiently.

346

'A day or two,' said Bauer.

'A matter of hours, if we work through the night,' said Fedorovich. Bauer shot him a dirty look.

The colonel took out his fob watch. 'It is now . . . seven minutes past midnight. You have until four o'clock to get the *Khimera* operational once more. Otherwise your next assignment will be the Siberian salt mines!'

'But the sun rises just after four!' protested Fedorovich. 'You're not suggesting I take the *Khimera* out when it's light?'

'Then you have an added incentive to get it repaired as soon as possible, haven't you?'

Fedorovich and Bauer hurried out to get to work cutting a new circle of glass for the viewing port.

Nekrasoff turned to Ryzhago and indicated Killigrew. 'Bring him.'

Ryzhago paid out one end of a pulley, lowering the hook from which Killigrew hung from the block and tackle above so he could unhook his manacles. As Nekrasoff headed for the door, Ryzhago took Killigrew by the arm and steered him out after the colonel. The big man gave him a shove in the back that sent him staggering after Nekrasoff. Caught off balance, and still woozy from Ryzhago's gut-punches, Killigrew stumbled against the wall of the gunboat shed. With his hands shackled in front of him, he had to twist to catch the worst of the collision against his shoulder.

The first part of the journey was carried out in a haze of pain and nausea. Killigrew could not tell how long it lasted or how far they walked. As they crossed a wooden bridge, the new sound of their footsteps on the planks after the scrunch of gravel helped to snap him out of his daze, and he realised he should be trying to remember the route so he could find his way back to the gunboat shed later.

Assuming he had a 'later' to look forward to.

They reached a T-junction with a large blockhouse in front of them. Nekrasoff and Ryzhago took Killigrew left, and then turned right, down the side of the blockhouse with a second building on their left. On the far side they crossed a triangular courtyard framed by buildings on two sides, passing between them into a second courtyard beyond which he could see the crenellated walls of the star-shaped citadel at the centre of Vargon. There was an optical telegraph tower off to their left, and they walked out through a gateway and between the open area beyond before the battlements of the citadel.

Off to the left he could see the starlight glittering on the Kronbergsfjärden, which meant they were headed south. Having had a chance to view Sveaborg from a distance, Killigrew was staring to get his bearings now. There was another wooden bridge ahead, spanning the narrow channel between Varfon and the next island, which he knew must be Gustafvard. Two forts that looked as if they had been constructed over the past few months stood on the shore to his right, and behind them a solid-looking structure with the word '*Magazin*' in bold Cyrillic script on a sign above the main door. Killigrew knew he was gaining invaluable knowledge of Sveaborg's layout if he ever got a chance to get back to the fleet before the bombardment started; except that the iron-roofed building looked so solidly constructed it was difficult to imagine any mortar shell falling hard enough to penetrate the roof before it exploded. Better yet, let him get inside the magazine for a few moments with a match, and he would make the Russians rue the day they had declared war on Commander Kit Killigrew!

But Nekrasoff and Ryzhago clearly had no intention of letting him get anywhere near the magazine. They marched him across the bridge on to Gustafvard, the southern-most of the five islands. Unlike East Svarto and Vargon, which were relatively built up, Gustafvard was comparatively open, apart from the artillery batteries down the west coast and a large, star-shaped fort at the south-eastern corner. Once inside the fort, they entered a labyrinth of inter-locking glacis, ravelins and blockhouses, where the paths became a narrow defile between the battlemented ramparts that towered above them.

They passed through a low but wide archway that became a tunnel, half built out of brick and half carved out of the rock. Killigrew saw light at the far end, but before they reached it Nekrasoff stopped abruptly by a recessed doorway and produced a bunch of keys, unlocking the stout, iron-bound door hidden in the shadows. He stepped through, and Ryzhago thrust Killigrew after him, down a set of stone steps carved out of the rock until they came to a small subterranean chamber at the bottom. A candle guttering in a lanthorn cast dim illumination over the iron door in the far wall. Nekrasoff banged on it with his fist. A grille opened in the door and a pair of piggy eyes peered out at them.

'Another prisoner for you,' Nekrasoff told him.

The eyes took in Killigrew and Ryzhago before the grille was slammed shut, and then the door was opened and Ryzhago thrust the prisoner through into an antechamber lit by two oil-lamps hanging from the ceiling. There were two soldiers in there, both husky men, the fellow who had opened the outer door for them and another, who was already in the process of unlocking one of the iron doors at the far end of the room.

A face appeared at the grille in another iron door further along. 'You there!' it called in French – the man's native tongue, if Killigrew was any judge. 'Our *enseigne de vaisseau* is an officer of the French navy, and as such should not be billeted with common *matelots . . .*'

The other gaoler smacked a truncheon against the bars of the grille, making the Frenchman jump back. 'Your precious *enseigne* will be billeted in conditions fitting his rank when he gives his parole not to try to escape, and not before!'

Killigrew was thrust through into a dank, unlit chamber that stank of urine. In the light that filtered through from the antechamber, he could just make out Stålberg and Lindström, hanging spread-eagled from the walls in chains, their feet not quite touching the straw-strewn floor. Nekrasoff kept Killigrew covered with a revolver from a safe distance while Ryzhago removed his manacles and then pinned him, spread-eagled, against the wall, while one of the guards locked Killigrew into the fetters. Once he was secured, the guard went out again, and chains clanked in the stout wall behind him as he was hauled off his feet. He gasped at the agony of the shackles on his already-chafed wrists, and the strain on his shoulders.

'I want you to exercise extreme caution with this one,' Nekrasoff told the guards. 'He may not look much, but he's tough and extremely resourceful. Don't listen to anything he tells you, and if you must let him down – which I strongly advise against – make sure you keep this door locked and two muskets levelled at him the whole time until he's chained up again – and be sure the men with the muskets keep their distance!'

'We know how to look after prisoners,' one of the gaolers muttered truculently.

'Perhaps, but you've never had a prisoner like this one before. Blink and he'll kill you. And if you let him escape, you'd best pray he kills you in the process, because he'll offer you a swifter, kinder death than I will if I come back in a few hours to discover he's gone.' Nekrasoff

349

turned to Killigrew. 'If it were up to me, I'd put a bullet in your skull myself and be done with it – I'd rather have you dead than risk your escaping while I try to think up a more imaginative death for you – but unfortunately Admiral Matyushkin demands that we observe the proper formalities while we're guests in his naval base. You are to be shot at dawn.'

'I don't suppose there's any point demanding to see the British consul?'

Nekrasoff smiled. 'Farewell, Mr Killigrew. The next time we meet, it will only be so I can watch you being put out of my misery.' He marched out with Ryzhago, and the guards slammed and locked the door behind them, plunging the room into darkness.

Killigrew's eyes slowly became accustomed to what little light came through the grille in the door, and he saw that both Stålberg and Lindström had been subjected to the Ryzhago treatment, if their dishevelled clothes and battered faces were any indication.

'Have you become a Hindoo, Herre Killigrew?' asked Stålberg.

'Eh?'

'You would appear to have a caste mark in the middle of your forehead.'

'Oh! Would you believe me if I told you that's where I shot myself?'

'I see,' Stålberg said dubiously. 'Any particular reason?'

'It seemed like a good idea at the time.'

'You did not do a very good job of it, did you?' remarked Lindström. 'I mean, you're still walking.'

Killigrew grinned through the pain of his wrists and shoulders. 'Thick skull. I don't suppose either of you gentlemen know a way out of here?' he asked, trying to sound breezy.

'We were rather counting on *you* to rescue *us*,' said Stålberg. 'Somehow I had a feeling that sooner or later you'd be joining us, one way or another. Is the Allied fleet still anchored south of Helsingfors?'

Killigrew nodded.

'So it's a toss-up whether the Russians execute us before the bombardment begins or *vice versa*,' said Lindström. 'How long, do you think?'

'The last time I saw the fleet, it looked as though they were making their final dispositions.'

'Then they could launch their bombardment any time now?'

The commander shook his head. 'They won't attack until dawn.'

'Why not until then?'

'We British always attack at dawn. It's sort of a tradition with us.'

'So, we have only a few hours to get out of here.'

Killigrew nodded, and looked about. 'This time last year, one of the men under my command managed to escape from a Third Section gaol using only a pair of woolly socks and a button.'

'A pair of woolly socks and a button?' echoed Stålberg. 'How in the world did he manage that?'

'Good question. I kept meaning to ask him, but unfortunately I never got round to it.'

After seeing Killigrew safely locked up in the dungeons below Fort Gustaf, Nekrasoff returned to the citadel on Vargon, where the ball was still going strong into the small hours of the morning. He had been to enough of these functions to know the dancing would continue until long after the sun had risen.

But he was in no mood to enjoy himself, and the taste of champagne, which should have been celebratory, turned flat and sour in his mouth. Killigrew locked up and scheduled for execution at dawn . . . it was too good to be true. The Englishman was a resourceful devil, and part of Nekrasoff wanted to go back to Fort Gustaf to make sure personally he did not escape this time. He tried to tell himself he was fretting about nothing, but he could not shake off a niggling feeling there was something he was forgetting, some X-factor he had not taken into account.

'Sir?'

He turned to see Ryzhago approaching through the throng. 'What is it?'

'We've found Lieutenant Kizheh, sir.'

'Ah, good. About time, too. Where is he?'

'He's dead, sir. They found his body stuffed in the bow locker of the ferry with that of a *matros*.'

'Dead?'

'Murdered, sir.'

Nekrasoff grimaced. 'I hardly thought he'd suddenly fallen victim to typhoid. How?'

'I'm no surgeon, sir. But from the bruises on his neck I'd say he was strangled.'

The colonel thought about it, and nodded. 'Well, it would tie in with what we'd already assumed. Killigrew gained access to Sveaborg by

351

posing as one of the guests coming to this ball. Didn't I always say this was going to be a security nightmare?'

'That you did, sir. There's something else you ought to know: the dead *matros* found with him was killed differently. Stabbed in the throat.'

Nekrasoff shrugged. 'So he stabbed one and strangled the other. Our Commander Killigrew is a versatile man.'

'Yes, sir. It's just that I can't help thinking that his accomplice who broke into Novaya Gollandia with him last Thursday used throwing knives to kill several of the guards.'

Nekrasoff felt as though he'd been stabbed in the stomach. He stared at Ryzhago in horror as the implications of his words sank in. 'He's not alone! Come on!'

The two of them almost had to fight their way through the crowd of drunken guests to get to the gateway. Fortunately, Ryzhago was the sort of man people tended to step aside for, drunk or sober.

Sergeant Obukoff was still on duty in plain clothes at the gateway, even though the guests had stopped arriving long ago. 'Sergeant, a man arrived here earlier tonight,' Nekrasoff told him. 'About five foot eleven, lean build, saturnine complexion, black hair, brown eyes, aged about thirty . . .'

Obukoff thought for a moment. He had a phenomenal memory for names and faces, which was exactly why Nekrasoff employed him for jobs like this. 'Sounds like Herre Ambrosius Ögren to me, sir.'

'Ögren! *Chert!* I don't believe it!'

'What's wrong, sir?' asked Ryzhago.

'I spoke to her! Damn it, I even danced with her!'

'Who, sir?'

'His accomplice: Fru Ottilia Ögren . . . if that's her real name, which I very much doubt. She's here, damn it! Brunette, brown eyes, good figure, late twenties or early thirties. I left her with Admiral Prince Zhirinovsky earlier . . .' Nekrasoff glanced back into the compound. 'Damn it, where's he got to?'

'They left the compound together, sir,' said Obukoff. 'I think he was taking her to his billet.'

'What do you mean, you think he was taking her to his billet? Did you hear him say so?'

'No, sir.'

'Then what makes you think they were going to his billet?'

'Well, he had an arm around her shoulders and . . . not to put too fine

352

a point on it . . . a bulge in his crotch like the Kamchatka Peninsula.'

'Thank you, Obukoff, I think we get the picture,' snapped Nekrasoff. 'When was this?'

'About thirty minutes ago, sir.'

'Thirty minutes! *Chert!* We must find her, damn it! I'll check his billet. Obukoff, round up all the men you can find – *matrosy*, soldiers, I don't care whose toes you have to tread on but get as many men as you can – and order them to search every inch of this base. Vargon, East, West and Little Svarto, Gustafvard – I want no stone left unturned, do you understand me? And I want guards on every bridge. Make sure they have descriptions of both the woman and Killigrew. When you've done that, I want you to go to Fort Gustaf and join the gaolers watching Killigrew's cell. You stay there and make sure he doesn't leave until I come for him, do you understand me? I don't care if the Grand Duke himself arrives ordering his release, you let no one past until I get there.'

'Yes, sir!' Obukoff hurried off.

Nekrasoff turned to Ryzhago. 'Come on!'

Aurélie made her way upstairs and found the bedroom, then closed the door again and tiptoed back across the landing in time to hear Zhirinovsky dismiss his servants. She re-entered the bedroom, closing the door softly behind her, and took up position pretending to re-arrange her hair in front of the cheval-glass.

The door opened and Zhirinovsky entered with a *schtoff* of vodka in one hand and two tumblers in the other. 'I thought perhaps a drink would help calm your nerves,' he explained.

'Oh, Samya! You are so thoughtful. However can I repay you?'

'I'm sure I can think of something.' He put the bottle and the glasses down on the dresser. When he turned back to face her, they stood barely inches apart. He could restrain himself no longer. He seized her in his arms and mashed his lips against hers, trying to force his tongue between her teeth.

Smiling, she pushed him gently away. 'Not so fast, darling!'

'I cannot help myself, Ottilia! I must have you now!'

'But do you not think that some pleasures are best lingered over?' she teased him archly.

He whimpered. 'Oh God, yes!' he moaned. He looked ready to burst.

She moved closer to him so she could whisper in his ear. 'Close your eyes. I have a little surprise for you.'

He closed his eyes. She moved behind him and picked up the stool from in front of the dresser.

'Can I open my eyes yet?' he pleaded.

'Not just yet,' she told him, hefting the stool over her head. She smashed it against the base of his skull.

He crumpled to the floor. 'I'll bet that surprised you, you gross pig!' she spat at his unconscious body.

She dragged him on to the bed and stripped his clothes off, tying his wrists and ankles to the bedstead. There was nothing like being naked and tied up to leave a man feeling vulnerable. Before she could revive him to start interrogating him as to the whereabouts of Stålberg and Lindström, however, she heard hammering at the front door downstairs.

She hitched up her skirts to pull the turn-over pistol from her garter and stepped out on to the landing in time to see the door burst open. Ryzhago stumbled through into the hallway below. She knew all about Ryzhago, of course: her superiors in Paris had a file on him a good two inches thick. She racked her brains, trying to remember something in that file that she could use against his superior strength, but the only thing she could remember from when she had studied it was a heartfelt desire never to meet him in person.

She raised the pistol and fired, but he threw himself on the floor, out of her line of sight. Nekrasoff followed him into the hallway, blazing up the stairs with his own revolver. A bullet smashed through the banister close to where she stood, and she cried out as splinters flew into her face, almost blinding her. She recovered in time to fumble with the turn-over pistol, rotating the second barrel into position. She squeezed off the second shot as Nekrasoff dashed for the cover of a doorway, and then Ryzhago had picked himself up and was charging up the stairs towards her.

She pulled the stiletto from its ankle-sheath, but there was no time to reverse her grip to throw it: she used it like a dagger, plunging it into Ryzhago's upper right arm. He gave a sob of pleasure, smiled beatific-ally at her, and then backhanded her across the face, knocking her down. When she looked up, Nekrasoff was standing over her, his revolver levelled at her. Ryzhago plucked the stiletto from his arm, buried it up to the hilt in the banister, and grabbed Aurélie by the hand, hauling her to her feet. She struggled in vain in his grip.

'Take her to the black house,' Nekrasoff told her. 'We'll let her stew for a while before I interrogate her.'

'Let go of me! Filthy pig!' she spat, trying to kick him.

Nekrasoff raised a hand to caress her cheek, and she jerked her head away with loathing.

He smiled. 'Still some fight in you, eh? We'll see if you're so feisty after my men have taken turns at you.'

# XXIII

# Countdown

---

The first traces of dawn were visible in the sky over Sveaborg when the ships of the fleet tolled seven bells. The boatswains' mates on each ship piped 'Wakey, wakey' and the seamen below decks rolled out of their hammocks, grumbling and swearing amongst themselves at the early start to the day. They lashed up their hammocks into tight rolls and carried them up on deck, where they were put in the netting on the bulwarks for added protection against shot and shell.

'Clear for action,' Captain Crichton told Commander Tremaine while the hands relieved themselves at the head.

'Aye, aye, sir.'

'Not that we'll see any fighting today,' Crichton added wistfully. 'Or rather, we'll see plenty of fighting – we just won't get to take part in it. Leave that to Adare and his lads in the *Swiper*; and the other crews of the gunboats and mortar vessels. Youth will have its day, eh, Mr Tremaine?'

'Yes, sir.'

'Still, we must be ready for any eventuality.'

'Do you think there's a chance the Russian ships will counter-attack, sir?'

'I doubt it, but who knows what tricks the Russkis have up their sleeves? Wait until our people have eaten breakfast, and then give the order to beat to quarters. Sir Richard's orders are for us to pray for a successful days' work at six, so we'll have breakfast an hour earlier. That should give the men plenty of time to get something to eat before divine service. Better have the holders start bringing up the day's victuals at once.'

'Aye, aye, sir.'

As Tremaine turned away, the first lieutenant emerged from the after hatch and saluted Crichton. 'Good morning, sir.'

'Good morning, Masterson. Looks like it's going to be a beautiful day, doesn't it?'

The lieutenant smiled. 'I suspect that depends upon your point of view, sir. I don't think the Russians will remember it as such.'

'That remains to be seen, Mr Masterson.'

A few minutes after sunrise, Rear Admiral Dundas left the *Duke of Wellington* with Commodore Pelham and hoisted his flag in the *Merlin*, in which steamer they made a tour of inspection along the whole line of mortar vessels. The *Duke* herself, meanwhile, hauled a few hundred yards nearer the line, so there would be less chance of any signals being misread; a danger that would become too real once the smoke of battle started to drift across the anchorage.

At six o'clock, the crews of the fleet – on ships of the line, mortar vessels and gunboats alike – raised their voices in song to the tunes of two dozen different hymns, accompanied by fiddles and harmoniums where players for these were available, wafting across to where they were heard in Helsingfors.

On board HMS *Swiper*, Lieutenant Adare chose 'Bound for the Promised Land' for the morning's hymn. Although not particularly religious for the most part, the men liked nothing better than a good hearty singsong, and they sang with gusto – always an indication that morale was high – while Molineaux played the chords on his guitar. He liked the tune, although he was not sure he cared for the implications of the words. He knew they were not planning a landing today, so Russia could not be the promised land, which only left one logical alternative . . . not that the prospect of an afterlife bothered him, as he did not believe in it; but he knew the way there, and did not care for that prospect one little bit.

HMS *Swiper* was a hundred feet from stem to stern, with a slim funnel rising between her two rakish masts. There were only sixteen inches of freeboard between the floatation line and the bottom of the entry port, and her flat keel gave her a draught of a mere six and a half feet, so there was little danger of her running aground in the shoals of the Baltic. Although she was designed to be small and manoeuvrable, the three sixty-eight-pounders on her upper deck meant

357

she packed a devil of a punch, and with a top speed under steam of seven and a half knots, she could get out of trouble just as fast as she got into it.

When they had finished singing, Adare read from *The Articles of War* in place of a lesson from the Bible, and finished off with the Lord's Prayer: the only prayer he knew, so far as Molineaux could tell. 'And for what the Russians are about to receive, may the Lord make them truly thankful!' he concluded with a grin, prompting huzzas from the crew. 'All right, lads,' he said once they had quietened down. 'Port watch make your way down to the mess to get some breakfast, starboard watch remain on deck to clear for action. Mr McGurk, be so good as to ask Mr Varrow to start getting steam up.'

'Hughes! Iles! Start spreading some sand on this deck!' ordered Molineaux.

'Sand?' echoed Hughes, a stocky, dark-haired Welshman with a pock-marked face. 'What's that for?'

'So we don't slip in the blood,' Iles told him.

'What blood?'

'Yours, if you don't stop asking stupid questions and do as I tell you!' Molineaux snarled at the Welshman. 'Look lively, there!' He turned to where Endicott stood over the fore hatch, watching the shells being brought up.

'All right, that's enough!' Endicott told his crew. 'We'll bring up the others as and when required.' He turned to Molineaux. 'God knows, it'd only take one going off on board this little ship to send her to the bottom!' A devout Catholic, he crossed himself piously. 'It's a good thing God's on our side, eh? I've a feeling we're going to need all the help we can get!'

'Yur,' Molineaux agreed sceptically. His mother had raised him and his brothers to be devout Baptists, except that the crowd he had grown up with at the Rat's Castle had not believed in God, and nothing he had seen from that day to this had convinced him that his mother was right and they were wrong. 'Of course, it'd be a lot more reassuring if I didn't know that just across the way the Russians are praying as fervently to the same God that *they'll* win. Let's hope your man upstairs don't granny Russian, eh?'

'You're a godless wretch, Wes, you know that? When you die you're going straight to hell.'

'Reckon I am, at that,' Molineaux agreed cheerfully. For him, this was not a crusade; nor was it about the Danubian Principalities, or the Eastern Question. It was about earning two pounds, fourteen shillings and thruppence a month, and trying not to get killed in the process.

He glanced at Endicott. 'You're in the larboard watch; aren't you going down to breakfast?'

The Liverpudlian shook his head. 'Not hungry,' he muttered.

'Not frightened, are you?'

Endicott drew himself up to his full height. 'Only of getting summat wrong, like. This'll be the first time I've been a gunner's mate in action; and I suppose I'm acting gunner on this tub. I don't want to make a muck-up first time out. Don't worry,' he added, seeing the concerned look in Molineaux's eyes. 'I'll be all right once the shooting starts. It's the waiting that bothers me. I just wish we could get on with it, you know?'

'Me too.' Molineaux checked his pocket watch. 'Only forty-five minutes to go now.'

Endicott cast an eye in the direction of the mortar boats. They should all have been in position over an hour ago, but even now some of them were still warping in. 'We'll never be ready on time.'

'Stop worrying,' Molineaux told him. 'The Ivans aren't going anywhere.'

From the outside, the only sinister thing about the black house was that it was built of granite rather than the red bricks that predominated throughout East Svarto, and was unpainted. Ryzhago had taken Aurélie down to a basement room with bare, whitewashed walls, tied her up in a chair and left her, locking the door behind him. That had been hours ago. She wondered what time it was now. After six o'clock, she guessed: more than sixty hours since the Allied fleet had dropped anchor off Helsingfors. She did not need to be a naval officer like Killigrew to know the crews of the ships had had more than enough time to prepare their bombardment.

If she had to die, she would prefer to be blown apart by the shells of her own Allies than taken back to St Petersburg for a show-trial and a firing squad. But she would have preferred not to die at all. While her work for military intelligence had often put her in a position where death was a very real possibility, she always managed to convince herself that it was something that only ever happened to other people. But she knew she had been lucky in that respect, and sooner or later her luck was bound to run out.

Was today that day? She felt sick at heart: she was not ready to die. She enjoyed life too much. Her patriotism always came second place to the pleasure she took in her work, outsmarting statesmen and soldiers who looked down at her, regarding her as fit only for bedroom activities, little thinking that a battle might be lost and won by their boasting. Looking back on her life, it was odd to think that the little girl from the back streets of Marseilles had grown up to make fools of some of the leading statesmen of Europe.

*Snap out of it*, she told herself. *Reviewing your life as if it was over. You're not dead yet . . .*

The door opened and three very large, very ugly men filed inside, the last one locking the door behind him and pocketing the key. 'Who's first?' asked one.

'Me,' said another, advancing on Aurélie.

Her superior in Paris had warned her about the various methods their enemies might use to break down her resistance under interrogation, and she had already suffered this one once before at the hands of the Austrian secret police. She was damned if she was going to undergo that ordeal a second time.

'Not so fast, boys,' she told them, trying to make her voice sound husky and seductive, although to her own ears it sounded as hoarse and harsh as the croaking of an asthmatic crow. 'I can take all three of you on at once.'

'That is not humanly possible!' muttered one of them. 'Is it?'

'Of course it is,' she told them. 'Just use your imaginations.'

They used their imaginations. Sweat broke out on their faces, although whether at the prospect of a gang-bang, or simply from the effort of thinking, she could not tell.

She flapped her hands at them. 'Just untie my wrists, and I'll show you how.'

'Don't do it, Sergei,' said one. 'It is a trick.'

'Oh yes? And what is she going to do against three of us? You can stand watch while Anatoly and I enjoy ourselves, if you're that worried. I reckon she can please two of us twice as well as three!'

Only a complete fool would have freed her arms. Fortunately, the sight of an attractive, helpless woman was enough to turn ninety-nine percent of men into complete fools. One of them unbuckled her wrist restraints. 'You're going to regret your offer, *golubushka*. I'll make you scream. Now, let's see what you've got under those petticoats of yours—'

360

'Let me show you.' She stood up, rubbing her chafed wrists and bent over, hitching up her skirts to reveal her legs, all the way up to her knees. Sergei and his friends were still gawping at her shapely calves when she flicked one of her feet into his crotch. He dropped to his knees with a hoarse scream, and she slammed the heel of a half-boot into his nose. Anatoly swung a fist at her, but she ducked below it, driving a small but well-aimed fist into his solar plexus. He doubled up with a gasp, and she lifted a knee into his face, throwing him down across Sergei's unconscious body.

The third man lumbered towards her, trying to grab her. She easily dodged aside and he stumbled on, allowing her to grab a fistful of his hair as he staggered past. She smashed his head against the wall and he sank down to lie on top of his two companions.

She stood there, breathing hard with her hands upon her knees. 'Told you I could take all three of you on at once,' she panted.

The reaction came at once. She recognised the symptoms – trembling, dizziness – and fought them off. Taking off their belts and socks, she tied and gagged the three men before retrieving the key from Anatoly's pocket, along with his revolver.

She unlocked the door with her left hand and threw it open, stepping to one side as she did so in case a fusillade of shots came down the stairs. But from above, there was nothing but silence.

With a supreme effort she picked up the unconscious Sergei – *nom d'un chien*, but he was heavy! – and propped him up against the wall beside the door, letting him fall across the threshold. No bullets thudded into him. Upstairs, all was silent. She peered cautiously around the door, keeping her head low, and saw no one. Gaining confidence, she staggered upstairs with the revolver in her hand. The house was as silent as the grave of a Trappist monk. The only sounds she could hear were the distant shouts of NCOs barking orders to their men somewhere outside. There was no sign of Nekrasoff or Ryzhago.

She found a washstand and a jug of water. The water was cold, but that was for the best: she splashed it on her face to revive herself. Three black leather greatcoats and wideawakes hung from a row of pegs in the cubby-hole beside the door. She put on a greatcoat and gathered up her hair, cramming it into the crown of one of the wideawakes.

She looked at herself in the mirror: she still looked like a woman in a man's clothing. She did not have the time or the facilities to do anything about that: all she could do was hope that she would pass muster if seen from a distance. Pulling the brim of the wideawake down, she tucked the revolver in a pocket of the greatcoat and went outside.

The sun was already well over the horizon, rising into a bright blue sky. What time was it? It could not be long until the fleet began its bombardment; but in truth she had no idea when that would be, if ever. All she could do was assume she still had time; otherwise, she might as well lie down now and wait to die.

Walking on shaky legs, she made her way through the houses of East Svarto. Occasionally she passed ensigns and *michmanis* running to and fro with messages, but they did not give her a second glance. *All your life you've wanted to prove you were just as tough and able as any man,* she reminded herself. *Now's your chance: you can either give up and lie down to die, or you can prove it.*

She forced herself to go on.

There were two soldiers on guard on the bridge across Artillery Bay. She thought about turning back, looking for some other way to Gustafvard – which meant swimming the channel – but it was too late: they had already seen her. Nothing for it but to brazen it out. Well, she was good at that.

She almost made it too: they were not paying much attention, and she got five paces past them before one of them called out after her.

'Stop!'

She froze. She could hear their booted feet on the wooden boards of the bridge as they came after her.

'Turn around,' ordered one. She turned and saw he had unslung his musket. '*Chert!*' he exclaimed. 'It's a woman!'

She grabbed the musket by the barrel, jerked it out of his hands, and slammed the stock back into his jaw. The other was still trying to unsling his own musket when she chopped him across the edge of the neck with the stock, bringing him down.

She tipped the two bodies over the rail into the channel, and just in time: a gaggle of guests from the ball appeared from the direction of the citadel on Vargon. She realised the music had stopped playing: the ball was finally over, the last of the guests drifting home-wards. They were too drunk and full of chatter to notice her. Slipping down the side of the citadel, she crossed one of the bridges on to Gustafvard.

She felt her second wind coming as she crossed the island to the fort at the south-east corner. Entering the maze of ravelins and bastions, she looked in vain for the entrance until she all but bumped into a lieutenant of artillery.

'What are you doing here?' he demanded. 'There are no civilians allowed on Gustafvard . . . wait, you're a woman!'

She pulled the revolver from her pocket and jammed the muzzle against his side. 'And you're going to take me to where they're holding the prisoners. Any tricks and you're the first to die.'

The colour drained from his face. He led her deeper into the maze, finally taking her into the tunnel under the fort where they descended the steps to dungeons.

'Knock on the door,' she told him at the bottom.

The grille slid open a moment after his knock. Standing behind him, she lowered her head so her face was hidden behind the brim of the wideawake. Two beady eyes peered out at the lieutenant, and a moment later the grille was slammed shut and a key turned in the lock.

Aurélie slammed the revolver's butt against the back of the lieutenant's head. As he crumpled to the floor, she stepped over him and threw her shoulder against the opening door. It slammed into the man on the other side, bowling him over. Aurélie dived through the gap, rolling on the straw-strewn flagstones beyond to rise on one knee. Searching the dungeon, she spotted the second gaoler and shot him twice in the chest. The man who had opened the door was starting to recover; she put her last bullet through his forehead.

The anxious face of a young man appeared at the grille in one of the cell doors. He was dark-haired, with a goatee beard and moustache in the Imperial style. 'What's going on out here?' he demanded in good French.

'It's called a rescue,' she grunted, taking a large ring of keys from the belt of one of the gaolers and unlocking his cell door. There were a dozen men in the cell behind him, big, burly fellows in the uniforms of *matelots* of *la Royale*, grubby from their incarceration.

The young man who had first addressed her wore an officer's uniform. '*Mon Dieu!*' he gasped. 'You're—'

'A woman, yes, I know. Please, let's not get into that now.'

'But . . . who *are* you?'

'Lieutenant Aurélie Plessier of Military Intelligence.'

He clicked his heels and bowed low to kiss her hand. '*Enseigne de Vaisseau* Paul Verne at your service, Mam'selle. They sent a woman to get us out?'

'Not exactly. Would you mind if we discussed it on the way? The fleet's about to start bombarding this place any moment now.' She peered past him at the astonished *matelots* who were rising to their feet to follow him out of the cell. 'Is Commander Killigrew here?'

'Commander who?' asked one of them.

She checked the other cells, until she found the one with Stålberg and Lindström in it. 'Mam'selle Plessier!' gasped the *friherre*. 'What are you doing here?'

'Answering a lot of foolish questions!' she snapped back, trying each of the keys on the ring until she found one that fitted the locks on their shackles. 'Have you seen Killigrew?'

Stålberg's face became grim. 'I am desolated, mam'selle . . .'

Her blood ran cold as she anticipated what he was going to say next.

'Nekrasoff came for him with that big brute he keeps in tow. They've already taken him.'

'How long ago?'

'A good quarter of an hour.' He clasped her by the shoulder. 'I am sorry, mam'selle, but they were taking him to a firing squad. By now he is dead already.'

An expectant hush reigned over the Allied fleet. On every ship and boat, from the *Duke of Wellington* down to the smallest dinghy, the petty officers had piped for silence. Gentle waves lapped at wooden hulls. Timbers creaked and hawsers groaned. Steam hissed from the engines of the gunboats like horses champing at the bit as they awaited for the signal to begin their manoeuvres, smoke rising into the clear blue sky from their slender funnels. Overhead, a seagull rose suddenly from a nearby skerry, mewing harshly. Startled, a seaman sitting in a cutter nearby swore vilely.

'Keep silence, there!' hissed the coxswain.

'Don't tell me!' muttered the seaman. 'Tell the bloody birds!'

On the gunboats and mortar vessels, all eyes were on Her Majesty's mortar vessel *Pickle*. The gun crew on the *Pickle* were in their positions around the squat, ugly mortar that dominated the upper deck, but their eyes were fixed on the screw frigate HMS *Euryalus*, moored abaft the line of mortar vessels with the other support ships. And on the *Euryalus*, all eyes were on the *Duke of Wellington*, moored halfway between the supply vessels and the fleet's ships of the line with Rear Admiral Dundas' flag back at the masthead.

'What the devil are they waiting for?' hissed the lieutenant standing on the *Pickle*'s quarterdeck next to Captain John Weymiss of the Royal Marine Artillery.

'Patience, Lieutenant, patience,' Weymiss replied. Only his eyes were fixed on the batteries of Sveaborg. 'All good things come to he who waits.'

'The *Duke*'s signalling *Euryalus*, sir,' reported one of the midshipmen.

'What's she saying?' Weymiss asked without taking his eyes off Sveaborg.

The lieutenant raised his telescope to one eye. ' "Is all ready?" Damn it, all's ready! It's been ready for fifteen minutes! I thought this bombardment was supposed to commence at seven? It's nearly half-past now!'

'There goes *Euryalus*'s reply,' said the midshipman.

' "Nearly; one boat shifting berth",' read the lieutenant. 'We're waiting on one boat?' he almost exploded.

'*Festina lente*, Lieutenant,' Weymiss remarked coolly. 'Can't go rushing into these things half-cocked.'

'Blindfold?' the lieutenant commanding the firing squad asked.

'For your men?' asked Killigrew. 'Capital notion!'

'For you, I meant.'

'He knows what you meant,' snarled Nekrasoff. 'Get on with it!'

Killigrew stood on the parade ground on East Svarto, in front of a whitewashed wall pock-marked enough to suggest that executions were not all that uncommon in Sveaborg. Half a dozen men of a regiment of line infantry were ranged before him a few yards away, standing rigidly to attention. They were in their full-dress uniforms: at least he was going to be executed with style, he noted wryly. He squinted up at the sky, a clear pale blue with only the occasional tuft of cloud. It was a glorious day to die.

He guessed it was past seven o'clock. He wondered what time the bombardment was due to start. Probably not in time to kill him before the firing squad did. Probably just as well: he was in no position to appreciate the thought of being killed by his own side, and besides, he preferred the quick, clean death of a bullet through the heart to the possibility of being horribly maimed by a shell. He was not afraid to die, did not feel he had not had a fair crack of the whip. He had lived life to the full and faced death so many times in the past, he felt as though he had been living on borrowed time for years now. His only regret was that he would not now get the chance to choke the life out of Nekrasoff with his own hands; although it was some consolation to know that the colonel's hours were numbered, if only Dundas and Seymour would get a move on and start the bombardment.

'Squad!' barked the lieutenant. 'Present . . . *arms*!'

Killigrew cleared his throat. 'You know, in my country, it's traditional to grant the condemned man a last request.'

'Yes, well, you're not in your country now, are you?' snapped Nekrasoff. 'I suppose you want to sing "Ten Thousand Green Bottles", or have the firing squad stand a little further back – say, five miles away – or some other witticism to show off how brave you are in the face of death.'

'I was only going to ask for a last cheroot.'

'With a poisoned dart in it to shoot the lieutenant here, I suppose? No, Mr Killigrew. It ends here and it ends now. No final tricks, no last-minute reprieves—'

The lieutenant cleared his throat. 'There's someone coming, sir.'

Nekrasoff turned to see a *michmani* hurrying across the parade ground to where they stood.

'I expect that's my last-minute reprieve,' said Killigrew.

'Somehow I doubt it,' said Nekrasoff. 'Carry out your duty, Lieutenant Rudenko.'

'Don't you think we should wait, sir? I mean, if it is a last-minute reprieve from the Grand Duke . . .'

'All the more reason to shoot the prisoner now, Lieutenant! I've tracked him for too long to let him escape me now. You have no idea how many times I've had this devil in my grasp, only for him to slip through my fingers! Well, not today. Today – this minute – he dies. Do you understand me?'

'Yes, sir.' Rudenko glanced dubiously at the *michmani*, who had completed his crossing of the parade ground during Nekrasoff's peroration and now stood behind the colonel, saluting.

'Colonel Nekrasoff?'

Nekrasoff closed his eyes as if in pain. 'Yes?' he hissed without turning to face the *michmani*.

'Rear Admiral Matyushkin wishes to see you immediately, sir.'

'All right. I'll be there in five minutes.'

'He did stress "immediately", sir.'

Nekrasoff rounded on the young man. 'If the Tsar himself wanted to see me five minutes ago, it would not drag me away from seeing this man finally get his just deserts!' he snarled, pointing at Killigrew.

The *michmani* quailed.

'Perhaps you ought to go, sir,' said Rudenko. 'With all due respect, we don't need your supervision to execute the prisoner.'

'Oh, what a brilliant notion, Lieutenant! In my hour of triumph, I'm going to walk away without pausing to witness Killigrew's execution! I'm just going to assume you carried out your orders without a hitch! No! I'm going to stand here and watch and see him die with my own eyes, if it's all the same with you.'

'We could wait until you get back—'

'No! No, damn it! I know what'll happen if I go and see what Matyushkin wants: when I get back I'll find you and your men all dead or unconscious and Killigrew will have mysteriously vanished! I think not! Shoot him now, damn it! If it hadn't been for all these damned interruptions, he'd be dead by now and I could be on my way to the rear admiral's office to report another job well done.'

'But if what the rear admiral wishes to discuss concerns the prisoner? Would it not be best to establish exactly what—'

'No! *No!* You're not *listening* to me, Lieutenant! Killigrew is *there*, the firing squad is *there*, and I'm staying right *here* until I've seen him die with my own eyes, do you understand?' Nekrasoff's voice had risen to a screaming pitch, but he made a visible effort to control himself. 'Carry out your orders, Lieutenant. I will take full responsibility.'

'As you command, sir.' Rudenko saluted with his sabre. 'Squad! Present . . . *arms*!'

'Any last words, Commander?' demanded Nekrasoff.

Killigrew shook his head, smiling faintly. 'You won't live long enough to write them down for posterity, anyhow.'

'Ready . . .' said Rudenko. 'Aim . . .'

'Wait!'

To Killigrew's astonishment, it was Nekrasoff who had interrupted. The colonel ran in front of the firing squad, and unbuttoned the front of the tunic Killigrew wore, groping inside his pockets.

'You know, it's customary to wait for a man to be dead before you rob his corpse,' Killigrew remarked mildly.

'Just making sure you haven't got a Bible in your breast pocket, or a cheroot case, or anything else that might stop half a dozen bullets.'

Nekrasoff moved out of the way of the firing squad. 'As you were, Lieutenant.'

Rudenko drew his sabre. 'Ready . . .'

The six soldiers raised the stocks of their muskets to their shoulders. 'Aim . . .'

They squinted down the sights on their muzzles at Killigrew's breast.

Raising his sabre, Rudenko took a deep breath . . .

# XXIV

# Hell on Earth

---

'The *Duke of Wellington* is signalling, sir,' reported the lieutenant on the deck of HMS *Pickle*. ' "Mortar vessel open fire with shell." And it's about time too, I should say!'

'You heard the man, Guns,' said Captain Weymiss. 'In your own time.'

The gunner proffered the lanyard he was holding to Weymiss. 'Begging your pardon, sir, but I thought you might like the honour of being the one to fire the first shot.'

'No, no. I wouldn't want to rob you of your duty. Carry on, Jones.'

'Aye, aye, sir.' Jones turned back to face the mortar and, beyond the prow, the batteries of Sveaborg in the distance. Standing with his feet spread, his weight distributed evenly, he grasped the lanyard and looked at Weymiss.

'Fire!'

Jones hauled the lanyard down with a jerk, bringing his left hand down smartly on his right. The hammer fell on the vent of the mortar, striking sparks from the friction tube. The powder flared in the vent, and a moment later the very air around the men on deck seemed to split asunder as the mortar roared, belching smoke and flame. The whole vessel shuddered under the impact of the recoil as the shell arced high into the sky above the fleet, trailing smoke from its sputtering fuse.

And then the other twenty-five mortar vessels in the fleet fired their shells as one.

All hell did not break loose. But the denizens of the infernal regions could only look on in envious awe at what was about to hit Sveaborg.

369

'Did you hear something?' asked Rudenko.

The soldiers lined up facing Killigrew still had their fingers on their triggers, waiting for the order to fire. Before any of them could reply, they heard a sound like a not-so-distant peal of thunder: one of those long, rumbling crashes that seemed to last for ever. The sound echoed off the walls and bastions of the islands, and even as that faded a new sound replaced it, a strange sort of whistling noise.

The muzzles of the muskets wavered and fell as the soldiers exchanged bewildered glances. The whistling sound increased in volume by the second.

Nekrasoff realised what it was. 'Shoot him!' he screamed, waving his revolver at Killigrew. 'Shoot him now! Fire, damn you, fire!'

'*Chert*!' Rudenko dropped his sabre and sprinted for the nearest cover, one of the barracks on the far side of the parade ground.

The whistling sound was rising in pitch to become an ear-splitting shriek.

The soldiers threw down their muskets and broke. Realising he still held the revolver and it was loaded and cocked, Nekrasoff aimed at Killigrew. Before he could squeeze the trigger, however, one of the fleeing soldiers had slammed into him, knocking him sprawling to the cobbles, the revolver flying from his hand. He started to pick himself up, and the ground shuddered under the impact of a terrific crash.

Nekrasoff whimpered and folded his arms over his head to protect it from falling debris after the explosion.

Except there was no explosion. He looked up, and saw a large hole had been punched through the cobbles about thirty yards from where he stood.

*A dud?*

He picked himself up, and took a hesitant step towards the hole, drawn towards it as a sailor was lured to his death by the sirens. He took another step . . .

. . . and the world was ripped apart around him.

Earth and cobbles shot up, shredding the air with a roar like a locomotive crashing through the side of a brick warehouse at full speed. A wall of hot air slammed into him, lifting him off his feet and hurling him several feet. A roar filled the air, the noise of twenty-five more shells shrieking earthwards, and then the cobbles thrown up by the first explosion rained down all around him, shattering with cracks like musket shots against the cobbles still in place to hurl shards like razors in all directions. One of them embedded itself in his cheek, but he was too relieved that none of them had landed on his head to care about that. He looked up, gazing to where Killigrew had been standing, waiting for the smoke to clear and the dust to finish sheeting down.

No debris had landed where Killigrew had been standing. The cobbles that had been beneath his feet were intact.

But the commander himself had gone.

More explosions erupted all over Sveaborg. Two shells had overshot the fortress altogether, exploding in the waters of the anchorage behind, while three more had fallen short to send up great fountains of spray before the batteries.

But the remaining twenty had landed on target, hurling fountains of dirt and debris high into the sky over the complex.

Nekrasoff noticed his cap on the cobbles at his feet. He stooped to retrieve it, brushing dust from the back of it with a kid-gloved hand, before placing it on his head with fastidious precision.

He took a deep breath . . .

. . . and whipped the cap off his head, hurling it down to the cobbles with all his might before kicking it across the parade ground. Lifting his face towards the heavens, he let out a bellow of primeval rage.

A moment later the guns of the Russian batteries – some nine hundred of them – spoke as one, spitting flame, shot and defiance in response to the Allies' opening salvo.

The bombardment of Sveaborg had begun.

Explosions erupted all over Sveaborg as Killigrew dashed between the arsenal and the barrack block behind it. His hands were still tied behind his back, but he was very much alive and determined to stay that way. He might have been living on borrowed time for years, but now he had been granted another reprieve he saw no reason to waste it. A grin crept across his face as it occurred to him that Nekrasoff had just saved his life: if the colonel had not spent so long arguing with Rudenko, the firing squad would have done their duty before the fleet could fire its first salvo.

Now they had the range, the gunners on the mortar vessels were concentrating on Vargon, throwing up a creeping barrage that steadily worked its way backwards from the west coast. They made no attempt to fire in salvoes, simply hurling shot at the island as fast as they could sponge and reload. The gunboats, meanwhile, engaged the batteries on the west coast, and the far side of the island looked like one wall of smoke and flames shooting high into the sky.

Killigrew emerged from the side of the arsenal and ran smack into a couple of artillerymen dashing towards the magazine on the far side of East Svarto. Before they could unsling their carbines, he kicked one in the crotch, and lifted his knee into the man's face as he doubled up, snapping his head back and throwing him down, unconscious. The other managed to level his carbine, but Killigrew knocked the barrel up with a high kick before smashing a heel into his kneecap. The man went down with a scream, and Killigrew kicked him in the neck, breaking it.

He dropped to the ground, sitting next to the unconscious man with his back to him so he could grope for the bayonet on his belt. Drawing it from its sheath, he wedged the tip in the ground so he could saw his bonds against the edge of the blade. Finally they parted, and he pushed himself to his feet, taking both men's carbines and slinging them over one shoulder. Pulling the last strands of rope from his chafed wrists, he ran to the bridge leading to Vargon.

Another round of shells burst across the island, throwing up fountains of bricks and dust. One shell overshot, landing in Artillery Bay and drenching Killigrew with spray as he ran across the bridge. On the far side he dashed between two buildings and emerged into the square beyond, only to run slap bang into half a dozen infantrymen emerging from the citadel. He unslung one of the carbines, but before he could even level it they ran straight past him. He gaped in astonishment, belatedly realising he was still wearing the dark-green uniform of a captain-lieutenant of the Russian navy; with shells bursting all over Vargon, everyone had too many problems of their own to want to stop him and check his papers.

He dashed past the telegraph tower, heading for the bridge on to Gustafvard, when he heard Nekrasoff screaming behind him. 'There he is! Kill him!'

Shots whistled through the air around Killigrew's head and he threw himself off the path, landing behind a low brick wall. Peering over the wall with the carbine, he saw three dozen infantrymen shooting at him from the side of the citadel, Nekrasoff blazing away with a revolver in his hand. Killigrew quickly ducked back down again as a bullet smacked against the brickwork inches from his head. Crawling on his belly to the end of the wall, he pointed the carbine around the corner and took aim at Nekrasoff. The carbine barked as he pulled the trigger, and he saw an infantryman standing several feet to the right of the colonel clap a hand to his shoulder and fall. Killigrew started to unsling the other carbine, but the infantrymen had already seen him, and he squirmed back out of sight as the bullets plucked at the greensward behind him. Glancing towards Gustafvard, he saw only 120 yards of open space: Nekrasoff's men would cut him down before he covered ten paces.

Another fusillade crackled to his right, and he saw a dozen more figures advancing through the trees of a coppice to the south of the citadel, firing as they came.

Except that they were firing not at Killigrew, but at the Russians. The commander did a double take, and realised the newcomers wore the bonnets and hooped guernseys of French matelots, while their leader wore the uniform of an *enseigne de vaisseau*. For a moment Killigrew thought the French had been crazy enough to attempt a landing, until he saw Aurélie, Stålberg and Lindström following them through the trees. Evidently the prisoners he had been on his way to free had grown impatient and broken out for themselves!

Realising that the French sailors presented more of a threat than a lone British officer, Nekrasoff's men directed their fire at the coppice, giving Killigrew a chance to bob up over the wall and take another shot at them. He saw his bullet pock-mark the masonry of the citadel, a foot above the heads of the Russians, but it was enough to convince them they were enfiladed. They fell back behind the angle of a ravelin long enough for Aurélie, Stålberg, Lindström and the *enseigne* to dash across the open space to where Killigrew squatted, firing revolvers as they went, while the twelve *matelots* gave them covering fire from the coppice.

Ducking down behind the wall, Aurélie flung her arms around Killigrew's neck and smothered his cheeks with kisses. 'Kit! I thought you were dead!'

'So did I! Steady on, old girl! There's a time and place for everything . . . and this most certainly isn't the time and the place for what you've got in mind!'

She pushed him away suddenly, bringing up a revolver in her left fist and squeezing off two shots. For a split second Killigrew thought she was shooting at him, that once again he had been betrayed, except that both shots missed; and even he could not have missed at that range. Hearing a thud on the ground behind him, he twisted to see the corpses of a couple of Russian infantrymen who had been trying to outflank them.

Stålberg, Lindström and the French officer crouched behind the wall; all three of them had a revolver in each hand, and they fired over the wall at Nekrasoff's men. Aurélie produced yet another revolver, and handed it to Killigrew.

'Where'd you get this?' he demanded.

'Armoury in Fort Gustaf,' she told him.

'And the Russians just let you take them?'

The French officer grinned. 'My men had to break a few Russian skulls. M'sieur Killigrew, I presume?'

'That's me. I'm afraid you have the advantage of me, M'sieur . . .?'

'Verne. *Enseigne de Vaisseau* Paul Verne of *La Mouette*, at your service. My men and I were captured raiding . . .'

The rest of his words were drowned out as a shell screamed down to explode in the ground between the low wall and the citadel. A great cloud of dust rose over the surrounding battlements, and as it sheeted down Verne gestured frantically to his men, signalling for them to dash across and join him while the curtain of dust hid them from the Russians' view.

When they reached the wall, Killigrew saw they were not so very different from their British counterparts: squat, brawny men with rough-hewn faces and tattoos on their forearms beneath a thick covering of hairs; not the sort of men you'd want your daughter to marry, but there were none better to have on your side in a fight.

'I'm not sure we're any better off,' Killigrew told Verne. 'We'll still be pinned down when the dust clears . . .'

'Look out!' yelled Stålberg, as the figure of a Russian infantryman appeared through the dust and smoke. Lindström shot him through the head, and when the cloud cleared enough for them to see a dozen more following behind him, Verne and his men picked off half of them while the remainder fled headlong for the safety of the ravelin where Nekrasoff crouched with the rest of his men.

Verne and his men ducked back down behind the wall to reload their muskets and revolvers. 'What's the plan?' Killigrew asked Aurélie. 'You did *have* a plan, didn't you?'

She nodded. 'Get on to East Svarto, steal the ferry and steam across to the fleet.'

Killigrew shook his head. 'The ferry will have high-tailed it for the south harbour as soon as the shooting started.' He frowned. 'But there's a gunboat in one of the sheds on East Svarto. If we can get to it, we might still have a chance.'

'But first we have to *get* to East Svarto,' said Lindström, and jerked a thumb over his shoulder to indicate Nekrasoff and his men. 'And with those pigs between us and the bridge, that's going to be easier said than done.'

'There *must* be another way to the bridge,' said Aurélie.

Killigrew looked about them, and his eyes fell on the two Russian soldiers she had shot earlier. 'There is! Those two got here: there must be a way along the east side of the island.'

'You four go ahead,' said Verne. 'Charrondier, take Ingres and Laval and go with them. The rest of us will stay here and hold them as long as we can.'

*'Oui, oui, mon enseigne.'*

Killigrew, Aurélie, Stålberg and Lindström crawled to the far end of the wall with the three *matelots*. There were about thirty yards of open ground to cross before they reached the cover of the next ravelin.

'We'll give you a volley to cover you!' Verne called.

Killigrew nodded, and Verne and the rest of his men bobbed up, blazing away over the wall. The commander motioned for Charrondier to go first, and as the *matelot* dashed across, Killigrew stood up and fired his revolver at the Russians. Aurélie, Stålberg and Lindström followed Charrondier, while Killigrew brought up the rear with the other two *matelots*. They had almost made it when a musket barked overhead, and one of the *matelots* twisted and fell. Killigrew looked up to see a Russian at an embrasure on the battlements above them. The other *matelot* raised his musket and fired, and the Russian fell back out of sight. Then he slung his musket across his back and helped Killigrew drag the *matelot* who had been shot past the angle of the ravelin.

Killigrew crouched over the wounded man. He had been shot in the chest and his guernsey was covered in blood. Killigrew felt for a pulse in his neck and found none. 'Sorry, *mon ami*; it's all up with your shipmate.'

The other *matelot* nodded. 'At least I got the Russkoff pig who killed him.'

Leaving the dead man where he lay, they followed the others as they crept along the side of the ravelin, Charrondier leading the way with his musket in his hands. They found themselves in a man-made canyon between the ravelin and a blockhouse with a battlemented roof. The canyon angled to the right, and Charrondier and the others dashed across to the far side so they could get right up to the corner, where Charrondier crouched down to peer around it.

375

'All clear!' he announced, stepping out from the side of the block-house and motioning the others through. 'Where's Ingres?' he asked Laval.

'Didn't make it, Maître.'

Charrondier nodded and brought up the rear with Laval while Killigrew and Lindström took a turn leading the way. They slipped between another blockhouse and a barrack house and came to a T-junction.

'Which way?' asked Lindström.

Killigrew was not sure. The pathways between the bastions, block-houses and ravelins were so mazy, even he had become disorientated. 'Left,' he decided, figuring that one way was as good as another.

Except that the left fork led them straight into Nekrasoff and his men. Charrondier fired his musket and Killigrew and Lindström blazed away with their revolvers, killing several of the Russians and putting Nekrasoff and the others to flight. But Killigrew and Lindström had exhausted their revolvers, and it was not going to take Nekrasoff long to realise that and rally his men.

'Fall back!' Killigrew told the others, gesturing with his empty revolver.

They sprinted back the way they had come only to run into Verne and the other nine *matelots*.

'Back, back!' yelled Killigrew. 'They're right behind us!'

Verne glanced nervously over his shoulder. 'Funny you should say that . . .'

With two sets of Russians closing in on them from two different directions, there was only one way they could go. Killigrew ducked through a low arch to his right, into a courtyard where he dashed up a ramp to the casemated battlements above. A lone thirty-two-pounder pointed through a loop-hole: it faced across the inner harbour, so there were no men manning it, but there was no other way down from the casemate except the ramp they had come up.

'It's a dead end!' one of the *matelots* exclaimed in despair.

Killigrew turned back to the ramp only to see the Russian infantry-men clustering beyond the archway below. Stålberg and Aurélie brought up their revolvers and blazed away, sending them diving for cover.

'*Tiens*!' exclaimed Aurélie. 'They've got us nicely bottled up now.'

'No they haven't.' Killigrew indicated the long gun. 'If we pull this back from the wall, we can crawl out through that loophole. It can't be more than a dozen feet to the rocks below.'

'You heard the man, *mes braves*!' Verne told his men. 'Put your backs to it!'

The Frenchmen cast off the side tackles, seized the train tackle and hauled it away from the loophole.

Below, a dozen infantrymen filed through the archway into the courtyard, lining up with their muskets levelled up the ramp. 'Throw down your guns and surrender!' Lieutenant Rudenko called up. 'There is no escape!'

Killigrew looked around desperately and saw thirty 32-pound round shot piled in a pyramid on a brass monkey beside the long gun. 'Ever played skittles?' he asked Aurélie.

She looked at him as if he was mad, but he was already snatching up a handspike, bracing one end against the flagstones below the brass monkey and using it to lever it up. With nearly a thousand pounds of solid shot on it, he could not shift it alone, but then Aurélie, Stålberg and Lindström saw what he was about and grabbed a handspike, ramrod and worm respectively. With a supreme effort on the part of all four, they managed to tip the brass monkey up far enough for the iron balls to cascade from it, thundering down the ramp to bowl over any Russian infantrymen unfortunate enough to stand in their path and scattering the rest.

Verne and his men had got the gun far enough from the wall for Charrondier to swing himself through feet first. Gripping the edge, he lowered himself down to the full extent of his arms and dropped the rest of the way. He stepped back at the bottom and waved up to where Verne stood at the loophole to show he was all right and it was safe to follow.

'You next, Mam'selle Plessier,' the *enseigne* called.

Aurélie went through nimbly, and Charrondier caught her at the bottom. Stålberg and Lindström followed her. The rest of Verne's men went through one after another, until only Killigrew, Verne and one *matelot* were left in the casemate.

That was when the Russians attacked again, charging through the archway below with bayonets fixed, Rudenko at their head with his sabre drawn.

Killigrew looked at the gun, saw there was a quill tube in the vent. 'Reckon there's any powder in this thing?' he asked Verne, shouting to make himself heard above the roaring of the Russians charging up the ramp.

Verne caught his drift at once. 'Get down, Gagneux!'

377

The *matelot*, who had been about to ease himself through the loophole, threw himself flat on the floor below it.

'Only one way to find out.' Killigrew grasped the lanyard of the cannon and gave it a firm tug. The hammer snapped, sparks shot from the vent as the quill tube ignited, and the whole thing shot back on its carriage as flames roared from the muzzle. Without the side tackles to secure it, it rolled back until the rearmost wheels crested the top of the ramp, and then the whole thing trundled down, the two-ton cannon inexorably gathering way as gravity accelerated it down the slope.

Rudenko and three of his men were able to escape death by pressing themselves against the wall to the left of the ramp, narrowly avoiding having their toes crushed by the wheels of the gun carriage. Most of the others managed to leap from the side of the ramp and sprawl on the flagstones of the courtyard below, but a couple were not so lucky: the cannon smashed through them, tossing one aside and carrying the other before it as it careered through the archway to slam into the masonry opposite.

Rudenko charged the rest of the way up the ramp with three of his men. Killigrew still had the handspike in one hand, and he used it to parry as Rudenko slashed at him with his sabre. Verne grabbed the ramrod, knocking aside a bayonet thrust and swinging the end of the ramrod against one Russian's ear, knocking him from the platform, before ramming it into the stomach of another and sending him sprawling back down the ramp. Killigrew parried another sabre-cut with the handspike, then caught Rudenko by the wrist and whirled him so that the fourth Russian was spitted on the end of the lieutenant's sabre. Letting go of Rudenko's wrist, he slammed his elbow back into his face, pulping his nose. Rudenko spun away with blood dripping between the fingers that clutched at his face. Killigrew took the revolver from the Russian's holster and kicked him up the backside so that he fell from the platform with a wail to land on the flagstones below. Rolling over, Rudenko picked himself up and limped out of the courtyard after the rest of his men.

Killigrew dropped the handspike, tucked the revolver in his pocket and followed Gagneux and Verne through the loophole, dropping down to the rocks on the other side. Aurélie and the others were already making their way up the east shore of the island. Killigrew walked a few yards away from below the loophole and turned. Drawing the revolver, he braced his right wrist with his left hand and took careful aim.

He did not have long to wait: one of Rudenko's men thrust his head out through the loophole. Killigrew squeezed off five shots in rapid succession, and at that range even he could not miss with all five bullets: the Russian slumped, his arms hanging limply down until his comrades dragged his body back out of sight. After that, the next man was reluctant to show his face. Killigrew pocketed the revolver and ran after the others.

Shells still exploded all over Vargon and Gustafvard; now one seemed to explode amongst the forts and blockhouses every two or three seconds, so that a new roar of sound boomed across the islands before the echoes of the last had died away. The return fire of the Russian batteries seemed to be slackening, and fires had broken out in several places, sending thick clouds of acrid smoke drifting between the buildings. Damage-control parties ran back and forth, carrying buckets of sand and beating at the flames with wet mops.

Killigrew soon caught up with the others and hurried to the head of the party, where Aurélie and Lindström led the way along the west side of Artillery Bay. The channel angled around to the left, and beyond they saw the bridge leading across to East Svarto, mercifully still intact. They waited for another damage-control party to run across, disappearing into the smoke in the direction of the citadel, and then Killigrew and his allies broke cover, dashing across the bridge and following the path past the arsenal to the gunboat sheds.

Killigrew kicked open the door of the first and dived through, rising on one knee with the revolver in his hands. The gunboat was still in the quay, with two *matrosy* on her deck. He shot one in the chest, aimed at the other and squeezed the trigger, only for it to fall on a spent cap. He threw the revolver, striking the *matros* square in the middle of the forehead and knocking him back against the far bulwark. An officer emerged from the after hatch, revolver in hand, and took aim at the defenceless Killigrew. But Verne had already followed him into the shed with the rest of his men, and Charrondier brought up his musket and killed him with one shot.

Killigrew vaulted over the bulwark on to the deck of the gunboat, followed by Verne and his men. 'Make sure he's dead or tied up!' yelled the commander, indicating the man he had knocked out, before descending the after hatch.

The officers' quarters below were small and poky. Killigrew found a door leading forward and entered the magazine, the shelves stacked high with flannel-wrapped cartridges. The next compartment beyond that was the engine room, the only light coming from the coals glowing in the furnace. He was looking for the pressure gauge on the engine when a burly, crew-cut figure in a vest stained with coal and sweat lunged out of the shadows and swung a shovel at his neck.

If there had been more space in the compartment Killigrew would surely have lost his head; as it was, the blade of the shovel clanged against part of the engine framing before the blow could land, giving Killigrew enough time to twist and throw a punch at the stoker's midriff. The man grunted and dropped the shovel, then caught Killigrew by the tunic and swung him painfully against the side of a coal bunker. Holding him there with his left arm, he threw a meaty fist at his face with his right. Killigrew managed to jerk his head far enough to the left for the fist to sail past him. It smacked against the iron bunker and the stoker staggered back with a howl of pain. Killigrew charged, catching him around the waist and slamming him back against the boiler casing, but then the stoker grappled him in turn and swung him against the furnace. The two of them wrestled, the stoker getting the palm of one hand under Killigrew's jaw and forcing his head back through the open door of the furnace.

Killigrew could feel the heat from the glowing coals sear the back of his neck. Out of the corner of his eye, he saw a small oil-can resting on one of the stanchions of the engine framing. He grabbed it, pointing the spout in the stoker's face and squirting oil in his eyes. The stoker screamed and let go of him, enabling him to step away, grasp the door in one hand and slam it shut on the stoker's head.

Verne and Charrondier charged into the engine room. 'Are you all right?' asked the *enseigne*.

Killigrew had burned his hand on the handle of the furnace door, and he clutched it with a wince. 'Where were you?'

Verne grinned. 'We found a couple more *matrosy* in the fo'c'sle who needed to be dealt with. I knew you could handle any stokers you ran into down here. What do you think? Can we fire her up?'

Killigrew found the pressure gauge. Like the one on the steam pinnace he had stolen at Novaya Gollandia, the engine had been made in London, and the gauge was marked in pounds per square inch. The dial pointed to fourteen.

'We need to get the pressure up to twenty-five,' he told Verne. 'Get a couple of your lads down here to stoke the furnace.'

Verne nodded. 'Charrondier, get Darlot and Fanton down here.'

The petty officer nodded and headed forward. Verne followed Killigrew into the magazine. 'How long will it take?'

'Ten, fifteen minutes? Depends on how fast your boys can shovel.'

'What if someone comes by while we're waiting?'

'Pray they don't . . . and put a couple of men on guard, just in case. Don't worry, the Russians have their hands full dodging shells and putting out fires; they're not likely to worry about what's going on in here. Take these,' he added, taking down a couple of the cartridges and passing them to the *enseigne*.

'What do you want these for? Or shouldn't I ask?'

'Best if you don't ask,' Killigrew told him, taking two more cartridges and leading the way back on deck. 'Just a little job I have to take care of next door. If I'm not back by the time that pressure gauge hits twenty-five, don't wait for me: just get the others out of here.' He took the other two cartridges back from Verne and stepped on to the quayside.

Aurélie intercepted him on his way to the door. 'Are you going where I think you're going?'

He nodded. 'Stay here with Verne and his men,' he told her. 'I can manage.'

She shook her head. 'This is an Anglo-French operation now, remember? And you'll need some of this.' She showed him the spool of fuse she was holding.

'Got any lucifers?'

She patted the pocket of the greatcoat she wore, and he heard the rattle of matches.

'You'll need these.' Lindström proffered a pair of revolvers. 'They're both loaded.'

Killigrew nodded, putting the gunpowder cartridges down on a table close to the door. 'We'll leave this stuff here while we make sure the other gunboat shed is clear, then come back for it,' he said, taking one of the revolvers from Lindström. Aurélie nodded and took the other.

He eased the door open a crack. What had been a bright, clear day less than an hour ago was now dark and overcast from the huge quantities of smoke that billowed up all around the complex, blotting out the sun. The roar of exploding magazines added their detonations to those of the shells that continued to burst amongst the forts and blockhouses, hurling masonry and debris high into the sky. The mortar vessels continued to focus their attentions on Vargon, but the barrage was steadily working its way back towards the channel, and it would not be long before shells started dropping on East Svarto too.

Killigrew waited for a damage-control party to dash past outside. Once it had disappeared into the smoke, he opened the door all the way. 'Come on, let's go! Close the door behind you.'

They hurried across to the next gunboat shed and stood on either side of the door, drawing their revolvers. 'Ready?' Killigrew asked Aurélie.

She nodded, her face pale beneath the dirt and grime on her cheeks.

'Let's hope we're not too late,' he said, and kicked open the door.

The *Sea Devil* was still in the dock, although the fact the water gates were already open and two *matrosy* were running back along the side of the quay to board the underwater vessel made it clear that Killigrew and Aurélie had only just got there in time. She brought up her revolver and fired twice, bringing down a *matros* on the dockside with each shot. A third *matros* stood on the back of the *Sea Devil*, preparing to lower himself down the hatch. Killigrew aimed two shots at him and missed with both, giving the *matros* time to jump down the hatch and slam it shut behind him.

The water astern of the *Sea Devil* became turbulent as the *matrosy* within manned the treadmills. The contraption slowly began to move towards the gates.

'It's getting away!' groaned Aurélie.

Killigrew looked around in desperation until his eyes fell on the chain-winch on the dockside. The chain ran from the barrel up to a joist on the ceiling, supporting a hook. 'The devil it is!' He began sprinting towards the overhead gantry. 'Man that winch!'

He ran up the steps to the gantry and swung his legs over the handrail, measuring the distance to the chain. No time to think: he jumped. It was only a few feet. His fingers caught the chain, slipped, and he felt himself falling. Then he had caught hold of the hook by one hand. He gripped it with the other and hung there, suspended over the dock.

There was no need to tell Aurélie what to do next: she had already begun lowering him to the deck of the *Sea Devil*. It was a race to see if she could lower him before the contraption left the dock: Killigrew won, but only by inches. 'More slack!' he yelled at her. 'I need more slack!'

Aurélie continued to turn the winch as fast as she could. The chain rattled through the overhead hoist, and Killigrew ran along the top of the *Sea Devil* until he reached the hatch. He looped the chain through the wheel that opened the hatch, and hooked it in place.

The *Sea Devil*'s bows had reached the open gates. It continued to move forwards, dragging more of the chain through the pulley, until Aurélie closed the ratchet on the winch and all the slack had been taken up. The pulley creaked under the strain, but it was more than a match for the treadmill-powered *Sea Devil*. The water astern of the underwater boat became still as the crew realised the futility of trying to escape.

'Now what?' Aurélie asked as Killigrew stepped back on to the dockside. 'It seems to me we've reached an impasse.'

Killigrew nodded. As soon as they left to escape on the gunboat, Lieutenant Fedorovich would simply climb out of the contraption, unhook the chain, and set off once more on his deadly mission. Killigrew crouched down behind some of the crates stacked on the dockside, and motioned for Aurélie to join him.

'Go and fetch the fuse and cartridges from next door,' he told her, and gestured at the *Sea Devil* with his revolver. 'I'll stay here and make sure they don't go anywhere.'

She nodded, ran across to the door, and slipped out. Outside, the shells continued to rain down and the constant succession of explosions rattled the windows. While she was gone, Killigrew wondered where he could put the cartridges to do the maximum damage. If all four exploded inside the body of the *Sea Devil*, they would rip it apart; but the damned thing had been built to withstand the pressures of the deep, and he doubted that four cartridges would be enough even to dent the outside if he exploded them on its back. If only he could somehow set them off under the *Sea Devil*, the rising blast would snap it in two. But, of course, the cartridges would be rendered ineffective if they were wet.

He glanced about the interior of the shed and saw the diving suit hanging on one wall. Of course! It was waterproof: all he had to do was fill the suit with powder, run the fuse through the air hose and somehow wedge the suit under the *Sea Devil*'s keel . . .

Aurélie returned, struggling to balance all four cartridges in her arms as well as the spool of fuse. 'Where do you want it?' she asked archly.

'Just put it down over there.'

She did as he bid her. 'Verne says the pressure gauge is up to twenty-two.'

'We've still got a couple of minutes, then—' Seeing her eyes widen in surprise, he broke off and started to turn even before his ears registered her cry of warning. He swivelled to see a *matros* charging along the dockside towards him with a knife in one hand, stripped to his shirtsleeves and sopping wet. Killigrew fired his revolver, hitting him in the chest, but then another wet *matros* had jumped down from the stack of crates above them to grab Aurélie from behind. Killigrew dared not fire for fear of hitting her, but it did not matter: she had dropped the equipment she was holding, stamped on the *matros*'s instep and rammed an elbow into his ribs. Breaking free, she whirled to face him, punching him in the throat, kicking him in the crotch and lifting a knee into his face as he doubled up.

She turned back to Killigrew. 'Are you all right?'

'Aren't I supposed to ask you that?'

She shrugged. 'If you like. Where did those two come from?'

'They must've used the air-lock to swim out underwater,' explained Killigrew, mentally kicking himself for not having anticipated that Fedorovich would think of such a trick.

The hatch on the deck of the *Sea Devil* was thrown open, and a *matros* bobbed up, levelling a revolver. Killigrew raised his own revolver and fired, tearing a lump out of the *matros*'s left shoulder. The *matros* slumped, and then seemed to find strength from somewhere and raised the revolver once more. Aurélie flung a bayonet across the shed, piercing the man through one eye. He crumpled, and was dragged back down through the hatch, only for Fedorovich and four more sailors to climb quickly up out of the hatch, intent on rushing the two saboteurs.

Killigrew squeezed the revolver's trigger repeatedly, knocking down one man with his first shot, the other two going wide. Then the revolver's hammer clicked on a spent cap. He scrambled over the crates and ran to intercept the rest, with Aurélie hard on his heels. The second *matros* thrust at him with a knife. Killigrew side-stepped and caught the *matros* by the wrist, spinning him around and smashing an elbow into his face before turning to face a third. As the fourth *matros* squared up to Aurélie, Fedorovich grabbed her from behind. Nothing daunted, she kicked the fourth under the jaw and somehow flipped herself backwards over Fedorovich's shoulder, landing on her feet behind him and throwing him into a stack of crates, which crashed down on top of him.

Squaring up to the third, Killigrew launched into the set-piece he thought of as the 'Killigrew special': right jab, right jab, left uppercut, right cross, and then the *coup de grâce* – that old left hook that came out of nowhere when they were too dazed to see it coming. It did not always work, but then Killigrew did not always find himself up against ordinary mortals. This one *was* an ordinary mortal, however, and he pirouetted neatly with a glazed look in his eye before measuring his length on the dockside.

Killigrew turned to Aurélie to see if she needed any help, but she merely stood over Fedorovich, dusting her hands off. As she walked across to where Killigrew stood, one of the *matrosy* groaned and tried to rise. She casually kicked him in the head as she passed, and this time he lay still.

Killigrew counted the bodies. 'Nine plus one in the *Sea Devil*: that's the lot. I'll climb inside, you start passing those cartridges down to me.'

He jumped on to the back of the *Sea Devil* and climbed down the hatch. Once he had made sure there were no living souls within, he climbed back up the ladder and stood halfway out of the hatch so that Aurélie could throw the cartridges to him from the dockside. He caught them one after the other and dropped them to the grating at the foot of the ladder. Climbing back down, he glanced around the interior of the underwater boat, trying to work out where to stack the cartridges to do the most damage. The enclosed space of the airlock seemed most promising: the blast should rip open both doors, and even if it didn't the valves would be smashed beyond repair. If the valves were smashed, then the air-lock was inoperable; and without the air-lock through which one of the sailors would get out to fix an explosive to an enemy ship's hull, then the *Sea Devil* was nothing more than so much scrap metal, to all intents and military purposes.

Having stacked the cartridges in the airlock, he crossed back to stand at the foot of the ladder leading up to the hatch. 'Can you pass the fuse down now?' he called.

There was no reply.

'Aurélie?'

'I'm afraid she's not in a position to answer you,' Ryzhago's plummy tones called back.

Killigrew's heart sank: it had been too much to hope he could destroy the *Sea Devil* and get away from Sveaborg without a final reckoning with the assassin.

# XXV

# The Road to Piccadilly

Killigrew climbed up the ladder to find Ryzhago standing on the dockside behind Aurélie with the chain of his pocket watch looped tight around her neck. She was still alive . . . for now.

'Throw down your weapons, or I'll leave another dead woman at your feet,' Ryzhago told him with a grin.

He did not seem to be carrying any kind of weapon, but then a man like Ryzhago did not need to rely on guns and knives. Killigrew climbed all the way out of the hatch to stand on the back of the *Sea Devil*. 'I'm unarmed. Let her go: this is between you and me.'

'If you insist.' Ryzhago threw Aurélie against the side of the shed. She crashed against the wall and slumped to the floor, lying still with blood oozing from a graze on her temple.

Ryzhago tucked his watch back in his fob pocket and strode across the dockside, grinning wolfishly. Killigrew jumped on to the dockside to meet him, and then backed away as Ryzhago continued to advance.

'The two of us can try to batter one another into submission,' he told Ryzhago nervously. 'But with the whole world being blown to hell, don't you think a couple of intelligent chaps like ourselves can find some way to come to a mutual understanding without resorting to fisticuffs?'

'No.' Ryzhago threw a punch at Killigrew's jaw, spinning him back against the railing at the foot of the steps leading up to the gantry.

Killigrew shook his head muzzily. 'Didn't think so,' he muttered, and threw a punch at Ryzhago's midriff. It had no effect, of course; unlike Ryzhago's next punch, which came damn' near to knocking

Killigrew's head clean off his shoulders. He thought about trying the old 'Killigrew special', and then decided against it: his knuckles had had enough punishment for one day. Instead, he feinted to the left, dodged to the right and skipped behind the Russian to smash a fist into one of his kidneys. Ryzhago cried out. *Not so invincible as you look*, thought Killigrew. Heartened, he hit him again, and again, and again, a succession of well-placed blows that would have had any normal man passing blood for a week. Each time his fist landed, the Russian gave a sob. *The bigger they are . . .* Killigrew told himself.

Ryzhago turned to face him. Killigrew was astonished and dismayed to see he was smiling dreamily.

'Hit me again.'

Killigrew shrugged. 'If you insist.' He threw a fist at Ryzhago's jaw, snapping his head around.

'Again!'

Killigrew punched him again.

'Harder!'

And again.

'*Harder*!'

Killigrew bunched his fist, reminding himself that this was the bastard who had murdered Araminta. He pictured her, tied to the armchair in his rooms, screaming as Ryzhago applied the red-hot poker to her cheek; and afterwards, her struggling on the bed as he throttled her with his watch chain, no doubt deriving the same pleasure from it that Killigrew himself had shared with her in rather more tender moments. Right on cue, rage and hatred welled up within him. He focused those emotions in his shoulder, putting all his strength into the punch that followed, whipping Ryzhago's head around.

When the Russian turned back to face him, blood was trickling from the corner of his mouth. He wiped it off on the back of his hand, and then licked it off, gazing at Killigrew with a crazed look in his eye.

'Harder,' he whispered.

Killigrew sighed. 'You want harder?'

Ryzhago nodded. 'Give me everything you've got!'

'You asked for it!' Killigrew flicked one half-boot into the Russian's crotch.

Ryzhago positively squealed with delight as he sank to his knees, clutching himself. Killigrew moved in close, grabbing a fistful of the Russian's hair and kneeing him in the face. Ryzhago was thrown back across the floor, laughing ecstatically.

Killigrew stood over him, resting with his hands on his knees, panting for breath. There was no satisfaction in thrashing someone like Ryzhago if the fellow was going to enjoy it.

The Russian stood up and pointed to his jaw. 'Hit me again!'

'You're insatiable!'

'Hit me harder!'

'Hit yourself, damn your eyes! My knuckles are raw!'

'Hit me!' Raging now, Ryzhago threw a fist at the commander's jaw.

Killigrew took no pleasure in inflicting pain, even on scum like Ryzhago, but he certainly had to agree that it was better to give than receive. He landed on his backside and was still sitting there, wondering if his jaw was broken, when he looked up to see Ryzhago standing over him. The Russian bent down, seized a fistful of the front of Killigrew's tunic, and hauled him to his feet.

'Hit me!'

Killigrew bunched a fist and drew back his arm, but his head was swimming so much it was difficult to focus on Ryzhago's face. Growling impatiently, Ryzhago hit him first. Killigrew's head was snapped round and he was sent spinning across the dock to crash into the wall. He clung on to a rail for support, and then realised it was not a rail at all, but a boat-hook resting across a couple of wall brackets. He lifted it out and whirled, swinging it at Ryzhago. It connected with the Russian's head and he gasped as the metal tip snapped off the shaft.

'That's more like it!'

Killigrew stared in dismay at the broken shaft, and then Ryzhago had grabbed the end of it, jerking it from his grip. He snapped it across his knee and tossed the two halves away. Advancing on Killigrew, he got his huge hands around the commander's neck and began to squeeze. Killigrew thumped him repeatedly in the stomach, but Ryzhago only laughed as if being tickled by a lover.

'Harder! *Harder*!'

'The devil with this!' Breaking free, Killigrew turned and ran.

He started up the steps to the gantry, but Ryzhago caught him by the ankles before he got halfway, tripping him so he landed heavily on his front. He twisted and slammed the heel of one half-boot into Ryzhago's face. The Russian cried out ecstatically, 'Yes!'

Killigrew turned and scrambled up as far as the gantry; but he knew he could not run for ever; and if Verne had any sense, he would not wait for him and Aurélie once the pressure gauge reached twenty-five. He

388

stopped in the middle of the gantry, grabbing one of the blocks and tackles that swung from chains overhead, and swung it at Ryzhago's face as he charged across. Ryzhago jerked his head aside, and the tackle swung harmlessly past.

He laughed. 'You missed!'

Killigrew arched an eyebrow. 'Did I?'

Ryzhago whirled to face the block and tackle as it swung back; except that it had gone wide, and was in no danger of hitting the back of his head.

But he had fallen for Killigrew's bluff, and turned his back on him for two vital seconds. Killigrew pulled Wojtkiewicz's watch and chain from his trouser pocket and jumped on his back. He drew the watch chain tight against Ryzhago's throat. Roaring, the Russian slammed him back against the railing of the gantry. Killigrew gasped, struggling to maintain his grip on the chain. He gave up trying to throttle Ryzhago and knotted the two ends together as tightly as the links would allow while the Russian flailed about wildly, trying to pitch him over the railing down to the back of the *Sea Devil* some forty feet below. Killigrew almost went over, and grabbed the first thing that came to hand to keep his balance: the hook at the bottom of the block and tackle.

'You enjoy pain?' he asked Ryzhago, digging the point of the hook under the fob chain. 'You'll love this!'

He swung himself over the railing and caught hold of the other end of the pulley. The links rattled through the block and tackle overhead, hoisting Ryzhago up to the girders above while gently lowering Killigrew to within inches of the *Sea Devil*'s deck. Pulled hard against the underside of one of the girders, Ryzhago made a ghastly choking sound, and then the knot Killigrew had tied in the fob chain came adrift, and the Russian plunged to the deck of the *Sea Devil*. He landed on his back across the wheel of the hatch, and Killigrew heard his vertebrae snap.

Killigrew stretched out his hand and the watch dropped into his palm. He tucked it into his pocket.

Still not dead, Ryzhago managed to raise his head a few inches to look at Killigrew. The commander moved to stand over him, one foot raised ready to stamp down hard on the Russian's neck. But Ryzhago's head flopped back to the deck and he lay still, a smile of blissful ecstasy frozen on his face for eternity.

Sobbing for breath, Killigrew jumped back on to the dockside and was relieved to see Aurélie regaining consciousness. He helped her to her feet. 'Are you all right?' he panted.

'I think so. What happened to Ryzhago?'

'Oh, I managed to fob him off . . .'

Before she could ask him what he meant, the whole building shuddered around them as a shell exploded next door, and there was a terrible crash from the adjoining gunboat shed. Killigrew and Aurélie exchanged worried glances, and the two of them left the *Sea Devil*'s shed to run next door.

The adjoining shed was a shambles: one wall had collapsed entirely, bringing with it several of the girders supporting the roof, two of which had slammed down on the gunboat's deck, smashing it down into the water of the dock. The far end of the dockside was in flames and smoke was rapidly filling the shed. Stålberg and Lindström were helping Verne and his men carrying the wounded on to the dockside.

'What happened?' demanded Killigrew, as he and Aurélie helped get the wounded outside.

'Not sure,' Verne slurred. There was a cut above his hairline and one side of his face was slick with blood. 'Shell hit the corner of the roof, I think. Laval's dead, and Gagneux and Fanton are badly injured.'

'Well, that gunboat's had it,' said Killigrew.

'Then so have we,' said Charrondier. 'I don't know about you, *m'sieur*, but I'm damned if I'll spend another minute locked up in one of their cells. I'm for taking as many of the bastards with us as we can.'

Verne smiled. 'I appreciate the sentiment, Charrondier; but you forget we have a woman and two civilians to concern ourselves with; and I doubt our Russian friends will treat any of them with the courtesies of war.'

'Don't worry about me, *m'sieur*,' said Aurélie. 'You forget I'm a military officer, the same as yourself, even if I don't fight in uniform. And if we must die fighting, there's one thing we can still do first: make sure the *Sea Devil* is out of action.'

Killigrew stared at her: then seized her by the shoulders and planted a kiss on her forehead. 'Aurélie! You're a genius!'

'What?'

'The *Sea Devil*! We can use it to escape!'

'What is the *Sea Devil*?' asked Verne.

'I'll show you.' Killigrew led the way back to the gunboat sheds, and the others followed, carrying Gagneux and Fanton between them.

Verne's jaw dropped when he saw the *Sea Devil*. 'What in the name of God is that?'

'The *Sea Devil*,' Killigrew explained. 'It's an underwater boat. My mission was to destroy it; but I don't think Lord Palmerston will object if I deliver it to the Royal Navy instead.'

'A boat that sails underwater?' Verne shook his head in disbelief. 'My brother Jules is never going to believe this!'

Killigrew removed the chain from the wheel on the dorsal hatch. 'Down the hatch, everyone!'

They climbed inside, lowering the two injured *matelots* through the hatch and making them as comfortable as they could in the cramped confines in the interior.

'Are you certain you know how to pilot this thing?' demanded Aurélie.

'How hard can it be?' Killigrew asked breezily.

Once they were all inside, he sealed the hatch and lit the candle in the hurricane lamp. 'Now listen carefully, everyone: we're going to have to work together to make this work. Charrondier, I want you to take the helm. It works just the same as the helm on any other kind of vessel. Aurélie, perhaps you'd be good enough to control the trim? You just use this wheel here: anti-clockwise lowers us by the head, clockwise by the stern, got it?'

'I think I can manage that,' she said drily.

'Verne, these pumps control the ballast: this one takes in water to make us sink, this one expels it so we float again.'

'You hope!'

'Trust me.'

'Do I have any choice?'

' 'Fraid not. Major Lindström, do you think you could keep an eye on the bathometer here? Thank you. The rest of you: the treadmills, if you please.' He climbed up into the observation cupola. 'If you're ready, gentlemen, we'll begin . . .'

Darlot and the other *matelots* began to turn the treadmills. The gears groaned and the *Sea Devil* began to move, slowly at first, but steadily gathering way as the *matelots* on the treadmills began to get a steady rhythm going. The vessel nosed its way out of the gunboat shed and into the channel. Through one of the portholes, Killigrew could see explosions ripping up the ground on the opposite side of Artillery Bay. It seemed as if the whole of Vargon was ablaze. There was so much smoke in the sky it was difficult to tell if it was day or night, although it could not have been past nine o'clock in the morning. And still the shells continued to fall relentlessly. One landed on the gasometer on West Svarto, and burning gas leaped high into the air with a terrific roar.

'Four points to starboard, Charrondier.'

'Four points to starboard it is, sir.' The *matelot* spun the helm, and the *Sea Devil* turned slowly until she was pointing towards the crossroads in the channels.

'Bring her amidships.'

'Helm amidships!'

Killigrew was startled to hear footsteps on the deck behind him; one flaw in the vessel's design was that there was no porthole facing aft from the cupola, so he could not see who it was. He scrambled back down into the body of the vessel. Everyone was staring up at the deck head, following the progress of the footsteps.

'What is it?' asked Aurélie.

'Someone on top,' said Killigrew. 'They must have swum out after us!'

'Did we leave someone behind?' asked Verne.

Charrondier shook his head. 'Only Ingres and Laval.'

The footsteps continued along the deck towards the hatch.

'You!' Killigrew picked out the brawniest of the *matelots*. 'Get up there and brace the hatch! Don't let them open it!'

The *matelot* nodded and scrambled up the ladder, gripping the wheel on the underside of the hatch. He grunted and strained with the effort of both maintaining his precarious perch and keep the hatch shut.

Killigrew looked around and found a pry-bar in a toolbox on the deck at his feet. He passed it up to the *matelot*. 'Here! Use this.'

The *matelot* slipped the pry-bar between the spokes of the wheel so that it was wedged against the coaming. 'There! That's got it!'

Killigrew continued to stare up at the hatch. After a few more seconds, whoever was on top gave up trying to open the hatch and made his way forward. Killigrew stepped over the two wounded *matelots* and scrambled up the ladder to the observation cupola. He could hear the person moving about, and a moment later a familiar face peered through one of the portholes at him.

'It's Nekrasoff!' he called down to Aurélie.

The colonel reached inside his coat, pulled out a revolver and levelled it at Killigrew's face through the glass. There was no time to get out of the way: Killigrew instinctively threw up his arms in a defensive gesture.

Nekrasoff pulled the trigger.

Nothing happened.

Killigrew could have laughed out loud: the powder in the chambers of his cylinder must have got soaked as he swam out after the *Sea Devil*.

Scowling furiously, Nekrasoff reversed his grip on the revolver and began to hammer on the glass. Killigrew had no idea how strong Bauer had made the portholes, but surely the glass could not stand up to the pounding Nekrasoff was giving it? Not that he would be able to squeeze through the port once the glass was broken; but if the glass was broken, they would not be able to submerge under the bridge between Vargon and West Svarto, and even if they could they would have to run on the surface all the way out to the Allied Fleet, with the Russian batteries no doubt throwing everything they had at the *Sea Devil* to stop it from falling into enemy hands.

Killigrew remembered the waterproof gauntlets and slipped his hand into one, grabbing Nekrasoff by the wrist. The colonel tried to pull his hand free, but Killigrew gripped him tightly.

'Oh, no you don't, you bastard!' he shouted at the glass. 'You're not getting away this time!'

'Kit!' Aurélie called from below. 'What's going on up there?'

'Just getting to grips with an old friend,' he told her. 'Stay by the trim control and stand by to dive.'

Nekrasoff took the revolver in his left hand and started pounding against the glass again. Killigrew slipped his other hand into the other gauntlet, and again caught him by the wrist. Now he had the colonel fast.

'Flood the ballast tanks!' he called to Verne. 'Aurélie, put five degrees of dive on her! Those of you on the treadmills, resume treading! Full speed ahead!'

The *Sea Devil* tipped forwards and water began to rise against the portholes. Realising his peril, Nekrasoff struggled furiously, but Killigrew had him fast by both wrists and was not going to release him even if his own life had depended on it. As the water rose around Nekrasoff's chin, he took a last gulp of air, and then the *Sea Devil* dragged him under. He blinked, his dark hair floating about like so much kelp. He stared wild-eyed at Killigrew through the porthole, his cheeks bulging as he fought to hold his breath. His face twisted with fury, and he braced his feet against the front of the cupola in an effort to break free. Killigrew thought of Araminta Maltravers, and all the others who had died because of the colonel's machinations, and if anything his grip became even tighter.

'What depth are we at, Major?' he called down.

'Eh? Oh! Two fathoms!'

'Right the trim, Aurélie . . . no, that's too much . . . back the other way . . . that's got it!'

Nekrasoff's expression became pleading. Killigrew just shook his head implacably. The look in the colonel's eyes turned to desperation. Killigrew saw his Adam's apple bob up and down in his throat as he gasped for air, but there was no air to be had. His eyes bulged in his head. The magnifying effect of the water enabled Killigrew to see the veins throbbing in his temples.

'Three fathoms!' called Lindström.

'That's enough ballast, Verne!'

The end came suddenly. Nekrasoff's jaw fell slack, and a stream of bubbles rose from it. The light in his eyes went out, and his body became limp, his lifeless face bumping against the glass of the porthole. Killigrew counted to sixty in his head before he finally let go, and the slipstream carried Nekrasoff's corpse past the cupola before he sank down to the depths below.

Killigrew could see rocks looming out of the gloom to port. 'One point to port, Charrondier!'

The *matelot* spun the helm to port, turning the *Sea Devil*'s nose to starboard. 'One point to port it is!'

Killigrew remembered to withdraw his hands from the gauntlet, and massaged his aching fingers.

'What happened to Nekrasoff?' Aurélie called up.

'He got out of his depth,' Killigrew told her grimly. 'In over his head.'


On the quarterdeck of HMS *Exmouth*, Rear Admiral Seymour dragged his good eye – the other still being covered with a patch after his little accident with an infernal machine – from the spectacle before him to regard the marine on duty at the ship's belfry, who watched the last grains of sand running through the hourglass. In less than a minute it would be time for him to ring eight bells at the end of the forenoon watch.

Such a thick pall of black smoke hung over Sveaborg, masking the

394

sky for miles around, it was more like midnight than noon. The shells from the mortar vessels continued to smash down on what was left of the complex of fortresses. In front of the mortar vessels, the gunboats steamed in small, tight circles, firing their guns when they were lined up on the fortifications and reloading them ready to fire again before they completed another circuit. The shrieking shells left smoking trails in the air, and grey smoke rings ascended amidst the dust and flames from each explosion. The noise of the bombardment was incessant and tremendous. Each explosion hurled chunks of masonry spinning through the air. The powder in the Russians' guns was clearly inferior, for their shots had hardly come close even to the gunboats, and they had not succeeded in hitting any. After the first hour of the bombardment, their batteries had begun to slacken: now they were too busy cowering in their bunkers to even bother returning fire.

'Of course, I said all along that all that talk about it being folly to send wooden ships against granite batteries was so much stuff,' Seymour said loftily, shouting to make himself heard above the incessant cannonade. He smiled to himself. For months now he had had to put up with the stigma of being associated with Napier's desultory campaign, but the wholesale destruction of Sveaborg would wipe out that stain. Now he could claim that it had been Napier who had held him back last year, and his support for Captain Sulivan that had led to the success of today's attack. A knighthood was as good as in the bag.

One of the seamen lining the bulwark, gazing across in awe at the vast inferno that seemed to stretch from one horizon to another, glanced down and blanched. 'In-infernal machine! There's an infernal machine!' He gestured frantically into the water.

'Where?'

'Right below us!'

Another seaman jumped up on to the bulwark beside him. 'I don't see nothin'.'

'It be there, I tells'ee! I seen it. Look!'

The second sailor glanced down again. 'He's right, there's something there . . . it's . . . it's coming up to the surface!'

Seymour ran across to the bulwark. Even as he looked down, a long, black shape surfaced below the *Exmouth*'s quarter.

'Stab me! It's a whale!' shouted someone.

'Bloody rum-looking whale, shipmate.'

Seymour saw the hatch in the back of the . . . the *thing*. 'That's no whale. Whatever it is, it's man-made. Corporal! Bring your men!'

A dozen marines crowded the bulwark, levelling their muskets at the iron contraption. 'Want us to open fire, sir?'

'Wait a moment, there's a hatch opening.'

The hatch cover was thrown back. A dozen muskets were aimed.

The barrel of a carbine emerged, with a white shirt tied to it. 'Whatever it is, sir, looks like it wants to surrender.'

A head emerged from the hatch, facing towards Sveaborg. Then the head turned, and Seymour recognised the face at once.

'Killigrew!' he spat in disgust.

The commander grinned up at him. 'Hullo, sir! Is this the right road for Piccadilly?'

'What the deuce is that thing?'

'It's an underwater boat, sir. The secret weapon I tried to warn you about back in January.' Killigrew climbed out of the hatch to stand on the back of the *Sea Devil*, and helped the others out after him. 'Lord Palmerston sent me to destroy it, but when I saw a chance to steal it instead, I could hardly pass it up. Oh, may I introduce Mam'selle Plessier, the Friherre Per Stålberg, Major Vidrik Lindström, and *Enseigne de Vaisseau* Paul Verne and his men from *La Mouette*?'

Seymour fumed and glowered as the *Exmouth* took the *Sea Devil* in tow, and the Frenchmen went on board the flagship with Stålberg and Lindström, until only Killigrew and Aurélie were left on the contraption. The commander slipped an arm around her waist and made to kiss her, but she pushed him away.

'Have you already forgotten what I told you? In espionage, it is not good to fall in love.'

He smiled. 'But now my mission's accomplished, I'm not a spy any more.'

She thought about it. 'In that case . . .' She threw her arms around his neck and kissed him.

And at that precise moment – on the dot of noon – a shell from a mortar finally penetrated the roof of the battered magazine adjoining the citadel on Vargon.

The resulting explosion was awesome. The concrete bunker was torn apart and a huge ball of flame seemed to engulf the citadel with a deafening roar. Rooftops, beams of timber, even the bodies of men were hurled high into the air, pitiful figures tossed up above the inferno like rag-dolls. Just as the fire began to turn to smoke, another explosion renewed it from within, and then another and another, as the shells and barrels of powder in the magazine exploded, a succession of overlapping blasts that poured flames into the sky and belched forth vast clouds of billowing smoke to add to the thick pall that already hung in the air for miles around. The eruptions merged into one long, dreadful roar, the astonishing conflagration lasting the best part of two minutes. The men on the deck of the *Exmouth* were too astounded by the cataclysm to cheer. Seymour had never seen anything like it, and he stared in open-mouthed fascination, appalled and amazed at the same time. The men in the gunboats and mortar vessels were so stunned by what they had done their guns fell silent for a few moments.

Killigrew and Aurélie broke off their kiss. 'Did you say something?' he asked her.

Laughing, she shook her head, and glanced up at the bulwarks of the *Exmouth*. No one was looking down at the *Sea Devil* any more: every eye on board was fixed on the vast cloud of billowing smoke and dust rising from the explosion on Sveaborg. Aurélie slipped back down the hatch and pulled Killigrew after her.

'Make the earth move for me one more time,' she invited him.

He closed the hatch firmly above them.

# Afterword

Both sides made extensive use of spies during the Crimean War, although usually on a local level. When the British bombarded Bomarsund in the summer of 1854, a Russian officer attempted to survey the Allied batteries disguised as a woman. The disguise fooled no one, of course, and he narrowly evaded capture. According to William Don – a hospital dresser on board the *Duke of Wellington* during the following year's Baltic campaign – the French captured some Finnish fishermen after the bombardment of Sveaborg and blackmailed them into surveying the ruins of the island complex to report on how much damage was done. Most intriguing of all, a man suspected to be a British naval officer arrived in Helsingfors (renamed Helsinki when Finland finally gained her independence from Russia in 1920) as the clouds of war gathered, posing as an ichthyologist and covertly attempting to recruit Finnish pilots for British ships.

There is a long history of secret policing in Russia. It is no surprise that it began when Ivan the Terrible founded the Oprichniki, a system of spies who kept a close watch on the boyar classes. The Third Section of the Imperial Chancery was founded by Nicholas I early in his reign. By the end of the nineteenth century, the Third Section had metamorphosed into the better-known Ochrana. The Bolsheviks quickly wiped out the Ochrana following the Revolution of 1917, only to replace it with the 'All-Russian Extraordinary Commission for Combating Counter-Revolution and Sabotage', or 'Cheka' for short. In time the Cheka was renamed the GPU, then the OGPU, which later became part of the NKVD before being detached again and being renamed the

KGB. In the Glasnost era, the KGB was renamed the Federal Security Service, or FSB. 'New name,' as Robbie Coltrane's character, Valentin Zhukovsky, wryly remarks in the film *The World is Not Enough*, 'same old friendly service.'

Having gained his PhD in mineralogy from the University of Helsingfors in 1855, Nils Nordenskjöld continued his studies in Berlin. In 1857 he made a speech calling for Finnish independence, and was exiled from the grand duchy by Governor-General Friedrich von Berg when he refused to apologise. The following year he participated in Otto Torell's expedition to Spitzbergen, and led further expeditions to the Arctic in the 1860s. In 1879, in the steamship *Vega*, he completed the first ever navigation of the North-East Passage. Paul Verne, meanwhile, retired from *La Royale* in 1859 and became a stockbroker. His brother Jules went on to make a name for himself as a writer.

James Tabard, QC is a fictional character, but inspired by the real-life 'Jem the Penman,' James Saward, QC, whose long career on both sides of the law came to an end in 1856 following his arrest for forgery. Saward is believed to have bankrolled the Crimean Bullion robbery – better known as the first Great Train Robbery thanks to Michael Crichton's book and film of that name – the previous year.

Wilhelm Bauer was a Bavarian artillery corporal who built his first submarine, *Der Brandtauscher* (Fire Diver) for the Army of Schleswig-Holstein in 1850. It sank due to a fault, and Bauer and his crew only escaped after five hours at the bottom of Kiel harbour by allowing water into the submarine to equalise the outside pressure of the sea so that a hatch could be opened. In 1851 he travelled to England, where Prince Albert gave him financial support to build a new submarine. For a time he worked with John Scott Russell, a distinguished shipbuilder who worked on the *Great Eastern* with Isambard Kingdom Brunel. Russell then cancelled his contract with Bauer, thinking he had learned enough of the Bavarian's secrets to design and build a submarine of his own. But Bauer was a cagey man who had always played his cards close to his chest, refusing to take out a patent for his invention because he felt he would have to part with too many of his secrets. Russell's submarine sank during trials and was lost with all hands; the submarine historian A. H. Burgoyne implies its failure may have been due to modifications introduced to the design by Lord Palmerston himself!

When the Crimean War began, someone in authority decided that Bauer's intentions were 'subversive' – it is possible he had already been contacted by Russian agents – and British Customs and Excise were ordered to confiscate his drawings and model if he tried to leave the country. Bauer, however, was tipped off by a friendly customs official from whom he had been learning English, and escaped unrecognised one night on a steamer heading for Hamburg. Within three hours of arriving in St Petersburg in the spring of 1855 he was in a meeting with the Grand Duke Konstantin, who was to be an enthusiastic supporter of Bauer's next project, the *Seeteufel*. The Russian Admiralty was less enthusiastic about the contraption, however, and there may have been some wry humour at play when they chose to call the *Sea Devil* the *Khimera*. The real *Sea Devil* was not completed until 2 November 1855, but the Admiralty delayed seven months before transporting it to Kronstadt for trials. There, during the coronation ceremony of Tsar Alexander II, Bauer submerged in the *Sea Devil* with his usual crew, and four musicians who played the Russian national anthem, accompanied by the singing of the crew. On the surface, they could be heard 220 yards away. Alexander II was so impressed by Bauer's work, he had the rank 'submarine engineer' invented for him, with a brevet and a special uniform.

Although the *Sea Devil* never engaged any enemy shipping – the first submarine to sink a ship would be the CSS *Hunley* some nine years later – it proved itself a success during 134 test dives. Later Bauer designed another, larger submarine for the Russians, with a steam-engine for surface running and a compressed air engine to drive her when submerged. She was also to be armed with twenty-four guns. When the Admiralty decided Bauer should complete his submarine in Siberia for security purposes, however, the engineer wisely decided that the time had come to leave Russia and return to Germany. His contribution to the development of the submarine is incalculable.

Brunel, meanwhile, really did design a 'jet-propelled' floating battery, to be sailed out of the opening bows of a specially converted collier (shades of the tanker *Liparus* in the film *The Spy Who Loved Me!*), for use in the siege of Sevastopol. Sadly – unlike the prefabricated hospital he designed – it was never constructed.

The Crimean War was also the first war to see the use of 'infernal machines', as sea mines were then known. The first models, designed by Professor Moritz Jacobi, were set off from the shore by electricity, although by the summer of 1855 the contact mines of Immanuel Nobel were in use. It was guilt over the use of his father's explosives in the Crimean War that prompted Alfred Nobel – who invented dynamite in 1866 – to found his famous prizes.

Rear Admiral Michael Seymour (later Sir Michael) dredged one of Nobel's mines up in his gig with Captain Hall, and took it on board the *Duke of Wellington* to show to Dundas. According to Captain Bartholomew J. Sulivan:

> They all played with it; and Admiral Seymour took it to his ship, and on the poop had the officers round it examining it . . . Some of the officers remarked of the danger of it going off, and Admiral Seymour said, 'O no. This is the way it would go off,' and shoved the slide in with his finger . . . It instantly exploded, knocking down everyone around it.*

Sulivan played a major role in the Baltic Campaigns: it was he who surveyed a channel through the Åland Islands, making the attack on Bomarsund possible in 1854; and in 1855 his surveying ship, HMS *Merlin*, went down in history as the first vessel ever to strike a mine; fortunately, the Russians did not put sufficient gunpowder in the devices to do any real damage.

The plan for the bombardment of Sveaborg was Sulivan's. The bombardment lasted for forty-four hours, from 7 or 7.30 a.m. (sources vary as to the exact time) on 9 August to 3 a.m. on the 11th, and even then it was only stopped when the mortars began to wear out.

It may seem like an overly convenient device to have the officers of the garrison throw a ball on the night before the bombardment, allowing Killigrew and Aurélie to gain access to Sveaborg by posing as guests, but the ball is a matter of historical record. It was held in honour of the Grand Duke Konstantin, who was visiting at the time; one of the first casualties of the bombardment was the wife of a naval officer who was injured leaving the following morning. The grand duke himself seems to have escaped the bombardment uninjured.

There is a marked discrepancy between the quoted numbers of Russian casualties incurred by the bombardment: all too willing to be misinformed by their reluctant Finnish spies, the British claimed 2,000 had been killed, whereas the Russian insisted the only victim was a single Cossack. More realistic figures are given by the Finnish historian A. W. Rancken (55 killed and 204 wounded) and the Russian historian Borodkin (62 killed and 199 wounded).

Henry Norton Sulivan, ed., *The Life and Letters of Admiral Sir B. J. Sulivan, KCB, 1810–90*, London, 1896.

William Don claimed in his memoir that it was the destruction of Sveaborg that convinced the Russians to come to terms the following year rather than risk a similar attack on Kronstadt, leaving St Petersburg open to bombardment. This is an exaggeration, certainly, but perhaps not as much of an exaggeration as all that. Previously the fall of Sevastopol has been seen as the turning point in the war, but from the point of view of the Tsarist government in St Petersburg, the Crimea was a far-flung outpost of the Russian empire, while the Gulf of Finland was right on their own doorstep. Only in recent years have historians begun to reassess the importance of the Baltic Campaign in the misnamed 'Crimean' War.